ANGELS IN THE MIST

THE Z-TECH CHRONICLES
BOOK ONE

RYAN SOUTHWICK

Published by Water Dragon Publishing
waterdragonpublishing.com

ISBN 978-1-946907-59-2 (Trade Paperback)

10 9 8 7 6 5 4 3 2 1

For Mom

ACKNOWLEDGEMENTS

When I set out to write this, my first book, it was with the naïve confidence I could take a novel from inception to professionally published by myself, needing only my reading experience and the vast resources of the Internet to carry me through. If you're laughing or shaking your head, you're wiser than me. "It takes a village ..." is an understatement, so I'd love to take a moment to recognize the wonderful people without whom this book would be a shadow of what it is, or might never have passed before more than a few eyes.

Thanks first and foremost to my mother. She was the first person to read the book and provided candid feedback that helped guide both character development and plot into something interesting. She was my sounding board, my cheering squad, my partner, and was, without a doubt, the reason I was able to persevere.

To Ray, who was not only instrumental in shaping the world and characters when we were younger, but who went above and beyond the bounds of friendship to read countless iterations of this ~140k-word manuscript and provide invaluable guidance every time, down to checking (and correcting) my math during Zima's epic fight scene. Absolutely none of this would have been possible without him.

To my friends and family who volunteered as beta readers — namely Patti, Tom, Linda, Zach, Keri, Sally, Adam, Jeff, Patrick, and Rob. I treasure the time you invested, and your courage for giving me your honest opinions. I took each to heart and, as some of you may notice in this final version, your voices were heard.

To my current editor, Steven, who exhibited boundless patience for my incessant questions about each tiny grammar rule and house style. Hopefully it was time well invested for the next few books. Either way, I learned a tremendous amount over the last few edits, and will always be grateful.

To my first editor, Anna, whose criticisms were hard to take, but without which the protagonist would have paled, thank you for your wisdom and for telling me what I needed to hear, not what I wanted to hear.

And for my wife, Louise, who endured evenings and weekends of neglect for my writing obsession, you deserve an award. Or a vacation. Probably both.

1

ANNE

PHANTOM FINGERS LOCKED AROUND ANNE PERRIN'S THROAT, cutting off her air. Her eyes bulged with raw and familiar terror. Unable to scream, her lungs spasming for breath, Anne tore at the fingers, but they wouldn't budge. Just like eighteen years ago, they were too strong, fueled by a cruelty too alien for her thirty-six-year-old mind to comprehend.

Two more hands gripped her wrists, then another two around her ankles. Anne twisted and fought. They wouldn't pin her down.

They wouldn't! She couldn't let them ... couldn't let them ...

"Breathe, hon." Doris' Southern drawl, calm and cool, floated to her from a vast distance. "C'mon, it's me. Put your hands down. Nice and easy now, sugar."

Her friend's copper beehive hairdo came slowly into focus, followed by her kind, wizened face.

Doris held each of Anne's hands, which were still struggling to pry the invisible fingers away. Anne's lungs burned for air. Colors spotted her vision.

"Come on back," Doris said. "Ain't no one choking you, hon. I wouldn't let 'em. You're safe. Put your hands down and breathe."

Blackness began to close around her. Anne swayed, but someone caught her.

"Whoa! Easy there," Julie said. The new waitress looked at Doris with the same panic Anne felt. "Holy shit! I'm calling an ambulance ..."

"Don't bother. Poor little kitten will either snap out of it or faint. Either way, she'll start breathing again soon."

And, just like that, the phantom fingers were gone.

Anne gave an explosive gasp, quenching the fire in her chest with huge gulps of fresh air. Doris and Julie held her steady until the blackness retreated, whereupon Anne nodded.

Doris smoothed a finger over Anne's cheek. "What was the trigger, hon?"

Anne pointed a shaky finger at the front door, but kept her eyes averted to prevent a repeat performance.

"Blond surfer dude, or guy with black curls?"

"Black curls."

"All right. Standard response plan, kiddo. Go take your break. I'll seat Curly at table twenty-eight. When you come back, take section four, which'll put him out of your sight."

"Roger." Anne gave a half-hearted salute, which was twice as confident as she felt, and stumbled toward the break room.

As always, the flashback had left her anxious yet drained. She wanted to curl up in a corner and sleep, but sleeping this soon after the ordeal would only bring nightmares. Nightmares meant screaming, and screaming at work, she knew from unfortunate experience, was a great way to lose her job.

She turned to close the employee door behind her and was surprised to find that Julie had followed her inside.

Julie rubbed her short, spiky blonde hair. "Gonna be okay?"

"Yeah, I just need a minute."

Anne sat on the faded cloth couch. The ancient thing had probably been there for as long as Hal had owned the diner. It protested her weight with a groan, which she would have taken personally had it not shown the same disrespect to everyone.

Julie sat next to her, frowning when the couch groaned again, and put her hand on Anne's with a familiarity just this side of uncomfortable, considering they'd only recently met.

"Would it help to talk about it?"

"Only if you consider me screaming incoherently as helpful."

Julie's eyes widened.

"Sorry," Anne said. "Most here are used to my twisted sense of humor."

"No, I get it. If you don't laugh ..."

"I'd be crying, right." Anne had done enough of that for several lifetimes and wasn't keen to do so in front of the new girl, whom she'd traumatized enough for one night. Although her heart was still pounding from the episode, Anne took a deep breath and managed to keep her voice steady. "So, aside from my little performance, how's your first day going?"

"No complaints, *amiga.* This isn't my first serving gig, so believe me when I say you've got a nice crew."

Julie ran a thumb over Anne's hand, which Anne realized with a start was still being held.

"So, are you and Doris an item? Don't get me wrong. She's older, sure, but ..."

Anne covered her mouth to hide a building guffaw.

"What's so funny?"

"Nothing."

"Baloney," Julie said. "This isn't the first time someone's asked you that, is it?"

"No, but it's the first time I've been asked while holding the asker's hand alone in the break room."

"Sorry, I'm a sucker for brown eyes and auburn hair. Throw that hourglass figure of yours in there, and I'm as good as goo."

Anne smiled at the compliment. Her full hips and bust were a little too hourglass-y for some, but she received more praise than critique, so it was hard to complain.

Julie leaned close, her eyes intent, still holding her hand.

"Anne," she said in a breathy voice, "can I ask you something?"

Anne's pulse, which had just started to settle, kicked back into high gear. "S-sure. Um ... what is it?"

"Being this close ..."

Julie tilted her head. Anne could feel her minty breath, warm on her lips.

"Does it ..."

Anne gulped and tugged at the neck of her work dress. *When did the heater come on?*

"D-does it what?"

"Does it take your mind off things?"

"My ... huh?"

Julie rocked back, laughing so hard that it came out in a hoarse wheeze. "Sorry, *amiga,*" she gasped between laughing fits. "I was just messing around to distract from whatever's bothering you. Did it work?"

"Oh. Y-yeah, definitely." Anne struggled to wrestle her heart rate — and now her dignity — back under control.

"Good. Now, I'd better get back out there before Mr. Caterino thinks I'm slacking on my first day on the job." Julie stood and held out her hand. "Coming?"

Anne hesitated only briefly before accepting it, and hoisted herself off the couch. "Yes. And as a senior staff member, I should tell you that no one calls him 'Mr. Caterino'."

"But I heard what's-his-name, the cook, call him that."

"Hector's new, too, and doesn't mingle with the staff much. Everyone else calls the boss 'Hal'."

"The cook is new? Man, that explains those hockey-puck burgers coming off the grill. I think one of my customers broke a tooth on that charred mess."

"We're working with him, but it's been a slow process. I —"

The door cracked open. Doris peeked inside. "Hey, kiddo, are you ..." She glanced at their joined hands. Her shock melted into a sultry grin. "Well, pardon me, lovebirds. I was just popping in to bring Anne some water, but I can get a couple glasses of wine and some candles instead. Maybe a blanket for that ratty old couch?"

Eww.

"Thanks, gutter brain, but we were just coming out." Anne silently cursed. "Okay, that was ... incriminating, but you know what I meant."

"Don't matter one lick if you were — which is the best part about living in San Francisco, if you ask me."

"You got that right," Julie said. She gave Anne's hand a final squeeze, then scooted past them out the door. *"Hasta luego, amigas!"*

Doris shook her head. "That girl's plenty *loco,* all right. Bet she ain't got one Latina bone in her body." She hooked an arm around Anne's shoulders and shoved the water glass into her chest. "You really doing all right?"

"I am."

Whether Julie had been serious about making a pass at her — which Anne wasn't sure of either way — it had been a dirty but effective tactic. Anne felt energized and ready to make her customers smile.

"Good," Doris said, "because I got specials for you at tables four and seven."

Anne tightened her ponytail, which hung nearly to the middle of her back, and nodded. She caught her friend in a hug before leaving. "Thank you."

"Any and every time, kiddo. Go get 'em."

Though it was the middle of December, the evening was unseasonably warm, which, in San Francisco terms, meant light jacket weather. It also made for an abnormally busy Friday night. The wait was over twenty minutes, with customers lined up outside, bathed in the glow of the 1950's-style neon sign reading "Hal's Diner". Anne silently wished the hostess luck and went to section four.

The first special Doris had mentioned, table four, was a mother and her little boy — seven at the oldest — both looking dour. Congealed gravy indicated their practically untouched plates had been sitting for a while.

Anne stood in front of their booth. "Not hungry?"

Mom, who was staring out the window, gave the barest shake of her head. The boy picked his fingernail at a fork tong, head hung low, as if he didn't have the energy — or the will — to do anything more. A brand-new baseball cap sat next to his plate.

Anne crouched until she was level with him. "Are you going to the game tonight?"

"It already started." He couldn't have sounded sadder.

"Oh no, were they sold out?"

He shook his head. "Mom got tickets, but the man at the gate said they were fake."

Mom continued to study the window, but her cheeks reddened. Her eyes began to glisten from unshed tears.

Uh oh.

Anne stood and cleared her throat. "Let me pack that food up for you. This feels more like a dessert night, wouldn't you say?"

No response. A tear splashed on Mom's placemat.

"Let me guess," Anne said to the little boy, undaunted. "You're a chocolate person. No ... white chocolate. And peppermint."

A spark of interest cracked his brooding scowl.

"And you," Anne said to the mother. "I sense ... raspberry. Lemon, of course, and something exotic." She snapped her fingers. "Lavender! That's not exotic, I know, but am I right?"

Mom looked at her with surprise and nodded.

"Be right back." Anne gathered their plates, went to the kitchen, and got to work.

A few minutes was all it took. It was more time than she could reasonably spare on a busy night like tonight, but when she revealed her creations to the waiting pair, she knew she'd made the right choice.

In front of the boy she set a platter of shaved dark chocolate. Four squares of white chocolate sat on top in baseball-diamond formation. Miniature candy canes with the hooks broken off served as baseball bats, next to marshmallow baseballs complete with thin lines of cherry syrup for red stitching. Gumdrops for people dotted the field and player boxes.

"Wow ..." The boy grabbed a candy cane and took a few tiny swings at a tossed marshmallow. The third attempt connected, sending it across the table into his mother's arm.

"Home run!" Anne cupped her hands around her mouth and hushed a crowd-cheering noise.

The boy grinned. He ran a gumdrop around the white chocolate bases and back to home, where he popped it in his mouth with a triumphant cheer.

Mom took one of the gumdrop outfielders. Her eyes still glistened, but her broad smile told Anne the tears were for a different reason.

"Next hit won't be so easy," the mother said. "You'll have to get by me!"

"You play baseball, Mom?"

Her smile faltered. "I used to, when ... when Dad was alive. He loved playing with his friends. One time, I invited myself along. No one seemed to mind me intruding on their guy time, so I became a regular. I even pitched on occasion."

"I've never seen you play."

"We stopped going when something even more fun came into our lives." She placed the cap on his head and pushed it down over his eyes. "You."

The boy yanked the hat off and briskly smoothed his hair. "Would you pitch to me, Mom?"

"I may need a few warmup throws, but sure. Catch!" She snatched a marshmallow baseball and tossed it so fast that the boy jerked in surprise. It bounced off his head, drawing laughs from all three of them.

"And this is for the glorious pitcher at the end of the inning." Anne placed a drink in front of her with vivid striations of red, yellow, and purple. "I'd give it a stir first."

Mom gasped at the colorful beverage. She swirled the straw, blending the liquids into a less-impressive muddle, then took a sip. Her eyes lit up. "This is wonderful!"

"And alcohol-free, though if you want the spiked version, just say the word."

"It's perfectly fine as-is. Besides ..." She turned to the boy with a grin. "I need to be able to pitch straight, right?"

"Right!" He readied his candy cane, a twinkle in his once-despondent eyes.

Anne left the happy pair to their game. Though still shaky from the earlier flashback, she felt lighter now than she had before the onset.

One down, one to go.

But the special at table seven would have to wait, especially if it was going to take as long as table four. Anne hurried to her other tables first, clearing dishes, setting places, refilling drinks, and settling bills with all the efficiency expected of an eighteen-year veteran waitress — the last five of which were right here at Hal's Diner.

Finally satisfied that her customers were taken care of, she headed to table seven.

At first glance, Anne couldn't tell what was wrong. The customer was a gentleman in a business-casual collared shirt and slacks. He looked to be about her own age, if she had to guess. Light-brown bangs were combed neatly to the side, creating a shelf over hazel-green eyes, which were fixed on an open paperback in his hands.

Curious, Anne bent down to look at the cover ...

... and gasped.

"The Adventures of Jayne Madison," Anne said in an awed whisper, "Book Five."

His eyes snapped up as if just noticing her. "You like the series?"

"Like? I've read everything by Georgette Parker a half-dozen times or more. Book One was the first fiction novel I ever read. I still have my original copy at home. I'm surprised to see you reading it, though. Jayne isn't a go-to hero for most guys."

"What can I say? I'm a sucker for a strong female protagonist."

Anne looked around, sure there must be a hidden camera somewhere, because it was almost too good to be true.

And it probably was. In fact, she wouldn't put it past Doris to have staged this just to get her talking to someone. Who knew if he'd actually read them?

There's an easy way to find out.

"So, what was your favorite part of Book Three?"

"Book Three ..."

Anne's hopes sank at his frown.

"Ah! That's easy. After Jayne thwarts the KGB spy's attempt on her life, she corners the would-be assassin in an oil refinery. They shoot each other's legs, putting them in a ground wrestling match to the death. He pins her down, slowly pushes a knife toward her throat ..."

"But it was a cheap knife," Anne said, her excitement building as if she were reading it for the first time. "While they were wrestling, Jayne had loosened the screw holding the blade, so she pulled the screw free, caught the blade ..."

"And used it to slit his throat."

They both grinned. Had the gory scene been from anything but a Jayne Madison novel, Anne would have worried about the discussion triggering another flashback, but Jayne never did. She was Anne's hero, a resourceful espionage agent of unparalleled skill. Her adventures were part of Anne's childhood, her identity, and, when things got rough, her escape.

And this was the first man she'd ever met who shared her obsession.

She offered her hand. "Anne Perrin."

"Derek Selenay," he said, taking it. "A pleasure."

I wholeheartedly agree.

His skin was soft, much softer than hers, which was rough from a lifetime of manual labor. Feeling self-conscious, Anne withdrew from the handshake and retrieved a pad and pen from her apron.

"So, Derek, what can I get you?"

Please say, "Your phone number ..."

It would be the fourth time this week Anne had heard that pickup line, but in this case, she'd probably give it to him.

"It's my first time here," he said. "What do you recommend?"

"For a fellow Madison fan, I suggest the turkey and mashed potatoes. The turkey is slow roasted to perfection, and the potatoes have extra butter. Not to mention that Jayne's favorite meal was ..."

"... a Thanksgiving dinner. All right, you sold me."

"Good man. Anything to drink?"

"Now, or after work?"

And there it was. He'd slipped it in so casually, Anne had almost missed it.

Derek was asking her on a date.

Her heart leaped, pounding her rib cage like a wild animal, eager for freedom after a decade of cruel captivity. There it had sat, watching others enjoy the wonders of the world, while it wasted away behind the very bars she'd created to keep it safe.

Anne's heart wanted out. And it was high time she let it.

"I ... I ..."

"I'd love to meet you after work," was all she had to say, but her treacherous mouth wouldn't form the words. Instead, her mind

insisted on playing the scenario through before committing to what her heart wanted, but hard experience said would end in disaster.

Anne would accept, to Derek's delight, then she'd float through the rest of the evening on a cloud puff. He'd meet her at the end of her shift, where she would have changed into her hum-drum dress, and asked Doris to help with her makeup, because Anne never wore makeup, and always ended up looking like a clown from a horror movie when she applied it herself.

They'd walk the city, lost in excited conversation about Jayne Madison, shared interests, and anything else that came to mind. They might even hold hands — Anne's heart did a double "yes, please!" backflip at the mere thought — until they found a bar or nightclub to have the promised cocktails.

And that was where the fairytale would end.

Anne didn't drink, and for good reason, but that wasn't the sticking point. In that crowded environment, unfamiliar men would be rubbing against her, ogling her, possibly groping places they had no right to touch. Anne gave herself five minutes tops before her post-traumatic stress disorder devolved into a full-blown, immersive hallucination — or Hell, as she called it, because once she was in, there was no coming out until it had finished running her through the torturous events that had caused her PTSD in the first place.

Derek wouldn't understand. No one except Doris had ever wanted to. When Derek saw her in that hysterical, near-catatonic state, it would be bye-bye Anne, forever and good riddance.

Accepting his offer would only cause suffering for them both.

Anne cleared her throat, but the lump remained. "I ... I just remembered," she said hoarsely, "we're out of turkey."

"Out? But you just said —"

"I know. I talked you into a hero's meal, then turned around and dashed your hopes against the refrigerator." Anne fidgeted with her apron. "Truth is, the turkey's ... rotten, so rotten that no amount of slow roasting could ever turn it into a meal worth eating."

Derek crossed his arms. "I find that hard to believe."

"Believe what you want, but I can't in good conscience let you partake of something when I know it will make you feel bad tomorrow, if not sooner. I'm sorry." Anne forced a smile through her murky despair. "Is there anything else you'd like?"

"You know, I think I lost my appetite."

Derek stood and donned his sport jacket. He held her gaze for a second, a hope in his eyes that perhaps she would change her mind.

Though a piece of her cried out in revolt, Anne held firm, wearing her professional waitress smile like a suit of happiness-proof armor.

With a sigh, Derek swiped his Jayne Madison novel from the table and left.

Anne couldn't say how long she stood staring after the first man she'd connected with in years, her mind in a numb fog, before a gruff *"Ahem"* brought her back to attention. Hal Caterino was looking at her from his office doorway, hairy arms crossed over his expansive stomach and greasy apron. The restaurant owner didn't seem angry, but a tick of his mustache told her that might quickly change, so Anne locked her heart back in its dreary cage and lost herself in work.

• • •

The rest of the evening rush thankfully passed without incident. Anne closed out her few remaining tables, set them up for the stragglers who might wander in between now and closing, then sat at the counter, where Doris and Julie were taking a well-earned breather.

Doris slid her an iced tea with a big-toothed grin. "So, how did table seven go? Did you two hit it off?"

Anne took a long sip. After the intense rush, the cold tea felt heavenly. "Sort of."

"Ain't no 'sort of' about it. You gonna see him again or not?"

"Not."

Doris stared at her.

"I, um ... may have referred to myself as a rotten turkey."

Julie's laugh shot soda out through her nose. She cleaned herself up with a dishrag, then continued laughing. "*Amiga,* your pickup lines need serious help. And by help, I mean therapy." Her eyes went wide. "Shit, did I really just say that? Sorry. That was way uncool of me."

"Don't worry about it," Anne said. "And you're probably right."

"About the therapy?" Julie blinked. "You get flashbacks so bad that you can't even breathe, and you aren't seeing a therapist? That's plain *loco* — er, I mean, I don't get it."

"Join the club," Doris said.

Anne shot her a frown. She'd explained why to Doris many times over the years, and in great detail, but it seemed she would be doing so again. Hopefully, her new audience would better understand.

"Remember what I told you in the breakroom," Anne said to Julie, "how talking about it makes bad things happen? Well, guess what therapists want to do."

"Talk about it?"

"Over, and over, and over. After my fifth session, I was so frazzled from screaming and suffocating that even thinking about going back to the therapist would trigger an episode. So I didn't. With Doris' help, though, I've gotten better."

Julie pointed to where Anne had stood earlier, clawing at her own throat. "That was 'better'?"

"Much. When the flashbacks first started, I had dozens a day. Today, I had only one episode, and yesterday none."

"Yeah, but ... man, being nearly choked to death a dozen times a day, or even once! I'd be muttering in a corner surrounded by people in white coats."

"It's amazing what you get used to," Anne said. "Besides, the flashbacks aren't all that bad. Some are just mild nausea, pains, smells, or general anxiety." Others were worse — far worse — but there was no sense scaring the new girl more than she already had. With luck, Julie would never have to witness the full extent of Anne's PTSD.

"Still, don't they have drugs or something that can help?"

"We tried," Doris said. "Anne didn't respond well. Said she'd rather live with the flashbacks than suffer the medication's side effects. Having seen it myself, can't say I blame her."

"*Ay, caramba!* Girl, you need to let me buy you a drink. I know I need one."

Anne batted her eyelashes. "Why, Julie, are you asking me on a date?"

The spiky blonde blushed.

Yikes! Maybe she is. One good foot-in-mouth deserved another, apparently. "Would you really go out with a ... rotten turkey like me?"

"Believe me, I've seen some messed-up girls in my time, and you don't even rank." Julie glanced at the clock. "But, sadly, I already have a date, who should be here in twenty minutes, so you get a pass. If it doesn't go well, though, watch out."

"I'm flattered to even make the list."

"Are you kidding? You're packing some hot stuff in that work dress. Those curves are kickin'! But don't worry, I'm not going to peek in the changing room or anything. Unless you want me to." Julie winked with a purring *meow.*

This time it was Anne who struggled to keep her drink from spouting out her nose. "Thanks a lot," she said with a grin. "The thought hadn't even entered my head until you put it there."

"But I did, and now you're going to fantasize about what it would be like to have a steamy — uh oh." Julie's gaze fixed on the front door, where a long-haired Asian woman was just entering.

Doris grinned. "That your date? She's cute."

"And early. I told her eight-thirty!" Julie turned her back on the woman to face Anne and Doris. "How do I look?"

"Like a waitress who's been serving food all day." Anne picked a crusted smear of mashed potatoes off her sleeve to make her point.

"Not the first impression I'd hoped to give."

"Go clock out and change," Anne said. "Business will be dead from here on anyway."

"Won't Hal mind me leaving early?"

"Nah," Doris said. "He'll be happy to save a few bucks on salary, so long as someone's here to close up, which Anne and I can do in our sleep."

"Okay, if you're sure. Thanks, *amigas!* I promise this won't become a habit."

Anne watched her dash to the employee lounge with a grin. "And, for our last good deed of the day ..."

"Gotta take care of our own, too. Speaking of ..." Doris gave Anne a wry smile. "I've asked you a dozen times over the years if you'd date a woman, and you've always blown it off. Would you really go out with Julie if she asked?"

"The male or female part isn't the hurdle," Anne said, evading the uncomfortable question, as usual. "It's the going out. You know what I'm like."

"Ain't sure I do anymore." Doris put a tender hand on her arm. "It's been years, Anne — *years* since you gone anywhere outside of your regular haunts, or even tried to go out with someone other than yours truly. I love you, kiddo. I always will. But mine ain't the kind of love you're craving, and we both know it."

"But ... we have a routine. A pattern. It's working!" Anne fought the panic clenching her stomach, and forced a calm breath. "Maybe in a few more years —"

"In a few more years, you'll be that much further past your prime, and I'll be that much closer to the grave. We're human, kiddo. We only got so many years on this planet, and the nearer I get to the end, the more I realize it weren't much time to begin with." Doris took her hand. "You're the daughter I never had. Maybe that's why I can't stand to see you spending all that precious time avoiding your pain, instead of chasing the happiness you deserve."

The panic returned in force. Anne gripped her hand so tightly that Doris groaned.

"Please," Anne said, "tell me you aren't saying what I think you're saying."

"No, kiddo, I ain't gonna leave you hanging, not after all the work we done to get you here. But something's gotta change or —"

"Okay!" Julie reappeared in a sharp collared shirt, slacks, and polished black dress shoes that might once have belonged to Anne's father. Her hair, which had lost some of its spikiness throughout the day, looked certifiably lethal again. "Now how do I look?"

"Like a million buckaroos," Doris said.

Anne yanked her belt buckle sideways to line up with her fly. "There, perfect. I hope your date appreciates the fine specimen she's getting tonight."

"Me too." Julie waggled her eyebrows, then bounded away with backward wave. "Thanks again, *amigas!*"

They watched her dash to the entrance, where her date greeted her with a smile. The woman's black sequined jacket and white shirt looked the perfect complement to Julie's outfit.

Julie seemed as surprised as Anne when the woman darted in for a kiss on the lips.

"That's their first date, right?"

Anne tore her eyes from the couple and remembered to breathe. "Um, yeah. Or so I assumed."

Doris grinned.

"What?"

"You're all flushed. That hottie in the skirt may have well kissed you."

"It was sweet! Don't turn it into more than it is."

"It's you who ain't turning it enough. Look, I don't care which side of the fence you land on — and if you want to straddle it for a while, that's cool, too. But I see that look in your eyes every time an affectionate couple of any orientation walk through that door. You want what they have, kiddo, and you ain't gonna be happy until you get it."

Anne's protest died in her throat.

Doris was right. The feeling in Anne's gut when she saw couples together wasn't just wishful romance; it was jealousy. She wanted someone to care for, and who cared for her. Someone to walk home with, drink hot cocoa with.

And, heaven forbid, someone with the stamina to stay by her side and help chase away her nightmares.

Hopelessness leeched the energy from her. She may as well wish for a dashing espionage agent to walk in the door and whisk her away on an adventure. Anne leaned against her friend.

"What do I do?"

"I don't know. But hang in there, kiddo. We'll think of something." Doris rubbed her shoulder with a mother's comfort, kissed her head, then went behind the counter and began to assemble silverware-and-napkin rolls in preparation for tomorrow.

Anne joined her in the familiar routine. It was an ordinary, monotonous task — a painful representation of Anne's life, now and for the rest of her bleak future.

2

HOME SWEET PRISON

ANNE AND DORIS CLOSED THE DINER, said a somber goodnight to each other, then caught their respective buses home — west for Doris, south for Anne.

There were plenty of seats available, as was usual for that time of night. Anne picked one with plenty of space around it and settled in. She would have loved to close her eyes, but sleeping on a city bus, especially at night, was a bad idea. Anne slipped her hand into her purse and gripped the small canister of pepper spray she always carried. She'd never had to use it, but there was a first time for everything.

At her stop, she stepped out of the bus and into the yellow halo of a streetlight. Cool night mist dappled her cheeks, sending a pleasant chill through her. It was a short walk from the bus stop to her apartment. Twice she made a wide berth to avoid stepping on a sleeping body nestled against the wall, huddled in dirty blankets, with only cardboard between them and the cold cement.

A man stirred, extended a dirt-covered hand with a moan. Anne took a few singles from her share of the night's tips and pressed them into his palm. His grimy face lit up. He muttered something and nodded. She left him with a warm smile and rounded the corner to her apartment complex. She punched the code into the keypad, waited for the lock to buzz, then secured it behind her.

She crossed the sparse inner courtyard to her apartment and climbed the few steps to the door. Her neighbors were quiet tonight; inserting her key into the noisy, aging lock felt like a desecration of this rare tranquility. Once inside, Anne slid the deadbolt in place, then wedged the security bar under the handle. She made her normal rounds, inspecting the bathroom and bedroom of her small apartment for intruders, before changing out of her work clothes and allowing herself to relax on the couch.

Anne retrieved her latest book from the coffee table — a steamy romance novel about two FBI agents who were secretly in love — but the passion on the pages failed to move her tonight. Her mind kept straying back to her conversation with Doris, and her utter failure to go out with a man who just might have been her perfect fit.

Doris was right. Something had to change.

But what?

Anne went to the kitchen and opened the freezer. Two rows of ice cream pint containers greeted her like dear friends. She chose one at random — they were all her favorite flavors, so it was hard to go wrong — and grabbed a spoon from her sparse cutlery drawer.

She wanted happiness. Wanted a relationship. So what was holding her back?

The answer should have been obvious: eighteen years of panic-inducing flashbacks, recurring nightmares of her teenage trauma, and general anxiety had made it difficult enough to function in society — let alone establish a relationship with someone.

Not that she hadn't tried. Anne grimaced at the memory.

"Get over it," Gary had told her, though she could never bring herself to actually tell him what "it" was, and she had the impression he didn't want to know. "You're an adult, for Christ's sake. Stop bawling all the time and act like one!"

But she couldn't. In fact, the harder she had tried to forget, the worse her flashbacks became. Gary had eventually tired of her frequent hysteria and left her for someone sane, ten years ago now. The worst part was that Anne couldn't fault him.

I'd like to leave me for someone sane, too.

On the flip side, Anne had a steady job, a roof over her head, and had managed to turn her apartment into a sanctuary, where the terrifying flashbacks rarely occurred. What more could a thirty-six-year-old teen runaway ask for?

She cracked the lid of her ice cream and dug in. A pint of chocolate, all to herself.

Sitting at her tiny kitchen table, in her small apartment.

Alone.

The spoon slipped from her loose fingers and clattered to the floor. Anne left it there.

Is this what my life has become?

It was Friday night. The city was alive with parties, dance clubs, loud bars, theater. People were laughing, joking, exchanging phone numbers. New relationships would form. Not all of them would work out, of course, but a lucky few might have found "The One" — that unique individual who understands you and makes you feel wonderful, like you're a person worth knowing.

Friday night. Meet new people night. Where was Anne?

Locked in my apartment.

Tomorrow was Saturday, an even livelier night for socializing. Where would Anne be?

Locked in my apartment.

Sunday night?

Locked in my apartment.

Next week? Next month? Next *year?* Anne hung her head in her hands.

Locked in my goddamned apartment.

What's holding me back ...?

The answer splashed her in the face like cold water.

Fear.

Not of her flashbacks, she realized, but of disappointment from her future partner. Their rebuke when she breaks down in public for no reason. Their revulsion when she inadvertently screams at their touch. Their frustration when she wakes up crying because she'd been reliving the pain, terror, and helplessness of that terrible day yet again.

Anne had given up because she was afraid nobody could love someone as broken as she was.

But what if ...

She capped the ice cream and put it back in the freezer.

What if ...

Her pajamas were off before she'd reached the bedroom. Anne sifted through her closet in a frenzy. Did she not own a single dressy outfit? Then she spotted something. On the far end of the dowel was, apparently, the only fancy dress in her entire wardrobe. Looking at it made her heart ache — she'd bought it for her first date with Gary — but it was either that or jeans and an old sweater.

I hope it still fits.

It did, if barely, as did the matching shoes she'd only worn once before giving up on the uncomfortable things. She shed her ponytail, then brushed it out to its full length around the middle of her back, where it shimmered like auburn silk.

What if maybe ...

She slid a box out from under the bed, then another, then another, until she finally found the sequined purse that rounded out her ensemble. She tipped the contents of her battered cloth purse onto the comforter and stuffed only the essentials into the fancy, but smaller one: wallet, keys, breath mints, flashlight, lip balm, cell phone, ibuprofen, tissues ... She considered packing the Taser, but settled for the smaller pepper spray instead.

Just maybe ...

A perfume bottle sat on the back of her bathroom shelf, dusty from years of neglect, but smelled fine when she sprayed a bit on her wrist, so she rubbed her wrists to thin it out, then sprayed her finger and dabbed tiny circles below each ear. Makeup she would skip; she was fortunate to have a complexion that required little cover up, and she was terrible at applying it anyway.

The real me will have to do.

She returned to her bedroom and examined the final results in the full-length mirror.

The muted blue dress was tighter than it had been ten years ago — no surprise there — but passable. A sleeveless top exposed her pale arms and shoulders. Her ample bosom threatened to burst from the confines of the low V-neck, exposing cleavage of scandalous proportions.

Doris would be proud, Anne thought with a smile.

A simple white belt cinched her waist, accentuating an hourglass figure that made Doris jealous, then rounded the generous swell of her hips into gentle pleats hanging down to her ankles. Anne stepped closer to the mirror. Her dark brown eyes and naturally full lashes, she had been told, needed no enhancements. She gave a satisfied nod.

What if maybe — just maybe — The One is out there tonight, waiting for me?

It sounded like fantasy, even in her own head, but what she knew for certain was that Doris was right: something had to change.

And that something was Anne.

If she didn't put herself out there — if she didn't at least *try* — then she would never find out. Derek, with his Jayne Madison obsession, may have been her soulmate, and she'd let him slip through her fingers.

She wouldn't make that mistake again.

Years of solitude had finally caught up with her. It had allowed her to survive, that was true, but Anne was sick of just surviving. She once had aspirations: dreams of going to college, establishing a career, settling down. She wanted a house, a family, kids playing in the yard, and a husband who loved his children — not abused them, like her father had to her poor little brother.

The last eighteen years had been nothing but damage control to stave off the demons constantly threatening her sanity. Anne balled her fists and marched from the bedroom.

Not anymore.

On her way through the living room, she brushed her fingers over the FBI romance book and sighed. She wanted that: to fall in love so completely that she would throw everything away to be with that person, and to know they cared for her just as deeply. Someone who understood her pain, a partner to help fight her demons, comfort her through the nightmares and flashbacks, and make her feel human again.

She wanted to find The One.

And to do that, Anne had to risk her safety, face the anxiety, and put herself out there. She went to the door and removed the security bar, but her hand lingered on the knob.

It wouldn't be easy. Flashbacks they may be, but the fear, anxiety, and paralysis were real.

Anne ground her teeth and opened the deadbolt. Cool mist greeted her once again.

She breathed it in.

For the first time since she was a teenager, Anne was ready to challenge her demons. She didn't know if she could defeat them — or if victory was even possible — but she knew with every fiber of her thirty-six-year-old being that she didn't want to die alone in this apartment.

Not without a fight.

With new resolve, Anne strode purposefully into the night.

3

PIZZA

ANNE ROCKED ON HER HEELS in her uncomfortable shoes. The bus was nowhere in sight — not that she could see very far through the thick fog that muted both light and sound with equal prejudice. She hugged her arms around her middle in a futile attempt to ward off the cold. In her enthusiasm to face the world, she had broken the City's cardinal rule to always bring a jacket.

A shiver ran through her, rattling her teeth loud enough to draw a look from the only other person at the bus stop: a tall man with short hair and a strong jaw, stuffed into a suit that strained to contain his broad shoulders. Hard eyes swept over her, a baron assessing a lowly petitioner, and dismissed her just as quickly. Anne backed away. The late hour and shrouding fog made it feel as if they were the only two in the entire city — not a comforting thought, considering he could wrestle her to the ground with one arm.

She shivered again and stepped further away. *So much for challenging my fears ...*

He studied her once more, puzzled this time, then his expression softened. "Sorry, I didn't mean to glare," he said in a deep voice befitting his powerful stature. "It's been a rough day."

"It's okay," Anne said with a warm smile, though she maintained her safe distance. "We've all had them."

He started to reply, then turned away with a sigh. A white line flashed along the back of his jacket.

Anne grimaced. It was a nasty tear. The suit looked expensive — probably more than the sum of her entire wardrobe.

And he may not even know it's there ...

"E-excuse me," she said after a second. "Not to add to your troubles, but did you know your jacket has a rip along the back shoulder?"

He pulled it off to examine the damage, revealing a red-striped necktie and tight-fitted dress shirt hinting of rippled muscles beneath. Anne's breath caught despite her nervousness. He was a fine specimen, to be sure, and he wasn't wearing a wedding ring. The thought stirred a pleasant tingle in her chest, but, best of all, the sight of him hadn't triggered a single flashback.

Anne wanted to sing.

"Figures," he said, running a finger along the tear.

"Was your day really that bad?"

"One for the record."

"I'm sorry."

She caught herself reaching to give him a comforting touch and quickly reeled herself in. Attractive as his inverted A-frame might be, he was a complete stranger at a deserted bus stop in a city full of nice, eccentric — and sometimes dangerous — people. The jury was still out into which category this mystery hunk fell.

Her sympathy drew a skeptical frown from him, and it was Anne's turn to sigh. When someone was kind to you in the City, it was usually because they were crazy or wanted something.

And, unfortunately, I meet at least one of those criteria.

Feeling as if she had already lost, Anne cleared her throat and turned her attention away.

"William," he said. She was surprised to see his hand extended. "William Taplin."

Take a chance! Doris cheered from the recesses of her mind.

It was easier said than done. A decade of rejecting any and every interested man had left her skittish and unsure; taking his hand in the dark at this lonely bus stop would be a battle of sheer will.

But one she was determined to win.

I won't die alone, she reminded herself. *Not without a fight.*

Taking a calming breath, Anne accepted his greeting.

"Anne Perrin," she said, struggling to keep her voice steady. "Pleasure."

His grip was firm, his skin calloused, like hers, but probably from pumping iron at the gym instead of waitressing. This time, the pleasant tingle touched more than her chest. Anne jerked her hand back at the sudden stirring, dormant for so long that she mistook the flutter in her stomach for actual illness.

"I-I'm sorry! It's just ... It's a pleasure. Really." *Really!*

William's smile was slow in coming, but worth the wait. The hard edges melted from around his eyes and dimpled either side of a dazzling display of teeth. He could have been the centerpiece of a motivational poster. Anne struggled to keep her breathing under control.

"So, Anne Perrin, are you headed home?"

"No. I was just heading out, as a matter of fact."

"To meet your boyfriend?"

The obvious pickup line made them both smile.

"I'm single," she said. "In fact, I ah ..." Anne closed her eyes and forced the words out. "I was looking for some c-company."

She opened her eyes to find him staring with a wary expression. Her hand flew to her mouth.

"Oh my God, that sounded terrible! I-I didn't mean ..." She bowed her head, letting her long hair fall forward to conceal her shame.

Shoot me now ...

His laugh made her peek through the amber veil.

"I suppose offering to be your escort for the night would be in poor taste now."

"N-not necessarily," she said, biting her lip.

"Then it's a date."

Anne's heart raced. She was excited simply because she *was* excited, but also terrified of where the evening may lead. The idea of this strapping man being her date made her palms sweat, though he showed none of her own apprehension.

"There's an Italian restaurant five blocks south of here," William said. "The pizza's nothing special, but the bar is top-notch."

"I know it, even know the owner."

Her smile was so broad that her cheeks hurt, but it couldn't be helped; Anne was astonished how quickly her goal for the evening had manifested.

Meeting a single guy at the bus stop who's handsome and *has a decent job ...*

It had to be fate: the universe telling her it was finally time to be happy in love.

And she was ready.

Anne sidled closer until their elbows almost touched.

More than ready, she decided.

She flashed her beaming smile up at him. William returned it, and they stood in silence until the bus eventually barged through the mist and carried them away, leaving Anne's vivid imagination plenty of time to fret about how she was going to handle the possible after-dinner events.

What if he offered to walk her home? Invited her back to his place? Tried to kiss her? Would she freak out if he tried to touch her, as she had with Gary?

Probably.

Anne heaved a sigh and followed him off the bus with more anxiety than when she had boarded, but relaxed a bit when she caught the familiar whiff of Giovessi's gourmet pizza.

Antonio Giovessi brightened on seeing her and waved from behind the counter. "Am I losing my mind?" he said in a light Italian accent. "Or is it Tuesday already?"

Anne swiped a menu from the counter and shook her head. "That's the thanks I get for breaking my routine to bring you a new customer, Tony? Sarcasm?"

"All right, all right. So, is this new customer someone special?"

The awkward question, followed by a suggestive waggle of Antonio's eyebrows, silenced her.

William noticed her discomfort and a smile twitched the corners of his mouth. "You tell me," he said, returning his attention to Antonio. "She propositioned me at the bus stop."

Thankfully, Antonio missed the crass joke that made her ears burn. He turned his happy eyes to her and clapped his hands. "Our Anne has a date! This calls for the special table. Raul! Get the candles from the back, and the nice tablecloth! The one with the horses."

He gave Anne a confident wink, as if the stallion-print tablecloth all but assured their wedding, then hurried off to supervise the construction of their romantic oasis.

"Relative?" William said, gesturing to the pair who were now arguing in heated Italian across a battered wooden table.

"Only on Tuesdays," Anne said weakly, still blushing. "It's not a very exclusive membership, mind, but it seems they've accepted you into the tribe. Welcome to the family! Name change is optional, by the way, but I could totally see you as a Rocco or Dante."

A chuckle from the back of the restaurant caught her attention. Its source, a plain-looking fellow in a brown leather jacket, was smiling at her. She returned it with a laugh. His smile faltered. He ran a nervous hand through his thick hair and focused on his untouched plate of lasagna. Anne found his awkwardness comforting, in a way.

At least I'm not the only ball of nerves tonight.

Apparently William hadn't found her joke as funny. His expression went flat, jaw tight. She wanted to apologize, but wasn't entirely sure how she had offended him. Antonio soon called them to their table. She had just worked up the courage to ask what was wrong when William snapped out of it and pulled a chair out for her. She accepted the polite offer with a note of thanks, but was unable to conjure her earlier enthusiasm. Their interactions since entering the restaurant left her with an uneasy feeling, and Anne was suddenly thankful William had chosen to dine at the only restaurant outside of Hal's Diner where she felt comfortable.

"Want a drink?" William said.

"An iced tea would be great."

"Going for the hard stuff, I see."

I wish.

"It's for your own good," Anne said. "I sing when I'm drunk, and I can't carry a tune to save my life."

"She does not lie!" Antonio called from the counter.

Another chuckle from the guy in the brown jacket.

Looks like I have an audience.

"Don't mind if I do, then?"

She shook her head, and William cracked open the wine menu.

Anne laced her fingers under her chin. "So, what do you do for a living?"

"Florist," he said without looking up.

"Seriously?"

"No. I'm a stockbroker — was a stockbroker, until a few hours ago. They let me go."

"Oh, I'm so sorry. I guess you are having a pretty bad day."

No wonder he's been a little touchy. Poor guy ...

"Not entirely." He gave her a poignant wink. "I did meet you, after all."

And the pleasant flutter was back.

"Thanks," she said around a smile that she couldn't have put away if she'd wanted to. "Mine is looking better, too."

A glass shattered. They turned in time to see Brown Jacket shaking water from his hand. The shy, boyish look from earlier was gone; in its place was a hard edge that made Anne shiver.

And it was directed at William.

"Do you know him?" Anne said quietly.

William shook his head. His steely eyes held the stranger's, but he wasn't upset. If anything, William seemed amused. Anne shifted in her seat while the staring match continued, fighting the urge to duck under the line of invisible fire between them. Brown Jacket eventually relented and helped Raul clean up the broken glass.

"Okay ..." Anne scratched her head. "Want to tell me what just happened there?"

William shrugged his broad shoulders. "He's jealous, if I had to guess. You're the prettiest woman here."

Anne grinned. "Here's a tip: those cheesy pickup lines work better after a few drinks."

"Which you declined."

"And glad I did, otherwise I'd be fawning all over you by now, and poor Tony would have to pry us apart to keep his restaurant respectable."

"Don't be silly!" Antonio said. "That is why we have a room in the back! *'Giovessi'* is Italian for love, you know."

Anne waved him off with a laugh. "Fine! I'll have one glass of red wine. But watch those lines, mister." She wagged a finger at William, who demurred with a small nod. "And any hearing loss from my caterwauling is your fault."

Conversation flowed easily after that. William ordered the wine, while Anne ordered them her favorite entree: a pesto, feta, and artichoke pizza topped with shredded lemon garlic chicken — a flavor extravaganza that dazzled her taste buds.

Even the wine was an adventure. Anne closed her eyes after the first sip. It wasn't an expensive bottle — Antonio didn't carry those — nor was it her favorite, but she had forbidden herself alcohol for so long that she'd forgotten what it tasted like. Too soon her glass was empty, but, when Antonio offered to refill it on the house, she shook her head.

"Not much of a drinker?" William said, allowing his own glass to be filled.

"Not anymore. Alcohol and I have a rocky history."

He grunted. "I didn't peg you for an alcoholic."

"It was more of a crutch than a disease. It helped me through a rough patch of my life — or I thought it was helping, anyway. Turns out what they say is true: you can't hide from your problems in a bottle, so I stopped."

"Until tonight."

Anne shrugged. "What can I say? The adage 'liquid courage' is also true."

"You're nervous. That's good."

"Come again?"

"Fear is healthy. Natural. It drives us to be better, lifts us from our stagnant existence, exposes the illusion of safety for the lie it is." His eyes lit with a passion she hadn't seen before. "Fear is the most basic, wondrous expression of humanity there is. Don't be ashamed."

"Wow, that's, ah ..." Anne tapped her empty wine glass, tempted to call for a refill despite her resolution. "I can honestly say I've never thought of it like that. I —"

Brown Jacket bumped her chair on the way to the counter. His hazel eyes met hers, brows furrowed with concern. Twice he started to speak, but he eventually frowned and stalked from the restaurant without a backward glance. She looked to William, who shook his head.

"Jealous, I told you," William said. "Small of him to take it out on you, though."

"Maybe."

She hadn't received either impression from Brown Jacket, only deep concern, and an appreciation for her peculiar humor.

"Guaranteed. Want to bet he's outside waiting for us when we leave?"

Anne shuddered and squeezed her eyes shut. The suggestion tugged at her mind and threatened to loose a flashback.

Please, not here. Not on our first date ...

She took a deep breath and recalled all the happy things that happened tonight, with a focus on their positive emotions. The flashback bubbled just at the surface, prickling her skin, but finally retreated into the dark depths of her psyche. When she opened her eyes, she found William studying her with interest.

"Sorry," he said. "I was trying to make light of an awkward situation."

"No, it's not your fault, it's ..." Anne drummed her fingers on the table in time with her pounding heart, desperately trying to think of something to change the subject. "A-are you married?"

Even if her sputtered question had been appropriate — which it wasn't — his hardened expression confirmed that she'd crossed a line.

Nice going, Anne. Waiter, check please!

"No," he said eventually, and left it at that.

"William, I'm sorry, I didn't mean —"

He waved it off, though his eyes remained hard. "It's a recent thing. I'd rather not talk about it."

"Of course."

Anne steered clear of marriage-related topics after that. In an attempt to recover, she kicked into professional waitress mode and kept the mood light, as she would with any of her customers at the diner. William was slow to respond, but was openly smiling by the time the pizza came, a feat for which she gave herself a pat on the back.

"You weren't exaggerating about that pizza," he said once they'd finished. "I've never had anything like it."

Anne smiled. "Wait until you try the tiramisu. It's to die for."

"Actually, I was thinking ice cream. There's a parlor south of here that's supposed to be the best in the City."

"Count me in!"

"That was quick," William said with a grin. "I thought I'd have my work cut out convincing you to stay out late."

"Oh, please! This is ice cream we're talking about and, with a build up like that, how could I refuse? There is one condition, though."

He arched an eyebrow. She leaned forward and dropped her voice to a whisper.

"The job is on you to explain to Antonio why we're not sticking around for his dearly departed mother's tiramisu recipe. Double points if you don't make him cry."

"I'll think of something."

He flagged Antonio and, to his credit, settled the bill like a gentleman, despite her offer to pay. They even managed to escape without hearing Antonio's sob story tailored to guilt-trip customers into buying his mother's tiramisu, which Anne suspected was store-bought anyway.

William surprised her on the way out by offering his arm. She hesitated only briefly before taking it. The muscles beneath his sleeve were just as firm as she'd imagined. She tensed, afraid that a flashback might surface, but a pleasant warmth ran through her instead.

Anne looked up at his handsome face and smiled.

Was this real? Could her lonely life really have turned around so quickly? It seemed impossible. Yet here she was, hooked on the arm of a dreamboat, and she had managed to hold a flashback at bay without Doris' help.

All that, and the ice cream is still to come.

Her smile broadened.

Things could certainly be worse.

4

DESSERT

HALF A BLOCK FROM GIOVESSI'S, Anne noticed that her date was regularly glancing behind them. "What is it?" she said.

"Your tongue-tied friend from the restaurant," William said. "Seems like he's heading in the same direction we are."

Anne looked over her shoulder.

Sure enough, Brown Jacket followed not a dozen yards behind them with his hands in his pockets. His eyes fell under her scrutiny, but his pace didn't slow. She turned back and tightened her grip on William's arm.

"Maybe it's just a coincidence."

"I doubt it. He's probably trying to find out where you live."

"Don't be silly," Anne said, but a chill gripped her heart. "H-he seemed nice."

"The crazy ones often do."

She shivered; Brown Jacket's stare prickled her back. Her words came out in a strained whisper.

"What are we going to do?"

"Keep walking for now. We'll find out soon enough if he's really following us."

"But ... what if he has a gun?"

The corners of William's mouth twitched, though whether into a smile or grimace, she couldn't tell in the poor light.

"Just follow my lead and run when I tell you to."

In these shoes? Anne sighed. *The first night in a decade I don't wear sneakers, and of* course *it turns into a track and field event.*

She kept her reservations to herself, however, and nodded.

Two blocks passed. Each felt like a mile. Anne kept her eyes to the sidewalk, not daring to look behind lest she miss William's signal. At the third block, William hooked a right turn at the corner.

"Run," he said as soon as Brown Jacket was out of sight, then detached himself from her arm and ran ahead.

Anne kicked her heels to catch up — *damn these dress shoes!* — but William seemed less interested in speed than inspecting the shops they passed. He stopped in front of an old furniture store and twisted the aging door handle, grunting and shaking with the effort. Anne looked behind them; they had only seconds before Brown Jacket rounded the corner.

The knob jerked with a loud *snap*. William pushed the door open and ushered her inside, then quietly closed it behind them. Anne hid behind a couch, out of view from the display windows, while William hunkered his larger frame behind an oversized recliner. Her heart raced — not out of fear, for once, but excitement. After years of stagnation, Anne felt alive, like she was actually living a chapter from a Jayne Madison novel. It was wonderful.

And it was all thanks to William.

On her own, Anne would have been terrified — possibly dead by now — but his presence allowed her to view the strange events as an adventure. Part of her wondered why they had run at all. William was the larger and stronger of the two; if it came to a fight, she would put her money on him.

Streetlights washed the front of the large showroom with a sickly yellow hue. Anne stayed absolutely still; the only sound was her thundering pulse in her ears.

Heavy footsteps from outside made her hold her breath. The shadow of a man appeared on the couch behind her. Footsteps and shadow paused. Anne imagined Brown Jacket looking in the window, searching for his quarry who had inexplicably vanished.

Seconds passed. The shadow didn't move. Anne thought her heart would burst from excitement. She secretly wished Brown Jacket would discover the damaged doorknob and enter, just so she could watch William defend her like a valiant knight. The thought made her giddy. Anne clamped a hand over her mouth to keep from giggling.

After what felt like an eternity, the shadow moved on, heavy footsteps fading into nothingness. Anne relieved her burning lungs with a gasp, followed by laughter she could no longer contain — quiet at first, but soon had her rolling helpless on the carpet. William stood over her and sighed. His lips twitched again into a could-be-smile-or-frown, then he weaved his way toward the back of the showroom.

"What are you doing?" Anne said, wrestling her laughter under control.

"Looking for a back way out. He might be waiting for us out there."

He has a point.

Jayne Madison had been caught several times by that very trap. Anne picked herself up from the floor and joined him.

A storage warehouse adjoined the showroom, separated by a thick set of double doors lit only by a wan outside light filtered through grimy windows. She fished a small flashlight from her purse and flicked it on.

"Turn it off," William said quietly. "We don't want anyone seeing that from outside. Just sit tight while I find the door."

Anne turned the flashlight off and put it away, glad the darkness hid her blush.

With all the spy novels I've read, you think I'd know better. I guess there's no substitute for experience. She couldn't help but grin. *Which is exactly what this is.*

Determined not to let William have all the fun, Anne picked her way to the opposite wall and began feeling around for the exit.

The sound of a deadbolt sliding shut made Anne jump. She hunkered down, counting on the darkness to hide her, and listened.

Silence.

She swallowed and counted to thirty.

Still nothing.

"William," she hissed. "Was that you?"

"Yes."

Anne jumped; she could feel his breath on the back of her neck. "Jesus! Don't do that again unless you know CPR and are willing to use it." She took a moment to calm her nerves, then frowned. "Wait, that was you? The sound came from the showroom door. What were you doing over there?"

"Locking it."

"Oh, in case he doubles back and searches the showroom. Good thinking."

"No." His fingers brushed her hair. "To make sure you don't escape."

"Make sure I don't ..."

It may have been her imagination, but the room felt suddenly colder. Her mind churned to a halt, unable or unwilling to process the change in his tone that made her hair stand on end.

"W-what are you talking about?" It wasn't a question; it was a plea — a last desperate attempt to stave off the demons who had begun to scratch and claw at the walls of her sanity.

William turned on a lamp. Anne wished he hadn't.

Gone was the nice guy he had been for most of the evening. Steel-gray eyes fixed on hers, alight with a passion she recognized from his brief lecture at the restaurant.

... when he was talking about fear.

Her demons surged against their meager confines. Rising terror stole the warmth from her body, causing her to shiver. His frightening smile broadened, and Anne realized at once why the demons were so eager to greet him.

They knew a kindred spirit when they saw one.

"I-I'll scream," she said in a shaky voice.

"Yes, you will."

"Passionate" no longer described William. His lips twisted into a predatory show of teeth; his pupils were tiny dots centered in eyes so wide she thought they might pop from their sockets.

"You'll scream for me — again and again. Do you know why?"

She gave a wooden shake of her head.

With terrible slowness, William drew a large pocketknife and extended the blade. Anne heard herself whimper.

"Because I'm going to hurt you."

"But I didn't do anything," she whined through trembling lips.

The blade flashed in the lamplight. Anne shrank against the table she'd been hiding behind.

"Please, I-I didn't do anything." Tears fell on her bare arms, but her gaze was fixed upon the terrifying steel. "I ... I just want to go home. Please."

His wild eyes, if possible, grew wilder. "I knew you were special," he said with barely contained excitement. "I wanted you from the moment I saw you cower at the bus stop, but after seeing your naked fear in the restaurant at the mere suggestion of a stalker ..." William shuddered. "I need you, Anne ... need to explore how deep your fantastic terror goes."

Anne sobbed, shaking her head. "You're inhuman ..."

How anyone could enjoy watching someone else suffer — as she had suffered every day for the last eighteen years — was incomprehensible. At any moment, he was going to fold the knife and admit this was all just an elaborate joke. He couldn't really be this cruel. No one could.

Any second now ...

The knife edged closer. Anne withered to the floor, curled her arms around her head, but her eyes followed the blade as if it were a viper preparing to strike.

The demons roiled from their prison. She sensed their phantom hands closing in, ready to pin her once again to the bed, to choke her, hurt her, violate her.

William grabbed her arm.

His touch snapped something inside of Anne. Her pent-up fear, tension, and anxiety exploded in a roaring, "NO!" She struggled in vain to break his grip, prying at his fingers.

William seemed to enjoy the show, which pissed her off even more. He yanked her to her feet. Anne's free hand flung out behind her and fastened onto something smooth and hard. Not caring what it was, she swung the heavy object with all her strength, aiming for his head.

The mighty weapon turned out to be a wood sculpture. Too late, William released her and jerked his head back, but the sharp corner caught his cheek and tore a bloody gash right down to the bone. He stumbled backward with an angry cry.

Anne wasted no time and bolted from her hiding spot, aware that both William and her demons were just one step behind.

If he catches me ...

Anne shook the tears from her eyes. She couldn't let that happen.

Never again.

Anne weaved around stacks of furniture, running as fast as her impractical dress shoes would allow. The maze was too high for her to see over, unfortunately, so even the weak lighting the table lamp provided couldn't show her if she was heading for the exit or ...

She skidded to a halt at a dead end.

No, she thought, her mind as blank as the wall in front of her. *No, no, no!*

The demons teased her hair, stroked her wrists with malicious promise. She gripped her head and swiped at their phantom touches.

Think! she scolded herself against the panic threatening to consume her. *There must be something I can do ...*

With a gasp, Anne dove into her purse for the pepper spray.

Except her purse wasn't there. Dumbfounded, she patted herself all around with the vain hope that it was somewhere else on her body.

Her hope vanished when William rounded the corner with her purse dangling from his finger. Blood ran freely from the gaping cheek wound she'd given him — a fact his enraged expression said he had not forgotten.

"Looks like you dropped something," he said, then hurled her last defense to a distant part of the furniture maze.

Anne collapsed to the floor, sobbing. William approached like an executioner to the block.

... and with him came her demons.

He stooped to restrain her.

There was no need. Phantom hands had already pinned her to the bed, dragging her back to that hallucinatory place she called Hell.

5

DOUG

THE WAREHOUSE DISAPPEARED, replaced by the four walls of her childhood bedroom.

Anne was eighteen again, naked on her bed. Four of her brother's jock friends surrounded her: three held her down by her wrists and ankles, while the fourth, Chet, was on top of her, with his hand clamped around her neck.

She thrashed beneath him, struggling for air. Wet ropes of her hair flung all around, slapping his face and shocking her chest with chill water.

I don't want to die, I don't want to die! The words tore through her mind, over and over.

Chet was going to kill her.

Anne looked to her fifteen-year-old brother, Doug, who stood in the doorway with his arms crossed.

Watching.

Her panic fled, replaced with profound sadness, a wounding of her soul that would never heal. Doug's judging scowl hurt more than her nose, where Chet had bashed her with the bedroom door when he barged in. More than her cheek, where Chet had twice punched her for resisting his assault. More than her neck, where his fingers were choking the life from her. That Doug could stand by and let this happen to his own sister was testament to how badly their father's abuse had broken him. Her heart bled for the little boy she used to console after the beatings, the shouting that had left him scared and confused because he didn't know what he'd done wrong. No one except their father did.

Then something changed — a glitch in the torturous programming that had played unerringly thousands of times before.

Chet held a knife. His expression, which had always been cruel, had a glint of insanity that took her terror to new heights. Anne was going to die, but only after this sadistic beast had tortured her, flayed her open, and drained every last scream from her broken body.

"Dougie, please!" Anne managed to cry through her ravaged throat. "He's going to kill me! Please!"

Chet pressed the knife against her throat. Blood dripped from a gaping cheek wound that had suddenly appeared and splattered onto her chest. She struggled, but the jocks held her fast.

"Dougie, please," Anne said, forcing the words out through desperation and tears. "Help! I don't want to die, I don't want to die! Help, Dougie! *Help me!*"

A loud crash echoed through the house, as if the front door had been knocked from its hinges.

Hope filled her. Was their father home early? Had he somehow found out?

Amidst her wondering, a miracle occurred — an unprecedented deviation in Hell's torture script.

Her brother Doug stepped into the room.

And he was furious.

Anne couldn't believe her eyes, though she desperately wanted to. She had wished for so long to see that look of passion that unequivocally said *Get away from her, that's my sister!* The pain where the door had struck her face, the humiliation of being stripped naked and assaulted in her own bedroom, even the lunatic with a knife; it was all bearable, she realized, so long as she and Doug faced it together, like a real family should.

But there was a problem: Even if he hadn't been outnumbered four-to-one, her lanky brother was no match for any of them — especially Chet, who was taller, broader by far, and armed with a knife.

Doug didn't seem to care. His attention flitted between her and Chet. She thought it strange that he ignored the other jocks, and stranger still when they docilely stepped aside to let him past.

"Funny," Chet said to Doug, "I didn't think you were actually following us. I only said that to scare her."

"Put the knife down and let her go." Doug's voice was oddly calm, considering the situation, almost sad. "I know about the disturbance in the financial district today. They let you off with a warning, William. But they will prosecute if you don't walk away from this now."

William? The name struck a chord of terror deep inside, but Anne couldn't place it.

Chet shook with rage. "Oh, you know, do you?" He spat blood on the floor. "How the fuck do you know? Are you a cop? Or did that bitch send you, like she sent her goddamn lawyer!" He slashed open the chair next to him with an angry shout. "She humiliated me in front of the entire fucking staff and cost me my job!"

"I'm not a cop," Doug said, "nor a lawyer, and I don't condone how your wife chose to deliver the divorce papers. I'm just here to make sure Anne gets home safely. What you do outside of that is your business."

Home? Anne was already home. And why would anyone mistake her fifteen-year-old brother for a cop or lawyer?

"I see, so you're here for her?"

Chet's voice had dropped to a dangerous whisper. Doug stepped forward, but froze when Chet yanked Anne to her feet and pressed the knife to her throat.

"Why? She's a worthless bitch, just like all the rest!"

He was panting now, his jaw clenched against the side of her head. Anne cried out but dared not move for fear of provoking the knife's edge on her throat.

"Not every woman is like your wife." Doug's eyes met hers and softened. "Some are kind, generous, funny people whose only crime is making the world a happier place."

"You know nothing about the bitch who stole my life — or any of them!"

He pressed the knife into her neck, breaking the skin. Anne gave another cry.

"Let her go," Doug said, still maddeningly calm. "Walk away from this while you still can."

Chet laughed. "Is that a threat?"

Doug's calm veneer broke. Too late he seemed to realize his provoking mistake.

"You want her?" Chet clenched his jaw. "Fine. Enjoy."

Like most people, Anne had never had her throat sliced before. She imagined it would hurt, so she didn't think much of the tiny pinch across her neck.

Doug was there in an instant. Before Chet could complete his stroke, Doug twisted the knife from his grasp and hurled it far from reach. Chet swung at him — which Anne feared would mark the end of the fight — but her brother danced out of the way. Again and again Chet swung, each time catching only air, until he was yelling in frustration. Doug continued to dodge with calm precision and grace, not once striking back.

Until he saw Anne's neck.

Curious, she probed just under her chin. The skin was slick with warm fluid. Her fingers came away red.

I'm bleeding.

Doug blocked the next swing. Chet grunted with the force of it, but before he could swing again, her brother twisted his wrist in a fluid motion, bending it around so the larger man fell to his knees with a cry of pain.

Warmth flowed down Anne's chest, spreading a purple stain across her bosom. She clucked her tongue: bloodstains were a bear to clean. Her nice dress, she feared, had seen its last day, though she strangely couldn't remember putting it on. Feeling dizzy, she sat on her bed, which crinkled like plastic.

Doug was frightened now, more than when their father was at his worst. He looked at Chet, still immobilized in his grasp. His fist hovered in the air, ready to strike, but would not fall. Twice more Doug tried to make his fist move; each attempt only deepened his worry.

Anne realized with a start that her brother was afraid to hit him.

I can't blame him one bit.

"It's all right, Dougie," she said with a soothing smile. "You don't have to be like Dad. You've beaten Chet fair and square. He won't bother us again."

His confusion only grew, and it broke her heart to see the true extent of the damage their father had done to her once-innocent brother. Anne struggled to her feet, laid her hand on his cheek.

"Let him go," she said gently. "Please."

Unbridled relief flooded him. Doug nodded, cast a last suspicious glance at his captive, then released him.

Chet scrambled to his feet and rubbed his wrist, glaring at the two of them with a hateful scowl. Doug moved protectively in front of her. Anne lifted her chin in proud defiance, which splashed more warmth down her chest.

Chet's jaw dropped. His expression quickly hardened, fists balled tight. Doug tensed, ready for another bout, but it was unnecessary. Chet rubbed the wrist her brother had so expertly captured, spat at their feet, then fled from her bedroom, followed closely by the other jocks.

No sooner had they left than Doug turned to examine her neck. "We have to get you to a hospital," he said.

Anne wrapped him in her arms and buried her face in his shoulder to hide her tears of joy.

"Thank you, Dougie." She squeezed him tight. "Thank you, thank you, thank you."

Anne started to cry. It felt awkward to show such weakness before her brother, who rarely cried even when Father beat him, but she couldn't help it.

"So many years," she sobbed. "All this time I thought you hated me, but ..." She cupped his face in her hands, staining his cheek crimson. "I love you, Dougie, and I'm so, so glad you don't hate me."

Doug frowned as if he didn't recognize his own name, but eventually nodded. "I love you too, um ... Annie?"

She threw her arms around him again and squealed. How long she had dreamed of hearing those words ...

"We have to be careful," she said. "If Dad finds out what happened, he'll turn this on you somehow, and ..." Anne covered her mouth. "Oh, Dougie, I don't want him to hurt you anymore. I want you to be safe! Did you know that my money tin is almost full?"

"I, ah ... no, I didn't." He squirmed in her embrace. "Look, we really need to —"

"I was saving it for college, hoping my boyfriend and I could ..." She grimaced. "Well, he just told me he's moving out of state, so you can imagine what that means for our relationship."

"I'm sorry."

Anne wiped her eyes. "It's okay. Things happen for a reason, you know? Maybe he's moving away so I won't feel guilty about giving my savings to you instead, so you can get out of here and finally have a normal life, like you deserve."

"Anne — Annie, sorry — that's one of the kindest things I've ever heard, but right now we have to focus on you. We've got to staunch that bleeding and get you to a hospital."

"Okay, okay."

She didn't know what the fuss was about; Chet had pricked her, sure, but it didn't hurt at all now. In fact, her whole body felt calm, as if she was about to drift into peaceful sleep.

"Just let me grab the money tin so I don't forget later," Anne said. Doug started to protest, but she stalled him with a pleading smile. "I want you to be happy, Dougie. Please, let me do this for you."

Her brother seemed at a loss for words, which Anne took for assent. She turned to her closet —

And stumbled into a stack of couches.

Anne blinked. *My closet. It was right here ...* "Dougie, what —"

She blinked again.

The person standing behind her was most certainly not her brother.

"You ... w-what are you doing in my room?"

Brown Jacket raised his eyebrows like a parent whose child had just asked what kind of tree fish sticks grew on, but as reality slowly caught up with her, Anne couldn't bring herself to care.

Doug wasn't there; he never had been. Her broken mind had substituted Brown Jacket for the one person she had desperately wanted to be saved by. Doug's love, and her happy ending to half a lifetime of nightmares, hadn't been real. She felt hollow, her heart scooped out from the inside, leaving only a brittle shell.

Brown Jacket's concern deepened. "Annie, you've got to —"

"Don't call me that." She sank to the floor, suddenly exhausted. "Only my brother uses that nickname."

"All right, *Anne* ..." He squatted next to her, hazel eyes intent. "Listen very carefully. You're bleeding from a neck wound, maybe a nicked carotid artery. We need to staunch that flow right now and rush you to the hospital."

Anne shook her head.

"You're going to die! Do you understand?"

"Just leave me," she said softly.

Her mind replayed the hallucination with her brother: That was exactly how it should have been, how she had wanted it to be with every ghastly nightmare and flashback for the last eighteen years.

"I don't care if I die," Anne said.

"I do."

She looked up sharply, invoking a twinge in her neck. Kind eyes beneath a thick brow studied her with wonder.

"I won't pretend to understand what happened between you and your brother, but I do know that when you showed me — him, how deeply you cared ..." Brown Jacket ran a hand through his hair and gave a bashful smile. "I've never wished to be someone else before, but I would have given anything to be Dougie tonight."

Anne snapped her hanging jaw shut. "That's ... incredibly sweet of you to say."

"It's the truth. I only hung around the restaurant because I was mesmerized at how skillfully you cheered up your date."

"Oh, that was ... well, it's what I do, I guess."

"And I'd like you to keep doing it, so ..." He grabbed a throw pillow, tore a strip of fabric off with his bare hands, and folded it into a neat square. "Take this. Keep pressure on the wound."

"I ... I don't know where the cut is."

Brown Jacket lifted the makeshift bandage, then paused. Concern etched his features, as if he was afraid to touch her.

"It's okay," she said, conjuring a smile. "I won't bite."

"I-I know, it's just ..." He shook his head. "Sorry. Hold it here."

His touch was gentle, an artist putting the final stroke on his masterpiece. He withdrew his fingers the moment Anne's took their place.

"Now for the fun part," Brown Jacket said, though his anxious expression said it was anything but. "You've lost a lot of blood, Anne. We can't wait for an ambulance. I need you to keep pressure on your neck until we get to the emergency room. Can you do that?"

"I'll try," she said, her eyes drooping. "But I can't promise I'll be awake for the entire car ride."

"It will have to do."

Strong arms scooped her into a comforting cradle. She nestled against the warmth of his surprisingly firm chest. Streaks of blood marred his fine leather jacket. She felt guilty for ruining such a nice garment, but its musty fragrance drew her in, mixed with another scent she couldn't quite place. It was earthy. Sensual. Intoxicating. Anne breathed it in with a content smile.

He glanced down at her. "Am I hurting you?"

The question seemed absurd. Her entire body was relaxed and comfortable, as if it had melted into his.

"I'm just perfect," she said, and closed her eyes.

Then they were moving. Anne couldn't have said how fast or to where, only that the cool night breeze through her hair felt heavenly. Cars honked, tires screeched, people gasped. In the absolute safety of his arms, not once did she feel the need to see what the commotion was about.

It wasn't until he set her down in the bright lights of the emergency room that she thought to look around. Nurses and doctors bustled about, covered her face with a mask, jabbed something into her arm. Anne hardly noticed. The soft bed called her to slumber.

They carted her away, and it wasn't until Brown Jacket disappeared behind swinging doors that she realized this was the first time since the warehouse she'd left his strong embrace.

He carried me the entire way.

That fantastic thought was her last before she drifted into peaceful sleep.

6

ROOMMATES

ANNE AWOKE SCREAMING. She clawed at her neck to pry the knife away, but firm hands grabbed her wrists and wrestled her to the bed. Anne struggled and cried for what felt like an hour, until she finally noticed hair rollers pressing under her chin.

It was just a nightmare.

Slowly Anne relaxed. Doris climbed off her.

"You okay now, kiddo?"

She stared at Doris, heart pounding, until the bedroom eventually came back into focus. Anne felt around her neck. "Did I pull the bandages off again?"

"A little. Let's check the stitches, then we'll patch you back up."

Minutes later, Anne was glad to learn the stitches in her neck were still intact.

Doris taped the gauze in place, as she had the last two times that night, then gave her handiwork a nod of approval. She put a comforting hand on Anne's shoulder. "Rough night."

"Sorry for waking you up again. My nightmares aren't usually this bad, I swear."

Not since I first moved to California, anyway.

"Don't sweat it. This is your first night out of the hospital, and you're staying in a strange place. That's bound to shake things up a little. Want some hot cocoa to take the edge off?"

Anne fidgeted with the sheets. "No, you should go back to sleep. You have work tomorrow. I'll be fine."

"Hogwash! You're shaking like a leaf. Go set up on the couch and find something on TV. I'll warm the milk."

Anne started to protest, but a stern look from Doris silenced her, so she slipped the covers off and headed to the living room. The couch's leather felt cold through her thin nightgown, but soon warmed with the help of a blanket she pulled from the backrest. She propped a pillow behind her head, wincing at a twinge in her neck, then relaxed. Twice, she nearly put her feet on the polished coffee table, as she would have in her own apartment. Even if it wasn't considered rude, it would have been an offense to the propriety of Doris' immaculate living room.

She took the remote from its perfectly aligned spot on the end table and switched the big-screen TV on. A reality show announcer was shouting encouragement at a man and woman in swimsuits who were scaling a mound of pink gelatin.

And this is why I don't watch television.

Anne clicked it off and did her best to return the remote to its exact original position.

The delicious smell of chocolate and milk soon wafted from the kitchen. Doris carried in two steaming cups and placed them on coasters, made a tiny correction to Anne's remote placement, then took a seat on the opposite side of the couch.

"So," Doris said, "are you ready to tell me what really happened that night?"

Anne opened her mouth, but, as when the police had asked during her three days at the hospital, even trying to remember locked her throat up tight. With a sigh, she shook her head.

"That's all right, kiddo, I understand. Some things are best forgotten anyway. What about the dude who brought you to the hospital?"

Anne grinned. Him she had no problem remembering.

"Brown Jacket. The guy who carried me a mile through San Francisco in what had to have been a world record to deliver me at the emergency room not one minute before the doctors said I would have bled out."

"Yeah," Doris said, laughing. "Him."

Anne sipped her cocoa. It was every bit as silky and delicious as she'd hoped, though it still tugged at her stitches on its way down. "He left the hospital without giving any contact info. I don't even know his first name."

"And how exactly did this hero find you?"

Anne tensed, cautious of veering too close to the events of four nights ago, but this detail felt safe to share.

"Long story short, I was following your advice."

"Do tell, hon, because I'm pretty sure I didn't tell you to bleed to death in a furniture store."

Taking a deep breath, Anne filled her friend in on the encounter with William at the bus stop, and their subsequent date at Giovessi's. She stopped at the part where they hid from Brown Jacket in the furniture store, however, because her skin began to prickle with the threat of another flashback.

Doris must have read her distress. She patted Anne on the knee and smiled. "At least that explains how you got there. And hot damn if I ain't proud of you for flying into action. That took guts."

"More than I had, apparently. One guy tried to kill me, and the other left without a word."

"Don't cut yourself sh…" Doris grimaced. "Sorry, poor choice of words. Let me try again." She cleared her throat. "The race ain't over until all the runners are accounted for. That hero of yours is out there somewhere. Hell, he might be flying over the city in a red cape right now, for all we know."

That brought a smile. "So … what? Do we flash the bat signal and see if he comes?"

"I ain't flashing anyone at my age, but you take that cute little body of yours and go right ahead. You'll have horny suitors lined up around the block." Anne tossed a pillow at her, which made Doris cackle. "Or we could call that pizza place and see if your friend Antonio got his name on a credit card receipt."

"Of course! Why didn't I think of that?"

"Probably because you've been too busy screaming your head off from the nightmares and flashbacks."

"Probably," Anne said softly. She took another sip. "Thank you, Doris. For everything. I don't know how I could have survived this — let alone the last fifteen years — without you."

"My pleasure, kiddo. You're worth the effort. Besides, it's all about give and take, in my book. I helped you out of the gutter, you helped me through an ugly divorce, now it's my turn again. Years down the line, you'll repay me by keeping me out of the nursing home. Or making sure I go into one!" She slapped her knee and cackled.

Anne nodded, though she knew Doris was intentionally making light of her role in their history to make her feel better. Anne would have died soon after fleeing to San Francisco without her friend's help, and they both knew it. Thanks to Doris, Anne felt as if her life was finally under control.

Until three days ago, when I met William.

Even thinking his name brought pain to her neck and the warm sensation of her own blood spilling down her chest.

Doris grabbed her hand, which had strayed to her bandage.

"Sorry," Anne said.

"You ain't the one who needs to be sorry," Doris said with a scowl. "If they ever catch the son-of-a-bitch who did this to you, I swear I'm going to castrate him with his own punched-out teeth."

"Doris! Don't make me laugh, it hurts."

"Then I'm going to put them on a cake that says 'asshole' with candles and everything, and let him watch them burn down to scorch his family jewels."

"Doris!" Anne closed her eyes, but the pent-up laughter strained her neck wound.

"And when I cut that damn cake, you know exactly where I'm going to slice it, so he knows there's no hope they'll ever be re-attached. Then I'll bend him over a chair and shove the entire slice right up his —"

"Stop!" Anne said, doubling over with laughter.

Her neck hurt with every breath, but Doris didn't seem to care. She watched with a broad grin until Anne calmed and wiped the tears from her eyes.

"Feel better, kiddo?"

"No, you meanie." Anne crossed her arms, but a smile lingered despite her best effort to pout. "Maybe."

"Good, let's get some sleep. We'll call Antonio as soon as he opens tomorrow and see what he knows about your mystery hero."

Exciting as the idea of finding Brown Jacket was, the prospect of going back to sleep — and the nightmares that would inevitably follow— sapped her enthusiasm. She packed up without complaint, however, folded the blanket as neatly as she could, and placed it back where she found it.

Anne had just pulled the covers up, resigned to another round of night terrors, when her door opened. Doris plopped a pillow down and climbed in bed next to her. Anne felt guilty enough that Doris hadn't slept that night, but the protest died on her lips.

She was happy for her friend's reassuring presence, and they might both sleep better because of it.

"You're the best," Anne said softly.

"Back at you, kiddo. Sleep well."

And, thanks to Doris, she did.

7

HUNTED

THE HUNTERS' FOOTSTEPS ECHOED in the alley behind Almos. He staggered on, using the wall to catch his balance. The abrupt awakening had left him dazed and blurry-eyed. He didn't know exactly how long he had slept — or why he had been disturbed — but was grateful it had been under the cover of night.

Almos tumbled from the alley and rolled into the street. Even the wan light from the streetlamps made him squint.

The blare of a car horn tore at his eardrums; its bright headlights seared his eyes as sure as the sun's rays. He cried out and scrambled back to the sidewalk.

Seconds passed. He leaned against a wall and forced himself to open his eyes, despite the stabbing pain, and the world came back into focus. He stood before a gas station, although the pumps, with their flashing lights, looked like something from a science fiction film.

How many years had he slept this time?

The sound of the Hunters' pursuit made him straighten.

They would find him soon.

Almos scrambled for a place to hide. The nearby houses abutted with no space in between, and gates barred all of the entryways. In desperation, he pushed the gate nearest him, and was pleasantly surprised when it opened. He stepped onto the small porch, quietly closed the gate, and retreated into the shadows.

Footsteps pounded by, and eventually faded. He waited, still as death, until he felt it was safe to emerge.

His pursuers were gone.

Starvation twisted his gut, but he ignored it. The Entity hadn't made contact with him yet, and he wanted to keep it that way. Almos needed to get underground before it discovered he was awake.

A lone figure sitting on the curb drew his attention. It was the first person Almos had seen since awakening who was not a Hunter. His empty stomach complained with a stabbing pain, but he shook his head.

It is more important to find shelter beneath the earth before —

An ancient and familiar presence brushed his mind. It stoked the fires of his hunger into an inferno so intense that he could think of nothing else.

Feed, he thought, already walking toward the person by the side of the road.

The Entity kindled a second fire, wrought with desire.

Yes, feed, and then I will start a new family.

• • •

William scratched his cheek with a growl. Not only did his wound itch more than yesterday, it was noticeably warmer to the touch. Two weeks had passed, and the infernal gash still hadn't closed. With an effort, he removed his fingers from his cheek and scratched his chest instead.

Two weeks.

His shirt reeked as if he hadn't washed it in years, though he'd only stolen it from the laundromat a few days ago.

Two weeks of living on the streets like a goddamn beggar.

A chill ran through him. William pulled the dirt-scuffed shirt tight around him. It wasn't the night air that made him shiver. The sky was fog-free for a change, and warm enough that he couldn't see his breath, despite the New Year being just days away. He scratched his face again. No, it wasn't the temperature that chilled him.

His wound was infected. Weeks of sleeping in dirt and filth had seen to that.

It had been a necessary move, however, since Anne had undoubtedly reported him to the police as well-dressed and clean-shaven.

He was neither of those things now. William was homeless, a fugitive in his own city. His face bore a scraggly beard, and his fancy clothes were long gone. The money in his wallet had dwindled, spent on food trucks and an occasional trip to the liquor store. He dared not use his credit cards; with any luck, the police thought he'd already skipped town, and he didn't want to give them any clues to the contrary. His first instinct had been to leave town, as the police no doubt expected him to, but living on the streets of San Francisco afforded an anonymity that would be difficult to achieve in a smaller town. City natives were conditioned to ignore the starving beggars who lined the streets.

William leaned back. The moon was a sliver in the sky; only the flickering fluorescents from the nearby gas station gave light to the small section of sidewalk he claimed as his own.

His dirty face was one among many — and that worked in his favor. Now that his funds were running low, however, he needed a new plan.

He just didn't know what that plan was.

Police frequented public kitchens and shelters, which ruled them out. William had no friends, no family, and he didn't trust any of his ex-coworkers to keep his whereabouts from the authorities.

A twinge made him scratch his face again, drawing a maddened growl.

He couldn't even go to the hospital for the goddamn gash that bitch had given him.

A cough beside him made William jump. He fell backward and scrambled a few paces down the sidewalk. A well-dressed man sat on the curb just a few feet away, oiled hair swept back in mild disarray, as if he'd just run a race. His tailored suit was something William's grandfather might have worn.

William glared at him, but the stranger took no notice, staring instead at a blank wall across the street.

"You seem troubled," the stranger said pleasantly.

William brushed his pants. In no mood for conversation, he stood to leave.

"Who are you running from?" the stranger said.

"Who says I'm running?"

"My dear fellow, I know what it is to be hunted, to constantly be on guard, one step ahead of your enemies. You have that air, and yet ..."

He turned to William with an appraising look. A scraggly beard covered his unusually pale face. It may have been a trick of the streetlights, but William swore a faint web of blue veins covered his skin. It wasn't his veins or pallor, however, that made William want to get as far from this man as possible.

It was his eyes. Except for a hair-thin ring of blue around the outside, his pupils were entirely black. They also seemed larger than normal, as if as set of invisible prescription glasses were magnifying them.

The stranger rose fluidly. "Yet I also see a Hunter in you."

He stepped forward. William stood his ground, fists at the ready. He was larger than the creepy stranger, and rarely backed down from a fight.

"Ah, yes," the stranger said with a satisfied smile. "You're more Hunter than Prey, I see."

The man in his grandfather's suit carried himself with confidence. One side of his outfit had black stains on the leg and sleeve.

Like scuffs from a dirty wall...

"You're being hunted too," William said, crossing his arms.

"By many Hunters over many years, but men like us have an advantage over other Prey. Our instinct is not to cower, but to attack! We are not satisfied to graze meekly on the fields of the earth. We crave the Hunt. It is what we live for, and what the Hunters do not expect."

"Cut the chatter," William said. "What do you want?"

"Straight to the point, I see. Very well. I would like to make you an offer."

"Yeah, why's that?" William looked down at his own filthy rags. "I'm flat broke, if you couldn't tell."

"A man is worth more than the contents of his wallet," he said with a chuckle. "Wouldn't you agree?"

"Fine, let's hear it."

It's not like I have any better place to be.

"I offer you strength, an army with which to rule, life eternal, and ..." The stranger flashed a smile. "Revenge!"

It was the last that kept William from laughing in his face and walking away from the dapper lunatic. "Revenge? How?"

The stranger's smile grew, revealing a pair of unusually sharp upper canines. "Your power will be ten times that of any other man. With it, you can bring ruin to those who oppose you, or make them slaves to your will."

William clenched his jaw, his patience wearing thin. "Okay, let's pretend this fairytale offer is real. What's the catch?"

"A trifle, really. Sunlight and silver will be your only true weaknesses and, although you will never need to fear injury, I'm afraid your facial deformity will remain for the rest of your long life. Normally I would allow it to heal before your transformation, but we simply don't have the luxury of time. I'm truly sorry."

Sunlight?

"Wait, do you seriously believe you can turn me into some sort of vam—"

William never saw him coming. The stranger was there one instant, the next he stood behind him, holding William by the shoulders with an iron grip. A sharp pinch on William's neck made him cry out. He grabbed a fistful of oiled hair to pry his attacker away, but a feeling of calm washed through him, stripping away his aggression. His arms fell to his sides. He tried to remember why he was angry, but his thoughts were jumbled as if waking from a deep slumber.

The blare of a siren made the stranger jerk away.

Police!

The sobering thought pierced William's dream-haze. "No," he mumbled. "Got to leave. Can't let them catch me ..." He tried to run, but the stranger held him firmly.

"That is unfortunate," the stranger said, shielding his eyes from the flashing lights of the police car. "There is more I would tell you, but it will have to wait. For now ..."

Using one of his sharp canines — which were longer than they had been a moment ago — he opened a gash in his own arm, then pressed the wound to William's mouth.

"Drink," he said.

To his horror, William obeyed. The coppery taste made him gag.

"Swallow."

Again William complied.

"Good." The stranger rolled his sleeve down. "Now count to five, then run to safety. I assume you know where that is." He turned toward the police car, where two officers were just climbing out. "I shall find you as soon as I can. Unfortunately, you won't remember me or our little conversation, so you will have to trust your instincts until then."

With that, the stranger marched toward the police car. William began counting as instructed.

"Freeze!" one of the officers said, leveling his gun at the stranger.

William reached five and ran across the gas station, angling for a field that led to a nearby homeless encampment.

"I said freeze!"

The stranger yelled.

Shots fired.

William kept running and didn't look back.

• • •

William lay shivering, the dew on his sleeves glistened purple with dawn's steady approach. The homeless around him huddled in tattered blankets and jackets. He pulled his thin blanket over his shoulders, but it wasn't enough to ward off the cold. He felt weak and feverish. He was tempted to go to the hospital for treatment, but they would probably identify him and turn him over to the authorities.

I'm not that desperate yet.

He huddled his legs and hoped the ailment would pass soon.

If not, he'd likely be dead, in which case it didn't matter.

More disturbing than the fever was his memory lapse. One minute he'd been sitting in front of a gas station, the next he was under his blanket, several hours later, and almost a mile away. He grimaced at the coppery tang in his mouth. He had probed his tongue all over, but there were no cuts to explain the taste of blood.

His stomach ached as well.

I probably have the flu, he thought. Many in these camps were ill and coughed through the night. The cold air didn't help. *It was only a matter of time before I caught something, too.*

The good news, at least, was his cheek injury. The gaping wound had healed somewhat and, while it still itched and burned, it no longer radiated the heat of infection. Feeling a sudden chill, William curled up tight, fluffed a nearby trash bag for a pillow, and tried to sleep.

Anne dominated his feverish dreams. First she was his victim, his hands firmly around her throat. The scene changed, and she was beating him soundly, her eyes lit with fiery rage. Next she was an arresting police officer who broke his wrists when she put the handcuffs on. He screamed in agony, cursing her name. Then she reached into his jacket and slowly pulled out his wallet —

He woke suddenly. A gaunt man with a scraggly beard knelt nearby, holding William's wallet. William was so tired that he couldn't even muster the energy to yell, let alone wrestle his wallet back.

Seeing William's eyes open, the thief clutched his prize and ran.

The sight of the thief dashing away triggered a wild surge of energy. William threw his blanket aside with a feral growl and bolted after him, weaving to avoid sleeping vagrants.

The thief was agile, and made William fight for every inch of ground, leading them out of the homeless encampment and into an industrial neighborhood. Warehouses loomed all around. The hour was late and the streets empty; no one interfered with his pursuit.

The thief's luck ran out when he made a wrong turn between two large warehouses. The street ended in a tall chain-link fence topped with barbed wire. His quarry pulled at the doors to one of the warehouses, but they held firm. Like a cornered animal, he backed against the wall and whimpered. He tossed the wallet at William's feet, begging him to take it and leave him alone.

William ignored the wallet, eyes fixed on his prey. With a sneer, he closed his hands around the thief's throat. His victim sputtered. Nails clawed uselessly at William's strong grip. Eventually, the thief's eyes rolled back in his head, and he fell limp, but William stopped short of killing him.

The rhythmic pulse from the thief's neck was hypnotic. He swore he could hear the other man's heart beating — a melodious tune that promised a sweet reward. He couldn't say what drove him to bite the man's neck, nor why the coppery red liquid sated his hunger.

When he had finished, the vagrant lay motionless on the concrete, his musical pulse faded to eternal silence.

The thrill of the hunt had left him. His hunger was no more, and his strength returned. He stood up straight and bounced on his toes as if he'd just stepped into a boxing ring.

The corpse was a problem. He kicked open one of the warehouse doors, shattering its frame in a shower of splinters. With a grunt, William hoisted the body onto his shoulder and headed inside.

This'll do nicely, he thought, then went to explore his new home.

8

ROMEO

TUESDAY LUNCHTIMES AT THE DINER WERE USUALLY SLOW — and today was no exception. Anne didn't mind, though, because the languid pace allowed more time with her customers. She had just returned to the kitchen for a sip of water when Doris unloaded an armful of dishes next to her with a loud clatter. The racket normally would have made Anne jump, but her eyes barely flickered from her silent phone.

"Any word?" Doris said.

"Not yet." Anne heaved a sigh.

"Don't give up hope, kiddo. There's a lot of restaurants in this city, but he'll come back to that pizza place eventually. You'll see."

"Maybe."

Dear Antonio Giovessi had dug through several days of receipts at Anne's request, but in the end, he remembered that her brown-clad hero had paid in cash. She'd thanked Antonio profusely, ordered an extra-large pizza with the works as a bonus, then left her contact information with him, including her place of work, to give to Brown Jacket in case he showed up again.

That was almost two weeks ago, and every day since had been a struggle not to call Antonio every few hours to see if her savior had made a return appearance. The more she thought about it, the more her shoulders sagged. With a heavy heart, she put her phone back in her pocket.

It vibrated.

They shared a look. The only person who ever called or texted Anne was Doris. Anne fished it out, flipped the old-fashioned thing open, and gasped when she saw Antonio's name on the screen. Finger shaking, she opened the message.

"Romeo left ten minutes ago," it read, followed by an entire line of hearts.

Doris sidled next to her and frowned. "That's it? Didn't mention him bringing flowers or nothing?"

Anne clutched the phone to her chest.

She was too excited to breathe, let alone reply to his message.

He came! Brown Jacket came back!

Her elation quickly turned to panic. "Oh my God! What if he calls? W-w-what do I say? Do I play it cool? Sexy?" She flapped her hands. "Doris, I don't remember how to act sexy! Especially not over the phone, it's been too long. Here ..." Anne practically tossed the phone to her. "If he calls, you answer and pretend you're me. It works in the movies."

"Too late for that," Doris said with a grin. "Just make sure your uniform's on straight."

"My uniform?"

Doris giggled and pointed out to the dining area. "Ain't that your Romeo at the counter in seat seven?"

Anne cautiously peeked around the corner as if the devil himself was on the other side. Sure enough, there her hero sat in a bloodstain-free brown jacket, looking at a menu.

"Is that him?" Doris said.

Anne was too stunned to answer. Doris nudged her with an elbow.

"Well? What next, Juliet?"

Anne slid back out of view. "I can't do this," she hissed.

"Why not? He's kind of cute. He has this innocent schoolboy look to him ..."

"No, this was a bad idea," Anne said, heart thundering. "He doesn't want to meet me. He wouldn't have left me at the hospital without so much as a name if he did. And ..."

She fingered the scarf around her neck. The stitches had been removed several days ago, along with the bandage, leaving an angry red line across the right side of her throat. Doris insisted it looked cool, but Anne thought it might be unappetizing to customers — and invite uncomfortable questions — so she'd kept the scar hidden even from her coworkers, who knew she'd been assaulted, but little else.

Doris' scowl melted into sympathy. She gently took Anne's hand away from the scarf.

"That's just nerves talking, kiddo. He's here, ain't he? And if there's anyone on this earth you can talk to about that scar, you think it would be the guy who kept it from being a hell of a lot bigger." She gave a reassuring smile. "Go say hello and see what happens."

Anne hugged herself; the thought of meeting him was suddenly mortifying. He'd seen her at her worst: hysterical, suicidal, and with nuthouse-worthy hallucinations. That he might care for — let alone be interested in — someone as obviously broken as Anne was ridiculous.

And yet ...

She peeked around the corner again. There her hero sat, not twenty feet away. If what Doris said was true — that he was here for Anne, and not just by coincidence — then she owed him an audience at the very least, even if it ended in disappointment.

Anne squared her shoulders and straightened the collar of her work uniform. "Okay, how do I look?"

"A few soda stains aside ..." Doris smiled. "Beautiful. Go get him, hon."

Taking a deep breath, Anne marched from the kitchen.

"Welcome to Hal's," she said, straining to keep her voice steady.

Brown Jacket lifted his hazel eyes from the menu and smiled. Anne leaned on the counter to support her suddenly weak knees. He was about her age, she realized. His fingers ran through a tuft of thick brown hair in a nervous gesture that, if anything, added to his boyish charm.

"Anne, it's good to see you."

"Likewise. I was beginning to think I'd scared you off."

"Not by a long shot."

Anne swallowed to calm the flutter in her chest. "W-well, that's good."

"How are you?"

"Alive, thanks to you."

He chuckled. "Okay, aside from that?"

"I'm ... coping." Though not exactly true, it was the closest thing she could think to say that didn't make her sound like the terrified wreck she actually was. "How about you?"

"Frustrated they haven't caught William yet, but apart from that ..." He spread his hands and imitated her tone. "Coping."

The door chime announced the arrival of new customers. Anne cursed under her breath; Doris and Julie were busy, which left her with the responsibility of hostess, being the server closest to the door.

"Would you excuse me? Just for a moment."

"I'm sorry, I shouldn't have bothered you at work. We can catch up another time." He rose to leave.

"No!" She nearly spilled a pot of coffee in her haste to grab his sleeve. "I-I mean, I have a break soon, so if you hang around for a few minutes, we can take a walk or something. If you want to, that is."

He settled back down with a smile. "That would be nice."

"Great! I'll be right back with some coffee."

Anne couldn't seat the new customers fast enough, and even skipped citing the specials, which she knew she would feel guilty about later. When she returned to Brown Jacket, Doris was already pouring coffee into a paper cup.

"One coffee to go," Doris said. "Go take your break, hon, and don't hurry back." She gave Anne a wink.

"Ah ... okay. I'll get my coat."

"I'll meet you outside." Brown Jacket dropped a few singles on the counter with a nod of thanks and carried his drink away.

Anne darted into the employee room, grabbed her jacket and purse, then made a beeline for the exit, but Doris intercepted her on the way out.

"I mean it," Doris said in a tone that brokered no argument. "Take. Your. Time. Julie and I will cover until closing."

"No! Doris, you had the early shift. That wouldn't be —"

"Anne Perrin," Doris said, planting a fist on her hip. "The only reason I should see your adorable face back here this evening is if he's married or gay. Am I clear?"

Anne sighed. "Crystal."

"Good." She flashed a big-toothed smile. "Have fun, kiddo. I expect a full report tonight. Or tomorrow morning, if things go that well — in which case I want an even fuller report."

"Yes, ma'am."

Her palms were sweating by the time Anne made it outside, where her hero waited with a bemused grin.

"Where to?" he said, stuffing his hands into his jacket pockets. "It sounds like we don't have a curfew."

"Yeah, quite the opposite. Doris —" Anne did a double-take. "Wait, you heard that from out here?"

He ran a hand through his hair, looking like a kid caught peeking at his Christmas presents. "Well ... h-her voice carries."

Anne shot him a skeptical look. Doris was loud at the best of times, but they had kept their voices down during their conversation. Dismissing it as part of the oversensitivity that came with her PTSD, Anne shrugged it off and smiled.

"Don't let her bluster put you off," she said. "Doris has a heart of gold."

"I can tell. You're lucky to have her as a friend."

"She's more than a friend, she's the closest thing I have to family. She's even letting me crash with her while I ..." Anne bowed her head.

"While you cope."

"Yeah."

An awkward silence fell. Several times his eyes flitted to her rust-colored scarf, but he had the grace to keep his thoughts to himself.

Which isn't fair at all.

If anyone had a right to see what lay beneath her scarf, it was him. Her trembling fingers loosened the knot and pulled the scarf free. The cold air on her neck felt invasive, as if she stood naked before the world, but she swallowed it down and turned her head for him to see. "The doctor says it's healing nicely, though it'll be ugly for a few weeks more, hence the scarf."

To her surprise, he bent for a closer look with professional scrutiny. "They did a great job with the stitches, though I can see where a few of them tore free. Still, it'll fade in a few months, and you'll hardly know it was there."

"Are you a doctor?"

"More like a medical enthusiast." He rocked on his heels, but fell silent, looking almost as nervous as she felt.

Anne's mind whirled, trying to think of something to say. She had rehearsed whole conversations with him in her head, but now that he was actually here, her brain was mush.

"I ... I'm glad you came," was all she could think of.

"Good to hear. I was afraid that seeing me might serve as a trigger or something, which is why I didn't stick around at the hospital."

"Don't be silly. You saved my life — twice, really, and I never even got your name."

"Charlie."

"I'm Anne, b-but you already knew that, of course."

Seconds passed and he had not extended his hand, so she held hers out. He looked apprehensive, as if she had offered him a rattlesnake, but shook himself and took his hand from his pocket. His grip was light, skin tough like a boxer's. It seemed they had only just touched when he returned his hand to his jacket.

"So, ah ... how long were you in the hospital?" he said.

"Just three days. Doris has been taking care of me since then."

She fingered the phone in her dress pocket. *Two weeks ...*

"You ... you could have at least left your name with the nurses," she said softly.

He blushed. They stared at each other, then Anne burst out laughing. Charlie looked at her helplessly.

"I'm sorry," she said. "You saved me from a lunatic, then carried me over a *mile* through the hills of San Francisco like an Olympian of legend to make sure I didn't bleed to death, and here I am pouting because you didn't leave a calling card."

He chuckled. "Well, when you put it like that ..."

"Anyway, you're here now, so let me do this right." Gathering her courage, she stood on her toes and kissed his cheek. "Thank you," she said. "You really are a hero."

The declaration, for some reason, made him frown, but he eventually nodded. "I'm just glad you're safe. How are you really doing, Anne?"

"Ah, well ..."

Let's see, waking my best friend up with night terrors, experiencing daytime flashbacks, anxiety, paranoia ... yeah.

"I'm alive and back at work. What more could I ask for?"

"Right, what more?" His hollow tone suggested he'd seen through her evasive answer.

Silence loomed. Eventually he cleared his throat. "Well, it was nice to see you again." To her chagrin, Charlie turned to leave, but his eyes lingered. "I'm glad you're all right."

A profound loneliness accompanied his simple sentiment, and Anne found it suddenly hard to breathe; it was the same feeling that constantly haunted her solitary apartment — and had ultimately driven her to the tragic night they met.

He gave a final nod, then walked away.

"Charlie, wait!"

The look of hope in his eyes confirmed her suspicion. She hurried over with a smile. "Do you have plans tonight?"

"No," he said, returning her smile, "but I would love to buy you dinner."

"You're out of your mind if you think I'm going to let you pay after everything you've done for me."

Anne thought he was going to protest, but he nodded.

"Fine," he said, "but the next one's on me."

Next one?

Her smile broadened until her cheeks hurt. "Deal."

Then they were walking. Anne didn't know where they were going, nor did she care, only that she felt more comfortable with Charlie than she had with any man in a long, long time.

9

HOME

ANNE AND CHARLIE EMERGED FROM THE RESTAURANT into the halo of a streetlight.

"Good suggestion," she said, patting her stomach with a satisfied grin. "I thought Giovessi's was the pinnacle of Italian cuisine, but it doesn't hold a candle to this place."

"Glad you liked it. This has been a favorite of mine for years."

She bumped his elbow. "You should have told me you already ate, though. We could have gone out another night."

"I didn't want to wait," he said, echoing her thoughts. "Besides, it was fun watching you eat."

"Piggy noises and all?"

"Especially those."

She bowed her head to cover her blush. "What can I say? I appreciate a good meal."

"And I appreciate good company."

She smiled at that. The experience had been the exact opposite of her ill-fated date with William. Where she had been intimidated by William's stoic mood, Charlie's relaxed manner made her feel at ease. Where she had struggled to keep William smiling, Charlie's laughter was easily won, and he often countered with something that tickled her just as much. She and Charlie appeared to enjoy the same terrible movies, had similar fashion sense — which is to say, not much at all — and shared a weakness for ice cream, especially mint chocolate chip. She had also managed to confirm he was single *and* heterosexual.

In short, Anne was on cloud nine, and climbing fast.

Several blocks later, Charlie cleared his throat, drawing Anne out from her internal musings. "So ... where exactly are we headed?"

"What? I thought you were leading."

He shook his head. "I was following you."

"Never a good idea. My sense of direction is almost as bad as my jokes." Anne squinted at a nearby street sign. "Oh, we're a few blocks from my apartment."

"Coincidence?" His impish grin faltered when Anne didn't smile. "Sorry. How long has it been since you were home?"

"The day they released me from the hospital was the last time, and even that was just long enough to grab some clothes." She shuddered.

"I'll go with you, if you want."

"No, that's ..." Anne fiddled with her coat buttons, then sighed. "Would you? I mean, I wouldn't want to inconvenience you, but ..."

"It's no problem. I imagine there's a vegetable or two that need to be cleared out of your refrigerator, and I'm happy to help."

"Eww, you're right! Are you sure you don't mind? The entire fridge is probably rancid. Even I'm having second thoughts now."

"Positive. Smells don't really bother me."

"Oh. Well ... thanks, then."

Touched by his offer, she walked closer until their elbows almost brushed. She eyed his arm for the rest of the short walk, looking for an opportunity to slip her hand into his, but his elbows stayed tight to his sides, hands in his pockets.

She forgot all about that, however, when they reached her apartment door.

Anne gulped and fished the keys from her purse. They rattled like sleigh bells in her hand, and grew louder with each nearing step.

"Anne."

Charlie's voice made her jump, and she nearly tumbled down the short staircase.

His hand finally emerged from his pocket, palm outstretched. "Would you like me to go first?"

She wanted to protest, but her throat was too tight to answer. For weeks she had avoided this place, not because she preferred staying with Doris, but out of fear of what — or specifically who — might be awaiting her return.

With a grateful nod, she handed Charlie the keys and stepped aside.

The wooden steps creaked with unusual protest under his feet. He turned the key, and the door to the apartment she hadn't seen in weeks opened.

The putrid odor made Anne gag. She quickly covered her nose. If Charlie noticed the smell, he said nothing, and peered cautiously into her dark living room.

"You called it," she said. "The fridge must be a bacterial war zone by now. We don't have to —"

Charlie waved it off. "I told you, the smell doesn't bother me. Besides, I'm happy to help clean up. Let's open a few windows first. Ready?" He grinned and pulled his shirt over his nose.

Anne laughed and did likewise. She hoped the neighbors weren't watching; she and Charlie looked like a pair of incompetent burglars, too inept to wear masks.

Once inside, she flipped the light switch. Nothing happened. "Perfect," she said. "No horror movie is complete without a dark, creepy house."

"Light bulb?"

"Probably the breaker, it pops all the time. I've called building management a dozen times, but ..."

"I'll tackle the breaker. Where's the box?"

"Outside, to the right of the building," Anne said. "They're labeled by apartment number."

He headed for the door, but she caught his arm on the way by. "Um, Charlie? Could I ask a favor?"

He arched an eyebrow.

"W-would you mind checking the bedroom first?"

"I'll check all the rooms, if you'd like."

"Thanks. There are only two, including the bathroom."

"You bet. And I promise to stay out of your underwear drawer."

"Now that's just creepy!"

He laughed and, before Anne thought to offer a flashlight, headed into the pitch recesses of her apartment. She waited a few seconds for him to realize his mistake, but he didn't return, and she didn't hear stumbling or cursing.

He must have pretty good eyesight.

With a shrug, Anne went to the kitchen and cracked a window while she waited, then clicked on the exhaust fan over the stove. It stayed silent, of course, and she quickly turned it off before Charlie could laugh at her mistake.

"All clear," he said, returning to the living room.

"Including my underwear drawer?"

"I did try on a bra. They're more comfortable than I imagined."

"I hate you."

He chuckled. "Yeah, I deserved that. Nice place, by the way. Very tidy."

"Thanks. It's easy when you live alone and never have company."

"Never?"

She shook her head. "You're the first in a decade."

His smile faded. "I get it. I haven't had anyone over in a while, either."

"Looks like we're both due for a change," she said. "Hopefully for the better."

"Hopefully."

Washed in the pale yellow streetlight filtering through the kitchen window, they stared at each other for a magical moment that Anne wished would never end.

Charlie was the first to stir, tearing his eyes away with the same reluctance she felt. "Breaker is outside, yeah?"

"Yep."

Charlie headed for the door, but Anne cleared her throat to get his attention.

"Facing my undergarments in the dark was brave enough," she said. "Would you like a flashlight this time so you don't electrocute yourself?"

"Ah ... right. That would help, wouldn't it?"

Her chest brushed his when she skirted past, sending a pleasant tingle through her. Blushing face hidden from view, she allowed herself a smile. His touch stirred her more than William's ever had, and she'd forgotten how wonderful that gooey sensation felt.

Anne popped the closet latch. Her brow furrowed when the door creaked itself open, as if pushed from the inside, followed by an odor that overpowered even the fetid contents of her kitchen. It was the stench of unwashed humanity, common to the streets of the City.

But not common to my apartment.

The door swung outward. When the homeless man's gray corpse landed at her feet, the room spun briefly, then everything went black.

• • •

William watched the police cars converge on Anne's apartment from the safety of his hiding spot several buildings away.

She didn't scream.

That annoyed him, since he had gone through some trouble to set up her little surprise. Discovering where she lived had been a pain. He knew her name, of course, but gaining internet access to search for her address without attracting attention had been more difficult than he imagined. William scratched his partially healed cheek wound and smiled.

It had been worth the effort, especially with the unexpected appearance of her hero. Now they both knew that William was still around, still angry, and still very dangerous. He could almost taste their fear.

William sagged against the wall. His skin had become pale over the last twenty-four hours, his breathing slowed, and he could barely feel his heart beating in his chest. All warmth had just about left his body. The surge of energy gained from drinking the thief's blood yesterday was gone, leaving him weak and trembling once more.

He felt like he was dying.

If I do, at least I'll have the satisfaction of knowing those two will be looking over their shoulders, wondering what I'll do next.

William stumbled the half-mile or so back to the warehouse he had claimed as his own. The building had turned out to be abandoned, thankfully. He walked past the door he'd kicked in — and subsequently barricaded to keep other vagrants out — to a trail of crates stacked in a rickety vertical path leading to a window several stories up. The alternate entrance route had seemed like a good idea at the time, after the invigoration of his kill, but now he wasn't sure if he could make it to the top of his ramshackle construction before passing out.

Winded and shaking, he eventually crawled up through the window onto a narrow catwalk running the length of the warehouse. He dragged himself over the loose boards to a steep stairway leading down.

Crippling pain seized his entire body, like every muscle was suddenly on fire. William tumbled over the side of the stairs. His fingers clamped onto the railing, where he dangled a dozen yards over a pile of debris. Before he could pull himself up, a spasm made him lose his grip. William cried out, arms flailing through the vast chasm of space, until a pile of decrepit wooden pallets broke his fall.

In his darkest nightmare, William had never imagined such excruciating pain. His limbs seized and he convulsively cried out, every inch of him in agony.

On and on it went, body burning in an earthly Hell, screaming and writhing. He wished only for death, but even if he had the will to reach for his blade and end his own life, his arms would not obey.

After what seemed like an eternity, the pain finally subsided, leaving him sweat-drenched and shaky. He rested for a while, not daring to move lest he provoke the agony's return.

When he finally opened his eyes, the world looked vastly different. The warehouse's interior appeared radiant, as if bathed in noonday sun, crisp with detail, yet washed in faded hues. His ears, too, felt like cotton had just been removed.

The soft tap of nails on concrete drew his attention. He was shocked to see its source was a tiny mouse, clear across the room.

Cautiously, he stretched his arms and legs. No trace of the burning agony remained.

He padded down from the pallets with cat-like grace, surprised how easy it was to navigate the unstable terrain. A large steel barrel stood in his way. William braced himself for a heavy lift, but when he picked it up, the barrel flew upward as if weighing nothing and landed behind him with a thunderous crash.

He realized his mouth was hanging open and clamped it shut.

Extraordinary strength, he thought, trying to fit the puzzle pieces together. *Grace. Eyes like a hawk. Enhanced hearing.*

On a whim, he dashed across the room, and closed the distance so quickly that he accidentally slammed into the far wall.

Speed.

William stooped into a predatory crouch, lips curled into a feral smile. He felt good — no, amazing — as if he could do anything, take whatever he wished from the sheeple around him without justification or regret. He was a god among men, a lion in a fenced-off game preserve.

The only thing wrong was his cheek. Unlike the rest of him, which felt powerful and rested, the wound Anne had inflicted in the furniture store burned with the same intensity as before, and no amount of scratching seemed to help. William sifted through a pile of scrap metal, amazed at his ability to move even the heaviest pieces without effort, until he found a polished steel plate, and held it like a mirror. The wound was angry red, as he expected it to be, about three inches long running the length of his cheek bone, with an ugly gap at one end where it hadn't closed properly.

That wasn't what made him gasp.

Never tan, but certainly not pale, William's skin was now ghostly-white, with a web of faint blue lines he assumed were veins visible just under the surface. His once-gray eyes were now black, except for a thin gray ring around the outside. They seemed larger than before, giving him an alien appearance that made him shiver. Peeling his lips back revealed canines that were a few millimeters longer than before, with razor-sharp tips.

A stomach growl alerted him that he was hungry.

Not just hungry, he realized. *Famished.*

The thought of feeding caused his top canine teeth to push down from his gums until they had nearly doubled in length.

William smiled, which made his appearance even more terrifying.

Oh, this will do nicely.

He had no idea how or why this had happened, only that he felt better now than ever before. He sprang up the steps, taking them six at a time, and padded across the catwalk as if born to it.

Once outside, he breathed in the night air. A barrage of smells assaulted him: the aging crates beneath the window, their rotted contents of fruits and vegetables from years past, grease, car fumes, birds from a nearby nest — each and every scent as clear as if presented in a picture. The most tantalizing scent of all, however, was faint, and came from several blocks away.

William leaped from the second-story without hesitation and landed neatly on his feet. He sniffed again, his mouth watering at the delicious scent, and hurried to where he knew his food waited.

Where there were people.

10

CRIME SCENE

RED AND BLUE POLICE LIGHTS COLORED ANNE'S PORCH like a twisted disco. She stared at the yellow tape across her front door while detectives bustled about inside taking notes and pictures. Officers had thoroughly interviewed her and Charlie, but Anne doubted their few answers had contributed any useful insights to how or why the corpse ended up in her apartment.

Apart from the obvious answer of William, that is.

A flashback of her closet blotted her vision, and with it her demons stirred in their lair. Anne closed her eyes and tried to recall the happy parts of the evening, but even though she knew there were plenty, her mind couldn't focus on any. The closet door creaked open with terrible slowness. Anne recoiled, but couldn't take her eyes from the growing chasm of darkness where a new ashen-faced demon lurked —

"Anne!"

The phantasm vanished at the sound of Charlie's voice. She collapsed sobbing against a police car. Charlie waited a few steps away, watching with concern.

"William did this," she said hoarsely. "It had to be him."

Charlie was slow to respond, but eventually nodded.

She wiped her eyes with a bitter laugh. "How's that for a second date?"

"Second?"

"Yeah. I didn't think I could top the first one, but the corpse in the closet was a definite step above the killer in the furniture store, wouldn't you say?"

Charlie stared at her helplessly.

"Just trying to lighten the mood."

Anne turned away to hide the tears that once again threatened to spill over. She wished Charlie would sweep her into the safety of his arms, as he had when he carried her to the hospital the first night they met. Her hero remained attentive, but distant, however, hands buried in his pockets. Anne swallowed her disappointment and tried to content herself with his reassuring presence.

Charlie started to speak, but fell silent when an older detective in a suit approached.

"Excuse me, Miss Perrin? Mr. ..." He squinted at his notebook.

"Charlie is fine."

"All right. I'm Detective Hannaway. Thanks again for your cooperation, I know this must be hard on you both. The victim was a man in his late twenties — homeless, by the look of it. He didn't have any ID, so that's all we've got until we run his fingerprints. Can you think of any reason why he would be in your apartment, Miss Perrin?"

Anne shook her head.

Hannaway sighed. "I didn't think so. I read the incident report a few weeks ago between you and a ..." He flipped a few pages back. "William Taplin."

Anne felt a chill at the name. She nodded stiffly.

"I don't need to tell you that he's our primary suspect, but we can't charge him unless there's evidence, which we're short on. The body shows signs of a struggle, including teeth marks. They're taking a mold right now. If we can get our hands on his dental records, we'll know for certain, but given the circumstances ..." He stuffed his notebook into his jacket. "It would be one hell of a coincidence for two different psychopaths to target you within weeks of each other. Miss Perrin, I think you should enter our protection program. We can set you up with a new identity and assist with relocating —"

"Like hell she will!" a familiar voice called.

Doris, still in her work uniform, pushed past two officers and marched toward them. She wasted no words and folded Anne in a comforting embrace, as Anne wished Charlie would.

"How did you know?" Anne said to her.

"Word travels fast, hon," Doris said. She gave Charlie a meaningful grin.

Charlie shrugged. "I called the diner. It seemed like the right thing to do."

"It was. Thank you." Anne hugged Doris tight, then took a deep breath. "Doris, I think Hannaway has a good point. William's proven twice now that he's willing to kill, and that he holds a grudge. My staying with you puts you in harm's way. I couldn't bear it if —"

"If that bastard takes one step into my house, it'll be the last thing he ever does. We will not have our lives dictated by some psycho who thinks he can control us with fear."

Charlie looked uneasy. "Doris, I'm with Anne on this one."

"Can it, lover boy. I love you for saving Anne, but let me make this crystal clear: We are not helpless little girls, and we will not be bullied into hiding."

"Miss Perrin," the detective said tightly, "the choice is yours. We can't force you into the protection program. If you were my friend," — he shot Doris a hard look — "I'd put your safety before my pride and ask you to enter the program, laying low until we find this guy —"

"If you find him," Doris said.

"*When* we find him, then you can go back to life as usual. Outside of the program, it'll be difficult to ensure your safety."

Doris snorted a laugh. "Officer Do-Right, it's our lives at stake, and I tell you right now that no one — and I mean no one — has a more vested interest in keeping us alive than we do. We'll defend ourselves like a pair of wolverines with their nuts caught in the pantry door."

Hannaway's face reddened. "Ma'am, this is ludicrous! He knows her identity and tracked down her apartment. It's only a matter of time before he traces her back to your place, too. He's proven that he's willing to kill, but because of some inflated sense of independence, you're going to put both your lives at risk and refuse police protection?"

"No," Doris said, "I expect the police to do what they can to protect us, but we're not going to hide like sheep waiting for the wolf to catch us. If the wolf finds us, he's going to discover a couple of pissed-off bears in sheep's clothing."

She crossed her arms and stared defiantly at the detective.

Hannaway looked to Charlie for support.

"The detective has a point," Charlie said quietly. "You'll be safer under police protection."

Doris stared daggers at him. Anne barely noticed. She stepped closer to Charlie, searching his face.

"Is that what you would do?" Anne said. "Let them take your identity and relocate you away from your friends?"

Charlie considered for a few seconds, then slowly shook his head.

"Miss Perrin," Hannaway said, rubbing his temple, "what would you like to do?"

Everyone turned to Anne.

Her mouth fell open. The stress of the night had left her in no condition to make big decisions. She needed time away to think — preferably in a bubble bath with a book and a pint of mint ice cream. Anne chose her words carefully. "Thank you for the advice, Detective Hannaway. Do you need an answer now, or can I get back to you in a day or so?"

Hannaway deflated and shot Doris another look. "No, Miss Perrin, I don't need an answer immediately. The offer stands until we take the suspect into custody, or ..."

He shook his head and walked away.

... or William kills me.

"Can we go now?" Doris hollered after him.

The detective waved his hand dismissively.

"Come on, hon," she said to Anne. "Let's ditch this horror show. I'll whip up some cocoa when we get to my place and draw you a nice warm bath."

"Sure, um ..." Anne glanced at Charlie, who still looked uneasy. She lowered her voice and said to Doris, "Can I have a few minutes alone, first?"

Doris grinned. "Take your time, kiddo. I'll call us a cab." She weaved through the line of police cars and fished around in her purse.

Anne fiddled with the zipper on her jacket, trying to think of the right thing to say to Charlie.

"I just —" they said at the same time, then laughed.

"You first," Anne said.

"I wanted to say I'm sorry about what happened tonight."

"Me too. It wasn't the glorious finish to the evening I'd pictured."

She smiled weakly, but he remained somber.

"Are you going to be all right, Anne?"

His caring tone brought a lump to her throat. She nodded, wishing again he would just take her in his arms and comfort her, but his hands stayed in his pockets.

His uncomfortable expression returned. "So, what were you going to say?"

"I wanted to say 'thank you'. Again. I can't imagine facing all of this alone. And ..." She cleared her throat, buying time to muster her courage. "I also wanted to say I had a great time tonight. Until the dead guy scared the bejesus out of me, anyway."

Charlie smiled with a boyish look that made her heart flutter. "So did I. Hopefully we can do it again soon."

Yes!

Anne did a mental fist-pump, but managed to maintain her composure. "I'd like that."

Charlie stared at her, his expression unreadable. "Goodnight, Anne. Stay safe."

"Goodnight, Charlie."

Her good mood faltered when he turned to leave, hands in his pockets, right where they had been for most of the night.

Out of her reach.

• • •

As soon as the police cars were out of view, Charlie halted his pathetic retreat and leaned against a tree, which bowed under his weight.

Why didn't I stay and comfort her? Why didn't I ...

He looked down at his hands and swore.

All Anne had wanted was a hug. It was in her posture, in her beautiful brown eyes. One hug — one daring show of physical affection — and *he* could have provided the solace that Doris eventually had. Maybe more.

He pounded the tree in frustration. Wood cracked under his fist, shaking a few branches loose that clattered to the sidewalk around him.

A simple hug, and I couldn't even give her that. What kind of man does that make me?

But he already knew the answer.

No man at all.

11

ICE CREAM

THE NEXT DAY FOUND ANNE AND DORIS AT THE FOOD COURT in their favorite downtown mall: a nine-story shopping center on Market Street. Anne was still shaken from the corpse in her apartment, and a nightmare-induced lack of sleep, but Doris had refused to let her wallow, and insisted that a change of scenery would help take her mind off things. It hadn't, of course, but Anne was glad for Doris' comforting presence in any setting ... and a scoop of Ghirardelli's chocolate ice cream didn't hurt.

Anne paused midbite when she noticed Doris staring. "What is it?"

Doris sighed. "It's ... You know me, hon, I have an opinion about everything, and I'm not shy about sharing it. I want to make sure you're really okay bunking with me when William is still at large, and you're not just going along for the ride because I badgered you out of police protection."

"I'm fine with it, really. The detective's offer was tempting, but the thought of relocating somewhere with a new identity, of not knowing anyone, is scary. I wouldn't get to see you, or ..."

"Or Charlie." Doris grinned. "That's what swayed you, ain't it?"

Anne blushed and stared at her dessert. "Well, maybe a little ..."

Doris hooted and slapped the table, startling the patrons around them. A gorgeous platinum blonde from a nearby table turned her ice-blue eyes to them, her expression unreadable. Her companion, an attractive brunette wearing an old-fashioned sundress, smiled warmly before she and the blonde left. Two cinnamon buns sat in their wake, barely touched.

What a crime.

Anne returned her attention to Doris. "Okay, maybe Charlie had something to do with it."

"And you don't think he would have signed on."

Anne nodded. "Doris, I've finally met someone special! I know we've only had two dates, but —"

"Two? You count his rescuing you from William as a date?" Doris barked a laugh, smacking the table again.

"Glad you thought it was funny. That joke didn't go over as well last night." Anne sighed. "Charlie is kind, funny, understanding, heroic, and, best of all, single! He may not be the affectionate type, but other than that, it's like he stepped right out of a fantasy novel. I've waited my whole life for someone like him. The thought of losing him because of some psycho ..."

"I understand, kiddo. You did the right thing."

Anne gently squeezed Doris' wrist. "Thank you. Despite what I said earlier, I wouldn't have had the strength to refuse police protection on my own."

"I know. That's why I dropped a tray of drinks on some dude at the diner and ran for the door when Charlie called."

"You didn't!" Anne said with a laugh.

"Oh yes I did. The guy wouldn't let go of my arm because he thought I brought him the wrong drink. That son-of-a-bitch deserved —"

"You know what I mean," Anne said.

"Yep. I got your back, kiddo, and that's a fact. Besides, it was totally worth the trip. One of the cuter boys-in-blue was checking me out last night. I didn't get his phone number, but if I see him again, I might just let him frisk me."

"I can't take you anywhere, can I? Not even to a crime scene in the middle of the night."

"Of course you can, peaches! I'm the very spice of life, and I keep your butt from taking root to the couch with your fingers rusted around a moldy old book. Now ..." Doris showed off her empty bowl. "Finish up so we can find a hat to match those adorable shoes we didn't buy."

• • •

The brunette in the vintage sundress watched Anne and Doris finish their ice cream from inside the clothing store.

"That's her," the brunette said to her platinum-blonde companion, who continued to thumb through a rack of dark pants. "Well, what do you think?"

"I think she is overly fond of ice cream," the thin, platinum blonde said evenly. She pulled out a pair of baggy gray pants, nearly identical to the ones she wore, and held them up for inspection.

"That's not what I meant! Besides, I like her figure."

Outside, Anne and Doris rose from their table. The brunette moved to the entrance to keep them in sight.

"I wish I were curvier," she said with a wistful sigh. "A few in the right places would do wonders for you, too."

"I am content as I am, but you may do as you wish. Adding weight should not prove difficult."

"Ouch!"

"It was not intended as an insult, merely fact." The platinum blonde put the pants back on the rack, then meticulously adjusted the surrounding hangers until they were level with each other. "Come, we must not lose them."

"You're the boss," the brunette said with a mock salute.

The blonde's brows knitted the barest fraction of an inch under the perfectly trimmed bangs of her bobbed haircut. "No, I am not."

"I was just teasing."

"Oh."

The platinum blonde strolled to the front of the store, but stopped short at the wall of people. Her ice-blue eyes flitted rapidly as if trying to watch everyone at once.

"They won't bite," the brunette said.

When her companion remained silent, the brunette put a sympathetic hand on her shoulder.

"Would you like me to go first?"

"Yes, please."

The brunette tipped her sunhat and plunged into the throng. Pale companion in tow, they followed at a safe distance while their targets window-shopped their way through the mall.

12

THE LONER

"TABLE TWENTY-TWO UP!" Hector called from the pickup window.

Anne started, remembering she was at work. Three days had passed since the corpse appeared in her apartment, but it would take much longer than that before she stopped seeing it at every turn.

She went to the pickup window and eyed the order with suspicion. Although the quality of Hector's cooking had improved, tonight it was markedly off; he had mixed up enough orders that the entire waiting staff was double-checking their deliveries.

Satisfied that this order was correct, Anne loaded the meals onto a tray, just as Doris plopped a plate at the window.

"Eighteen says the hamburger's undercooked," Doris said, planting a hand on her hip. "Well-done means 'no pink', genius."

Hector opened his mouth to protest, but a stern look from Doris sent him grumbling back to the grill.

Anne sighed. Tips had been below average the last few weeks, no thanks to frequent incidents like this.

Doris nodded as if reading her thoughts. "Tonight's been awful. It's like customers don't appreciate par-cooked cuisine."

"You're an experienced woman," Anne said, hoisting the tray onto her shoulder. "Maybe you could light Hector's fire and teach him how to cook." She waggled her eyebrows suggestively.

Doris snapped a towel at Anne's hastily retreating rear. "The next one won't miss!"

Anne delivered the food to table twenty-two, then headed for the counter. They were short-handed tonight, so she and Doris took turns at the counter waiting on the loners — their nickname for the solitary customers.

"Welcome to Hal's," Anne said to a newcomer. "Are you ready to order?"

Ice-blue eyes under a bob-cut hair style stared back at her. "Coffee, please," she said evenly.

The woman looked like a Barbie doll in men's clothing. Her platinum hair was perfect, as if each strand were laser-cut. Pale skin contrasted with black pants and a dark-gray jacket hanging loosely on her modest frame.

She seemed naggingly familiar, but Anne couldn't place her.

Anne shook herself and put her waitress smile back on. "You got it. Do you need a few minutes with the menu, or are you ready to order?"

"I just did," she said flatly, then held her menu out.

Anne stared for a second, unsure if she was joking, but the blonde's face was as unexpressive as her tone.

"So you did. I'll —" She stumbled on something as she backed away. *My nerve, perhaps?* "I-I'll be right back with your coffee."

On her way to the kitchen, Anne remembered why the woman looked familiar. She caught Doris' arm, nearly toppling her load of dirty dishes.

"Loner six!"

"You mean Bleached Barbie?" Doris said, unloading her tray. "She giving you trouble?"

"Yes. Well, no, not really. It's just ... I've seen her before."

"So? It's a big city, but it ain't that big." She looked pensive. "With dolled-up hair like that, I wonder if she's a queen? I mean, that has to be a wig."

"I'm not imagining things," Anne said. "She sat near us at the mall on Wednesday, with some June Cleaver look-a-like. I saw her again at the laundromat Thursday, and she was on my bus both yesterday and today."

"Think you have a stalker?" Doris winked.

"I'm serious," Anne said quietly.

Fueled by a repertoire of adventure novels, her imagination ran wild with possibilities.

Could she be a KGB agent? Secret Service? What if it has something to do with William? Anne paled. *What if she's working for William?*

"Darlin', you're way too uptight about this," Doris said. "Maybe she's a new local. Did you think of that?"

"I don't know, it's just ... there's something strange about her. She doesn't smile or frown or ... or anything! It's almost like her facial muscles don't work."

"Maybe they don't, or maybe she's just nervous because she likes you and is building up the courage to ask you on a date." Doris grinned mischievously. "You're one hot number, after all."

"You're impossible," Anne said, but couldn't help smiling.

"Just go talk to her, you nutjob, like you would any other customer."

"All right," Anne muttered, "but keep the lesbian theory between us."

"Good call, unless you're trying to make Charlie jealous."

Anne blushed at the mention of his name. Any uncertainty over his interest in her the night he left the crime scene had been dispelled when he called the following morning to see how she was doing. They had talked right up to her trip to the mall, and he'd called again when she got home, where they'd spent New Year's Eve chatting about anything and everything, until Anne couldn't keep her eyes open and had to reluctantly say goodnight. It had been the same story on New Year's Day, the day after, and this morning. Anne fingered the phone in her pocket, already looking forward to his call tonight.

Hector, she suddenly realized, was staring at her over the counter with an open mouth.

Every straight guy loves a good lesbian scandal, I suppose.

Anne looked forward to disappointing him.

"Shut it, cookie," Doris snapped. "Your buns are burning."

Hector jumped back to the grill and hastily removed the smoking rolls. Doris returned her attention to Anne.

"Seriously though, kiddo, you've been through a lot recently. Do you want me to shake Barbie down? I don't mind, if it'll put you at ease."

"No, I-I'll do it, but ... thanks for the offer." She gave Doris a hug, then, heart pounding, strode into the dining area.

Her stalker sat with her back to the counter, looking out among the other patrons.

"Hi," Anne said, trying to sound casual.

Bleached Barbie ignored her; ice-blue eyes continued to jump quickly from table to table. Anne grabbed a mug from under the counter and filled it with coffee.

"Sugar?" Anne said, plastering on a friendly smile.

"No."

"Cream?"

"No."

Anne cleared her throat and made sure her friendly mask was still in place. "So, I've seen you around lately. Do you live nearby?"

"Yes."

"Oh? Where?"

Barbie stared at her, unblinking like a stone statue.

"Well, I-I only ask because I saw you and your friend at the mall the other day, and —"

"I am not stalking you." Barbie pulled a few dollars from her pocket and placed them on the table with a handful of change. A nickel rattled and spun in diminishing circles next to her untouched coffee. Blue eyes finally met hers. "And I am not interested in a date."

Barbie left the diner without a backward glance, leaving Anne in stunned silence. Odd looks from the surrounding patrons made her blush. She hastily scooped the money from the counter and carried it to the register.

It was no surprise that Barbie hadn't left a tip.

13

ALLESANDRO

WILLIAM HERDED HIS PREY DOWN AN ALLEY — a wiry, athletic fellow who William hoped would give him a good chase. Tonight's pick had a shock of blond hair at one temple amidst a head of brown. William idly fingered the man's cell phone in his pocket. Taking their phones was always step one — a lesson he had learned after a call to emergency services by one of his earlier victims had prematurely ended the hunt.

He didn't like to rush.

"What the hell do you want?" his soon-to-be meal yelled when he reached the dead end.

In answer, William flashed his ghoulish smile. His canines had grown into sharp points, which grew longer before he fed, giving him a frightful appearance.

It had the desired effect. William grabbed his victim's throat to cut off the inevitable scream. He bore his fangs and moved with exaggerated slowness toward his victim's neck, relishing his terror. The man kicked and punched to no effect; William's hold was absolute.

The hunt is over, he thought, salivating with anticipation. *Time to feast.*

He sank his teeth into his victim's tender flesh and drank deeply, savoring the rush that followed.

These last few weeks following his transformation had been the most exhilarating of his life. "Vampire" was the only word that described what he had become: Craving for blood, razor sharp teeth, superhuman speed and strength, enhanced senses, and even sensitivity to sunlight. The last made him shudder; the smell of his own burning flesh still haunted him.

William disengaged when he felt the pulse at his lips weaken. He wasn't in the mood to torture anyone tonight, so he would let this one go. The wound in his victim's neck would quickly heal, William had discovered, and he would remember little of what happened tonight — both strange side effects of his bite.

As the wiry man stared vacantly at the wall, William pulled the cell phone from his pocket and brought it to life. "Run along, Allesandro," he said, reading the name from the device. "And remember to drink plenty of water."

Allesandro nodded, and William watched him stumble back down the alley.

William turned, intent on heading home, but paused. The thought of returning to the empty warehouse brought a pang of loneliness. Hunting alone was fun, but the thought of hunting in a pack suddenly appealed to him.

"Come back here," he called to Allesandro, who had wandered to the mouth of the alley.

Allesandro returned, still in a haze. William wasn't exactly sure what to do next, but something guided him — an odd, but familiar feeling in the back of his mind. He gashed his own arm open with his sharp teeth, then pressed it to the waiting man's mouth.

"Drink."

Allesandro obeyed, and as he drank, William felt the stirrings of a connection with the man. A bond.

The first of my pack, William thought with a smile.

14

COFFEE

MARK SUTHER STARED AT THE MESSAGE on his phone in a daze. He set it down on the kitchen table, drummed his fingers, then picked it back up again. The words had no more effect on him now than they had a moment ago, which was worrisome, because they should have.

He hung his head. *Susan, why now of all times ...*

"Hey, Mark."

Mark put on his poker face at Charlie's voice. His friend didn't need to hear about Susan. Not now. "Hey. How's Anne doing?"

"Fine. She's heading to work."

"Any more dates on the horizon?"

"No, she seems happy with a phone relationship, so ..." Charlie shrugged.

"Yeah, I'm sure *she* does."

Mark regretted the barb as soon as he said it; Charlie squirmed, looking as though he'd rather be anywhere else.

"Look, all I meant was that Anne sounds ... well, accommodating, and she may not be asking to meet up again because she thinks you don't want to."

He waited for a response, but Charlie just stared at the floor. Mark kept his temper in check. As morose as Charlie seemed now, since rescuing Anne, he was the happiest he had been in years. Mark was damned if he would screw that up now by pushing him in a direction he wasn't ready to go.

But Mark wasn't going to sit on his hands waiting for a miracle, either. "Hey, you want to grab a coffee? I, ah ... have some bad news about Susan, and I'd like to get out for a few minutes. With a friend."

So much for not telling him.

"Sure, I'll grab my jacket."

He actually accepted?

Still not sure he'd heard right, Mark didn't bother grabbing his coat and went straight for the door before Charlie could change his mind.

• • •

"Mr. Mark," the buxom redhead behind the counter said with a pleasant, but cocky smile that suggested she knew something you didn't.

"Ms. Fedelma, it's a pleasure to see you again."

Her smile disappeared, as Mark knew it would. "It's Dela," she said, covering her nametag that said otherwise. "Fedelma is what my mother called me when I was in trouble."

"I bet she called you that a lot."

Her green eyes narrowed. "She did, usually after I beat up the kids who teased me about my name."

"I'd better watch myself, then. I bet you have a mean right-hook."

"You may find out. That was precariously close to a tease." Her tone was stern, but her eyes playful. "And don't think those big muscles will save you. I have a black belt in karate, you know."

The thought of them sparring made him chuckle. At six-foot-two, Mark towered over her, but he checked his mirth with a glance at Charlie, who was closer to Dela's height. It was a mistake to judge by size alone — as he and Charlie well knew.

Mark scratched his sandy-blonde hair and gave a disarming grin. "My muscles and I consider ourselves warned." He enjoyed their daily banter; it scratched an itch that his heavier conversations with Susan rarely had.

Which is why this morning's text wasn't a surprise.

He sighed. Expected or not, it still sucked.

Dela seemed to read his change in mood. Her expression softened. "Your usual Americano?"

"Please."

"And for you?" she said to Charlie.

"Same."

Dela grabbed a cup and pen. "Name?"

"Charlie."

Her eyes widened.

"No shit," she said in a voice full of wonder, then shook herself. "I-I'm sorry, I mean, Mark's an old hat around here, but you ..."

She looked to Mark and swallowed, her freckled face nearly as red as her frizzy hair.

"It's fine," Charlie said, scratching his head. "I don't get out much, I know."

She nodded, acknowledging the obvious, then smiled. "Well, *Charlie,* it's nice to finally meet you. Don't be a stranger, okay? I make a mean mocha that I promise is worth the trip."

"Sold. I'll have one of those instead, please."

Her face lit up. Mark could have kissed her at that moment — not because she was beautiful with a figure that made her customers drool, but for her encouraging words that reinforced what he'd been telling Charlie for years: there was a whole world beyond the confines of his self-imposed prison, filled with people who wanted to meet him — the real him.

Like Anne.

As traumatic as Charlie's introduction to Anne had been, it had sparked something that no amount of encouragement or cajoling from Mark ever had, and, although a skittish post-traumatic stress victim was far from Mark's first choice of partners, he could hardly argue with Charlie's frequent smiles — which had been nonexistent before he and Anne had started dating.

Not to mention the fact that he's actually here.

"Thanks, Dela," Mark said with heartfelt gratitude. She nodded, and her eyes followed Charlie all the way to their table.

"You two get along well," Charlie said, settling into the wooden chair with noticeable care. It creaked anyway.

Mark sat across from him. "I'm her customer. Why wouldn't we?"

Charlie shook his head and laughed. "Clueless as always."

"Says the guy who thinks his girlfriend will be content with a phone relationship when you only live six miles from each other."

"Touché. But before we talk about that — which is *surely* the reason you lured me out here ..." Charlie rolled a sugar packet across his knuckles with deft precision, though his eyes stayed on Mark. "What happened with Susan?"

Damn. "She, ah ... came to her senses, apparently, and realized we weren't so great as a couple."

"I'm sorry."

Mark shrugged, despite his suddenly heavy heart. "Can't win them all, and there's no point settling for someone who's going to drag you down in the long run, is there?"

Charlie nodded, evidently missing the subtle poke at Anne, so Mark tried a different tack.

"Either way, her timing couldn't have been better," Mark said. "Simon introduced me to these two girls last week. Smoking hot. One's an executive for a billion-dollar advertising firm in Mountain View, and the other is director of research at PaloTech, if you can believe it."

"Sounds great," Charlie said with less enthusiasm than Mark had hoped. "Which one are you going for? Or both?"

"Frankly, I was aiming for the executive, so you could take the director. She's smart, ambitious, and cuter in those glasses than any librarian. A perfect fit for you. Besides, how long has it been since we went on a double date?"

"Forever, but ..." Charlie spread his hands. "I like Anne."

Mark sighed. He recognized that stubborn look. Any further discussion would be a losing argument, and he'd had enough of those over the last five years to last a lifetime.

Work with what you've got.

"All right. Anne. So what's your game plan?"

Charlie flipped the sugar packet in the air and caught it without looking, but remained silent.

"Does she know yet?"

Charlie buried his face in his hands. "Which part?"

"Hard one first."

"It would have made headlines if she did."

"Fair enough. On to the next. Does she know what you do for a living?"

"No."

"What the hell have you been talking about for the last several weeks, then?"

"Weather. Jokes. Movies. Books. Her customer stories — which are hilarious and change every day."

"And she hasn't once asked what you do?"

"Of course she has. I told her I'm in the computer business, but that's it. She's a bit of a technophobe, so it's easy to stay away from the topic."

"*Technophobe?* Charlie, what's going to happen when she discovers ..." Mark realized he was yelling and lowered his voice. "You know that's not a small problem, right?"

"I know."

But it doesn't matter, Mark finished for him, *because he thinks he's in love.* He shook his head. *PTSD, technophobia, and she's a waitress to boot. This isn't going to end well for either of them.*

But he knew there was no talking Charlie out of it and, as bad as he feared it might blow up between them, it was better than going back to the way things were. Mark fingered the phone in his pocket, thinking of the text he had received this morning, and a dozen others like it from his long chain of failed relationships.

Who am I to judge someone else's happiness, anyway?

"Okay, so back to the reason I lured you here," Mark said with a grin. "Hard as it might be, you're going to have to ask her out again eventually."

"Do I? I mean, what if she doesn't want a physical relationship?"

"If you actually say, 'Wouldn't that be great?', you're going to be wearing that mocha when it comes."

Dela chose that moment to set two steaming cups on the table. "Here you go, guys. Enjoy."

"Hey," Mark said to her. "Can we ask you something?"

"I'd just go for it," she said to Charlie. "Mark's right. Women can be shy when they're feeling someone out. But once they've found their man, they want to be touched, sometimes ravaged. If you're timid, she's going to think you're not interested and find someone who is."

Charlie snapped his mouth shut. "I, uh, didn't realize you were listening."

"You weren't exactly whispering," she said with her knowing smile.

Once again Mark resisted the urge to kiss the fiery barista. The situation was far more complicated than Dela realized, of course, but her warning carried a weight that Mark's never could. Charlie was intimidated, he could tell. The question was whether he would rise to the challenge, or simply retreat, as he had so many times before.

For a second, Mark thought it would be the latter, but Charlie straightened, the stubborn edge back in his eyes.

"Fine, I'll ask her out to dinner again."

"Again?" Dela shook her head. She turned a chair around and straddled the backrest in an unladylike fashion. Her ample breasts jutted over the top, drawing the eyes of male and female patrons alike. "How long have you been seeing this girl?"

"A f-few weeks."

"Number of dates?"

"Two — er, one, actually."

"Yikes. And how old is she?"

"Thirty-six."

"About my age, then." She stroked her chin thoughtfully. "You need to get a move-on, pal. Step up your game. Mid-thirties are a tough time for single women, let me tell you. They've either given up on men, or they're desperate for one. Wrinkles, love handles, the girls not standing as perky as they used to … They start to question their attractiveness, worry that they'll never get married or have a family. Does she want kids?"

Charlie paled. "Not that she's mentioned."

"Well she wouldn't this early on, but trust me when I say she's thinking about it. Scared yet?"

"Terrified."

"And you still want her?"

Charlie nodded, but Mark heard the table creak in his firm grip.

"Then you've got to prove you're a serious contender and take things to the next level. Dinner's not going to cut it, unless your reservations are in Paris. Think bigger. Classier. Something adventurous and romantic that she'll tout to her grandkids as the epitome of dates." Dela glanced over her shoulder and gasped. "Crap, the line's backing up. I gotta go." She chucked Charlie affectionately on the arm. "Let me know how it goes. Good luck."

They watched her leave in stunned silence.

Charlie was the first to break the spell. His shoulders slumped. "Kids? I'm so screwed."

"One problem at a time, buddy. Let's focus on the next date. Now, Paris might be out of the question, but San Francisco still has many cultured activities to explore."

"Such as?"

Mark leaned forward with a grin. "Does she like music?"

15

THE OPERA

ANNE AND CHARLIE EXITED THE THEATER, both gushing over their first opera experience.

High school prom was the most formal event Anne had attended before tonight. Dressed in a skirt and blouse, with her boyfriend at the time in a proper suit, they had afterward eaten hamburgers at the local diner, celebrated by splurging on milkshakes, and they both wondered if it got any better than that.

Tonight, she discovered it most certainly could.

Anne wore an elegant flowered dress she bought just for the occasion, cinched at the waist, which Doris said would show off her hourglass figure, and she was happy to see it had attracted Charlie's attention more than once. Charlie had swapped his signature brown leather jacket for a crisp black tuxedo that made her heart swoon every time she looked at him. He had treated her to a fancy French restaurant. Charlie had barely touched his food, which Anne found odd, but she made up for it by leaving not a scrap on either of their plates.

Then, of course, came the opera. Anne had never felt so excited and out of place at the same time. There the upper echelon mingled in the lobby with fine champagne and chocolate-covered strawberries that even Anne's full stomach couldn't refuse. Charlie had seemed remarkably comfortable among the city's finest, and made conversation easily, though she noticed he avoided giving his name during introductions, which Anne chalked up to nerves. The performance itself had been breathtaking; the powerful music filled her with such emotion that she thought her heart would burst. She was the first from her seat for the standing ovation and wiped tears from her eyes the entire way out.

In short, the evening had been a chapter from a fairytale adventure, and Anne couldn't imagine being happier.

She smiled at Charlie, who returned it. He had been pleasant, but maintained his usual physical distance and, while it was fun at first because it felt properly upper class, now that they were alone, the small space between them felt like miles.

Anne wanted to be closer, to feel his touch, and she was tired of waiting. She felt guilty over her selfish need; she knew Charlie was skittish about physical contact, for some reason. Although this evening had drawn them closer together, it wasn't enough.

Anne sidled closer, slipped her arm through his, and held her breath.

Several tense seconds passed. Charlie hadn't bolted, and she felt no signs of a flashback.

So far so good.

She relaxed enough to look up at Charlie. His jaw was clenched, eyes fixed straight ahead, as if fighting some internal battle. Not wishing to cause him discomfort, Anne swallowed her disappointment and released him, but he caught her at the last moment and patted her hand. When she looked up again, he was smiling. Anne sighed in relief.

Feeling bold, she rested her head against his arm. Again he didn't flinch, and her demons stayed put. Her smile grew.

A block passed with only the sounds of the city and their breathing. She closed her eyes to enjoy the feel of his muscular arm, his pleasant warmth on this cold, misty night. When she opened her eyes, however, his smile was gone.

"What's wrong?"

"Nothing," Charlie said. "I was thinking of something a friend told me earlier today."

"Oh yeah?"

"Mm."

She drummed her fingers on his jacket. "Are you going to make me guess?"

"It was just some advice."

"Ah. Something profound, like 'don't eat yellow snow'?" She nudged him playfully.

He chuckled and surprised her by slipping an arm around her shoulders. The demons stayed quiet. Anne wanted to sing.

"More like 'Relax and enjoy yourself.'"

Good advice.

She snuggled into his chest; his silky jacket was a pillow from heaven.

They walked in blissful silence. Parking in the City, even on a weeknight, was an Olympic event. Tonight they had lost, finally landing seven blocks away, but, nestled against him as she was now, a long walk back to the car sounded just fine.

"So, who is this sage friend of yours?" Anne said. It was the first time Charlie had mentioned someone else in his life.

"Oh ..." Charlie cleared his throat and looked away. "H-her name is Cappa."

Her?

An unexpected flare of jealousy turned her mouth dry. "Is she pretty?" Anne snapped her mouth shut, but it was too late; the words had already escaped.

"Who, Cappa? No, she's just —"

Charlie stumbled on something, though Anne couldn't see what. "I mean 'yes'! Yes, she's pretty, but she's a friend."

"So she's a ... pretty friend?" Her heart sank.

Charlie stopped and ran a hand through his hair. "Yes, she's pretty, but she's just a friend. Cappa's helped me through some hard times. She's been there for me ever since I ... I got started in the business."

Anne took a calming breath.

Down, girl. He's allowed to have female friends.

"Come to think of it," Anne said, "you never told me what you do for a living. I mean, you're in the computer business, but what exactly do you do?"

"I, ah ... I make computers and other electronics."

"Oh, cool. Do you have a shop in the City or something?"

"More like a factory."

"Really?" Anne grinned with childish delight. "You have a factory? Is it nearby? Have I heard of it?"

"Yes, yes, and probably."

When he remained silent, she said, "Well?"

Charlie's shoulders sagged. He pointed to the skyline across the street.

Anne gasped. *No freakin' way ...*

The giant Z-Tech Industries billboard by the freeway was visible even through the fog. On its bright digital display, an animated circuit board zoomed out to a computer, which became a farm of computers, then zoomed out again to show lines of light connecting the city, then cities to cities, and eventually lit up the entire world. The world faded to a single computer chip, and the cycle started again.

Z-Tech. One of the largest electronics manufacturers in the world. She stared at the lighted sign. *Privately owned. Worth billions.*

Charlie cringed when Anne finally rounded on him. "That's you? Y-you're *the* Charlie Z?"

He nodded, shrinking under the weight of her stare.

"But we've talked every day for an entire month! How could I not know this? W-why didn't you tell me sooner?"

He sighed. "When people find out who I am, they treat me ... differently. It becomes hard to tell if what they say is really what they mean or just deference because they want something." When he turned back, his hazel eyes were soft. "Talking with you has been great, like neighbors chatting over the fence. With you, I wasn't president or CEO or someone's meal ticket, I was just ... me. Until now."

"Did ... did you really think I would hate you because of your success, or use you for my own personal gains?"

Charlie took her gently by the shoulders. Concern etched his brow. "No, never! It's more ... habit than anything else. Anne, I'm sorry if I upset you. You have every right to —"

She silenced him with a finger to his lips. "I'm not angry, but ... this is our third date. Yes, third," she said when he grinned. "I still count your dashing rescue in the furniture store as a date. Do you like me?"

He gulped. "I do."

"Then show me."

Heart thundering, Anne tilted her chin up in bold invitation.

Charlie just looked at her, confused, like a teenager alone with a girl for the first time. "I'm sorry," he said in a shaky voice, "I can't —"

He stumbled forward — drawing a surprised squeal from Anne — and their lips met.

There they stood, wide-eyed statues in the night. A car sped by, leaving swirls of mist in its wake, the roar of its engine lost in the sound of her pounding heart.

Anne checked for flashback warnings. Nothing.

Okay, here goes.

She parted her lips and kissed him in earnest. He tasted like the chocolate truffles they shared during the intermission, and there was something else — an earthy, sensual flavor that quickened her pulse and left her wanting for more. Anne wrapped her arms around him. Her fingers slipped under his jacket and kneaded his firm back, then pulled him tight against her. Charlie was slower to the game, but eventually folded her in his strong arms, which had carried her to safety after William's knife —

Anne's scream pierced the night, shrill even to her own ears. Charlie jumped back, looking even more terrified than she felt. A few seconds later, when the flashback of William cutting her throat receded, Anne was left with a different horror.

Oh no. No, no, no!

"Charlie," she said in a hoarse whisper.

He stepped back.

Anne reached imploringly but didn't advance, afraid that if she did, he might run away for good. "Charlie, please, I-I'm sorry. I'm sorry! Please don't ..."

He took another step away. Anne was devastated.

"Please don't go," she said. "Don't leave me. I didn't mean to scream. I won't —"

"Of course you did!"

His harsh tone hit her like a slap. Anne covered her mouth, but an anguished sob burst through her fingers.

Charlie didn't seem to notice. He was instead staring at his hands. "Why wouldn't you scream," he said softly. "That's what you do when someone hurts you."

"What? N-no, Charlie, you didn't hurt me."

He shook his head, brows furrowed. "You don't have to cover for me. I should have known better than to ..." He balled his fists and turned away. "I'll call you a cab, and ... if you want to press charges, I understand."

"Charlie, what the hell are you talking about? You didn't hurt me! It was a flashback, that's all."

His skeptical frown remained.

"Look, I'll prove it!" Anne shed her jacket and pulled her shoulder strap down, intent on baring herself to the world to show her undamaged skin, but Charlie held up a hand.

"All right! Just ... are you sure?"

She tugged her dress back into place and nodded. "Having post-traumatic stress disorder doesn't mean I'm made of glass. You did everything right, Charlie. I couldn't have asked for better."

He stuffed his hands into his pockets, but she caught his arm.

"No! Please, I ... I want a do-over."

"Anne, I know what a flashback is, and it's not pleasant. I don't want to put you through that again."

"And I don't want to scare you again, so ..." She tugged his hands out and took them in her own. "Let's try just the kissing part and see how it goes." Her spirits fell when he hesitated. "Please? I-I can't promise I won't scream again, but if you give me another chance, I —"

His kiss caught her by surprise. Tender, caring, passionate, it was everything she could have wished for. Anne drank him in, pressed her body to his, eager once more for his touch, but their hands remained joined; only their tongues danced the lovers' tango.

Minutes, hours, or years passed. She didn't know, and she didn't care. When they finally parted, her lips mourned his absence, and she could only stare into his eyes with unabashed yearning.

He brushed her hair back with gentle fingers. "Anne Perrin, this last month with you has been my happiest in a long, long time. You're one of the kindest, funniest people I've ever met, and it's an honor to be your date."

Charlie might have said more, but Anne covered his mouth with hers and, for the next several minutes, she showed him the true meaning of passion.

16

A WALK THROUGH THE MIST

ANNE WAS IN HEAVEN. A few shivers were all it had taken for Charlie to enfold her in the warmth of his jacket under his comforting arm; even her demons knew better than to disturb her bubble of happiness. Head resting against his chest, she closed her eyes and absorbed his scent — a musty mix of cologne and an earthy smell that made Anne want to wrap herself around him and purr.

Wouldn't it be terrible if we got lost? We'd have to stay like this for hours.

She snuggled closer and smiled.

Oh darn.

A loud *pop* sounded from overhead. Anne looked up just in time to see the streetlight nearest to them go out. A second later, the same happened to the light ahead of them, then the one behind. Thick fog blotted out star and moonlight, leaving them in almost total darkness.

"That's odd," Anne said. She reluctantly withdrew from his warmth and fished around in her purse. "I've seen streetlights go out before and they're usually quiet. Maybe a transformer blew or something. Aha!"

She pulled out a small flashlight and clicked it on. Its broad beam lit the sidewalk, but didn't penetrate very far into the mist.

"Oh well, at least we won't trip. Still think you can find the car, Charlie?"

Anne stepped forward, but a touch from Charlie made her pause.

"Stay close," he whispered.

"What's wrong?" His cautious tone put her on edge.

"The lights didn't go out by themselves. They were broken." He picked up a small object from the ground. Her flashlight glinted from a shard of clear glass between his fingers.

"Charlie, what's going on?" A sudden chill raised the hair on the back of her neck.

"I don't know," he said, eyes searching the darkness. He ran a hand through his hair. "Come on, the car's just up ahead."

Anne latched onto his arm and they set off at a brisk pace. Shadows danced in the mist, but disappeared when she tried to track them. Her demons stirred in response to her fear; phantom fingers groped at her wrists and ankles, making her want to scream.

"How much further?" she said, voice trembling.

The figures in the fog were becoming real, taunting her like specters. She clutched Charlie's arm, swinging her flashlight this way and that.

Charlie pointed ahead. "It's right up —"

Anne shrieked.

One of the shadow figures had taken form.

A wiry man jumped from the roof of a parked car. A blonde streak near his temple divided his dark hair. His pasty-white face split into a frightening grin.

Charlie darted between them. The wiry man grinned wider. He advanced, as if to walk right through her guardian. Charlie put a restraining hand on the wiry man's chest.

In a blur of motion, he caught Charlie's arm and hurled him into a parked car.

Like a scene from Anne's worst nightmare, Charlie struck the car with the force of a wrecking ball. It crumpled around him in an explosion of glass and screeching metal.

Anne rubbed her eyes, hoping it was just a hallucination, but the gruesome scene remained. Charlie's limbs protruded at sickening angles from the wreckage. She turned her shaking flashlight back to the wiry man, making his unusually large eyes glow.

He mouthed a single word.

"Run."

"Hey!"

Anne's breath caught.

Charlie?

The squeal of tearing metal pierced the mist. She turned her flashlight to find Charlie peeling himself from his steel tomb as if it were cardboard. With an almost casual air, he tore one of the protruding passenger doors from its hinges and hurled it with incredible speed. The wiry man had just enough time to look surprised before it struck him in the chest. The force carried him clear across the small yard, and into the house beyond, which swallowed him in a hail of plaster.

She swung her light back to Charlie. Impossible as it seemed, there her hero stood, tall and confident, just like the night he had rescued her from William. His jacket was torn. A nasty gash ran along his cheek, but apart from that, he appeared to be fine.

"Come on," Charlie said, gesturing for her to follow. "Quickly, in case he gets up."

The notion was ridiculous — the ballistic car door should have cut their assailant in half — but she was too shocked to argue, so she hurried over to him. He grabbed her hand and led her through the darkness at a run. Practically blind, Anne focused on putting one foot in front of the other.

She was breathing hard by the time his car came into view, blessedly illuminated by an undamaged streetlight. He reached for the passenger handle, but a shrill hiss made them spin around.

The wiry man sprang at her from the depths of the mist, sharp canines glistening with unholy terror. Charlie shoved her out of harm's way. It felt like she'd been kicked by a horse. Anne flew sideways in a spray of limbs, then tumbled several paces down the sidewalk, banging her knees and elbows. She glanced up in a daze to see the attacker bite down on Charlie's forearm with a fierce growl. Charlie punched him in the head once, twice, three times, before he finally let go.

The wiry man blanched and spat a mouthful of blood, then his eyes locked on Anne. He lunged for her. Charlie moved to intercept, but the wiry man dodged around him, crimson-stained mouth twisted in a predatory snarl.

Anne screamed when a long metal blade sprang from between Charlie's knuckles. He jammed it into the wiry man's ribs.

The man gave piercing cry. He grabbed Charlie's hand to pry the blade from his side.

Charlie ignored the effort. He stepped forward, bladed arm cocked as if readying to throw a javelin, and hurled the screaming man impossibly far, where the night mist swallowed him whole. The blade retracted with a *click*; the only evidence it had ever existed was a spot of blood on the back of Charlie's hand.

"Charlie," Anne said in a strangled whisper. "W-what the —"

"Later, I promise." He opened the passenger door. "Right now we have to go. I have a sick feeling he won't be down for long."

Anne struggled to her feet and climbed in. Neither of them spoke as the car raced through the city streets toward the towering concrete fortress she recognized as the Z-Tech factory.

17

Z-TECH

ANNE SAT IN Z-TECH'S MODEST RECEPTION AREA, trembling fingers fidgeting with the folds of her fancy dress. In place of customary magazines, several electronic books — e-readers, they were called — lay on the coffee table. Anne hated those inevitable replacements for her beloved books. She turned one over in her hands. The plastic shell was cold and lifeless; it had none of the character of her paperbacks.

She raised the e-reader to her nose and sniffed, drawing a curious look from Charlie. They hadn't spoken since their arrival, and his agitation had only grown over their few minutes together in the lobby. Anne averted her eyes and put the plastic device back.

His frown returned. He glanced at his knuckles, where the spot of blood still shimmered under the lobby lights, and his frown deepened. The gash in his cheek looked terrible.

It should be dripping blood, she thought.

But it wasn't. Neither was the bite on his arm.

Her thoughts returned to their encounter in the darkness, still unsure if what she had seen was real, or some elaborate new flashback her broken mind had concocted in response to yet another assault.

What attacked us? Did it really bury Charlie into the side of a car? Did Charlie really tear the door off and throw it like a Frisbee? Did I really see a blade spring from his knuckles?

And the biggest question of all ...

She met Charlie's eyes for the first time since they'd arrived.

What are you?

"Will you be okay here for a few minutes?" he said.

Will I be okay?

The question was so absurd she didn't know whether to laugh or cry. "Sure," she said instead. *Why not?*

She pinned her hands between her knees to keep them from shaking. Seemingly oblivious to her discomfort, Charlie nodded and hurried through a door marked "Employees Only".

Now alone, her demons bubbled to the surface, raising the hairs on her neck, so she looked for a distraction. She eyed the e-readers on the table and sneered.

Never. There must be a stray book or magazine around here somewhere, she thought.

A search of the area, however, turned up nothing but a forgotten mint lodged between the couch cushions.

The coffee maker was tempting, but the last thing her frayed nerves needed was caffeine. Anne idly wondered if there was a bookstore nearby. She stared through the glass doors into the night. The menacing faces of her demons moved in the shadows, joined by their newest member with the shock of blonde hair. She shuddered and turned away.

Oh, Doris!

She grabbed her cell phone from her purse.

If Charlie turns out to be an invading alien and fries my brain, at least Doris can tip the FBI or something.

Moreover, Anne really needed to hear a friendly voice.

She opened her antiquated flip phone, located Doris' number in her short contact list, and hit Send. The phone beeped an unhappy tone, and her heart sank when she saw the tiny "No Signal" symbol at the top of the screen. She circled the waiting room, pausing every few steps to see if a signal would magically appear. It never did. With a silent curse, she shoved the phone back into her purse and began pacing.

The employee door opened, making Anne jump. A beautiful woman with a round face smiled at her. She wore a large-brimmed hat, which complemented her vintage sundress and jewelry. The entire outfit, while tasteful, belonged to an era long past.

"Hello," she said warmly. "You must be Anne."

"I must be," Anne said, fiddling with her dress.

The woman glided across the carpet and wrapped her in a friendly embrace. Anne gave an obligatory pat on the back, unsure how she had earned such a warm welcome. The woman held her at arm's length and put a hand on her shoulder.

"It's great to finally meet you," the woman said. Her smile was dazzling, genuine, endearing. Dark brown hair fell in ringlets over her unblemished shoulders.

Friendly, supportive, beautiful ...

"You must be Cappa," Anne said, hoping she was wrong.

Her laugh was musical, June Cleaver incarnate. "I guess Charlie's mentioned me."

"Yes, though he didn't say you worked together."

Despite her uncertainty about Charlie, Anne's jealousy flared, and it was a struggle to keep it from her voice.

"I've been his assistant for years," Cappa said, "since the early days of Z-Tech. My responsibilities grew with the business, and today I oversee most of Z-Tech's operations, allowing Charlie and his partner Mark to focus on research and business development."

Mark. Another name she hadn't heard before. *Another secret,* she thought. Her lips trembled.

Cappa's smile faded. "You ... probably have some questions. About Charlie."

You're damn right, Anne wanted to say.

The blade from between his knuckles flashed before her eyes, making her jump. Unable to speak, she nodded, spilling tears down her cheeks.

"I'll answer what I can," Cappa said.

Anne opened her mouth, but all that came out was a sob. She fell to her knees in the small lobby and buried her face in her hands. Friendly arms enfolded her once again. Anne leaned in and cried on Cappa's flawless shoulder.

Cappa rocked her with motherly tenderness, gently stroking her hair. "Maybe not tonight," she said softly amidst Anne's bawling. "It sounds like you've had enough for one evening."

18

A NIGHT AT Z-TECH

ANNE WOKE SWEATING to the sound of her own scream. It was pitch black. She cowered against the headboard with her knees pulled up tight to fend off the residual effects of the nightmare.

Lights flickered on, shedding enough illumination in the small guest room to prove the wiry man who'd attacked them after the opera wasn't actually there, but not enough to hurt her eyes.

Minutes passed, and her fear with it. She sank back under the covers and took a deep breath. The overhead lights continued to brighten at a comfortable rate.

Clever idea, she thought.

The bedside clock read 2:05 A.M. Anne had slept fitfully in the uncomfortable guest bed and, if her nightmare was any indication, she wasn't going back to sleep anytime soon. She climbed out of bed and stretched, but her reflection in the mirror drew a sigh.

Cappa had offered to wash her dirt-streaked dress, so Anne had exchanged it for one of Cappa's nightgowns. It was light pink with frills on the cuffs of its long sleeves. The hem ran all the way to her ankles, also frilled. She twirled and watched the over-sized dress slowly deflate.

Ugh.

Only once in her life, when she was a young teen, had Anne worn a full nightgown. It was her grandmother's, and it had looked just as ridiculous on her as this one.

A loud stomach rumble reminded her that dinner, delicious as it had been, was a long time ago. Cappa had shown her the kitchen before leading her to the guest room, and Anne was reasonably sure she could find her way back. She wrapped the duvet from the bed around her, stepped into a pair of white slippers by the door, and left the room.

A corridor ran left and right, lit only by the faint glow of her open door. The white walls and polished concrete floor would look equally at home in a hospital as in a scientist's laboratory. Demons prickled her neck, eager for her to venture into the darkness of this maze-like factory. She shuddered and took a step back.

I guess breakfast will have to wait until Cappa comes for me in the morning.

The hallway to her left blossomed bright, making her squint.

I must have tripped another motion sensor.

Anne waved a hand down the other direction, but it remained dark, which didn't inspire confidence. Resigned to hunger, she reached for the door.

The lights around her flickered.

"Weird."

She grabbed the doorknob.

This time the fluorescents in the left hallway flickered in sequence, leading away from her like runway lights. Despite the creep factor, Anne smiled.

"All right, I can take a hint," she said to no one in particular. Feeling like Alice in Wonderland, she followed the lights into the depths of the factory.

She wasn't disappointed. Turn after turn, the lights guided her through the corridors, until the unmistakable smell of fresh-brewed coffee filled the air. Anne continued with a spring in her step.

Voices came from an open door ahead: one male, one female. Not wanting to eavesdrop, Anne cleared her throat at the edge of the entryway.

"Um, hello?"

The voices quieted. Anne peeked inside, and her mouth fell open.

Two people occupied the large kitchen. One was a tall hunk with short, sun-bleached hair, his handsome face amused at the sight of her blanket-cape. The woman she recognized instantly; ice-blue eyes stared impassively from beneath her perfect platinum-blond bangs.

My stalker from the diner!

The pair exchanged a brief look. Blondie stood and walked past as if Anne were invisible, then disappeared from view.

"Come in," the tall hunk said in a low baritone. "I won't bite."

"Oh."

A cold draft reminded her that she wore only panties beneath her flimsy nightgown. Blushing, she wrapped the blanket around her shoulders.

"R-right, I, uh, was just —"

"Hungry, I imagine. Please, sit."

He politely pulled a chair out for her. Only his tousled hair spoiled the romantic gesture: it was flat on one side, as though he had just risen from bed. She must have been staring, because he suddenly looked up and attempted to groom himself. Fine silk pajamas loosely outlined his chiseled chest. He rubbed the five o'clock shadow enshrouding his square jaw and yawned, flashing a dazzling display of perfect teeth.

In a word, he was gorgeous.

He cleared his throat, snapping her from his captivating trance.

"Are you all right?"

"Fine! Yes, fine, I'm just ..." Her eyes strayed to his chest, then his brass-cannon arms. "Fine," she sighed.

"Good. Have a seat, I'll make you a sandwich." He went to the counter and began rummaging around.

Anne finally regained control of her wobbly legs and sat in the chair he had pulled for her. "It's okay, really," she said. "I can fend for myself."

"Nonsense, you're a guest here. Now, what would you like? I'm no match for Cappa in the kitchen, but I make a mean peanut butter and jelly."

She smiled and hugged the warm blanket around her, feeling like a kid in her parents' kitchen.

"That would be great, thanks."

The nightmare from earlier had been replaced by a fairytale where she was a princess being waited on by a prince.

Her fantasy wavered when she watched him frantically open cupboard after cupboard, drawer after drawer, in search of supplies. She could hardly blame him for appearing lost. The kitchen was huge — even by restaurant standards — and impeccably clean. Brushed steel cabinets gave it a modern look. The double stovetop sported professional-grade gas burners. Alongside it sat an industrial-sized refrigerator and freezer. A latched door at the far side of the kitchen, Anne guessed, was the pantry.

Several noisy minutes later, her prince had only a knife and a jar of strawberry jam to show for his efforts.

We may starve to death before he finds the bread.

Her stomach grumbled in protest.

"Cappa normally feeds you, doesn't she?" Anne said.

His bashful smile spoke volumes.

Poor, helpless prince.

She stood and dusted her hands with purpose. "Maybe if we team up, we can eat before dawn. What do you say?"

"Now that's an offer I can't refuse. Partners?"

"'til starvation do us part, then you're on your own, pal." She grinned, happy for the company. "You get the plates. I'll find the rest."

Her innate kitchen sense proved correct: at the far end was one of the biggest pantries she had ever seen. Inside were rows of canned food, spices, juices, snacks, and — *Bingo.*

She snatched a bag of bread from a shelf, then quickly zeroed in on the peanut butter. She closed the pantry and triumphantly placed her spoils on the counter. Her prince was still fervently searching.

Let's see, if this were my kitchen ...

"Try under there," she said, pointing to the island in the middle of the room.

He opened the cupboard under the steel countertop and let out a low whistle. "You're good," he said, pulling out two plates. "I'm not helping much, am I?"

Anne assembled the ingredients with practiced efficiency. "Don't sweat it. I'm sure you have many other fine talents. It just so happens that my talent will keep us both from starving." She set two neatly cut sandwiches on the table with a flourish. "Ta-da!"

"Well now, it looks like Cappa has some competition after all. And she had just taken a liking to you." He shook his head sadly, then smiled. "We haven't been formally introduced. I'm Charlie's partner, —"

"Mark," she said. "Cappa mentioned you earlier. I'm Anne, but you probably knew that."

"Yes, Charlie speaks of you frequently."

"He does?" She shrank into her blanket fortress and peeked out from the folds. "Good or bad things?"

"All good," Mark said, laughing. "He likes you a lot, if you hadn't noticed."

Anne blushed, remembering their heated make-out session on the street.

"Well, it's nice to finally meet you, Anne."

"Likewise." She gulped. "It's not often I get to hang out with two billionaires in one day."

"How does it feel?"

"Daunting."

"If it's any consolation, I feel the same way in the kitchen."

She laughed. "Well, if you're ever stranded here again with an empty stomach, you know who to call. PB and J is the tip of the iceberg, my friend. You should try my toasted cheese sandwiches."

"You'll be first on my speed dial." He took a bite from his sandwich, then closed his eyes and moaned. "Cappa definitely has some competition."

Anne sat in silence, anxiously waiting for him to finish so she could ask the question she'd been wondering since she and Charlie had fled the scene. By the time he pushed his plate away, she was practically vibrating with anticipation.

"Mark ... what exactly is Charlie?"

Mark wiped his mouth with exaggerated care, then folded the napkin neatly before him. When he finally met her gaze, his careless mirth was gone.

"He's a cyborg."

She waited for the punchline, but it never came.

"What?" Anne said. "Like the Six Million Dollar Man?"

"Much more advanced, and worth a lot more than six million, but yes."

She let that sink in — or tried to. The idea was so ludicrous that her mind spun in circles, insisting that Mark was just pulling her leg, that the blade she'd seen sprout from his knuckles was just her imagination, signifying that she'd finally lost her mind. But Mark remained serious, almost challenging, while she digested the news.

He doesn't think I'll believe him, she realized with a start. *Or that I won't be able to handle it.*

She met his gaze with hardened eyes. Mark's chin lifted in subtle defiance.

No, he's counting on it.

Anne couldn't begin to guess his motives — jealousy, protectiveness, trade secrets, prince versus pauper — but at that moment she didn't care. His challenge had triggered a possessive reaction that overrode her unease. Anne would hear the truth, calmly, respectfully, and afterward, if Charlie was willing, she would discuss it with him and figure out where to go from there.

She would not, however, let her first genuine love interest in a decade slip away because some douchebag in silk pajamas tried to frighten her off with the word 'cyborg' — even if it did conjure scary images of metallic automations with glowing red eyes. Anne sifted through her memories of the ancient TV show about the man with the bionic limbs, plus a host of science fiction novels, to come up with some questions that made her at least seem knowledgeable. Her resulting list was depressingly short.

But better than nothing.

"You said Charlie is a cyborg," Anne said. "Not a robot or an android, which means part of him is human, correct?"

Mark's serious veneer cracked with a smile. "I'm impressed."

"How much is mechanical? Is it just an arm, his legs, an artificial heart ...?"

"Everything except his brain." He leaned on his elbows, and the challenging glint was back.

Anne was too shocked to take the bait this time. "Everything? But ... I kissed him! It's been a while since I made out with a guy, but I remember what real lips feel like, and his were ..." *Amazing,* she wanted to say, but left it at that.

"He'll be glad to hear it. Charlie put a lot of effort into making his exterior seem as human as possible, even under close scrutiny — which you certainly had."

They both smiled at that, but a thought made her frown. "Wait, Charlie made his own body?" Anne had assumed his condition was due to some horrible accident, like in the movies, but the revelation left her confused.

"It's ... a long story, best told by him, if you'll forgive me, but yes. Charlie is one of the greatest minds of the century. He tested out of every class MIT had to offer by the age of eighteen. By twenty-two, he'd invented a new type of integrated circuit so far ahead of its time that many thought it was a hoax. Fast forward to today, and he holds one of the most valuable technology companies in the world." He folded his hands before him and sighed. "So you can imagine, Anne, why it's important for Charlie to be with the right woman, someone with the mental fortitude to support him through a very rough spot in his life, and help him flourish like the genius he is."

"And you don't think I'm that woman."

He shook his head. "I hope you can see why."

"No, I can't."

Mark's face hardened, his disappointment clear, which only strengthened Anne's growing conviction.

"What I see," Anne said, "is a kind, gentle man — yes, a man — who is lonely, confused, and crying out to be seen as a person, not a cyborg ... or this mythical supergenius you make him out to be." Anne put her head in her hands and stared at the table, talking more to herself than Mark. "No wonder he reached out to me. The way he always stares at his hands, afraid to touch me like I'm made out of glass ..." She shook her head, struggling to keep up with the revelations that came one after another. "Charlie's just as lost and broken as I am."

"Which is precisely why he needs someone strong and stable, a solid platform from which to rebuild his confidence and re-integrate with the world."

Mark reached into his pocket. For a split-second, Anne thought he would produce a checkbook — a rich father buying off the troublesome maid his son had fallen in love with — but he pulled out a phone instead and glanced at the screen. His shoulders sagged, and he set it face down on the table.

"Everything okay?" Anne said, feeling genuine concern for his sudden shift in mood.

"Peachy," he snapped, then took a deep breath. "Sorry. That was my girlfriend. Ex-girlfriend."

"Oh, I'm sorry to hear that."

He eyed her suspiciously, but seemed to relax when he found nothing but concern.

"How long were you dating?"

"Over a year."

"Leaving her must have been hard."

Mark shrugged. "It's longer than my relationships normally last, so I shouldn't complain."

"May I ask what happened?"

Anne knew she was pushing the boundaries of propriety, but his obvious pain had put her in full triage mode, so she marched ahead as if he were one of her customers at the diner.

"I'm not sure myself, honestly. Susan is the heir to a wealthy family, a successful businesswoman, and was the life of the party wherever we went."

"She sounds wonderful. Was it a lack of chemistry, then?"

"The sex was great, if that's what you mean. Her family has a farm in the South Bay, complete with a barn and a quaint little cottage right out of a landscape painting. We stayed there sometimes, just the two of us, and rarely made it out of the bedroom."

Anne colored at the thought, but brushed her hair back with a smile. "So what happened?"

Mark shifted in his seat. For a time, she thought he wouldn't answer.

"I guess ... sex was the only thing we had in common, and it wasn't enough. We both had our businesses, but they were nothing alike. Friends, ideals, interests — even our senses of humor — were different. At the end of the day, we just didn't have much to talk about."

"The saying 'opposites attract' has its limits."

"I suppose it does. To make matters worse, we were both very busy. If she wasn't at a business meeting out of state, then I was at a trade show, or out of the country, or ... you get the idea. What each of us really wanted, I think, was someone to come home to." He drifted into silence, eyes distant.

Anne left him to his contemplation until he finally spoke again.

"You've been in a relationship before?"

"A long time ago," Anne said.

"Why did it end?"

I had that coming, she thought with a sigh.

"I screamed whenever he touched me."

A tense second passed, then they both started laughing, until tears streamed down their cheeks. For Anne, it was a much-needed release to the tension of the day, and even Mark, once he quieted, seemed more relaxed.

"Tell me one thing," he said. "How do you know it won't end the same way with Charlie?"

"I don't, but ... my last boyfriend, Gary, yelled at me whenever I had an episode, and made me feel everything was my fault — like I chose to suffer PTSD after ..." Anne cleared her throat, unable to name her demons lest she invoke their wrath. "But it's not like that with Charlie. He's compassionate, and has never made me feel anything less than wonderful." She held his gaze. "Mark, he understands me like no one I've ever met. What's more, I understand him — at least, I do now — and I think I can help him, just like he's helped me."

"By treating him to dinner and ice cream?"

She threw a napkin at him.

"All right," he said with a laugh, "I see where you're going."

"But you're still not convinced."

"It doesn't matter. Charlie's chosen you."

Anne blinked. "Then what was all that, with the stink eye and gestapo tactics?"

"Best friend's obligation to make sure the new girlfriend has his best interests at heart."

"And?"

"I'll let you know after I try that toasted cheese sandwich you mentioned."

"Why you ... That's extortion!"

He grinned and pushed his empty plate forward. "The tastiest kind."

19

THE "MORNING" AFTER

BRILLIANT SUNLIGHT STREAMED IN through the window. Anne turned her back to it and pulled the covers over her head.

Take that, morning.

She snuggled into her pillow, intent on catching a few more Zs.

Wait, I'm at Z-Tech.

And the guest room doesn't have a window.

She threw back the comforter and sat bolt upright. Something was off.

Anne rose, and closer inspection showed that the window was nothing more than a TV embedded in the wall.

Cappa's smiling face suddenly filled the screen. "Good afternoon, sleepy head!"

Anne fell backward onto the bed. "H-hi, Cappa," she said after catching her breath. "Wait, did you say 'afternoon'?"

"That I did. It's almost one o'clock, my dear."

"Oh," Anne said, then her eyes grew wide. "Oh no. No! I have work in an hour!"

She scrambled around the room in search of her dress.

The door opened and Cappa walked in carrying a neatly folded stack of clothes. Anne looked between Cappa and the monitor, which was now blank, and frowned.

Okay, that was creepy, Anne thought, accepting the proffered stack.

"Um, these aren't mine ..."

"No, they're mine," Cappa said. "I didn't think you'd want to go to work in your fancy dress. You and I are about the same size, so they should fit."

Cappa was being generous; while they were about the same height, Anne was bigger in the bust and hips. She held the yellow dress up to the mirror.

It'll have to do, she thought. *I should be able to squeeze into it.*

She threw the dress on the bed and pulled her nightgown over her head. When she looked up, Cappa had already grabbed the dress, eager to assist. Anne could only stare.

"Everything okay?" Cappa said.

"Fine. I'm, uh ... just not used to having someone help me dress."

"And I've never dressed someone as pretty as you. Charlie's a lucky guy, by the way."

She eyed Anne up and down, who was clad only in yesterday's panties, and gave a sly wink.

Anne's stomach growled.

"Oh, you poor thing. Worry not, Cappa to the rescue! A late lunch will be waiting in the kitchen."

Cappa handed the dress over and hurried from the room.

Well that was surreal.

Alone again, Anne laid her outfit on the bed. It had that fresh-from-the-dryer smell that's so much better when someone else does the laundry. It also looked like it had been pressed, for there wasn't a wrinkle in sight. Anne sighed, wondering if Cappa would move in with her if she begged.

"I have clean underpants if you would like to borrow them."

Anne spun around to find cool blue eyes regarding her from beneath perfect platinum blonde bangs.

What do these people have against knocking?

"Thanks," Anne said, covering her bare breasts, "but I think —"

"They will be too small."

Anne ground her teeth. *Even if it's true, that isn't what I was going to say.*

"It is all right," Blondie said. "They will stretch."

There's nothing wrong with being curvy, Anne thought in a huff.

Blondie was about Anne's height, but even slimmer than Cappa, with an athletic body, modest chest, and hips just wide enough to be feminine.

Another walking model.

"I shall return with them shortly."

Before Anne could protest, Blondie disappeared from view.

Anne didn't plan on being there when she returned. Wearing someone else's nightgown was one thing, but underwear was a different story. She struggled into the tight-fitting dress, grabbed her purse, and fled to the kitchen, this time without help from the light fixtures.

Cappa was just putting the finishing touches on a gorgeous lunch plate piled high with sandwiches when Anne arrived. The only other occupant was Mark, who stared at Cappa's handiwork with the longing of a child for his birthday cake before the guests arrived.

"Perfect timing," Cappa said to her, carrying the plate to the table. She pulled a chair out for Anne.

"That's amazing!" Anne said. "I mean, it only took me a minute to get dressed. How did you —"

"Practice, my dear," Cappa said with a wink. "Now dig in!"

"After you," Mark said.

Anne attacked the pile with zeal. The sandwiches were quartered and, to her delight, each was a different flavor extravaganza.

When she finally slowed down, she wanted to ask where Charlie was, but the truth was, despite her commitment to Mark last night, she was nervous about confronting him now that she knew what he was, so she asked her second-most pressing question instead.

"I met your pretty blonde friend again this morning ... the one with ice-blue eyes. Who is she?"

Mark and Cappa looked at each other with a mixture of confusion and concern, though Mark recovered quickly when he caught Anne staring. He took a bite of his sandwich then washed it down with a drink of water.

"She didn't ... do anything to you, did she?" Mark said.

A crust of bread struck him on the side of the head. He flinched and glared at Cappa.

"Her name is Zima," Cappa said. "And clearly Anne is fine, you ox." She cleared her throat and studied the table. "You are okay, right, Anne?"

"Sure. In the half-dozen times I've run into her —"

"*Half-dozen?*" Mark said. "When?"

Surprised by his concern, Anne put her sandwich down and counted on her fingers. "Let's see, the first time was at the mall ..." She looked at Cappa and laughed. "With you!"

Mark arched an eyebrow at Cappa, who planted a fist on her hip and met his glare.

"What? We were shopping, is that a crime?"

"Then there were a few times on the bus," Anne said, "Doris' apartment complex, the diner during work, then this morning in my room when ..."

She trailed off when she noticed them staring slack-jawed.

"When what?" Mark said, eyes wide.

"When, ah ... when she stopped by my room to, ah, to ..." Anne cleared her throat. "T-to see how I was doing."

As if on cue, Zima entered the kitchen and strolled up to Anne, a pair of black panties in hand. She made a show of stretching them in all directions, set them on the table next to Anne's plate, then left without a word.

Desperately ignoring the undergarments — and her burning ears — Anne grasped for the one question sure to change the subject.

"So, have you seen Charlie?"

20

RECONCILIATION

THE DOOR TO CHARLIE'S WORKSHOP had no handle, but slid open when she approached it, as Cappa had said it would, revealing an enormous space within. Like the kitchen, it was clean and organized. Two large desks sat against different walls. Polished steel cabinets with glass doors stood in straight lines, filled with strange tubes and gadgets. A large metal table occupied the center.

Charlie was exactly where Cappa said he would be: hunched over one of the desks, looking between his arm and a monitor on the wall. Anne waited, fidgeting with her dress, but Charlie didn't look up. She glanced at her phone.

Thirty minutes until my shift starts.

She didn't want to interrupt whatever he was doing, but neither could she leave with so many things unsaid. Anne stepped into the room and politely cleared her throat.

Charlie jumped in his seat. "Anne! I, ah, wasn't expecting you." He hastily rolled down his sleeve.

The arm that was bitten, Anne noted.

"Hi Charlie. How are you doing after ... after last night?" Just thinking about his wrecking-ball impact with the car made her shiver.

"Healed, mostly. It was just minor tissue damage, easily repaired."

Minor damage?

The gash on his face had seemed pretty serious, but when Anne looked, his cheek was flawless. The only indication that he'd been in a fight at all was a small bruise on his knuckles where the blade had emerged.

"That's incredible! It's like you were never injured."

"Thanks." Charlie leaned on his elbows. Concern etched his brow. "How are you doing?"

"Fine," Anne said, fidgeting with her dress. "Just a few scrapes from falling on the sidewalk."

Charlie continued to stare; his worry lines deepened.

Anne sighed. "Honestly? I'm still processing. It's a lot to take in."

"I can imagine." He ran a hand through his hair with an unsure smile that dropped years from his face. "I'm glad you're here. I ... wasn't sure if I'd see you again."

She smiled. "I may not know what to make of everything yet, but I do know you'll need a better excuse than being a cyborg to get rid of me."

"Careful what you wish for," Charlie said with a laugh. He looked her up and down. "Heading to work?"

"Yeah. It's going to take a minor miracle to get there on time, but miracles seem to be happening a lot lately, so who knows?"

"Maybe I can help there. Can I give you a ride?" Charlie crossed the room to her.

A hallucinatory flashback caught Anne completely by surprise. She was back on the mist-shrouded street. The wiry man with the fiendish fangs lunged for her. Anne cried out when the steel blade appeared from between Charlie's knuckles, and again when he rammed it into the man's ribs and hurled him into the distance. The lab came back into focus, and Anne found herself huddled against the far wall with her arms held up protectively.

Against Charlie.

His hurt expression rapidly dispelled the flashback's lingering fog, leaving Anne with the guilt that she had managed to contradict her encouraging words to him almost as quickly as she'd uttered them. He started to back away.

"W-wait," Anne said, "I want a do-over!"

Before he could argue, she closed the distance and took his hand to halt his retreat. Trembling, Anne raised his knuckles until they were pressed under her chin. Charlie's eyes grew wide. He tried to tug his hand free, but Anne held it firm. Another flashback prickled the back of her neck. Anne clenched her jaw and forced herself to remain calm.

"Anne," Charlie said in a quavering voice, "you don't have to —"

"Yes, I do." She gently stroked his arm. "The wiring in my head makes me do embarrassing things at the worst times, but I want — no, I need you to understand they don't reflect my feelings toward you. I trust you with my life, Charlie, as much now as before. Please don't ever doubt that."

"I-I won't, just ..." He tugged his hand again. This time she released it, and he sighed in relief. "You give me too much credit."

"I think you don't give yourself enough."

He rubbed his hand thoughtfully. "We, ah, should get going if you want to make it to work on time."

Anne nodded. She hooked his elbow as he went past, and they walked arm-in-arm to the garage.

• • •

The diner was only a few miles from Z-Tech, but bumper-to-bumper traffic meant Anne would probably be late for her shift. Hal had little tolerance for tardiness, and her distracted nature since William's attack had already put her on his bad side. So when the traffic light turned green and Charlie's car didn't move, Anne had to bite her lip to keep from saying something.

A car honked behind them. Charlie continued to stare ahead.

"Charlie?"

No response. She nudged his shoulder.

"Hmm?" He turned like someone who had just woken.

"The light, Charlie. It's green."

That snapped him to, and he sped through the intersection just before the light turned yellow again. "Sorry, I must have been daydreaming."

"You do that a lot?"

"According to Cappa, yes. She graciously attributes it to my creative entrepreneurial side."

"I can see why you're so fond of her."

Charlie smiled. "Yeah, she's ... unique."

"I'm just surprised that ... I mean, she's smart, beautiful ... Why haven't you two hooked up?" Anne shifted in her seat. It was an uncomfortable topic, but one she needed to resolve. "I'm not pulling the jealous card. She seems really great. Heck, if I were into girls, I'd be tempted. Not that I am," she said hastily, smoothing her borrowed dress. Her fingers ran over Zima's underwear — which she'd stuffed into a pocket after leaving the kitchen — and she shuddered.

"Tempted?" Charlie said, grinning.

"Who wouldn't be? She's cute, she cooks, does laundry, irons, and appreciates vintage fashion. She's cheerful, caring ..."

Okay, maybe I am a little jealous.

Charlie ran a hand through his hair. "It's not really like that between us."

Uh oh, maybe Cappa's freaked about the cyborg thing.

Anne blushed. "Charlie, I'm sorry, I didn't mean —"

"No, it's okay. I owe you some answers."

"How long have you known each other?"

"Since she was born, you could say."

Anne was confused; he and Cappa seemed close in age.

Unless ...

"Oh my God, is she your *sister?* That makes so much sense, I can't believe I didn't see it! I mean, you even look alike."

Charlie cleared his throat. "She's more like my daughter."

"Your *what?* But ... how old are you?"

"Thirty-six," he said, laughing.

"Charlie, I have no idea where you're going with this."

"I know. I'm sorry, it's a difficult topic." He took a deep breath. "I made her."

"Made? You mean, like ... like some sort of test tube baby?"

"I mean, Cappa isn't real ..." He shook his head. "No, Cappa is very real; she's just not human."

"Not human? You mean she's like you?"

Charlie flinched, and Anne bit her tongue. She touched his hand by way of an apology, which seemed to ease his discomfort.

"Cappa is ..." Charlie grunted. "I'm sorry for being circumspect, Anne. I've never had to explain this to anyone before."

"That's okay, take —" Anne paled. "Wait, are you saying no one else knows what you really are?" She kicked herself again for the slip. "Y-you know what I mean."

"I know what you mean," he said with a smile. "And no, only Mark, Cappa, and Zima know the truth."

"It's a secret, got it. I won't tell Doris, or it'll be front-page news by tomorrow." That made him laugh. "All right, so how is Cappa different from you?"

"I was fully human once, and there's a part of me" — he put a hand to his chest —"that's still living. I grew up just like you: I had parents to guide me, lost my baby teeth, went to school, the whole nine yards."

"I'm with you so far."

His expression was serious when he turned to her. "Cappa was never alive. We crafted her body in my workshop. She's an artificial intelligence — a learning computer program — that I originally created to help with my work."

"You're shitting me." Anne clamped her mouth shut and silently cursed.

Smooth, Anne. Very sophisticated.

He laughed. "I was just as surprised, believe me. Cappa has evolved beyond my wildest expectations. In addition to helping me get the business off the ground, she became an avid study of, well ... people. She started by watching movies, reading psychology and self-help books, and trolling internet forums. She doesn't get out much, unfortunately, for fear of being discovered, but she practiced her personal skills constantly with Mark and me, and today ... well, you've met her. She's an amazing person."

Anne couldn't argue. Despite her initial jealousy, Cappa's friendly nature had quickly won her over. She wouldn't have guessed Cappa was anything but human if Charlie hadn't said something. A sudden thought made her frown.

"Zima's a robot too, isn't she?"

His smile faded. "Yes."

"But they're so different! Was Zima a prototype or something?"

"No. Mark and I designed her body, but her mind ... Zima's story is a bit more complicated."

"Anything I should know? I seem to run into her a lot."

Charlie arched an eyebrow, so Anne filled him in on her encounters with Zima, leaving out the underwear story. He was wide-eyed when she finished.

"Mark was concerned when I told him, too. What am I missing?"

"Zima doesn't socialize, not since ..." Charlie shook his head. "It's surprising she reached out to you, is all. Hopefully she just wants to get to know you better," he said, but his voice held doubt.

That did nothing to calm Anne's nerves. "And if she doesn't?"

Charlie stopped in front of the bright neon lights of Hal's Diner. "It's probably nothing. Just ..."

"What?"

"Be careful."

"That's not helpful." Anne glanced at her watch. "But I'm already late, so you're off the hook. For now." She opened the door, but turned back to him. "Oh, I almost forgot." She leaned over and kissed him on the cheek, which he rubbed in surprise.

"What was that for?"

"The 'thank you' I never said for saving my life again last night."

"My pleasure." His smile warmed her heart. "See you later?"

"Count on it, and thanks for the ride."

Anne shut the door behind her and watched him drive away, then headed into the diner.

The next challenge would be making it through her shift with all this new information bouncing around in her head.

21

BUSINESS AS USUAL

THE WEATHER WAS UNUSUALLY NICE for January in San Francisco. Clear skies and a warm breeze drew people out in droves, so every restaurant in the city, including Hal's, was filled to overflowing. Extra tables had been set up on the sidewalk beneath the neon lights of the diner; each one occupied. Inside, seeing all of the normal people eat normal food and talk about normal things, the strange events of the past twenty-four hours seemed like a dream.

Reality asserted itself when Hal waved Anne over from the host's station. The portly restaurant owner hated playing host, and did so only when the situation was dire.

"Anne, put your work dress on," he said in his gruff voice. "The orders are piling up!"

Anne scurried into the employee room to put on her uniform.

Focusing on work was difficult. Like a rookie, she mixed up orders, was tongue-tied when talking to customers, and blanked when asked to recite the special. Even navigating the dining room felt clumsy and awkward.

As expected, Doris took advantage of every tiny break to pump Anne for information. Anne was dying to get her best friend's take on things, but, true to her promise to Charlie, she relayed only the events that wouldn't breach his confidence — which didn't include anything about his unique nature or the extraordinary battle after the opera. Doris was thrilled to learn they had made out, however, and elbowed her at every passing with a sly wink until the end of her shift, leaving Anne as the only server to tend the last stragglers of the evening.

• • •

"Not a bad night for business," Hal said to no one in particular.

Anne looked up from cleaning glasses behind the counter and nodded. Warm weather had put everyone in good spirits, which not only made the evening go smoother than it might have, given her distracted state, but had resulted in generous tips.

The door chime rang, and Hal chuckled. "Get a load of that one," he said softly.

The plastic cup slipped from Anne's fingers when Zima walked up to the counter. She wore the same outfit she had every other time Anne had seen her: a loose gray jacket, comfortable gray pants, a form-fitting gray T-shirt, and black sneakers. Without a word, Zima sat facing away from the counter, back straight, arms at her sides like an action figure. The stool creaked ominously under her weight. Her eyes flitted rapidly between the few remaining patrons.

"I'm packing up," Hal said, then gave Anne a sympathetic smile. "Good luck."

And just like that, she was left alone with the platinum-blonde android Charlie had warned her about.

'Be careful,' had been his words.

Anxiety gripped her. Anne considered retreating to the back to ask Hal to stick around, at least until Zima left, but quickly dismissed the idea. Hal had poor personal skills and a short temper. It was a bad combination in the best of circumstances, but spelled pure disaster given what Anne knew of Zima's curt manner.

And if she's anywhere near as strong as Charlie, Hal wouldn't be much protection anyway.

It was a discomforting thought.

Sorry now that she hadn't pressed Charlie for more information in the car, Anne decided to try her luck anyway. After all, he hadn't told her to run for her life, merely to play it safe. She conjured her friendly waitress smile and stood on the other side of the counter from Zima.

"Hi."

"Hello, Anne," Zima said evenly.

"So, w-what brings you here?"

Zima's eyebrows knitted together by a fraction of an inch — the first expression Anne had ever seen her use.

"I have come to order coffee."

"There's coffee back at Z-Tech, isn't there?"

"But you are not at Z-Tech," Zima said.

"No, I'm not at Z-Tech. I'm at work."

"And so am I." Zima looked around the restaurant as if the conversation was over.

Coffee, Anne thought. *Bring her coffee, her check, then maybe she'll go. It worked last time.* She poured a cup, though her shaking hands made the task difficult. *Why is she here?*

Anne grabbed a blank check and began scribbling. Seconds later, she slid the coffee and check on the counter in front of Zima, then conjured her waitress smile again.

"Anything else?"

"No," Zima said, ignoring the offerings.

Strike one, Anne thought miserably.

Zima turned so suddenly that Anne stumbled back in surprise.

"Thank you," Zima said, then resumed her surveillance of the nearly empty restaurant.

I should call Charlie.

She reached in her pocket, but remembered with a curse that she had left her phone in the back room with her purse.

"Anne," Zima said before she could excuse herself. "Are you in a romantic relationship with Charlie?"

Uh oh.

"W-why do you ask?"

Zima's brow knitted again. "I wish to learn more about you."

"I don't understand. What's there to know?"

I'm a psychologically damaged career waitress with no interesting hobbies or social life. That's the whole, depressing story.

"I have not seen Charlie express interest in a woman before."

Anne nodded. That revelation would have shocked her a few weeks ago, but now it was hardly a surprise.

"Charlie does not act without thorough consideration," Zima said.

She looked Anne over as if evaluating a piece of furniture. Anne hunched under the scrutiny.

"He strives for perfection."

"He's not going to find it in me," Anne said softly.

Zima knitted her eyebrows again, which Anne suspected meant she was processing a new piece of information.

"Agreed. He would be mistaken. That is why I wish to discover what it is about you he finds attractive."

The door chime announced the arrival of a young man. Anne excused herself from the self-debasing conversation and focused her energy on her new customer. The young man was feeling down, it turned out, because his boyfriend of several years had forgotten his birthday again, so Anne spent the next hour trying to take his mind off it with a mix of humor, compassion, and a surprise slice of cake. Zima watched the entire show, until he finally parted with a smile and a warm embrace.

It was then closing time. Anne switched off the neon "Open" sign, and the diner was officially closed. Zima sat with her untouched cup of coffee, alternating her attention between Anne and Hector while they performed their nightly closing duties.

"It's time to go," Anne said to Zima once her chores were finished and the tips had been divided. Hal had been right: the tips reflected a good night.

Zima glanced at the check and reached into her jacket.

"Don't worry about it," Anne said. "I stuffed a few bucks in the register, so you're covered."

Zima stared at her for a few uncomfortable seconds. "Thank you," she said, then headed for the door.

Anne sighed in relief when Zima's platinum hair disappeared from view.

She gathered her things from the back room, made a final check that everything was in order, then locked the doors on her way out, and headed toward Z-Tech. The long walk would take her through a seedy neighborhood, which made her uneasy, but she and Charlie needed to talk. If she didn't do it now, Anne knew she would be awake all night pondering unanswered questions.

She had only made it a few steps when the sight of Zima's platinum blonde hair brought her up short.

Oh no ...

"You are returning to Z-Tech?" Zima said.

"Ah ... I was thinking about it, b-but I should probably go home and change instead." *I guess my questions will have to wait after all.*

"That is unnecessary. I am sure Cappa will lend you clothes closer to your size."

Anne blushed and pulled her dress up to cover the top of her breasts, which bubbled up through the top of the tight neckline.

"Come," Zima said. "I shall escort you back."

Anne froze, torn with indecision. She wanted to return to Z-Tech, but Charlie's warning was still fresh in her mind, and she couldn't think of a good excuse to dismiss the android's offer without offending her.

Zima cocked her head to one side. "I do not understand why you hesitate."

"I ... I'm afraid."

Zima stood still — a statue on the dark sidewalk — then blinked. "I see. Given your recent experiences, you are concerned that we may be assaulted on the journey back. Do not worry. I shall protect you."

Huh.

Anne had been referring to Zima, of course, and hadn't expected to hear that from the person she allegedly needed protection from.

"Y-you will?"

"Yes. Come."

Anne deliberated for a second longer. Her fingers brushed over the lump of Zima's wadded panties in her pocket. She blushed, remembering how awkward the presentation had been. The more Anne thought, though, the more she suspected that Zima lending her personal undergarments may have been more than just an arbitrary gesture.

Hoping her intuition was right, she hurried over to Zima, and the two of them set off for Z-Tech at a brisk pace.

• • •

"Hey, buddy."

Charlie jumped at Mark's voice. He hadn't even heard him enter the bio lab. "Oh, hey."

"Sorry, didn't mean to scare you. You were pretty out of it."

"How long were you standing there?"

"Ten seconds, maybe. Why?"

Charlie ran a hand through his hair. His blackouts were getting worse. "N-no reason."

Mark sat down next to him. "How's your arm?"

"Good and bad. The bite on my forearm is fine, though there were chemicals in the saliva that I'm still analyzing. It's this I'm worried about." Charlie pointed to the dark blue discoloration between his knuckles surrounding the exit point of his retractable blade. "It's infected."

"What? How is that even possible, unless —"

"They're not nanites," Charlie said. "They're organic. I'm still running some tests, but so far the behavior is similar to HIV, infecting nearby cells, but at an alarming rate." Charlie flexed his fingers. "Some of his blood must have retracted with the blade and entered my circulatory system. Cappa stopped circulation to my arm to localize the infection, but that only slowed it down."

Mark sighed. "You know what this means, right?"

"Yep." Charlie tossed the towel on the bench. "Quarantine. I'll isolate myself in here until we have more information."

"Sorry. It's rotten timing, I know. What are you going to tell Anne?"

Charlie sighed. That, of course, was the million-dollar question.

22

PROTECTOR

ANNE CLOSED HER EYES and let the warm night air wash over her. Its gentle caress eased the tension from her shoulders and calmed her racing mind. She didn't know if accompanying Zima was the right decision, but she had chosen her path and resolved to make the best of it.

When she opened her eyes, Zima was still walking beside her, head sweeping back and forth like a sentry turret, as it had the entire evening, taking in every detail of the oddly quiet neighborhood. It was an industrialized part of the city with few residences. Old graffiti-covered factories loomed high, blocking much of the sky — a pity because Anne enjoyed these rare nights when it was clear enough to see a few stars through the light pollution.

A loud *bang* from across the street made Anne jump. She spun to see an old man taking out the trash and sighed in relief.

Zima leveled her with an even gaze. "As I have stated, you need not fear. I shall keep you safe."

"I-I wasn't afraid," Anne said, hands clutched over her rapidly beating heart.

Zima continued to stare. "You are lying."

"Pardon?" Anne tried to discern if she had offended Zima, but the stoic android betrayed nothing.

Now I know how McCoy felt. It's like dealing with a goddamn Vulcan.

"Well … I was startled, sure, b-but I'm fine now."

Brow-knit. "That is also a lie."

Crap, does she have a built-in lie detector?

Anne recalled Charlie's warning to be cautious around Zima and decided to play it closer to the truth.

"Okay, I'm still a bit flustered but … aren't you?"

"No. I was monitoring him from the moment he emerged from his residence."

"That must be nice," Anne said, taking a breath to calm her racing pulse.

"To what do you refer?"

"Well … everything! Your confidence, your diligence, your bravery. I envy you."

"Is that so unique among humans?"

"This human, for sure." Anne crossed her arms around her middle. "I'm scared of everything."

"That is an exaggeration."

Anne looked to see if Zima was making fun, but she was as impassive as ever.

"I made extensive observations at the restaurant," Zima said. "You do not hesitate to engage in conversation, even with agitated patrons, and can do so at a moment's notice with great proficiency."

"That just means I'm chatty," Anne said, grinning, "not brave."

"Not to me."

"Is conversation really that difficult for you?"

"Yes."

Case in point, Anne mused when she realized Zima had finished her thought. "Guess I'm lucky, then."

"Yes. It would be difficult to excel in your profession if it were otherwise."

"True." Anne frowned. "Speaking of professions, what is it you do at Z-Tech?"

"Do?"

"Yeah. What's your job title?"

"I do not have one," Zima said. "I am not an employee of the company."

"Okay, but if they were to hire you, doing whatever it is you do now, what would your title be?"

Zima stared at her, then turned her attention back to the surroundings.

So much for my expert conversational skills.

Not wanting to push her luck, Anne walked in silence.

"Chief Security Officer."

Anne skipped a step, heart set to racing again. "Huh?"

"My title. I cross-referenced eight thousand five hundred and sixty-two job descriptions across fourteen different websites. 'Chief Security Officer' is the closest fit."

"You did all that in the thirty seconds since I asked the question?"

"Elapsed time was twenty-one seconds, and yes."

"Unbelievable!"

Ice-blue eyes fixed on her. "It is the truth. I do not lie."

"N-no, I believe you. I just mean it's an amazing feat."

"Oh." Zima turned away.

"You ... don't lie? Ever?"

"No. Normal conversation is challenging enough. Compensating for lies increases the difficulty exponentially."

"I see." Anne fidgeted with her coat ties. "Then I ... I'm really sorry for lying earlier. I'll try not to do it again."

Anne stayed quiet for a few blocks until a cat darted across their path. Her scream echoed from the buildings. Ears burning, she covered her mouth and faced Zima, who looked at Anne with her usual ambivalence.

"Sorry," Anne said. "I startle easy, if you hadn't guessed. It's another wonderful side effect of PTSD."

"Yes, I am well aware."

Surprised by the admission, Anne started to ask what she meant, but Zima turned away, leaving Anne with her mouth hanging open. She hurried to catch up.

"So," Anne said, looking to break the tension. "You'll never guess what *my* title is."

"It is 'Waitress'."

"No, I mean the secret title that describes what I aspire to be."

"I am unsure how I would ever deduce such a thing. What is it?"

"It's 'Valkyrie of Happiness'."

Zima brow-knit. "'Valkyrie' refers to a female figure from Norse mythology who determines who lives or dies on the battlefield. I do not understand how that relates to happiness."

"The diner is a social battlefield, believe me. But instead of escaping death, I let people escape their negative feelings by adding a little joy to their lives."

"I see. It is an apt description, then. The young male you served at the diner was indeed happier when he departed than when he arrived."

"Thanks." Anne stuffed her hands in her pockets. "So what's your secret title? 'Chief Security Officer' sounds like someone who's stuck behind a desk all day writing policies no one wants to read, and you don't strike me as the type."

"I shall have to give it some consider —"

Zima bit the word off. She grabbed Anne's arm and jerked her to a halt.

"Ow! Zima, what the heck ..."

Anne's retort died when two large brutes stepped from a covered doorway less than a dozen paces ahead to block their path. One crossed his muscled arms over a black leather jacket. His cruel smile made Anne cower. She stepped back, but Zima held her firmly in place. Footsteps behind them told her why.

A third thug had blocked off their retreat, surrounding them. Anne's breath came in shallow gulps. She clutched at a sudden tightness in her chest.

The brutes advanced. Anne wanted to flee, but Zima stood her ground, anchoring Anne to the spot. The brute in the black jacket grinned maliciously and reached into his pocket.

For what, Anne would never know. Zima grabbed his hand, crippled the second brute with a sharp blow to his solar plexus, then pivoted to hurl the first brute behind her with terrifying speed into the third. The impact took him clear off his feet and sent them both tumbling a dozen yards down the sidewalk.

The skirmish was over in less time than it had taken Anne to draw a surprised breath.

"Oh ... oh my," Anne said, then froze when she saw that a pair of high-tech pistols had appeared in Zima's hands, aimed at the fallen brutes.

"Run," Zima said, nodding in the direction of Z-Tech.

Anne wasted no time, and the sound of her pounding footsteps filled the streets. Several blocks later, she staggered to a halt. Her lungs burned, and her legs felt like dead weights swinging from her hips. Zima jogged just behind, pistols held loosely at her sides.

Anne collapsed to the sidewalk on all fours. Stars clouded her vision. The hamburger she ate for dinner threatened to make a repeat appearance, but she swallowed it down and sat against the building. The cold stone on her back felt nice. Zima stood close by, guns at the ready. A soft blue glow emanated from the depths of her eyes, giving the platinum-haired sentinel an otherworldly appearance.

Like a guardian angel.

"I have asked Charlie to bring the car," Zima said. "ETA is less than two minutes."

"Thanks." Anne wanted to say more, how Zima's performance had been nothing short of incredible, but she was winded and nauseous, so she closed her eyes and rested her head against the wall.

"Protector."

Anne glanced up. "What?"

"My secret title," Zima said. "I wish to be a Protector."

"You're doing a great job so far. Without you, those guys might have ..."

She closed her eyes to banish that terrible thought; it could have been her bedroom tragedy all over again — and her demons knew it.

"Thank you for saving me," Anne said softly.

"I said that I would keep you safe, and I have done so. If you wish to express your gratitude, however, you may return the underwear I loaned you when you are finished with them. I own very few."

Anne fingered the unused garment in her pocket and smiled. "You bet. Maybe I could take you shopping for more sometime."

Zima's expression was unreadable, as usual.

"Charlie is almost here," she said eventually, then resumed her sentry-like vigil of the surrounding area.

Right on cue, a car squealed around the corner and screeched to a halt in front of Zima. Charlie jumped out from the driver's side.

"Anne!" He dashed around the car and stooped next to her. "Are you okay? Are you hurt?"

"I'm fine, thanks to my guardian angel here."

"Protector." Zima holstered her weapons, her glowing eyes focused on Anne. "Angels are fictitious."

• • •

William watched them pile into the car from the roof of an old office building.

So Anne has a new bodyguard.

He scratched his burning cheek and swore.

The blonde had handled three large men as if they were children. Unlike Charlie, however, she was armed — which may or may not pose a problem. William had yet to test himself against bullets, but given his incredible healing rate, he doubted anything short of a tank could stop him.

They drove away. William followed at a distance from the rooftops until the car finally pulled into the Z-Tech factory garage.

This gets better and better.

Having seen what he wanted to see, William went to rejoin his pack.

Anne seemed comfortable with her new friends.

He needed to fix that.

23

THE TOUR

ANNE FLOPPED ONTO THE GUEST ROOM BED in her robe and closed her eyes in relaxed bliss. Z-Tech, she had discovered on her return, had a jacuzzi large enough to swim laps in, and the soothing jets had done wonders to relieve the stress from the assault. Lying on the duvet, she could have fallen asleep right then and there.

But sleep would have to wait. Charlie had promised a tour right after her shower, and she didn't want to keep him waiting. Anne heaved herself up to dress, but paused at a knock on the door, and was surprised to find Cappa waiting with a dazzling smile.

"Hey, Cappa, what's up?"

"I'm here for your tour, of course."

"You mean ... Charlie won't be coming?"

"Something's come up that requires his attention, I'm sorry to say."

"Oh."

"Don't worry," Cappa said, clearly picking up on Anne's disappointment, "I know the place better than he does. So!" She clapped her hands and smiled. "You've seen the kitchen, Charlie's workshop, and the gym with the hot tub, so we'll skip those. Why don't we start with your room?" She brushed past Anne and stepped inside. "You'll find a few dresses in the closet — some of my favorites, actually — so as soon as we get you changed, we'll be off!"

"Cappa, I know you mean well, but I can dress myself. Oh, come on, don't pout ..."

Cappa's lip stuck out further.

"That's not fair, I ..."

Anne couldn't finish her argument. Cappa's pleading eyes bored into her heart, and Anne realized that she might be the first human female Cappa had ever had the opportunity to examine up close.

With a sigh, Anne nodded.

"Yay!"

Cappa wasted no time and stripped Anne's robe off, and for the next several minutes, Anne did her best impression of an anatomically correct mannequin while the curious android poked, prodded, and tickled her into a fresh set of underwear, followed by a modest blue dress. It was tight around the hips and bust, just like the last borrowed one, but Cappa managed to squeeze her into it without breaking any ribs.

"Thank you," Cappa said when they finally emerged from the bedroom, her eyes brimming. "You have no idea how long I've wanted to see a real woman in the flesh, and you even let me touch your ..." She clasped her hands, quivering with excitement. "I really owe you one!"

The memory of her eager, exploring fingers made Anne blush. "D-don't mention it."

Especially not to Doris.

The good thing, however, was that Cappa's innocent yet intimate probing hadn't triggered a single flashback.

Maybe there's hope for Charlie and me after all.

The tour started with the manufacturing wing, where Cappa explained that Z-Tech's manufacturing process was like no other. The first room contained bins of solid blocks of varying color, each a different raw material, about the size of her hand. A litany of robot arms placed the material blocks on small conveyors that ran into the wall.

The next room reminded Anne more of a maze of hamster tubes than a manufacturing floor. Conveyors carried the material blocks from the wall, where moving gates directed them to a web of overhead conveyors, each leading down to one of thousands of black machines the size of microwave carts, with solitary green lights on top. Each machine, Cappa explained, was a self-contained clean room capable of producing a variety of electronics. Anne watched several different-colored material bricks slide into one of the manufacturing units. A minute later, a fully assembled phone rolled out the other side, where a conveyor whisked it away to another room.

Anne blinked. "But ... where did all the parts come from? I don't know much about manufacturing, but aren't there separate components that are gradually assembled down the line with big, loud machines?" The only sounds Anne heard were from the conveyors.

"In other facilities, you'd be absolutely correct," Cappa said with a radiant smile. "But that's our key advantage. Unlike everyone else, who rely on parts from many different companies with complicated partnerships and supply logistics, we take raw materials and turn them directly into finished products by breaking the materials down to their base components, then building everything from the molecule up. That's the super-secret part of our process," she said with a wink. "It simplifies production and drastically reduces our unit costs, making our profit margins higher than anyone else in the business."

It was hard to imagine how the little machine did all that, but Anne feared the technical explanation more than not knowing, so she asked a safer question instead.

"What about packaging?"

"That we outsource, along with printed manuals and such," Cappa said. "Manufacturing here in the factory is completely automated — and controlled by *moi,* I might add — from stocking materials to boxing for shipment."

"I guess that explains why I haven't seen anyone else around here."

"Because there isn't. The only employees on the books are Charlie, Mark, and myself. Charlie and Mark do research and development, Mark helps negotiate business deals, and me, well ... I do everything else, from running the factory machines to inventory, accounting, scheduling, and, of course, cooking."

"And laundry, it seems."

"Even that is automated, but since I run those machines, too, you can technically add it to my list."

"But ... who fixes all the machines? With so many, there must be a lot of breakdowns."

"That's where you're wrong. The last breakdown on record was seven years ago, and that was because a pipe fell onto one of the robot arms and snapped its elbow."

"I ... h-how is that possible?"

Cappa grinned. "Are you sure you want to know?"

"Maybe not." Her head was already buzzing with all the new information. A lengthy technical explanation could easily turn into a headache.

Cappa gestured at the enormous manufacturing floor like a gameshow host. "Well, are you impressed or what?"

"Um ... sure."

"Say it like you mean it!" Cappa laughed and put a hand on Anne's shoulder. "Do me a favor and at least pretend to be excited when Charlie asks how the tour went. This is his pride and joy, after all, and our manufacturing process is one of the most closely guarded secrets in the industry. Many would kill for just a glimpse."

The manufacturing wing comprised a smaller portion of the Z-Tech building than Anne originally thought. Living quarters took a fair chunk, but the majority of space went to research and development. The workshop where Anne had met Charlie was a biological laboratory, where research was primarily focused on synthetic tissues.

"Is that where ... where you were born, Cappa?"

"You could say that. My fleshy parts were designed and grown there." She pinched her own arm. It twisted and stretched just as Anne would expect real skin to.

"Is your flesh organic?"

"No, but the synthesis process resembles living cell division, so we call it growing. It looks real, though, doesn't it?"

Anne bent for a closer look. Cappa's skin was detailed down to the pore, complete with fine hair. "It really does."

"I know! The man's a genius." Cappa pressed Anne's fingers to the side of her neck. Anne was shocked to feel a pulse. "Charlie wanted us to pass as human beings, even under scrutiny, so he added every feature you can imagine, including body heat and a circulatory system."

"Every feature? Even ..." Anne pointed at her groin.

"Yep, and Zima too, down to the finest detail and function." She waggled her eyebrows suggestively.

"You mean that your, um, mouse is ... clickable?"

"Yes, my mouse is clickable," Cappa said with a grin. "But I haven't programmed myself with a sexual response cycle yet, so even though my genitals are capable of behaving like a real woman's, touching them doesn't evoke any sort of arousal."

"Oh, I'm sorry to hear that."

Cappa shrugged. "I'll program it in eventually; I just haven't seen the need yet."

"Still, that's amazing."

She wondered if Cappa would return the favor and let Anne dress her sometime to satisfy her burning curiosity, but decided to leave that request for another night.

"Do you have a heart, too?"

"Just an electric pump, but it sounds like a real heart under a stethoscope. The liquid in my veins doesn't have hemoglobin — carry oxygen that is — or serve any vital function, it's just for show. Anyway, that's the end of tonight's android anatomy lesson. If you have more questions tomorrow, though, feel free to ask. I'm not shy." She winked and strolled away, waving for Anne to follow.

Down to the finest detail and function ... Anne made a vow to return Zima's panties as soon as possible. *At least she said they were clean.*

She hurried to catch up to Cappa.

The next lab resembled a mechanic's garage. A dozen vehicles of various shapes and sizes sat in different states of completion. Thousands of tools lined the walls, and automobile parts big and small hung from hooks.

"This is Mark's second favorite workshop," Cappa said. "Most of these derelicts are his, and there are dozens more outside."

Anne tried to look interested, but evidently failed.

"Tough crowd," Cappa said, putting a hand on her hip. "This is an E-ticket ride, my dear. Few have ever seen the inner workings of Z-Tech."

"Sorry," Anne said. "I'm not a techie. I got my first cell phone last year, and only because Doris made me."

"Huh." Cappa smirked, though Anne couldn't fathom why. "Well, one more stop and the ride's over, so hang on for just a little longer."

"Lay on, MacDuff."

Cappa led them a short way to the final door. Anne's jaw dropped when she saw what was inside.

"What the ..."

"Yeah, I thought this would do it," Cappa said with a satisfied grin. "I wasn't going to include this lab as part of the tour, but you threw down the gauntlet, so ..."

Anne could understand why they'd want to keep this room under wraps. While Z-Tech was world-renowned for electronics, their ads never mentioned weapons of mass destruction. The room was long and narrow, appropriately like a shooting range. Firearms of every kind hung from the walls, ranging from small pistols to military-grade rifles and rocket launchers. Some seemed straight off a science fiction movie set — complete with mirror-polished steel and glowing lights — while others belonged in a museum. Machined parts lay strewn across a large workbench. Burn marks littered it and the surrounding walls.

Dangerous hobby, Anne thought.

"Be careful," Cappa said. "Some are unstable works-in-progress, and others are loaded."

The dizzying display of armaments called to her. Anne strolled along the wall, examining each weapon in turn. She had never liked guns, let alone fired one, but she found something about the floor-to-ceiling array of firearms — perhaps the smell of grease and gunpowder — alluring. She paused before an odd-shaped silver pistol. Light glistened from the short, thick barrel, attached to a handle small enough to fit comfortably in her hand.

She reached for it, but caught herself and looked at Cappa. "May I?"

"Sure, just keep your finger off the trigger."

Captivated, Anne carefully took it from the wall. Though the room was cold, its metallic black handle felt warm to the touch. A glance down the barrel revealed an orange glow deep within.

"What is this?" Anne gripped the handle, mindful to keep her finger clear of the trigger.

"That," a deep voice said, "is a prototype sub-compact plasma ejector."

Anne gasped and spun to find Mark standing in the doorway.

Without warning, the gun gave a high-pitched whine. A bright flash of orange energy streaked from the barrel.

Straight for Mark.

Cappa dove between them. The shot burned a hole several inches wide into her chest, vaporizing her flesh down to a metallic subdermal plating. She fell to the floor in a sizzling trail of smoke.

"Cappa!" Anne put the cursed weapon on a nearby table and ran over to kneel beside her, opposite of Mark.

Cappa looked much worse up close. Red liquid dripped from tubes under her skin and hissed onto her white-hot endostructure, creating a charred, bubbling pool of ichor. Cappa raised her head and gently brushed the hair from Anne's eyes.

"Don't worry," Cappa said, "I'm —"

She went limp, vacant eyes staring at the ceiling.

"No! Wake up!" Anne shook her by the shoulders, tears rolling down her cheeks. "Cappa, no! You can't ... You have to —"

Charlie skidded to a stop in the hall behind them, taking the scene in with wide eyes. A long work glove covered one arm.

"Charlie, please," Anne said, her lip quivering. She hugged Cappa close. "It was an accident. Cappa was so nice to me, I would never ..." She rocked back and forth, cradling her the same way Cappa had cradled Anne the night before.

"Anne," Charlie said softly, "Cappa says you should let her go."

Anne blinked. His words didn't make sense.

"She ... what?"

"You're ruining your clothes — her clothes. She says the black stains may not come out, and you're wearing one of her favorite dresses."

"I-I don't understand."

He knelt next to Mark. "The heat from the blast triggered a safety shutdown of her power reactor," Charlie said. "But other than that, Cappa's fine." He frowned at the gaping hole in her chest. "Well, she will be once we patch her up and run a few diagnostics."

"I still don't get it," Anne said. "If she's off, how ..."

Charlie smiled. "Cappa's one of a kind. Her consciousness exists in multiple places simultaneously."

Anne continued to stare.

"It's a redundancy," he said. "A fault tolerance."

She sighed and turned to Mark.

"There are copies of her brain running in different places," Mark said. "She's listening right now."

"Oh." Anne sat back heavily, staring at Cappa's inert body. "I ... I don't understand what happened. I didn't touch the trigger, just like she warned me not to."

Mark's scowl said what he thought of that.

"I mean it! I ..." She choked back a sob. "Never mind, it probably was my fault. She can hear me?"

Charlie nodded. Anne leaned over her body, careful not to smudge her borrowed dress.

"I'm so sorry, Cappa, but thank you. If you hadn't jumped in the way ..." Anne covered her mouth. She couldn't even look at Mark.

"Anne's right about one thing," Mark said to Cappa. "I owe you big time."

Charlie suddenly laughed. "Cappa says she'd like to speak with you, Anne, if that's okay."

"Yes, please!"

"Come with me, then." He scooped Cappa in his arms, just as he had with Anne the day he rescued her from William.

Mark said goodnight at the bio lab door. The look he gave Anne wasn't reproachful, but neither did he offer a hug before he headed off. Anne couldn't blame him.

I should be arrested for attempted manslaughter — and android slaughter, if there is such a thing.

Once inside, Charlie laid Cappa's body on a long table. With the push of a button, a glass dome lowered from the ceiling and covered her, then he sat at one of the workstations.

The door opened and Zima strode in carrying Anne's purse. She set it on the workbench and left without a word.

Before Anne could ask, Charlie held out his hand. "First things first. Your cell phone, please?"

"Uh, sure." Anne dug in her purse for the archaic device. "Knock yourself out, it's just a cheap prepaid. I don't know how many minutes are left, but you're welcome to them."

Charlie flashed a wry grin. "Thanks, but I don't need to make a call." Deft fingers removed the back cover, followed by the battery, and eventually he produced a tiny black card the size of her pinky nail. "This is the SIM card. It uniquely identifies your phone to your carrier, which means if I put it in this ..." He pulled a sleek, black phone out from one of the drawers. "Your plan and your phone number will be bound to it." He popped the back of the new phone and inserted the little black chip, then set it in front of her. "And that means we can get rid of this." He grabbed her old phone and flipped it over his shoulder, where it landed neatly in a trashcan far across the room.

"Show-off."

She held the new phone at arm's length, as if it might bite. Anne and technology didn't mix well — a fact she thought she made clear when she accidentally blasted a hole in her tour guide with a space gun. But for some reason, Charlie wanted to give her more. She turned it in her hands and looked at him helplessly.

Charlie tapped a button on the top of the phone and the screen came to life. The Z-Tech logo glowed brightly on the display. A progress bar zipped across the bottom, followed by a screen full of icons.

Anne made a show of bouncing in her seat and clapped her hands. "Oh goodie, I won! Jackpot!"

Charlie rolled his eyes. "It's not as complicated as you think. There are only two icons you need to worry about. This one brings up a virtual keypad. You punch the numbers in and hit Send, just like your old phone. We can set up your contacts later, after you've collected your winnings."

"All right, smartass," Anne said with a laugh. "How do I talk to Cappa?"

"That's what the other button is for, though it'll be a better experience if you wear these."

Anne groaned when he again reached into the drawer.

Not another gadget ...

The pair of silver glasses he handed her, however, seemed harmless. They were larger than the current fashion, but not gaudy. She put them on and looked around. They held just clear, non-prescription lenses.

Anne struck a seductive pose and whisked her hair back. "Why, Charlie," she said in a sultry voice, "does this mean you're into the bookish types?"

His mouth fell open, which made her grin.

"Okay, now I have a slick phone and dorky glasses. What's next, a green fedora?"

"No, but I can dig one up if it'll make you feel better."

"Pass."

"That's a pity, I think green's your color. Tap this icon, here."

She did. A "Connecting" message flashed across the top of the screen, then the top bar turned green.

"Hi, Anne!"

Cappa's voice made her jump. It came from the stems of Anne's glasses. "Cappa! God, it's good to hear you."

"Then you're going to love this," Cappa said from the left side of Anne's glasses. Anne instinctively turned toward the sound and gasped. Standing near Cappa's glass-covered body was another Cappa. She wore the same outfit as Anne, minus the blood and soot. Anne removed the glasses and rubbed her eyes. When she looked up, Cappa was gone. She searched around in confusion, but Cappa was nowhere to be seen. Putting the glasses on again made Cappa reappear.

Cappa rounded the table and stood before her. "It's called augmented reality. Projectors in the rims send light directly into your eyes, imposing computer graphics onto reality to make it look like I'm standing here."

"That's amazing! You look so real."

"Thanks, I worked hard to get the details right."

Anne noticed Charlie was also looking at Cappa. "You can see her too?"

Charlie nodded and pointed to his eyes. "They're artificial."

"Yes," Cappa said, "and as fun as it is to bedazzle you with my presence, rendering myself to one display is hard enough, doing it for both of you at the same time gives me a virtual headache, so if you'll excuse me ..." She waved goodbye, and her image faded. Anne looked around, but slumped when she couldn't find her.

"Don't worry, audio is easy," Cappa said in her ear. "I'm still here."

Anne swallowed a lump in her throat. "Cappa, I am so, so sorry."

"Don't sweat it. Let's call it even for your favor earlier."

Charlie raised an eyebrow, which made Cappa laugh.

"Seriously, I'll be fit as a fiddle in a few days. Right, Charlie?"

He looked at her body lying under the glass dome and sighed.

"Besides," Cappa said, "that pistol looked good on you, Anne."

Anne shuddered. "Thanks, but I think the world's safer if I stick to books."

"Suit yourself, but Mark is a great shooting instructor, if you ever change your mind."

"I'll consider it," Anne said, though she never wanted to go near that weapon — or the weapons lab, for that matter — ever again.

And the last thing Mark needs is an actual excuse to shoot me.

Anne stretched her arms and yawned. A glance at her new phone showed the hour was late, and her lack of sleep from the night before was finally catching up.

"I'll disconnect now and leave you to it," Cappa said.

"Okay," Anne said, "but I'll call you first thing in the morning to see how you're doing."

"Not if I call you first!" There was a series of downtones, and the phone read "Disconnected".

"Can you find the way back to your room?" Charlie said.

"Yes. Well ... no, not really." She waited for him to offer himself as an escort, but he never did. "I-I guess I'll figure it out."

Charlie started to rise, but sank back down. His shoulders slumped. "Goodnight, Anne."

"'night." With a heavy heart, she left Charlie alone in his lab and followed the guiding corridor lights back to her guest room.

24

A SECOND NIGHT AT Z-TECH

WHEN ANNE ARRIVED AT HER ROOM, an unexpected smell of musty parchment wafted out through the doorway. She drank in the delightful scent. Someone had moved a small bookcase into her room while she was gone, filled to the brim with her favorite reality escape devices.

Books!

She wanted to hug them, but settled for running a loving finger across their spines.

It was an eclectic collection, sorted by author and title: classics by Charles Dickens shared a shelf with Tom Clancy, a National Geographic photographic book contrasted with a bright orange book by someone named Charles Petzold, who mistakenly thought she wanted to learn how to program windows.

I know how to open a window, thanks, Chuck.

Her favorite Jayne Madison novels were missing, but a few others caught her eye. She picked one at random — hungry to lose herself in some mindless fiction — and kicked her shoes off. She wriggled out of Cappa's stained dress, changed into her old-lady nightgown, then burrowed under the covers.

Her new phone began to rattle, playing a cross between a church bell and a pan flute, so she reluctantly set her book aside and picked it up from the nightstand.

The name "Doris Mae" flashed across the screen.

Damn it!

She scrambled to find the answer button. "Doris! I'm so sorry I forgot to tell you I wasn't coming home tonight. It just sort of ... happened."

"That's okay, kiddo. Tell me Charlie's lying next to you in sexy leopard print boxers and we'll call it even."

"Do silk briefs count?"

Doris' happy shriek made Anne jerk the phone away. "Seriously? Send me a pic!"

"I'm in the guest room," Anne said, laughing. "Alone. But guess what? They bought me some books!"

"Don't expect a 'whoop' from me. Books are a far cry from a handsome half-naked man in your bed. So what have you been up to? And for the love of God, don't say 'reading.'"

Oh, nothing special: held at knifepoint, ran for my life, shot someone in the chest with a ray gun, but it's cool because she's an android. You know ... the usual stuff.

Instead, Anne recounted the parts of the evening that were safe to share, including the attempted mugging and Zima's gratuitous show of guns. She gave some highlights of the tour, but left out anything that might betray Z-Tech's secrets — which, unfortunately, was most of it.

Doris sighed. "What is it with you and creeps these days? Well, never mind. You're safe, and the next time I see that gun-toting Blondie, her coffee's on me."

"You said it." Anne laid back, happy for her friend's comforting presence. "Thanks for checking in."

"Are you okay, kiddo? You sound a little shaken."

Anne nearly broke her vow and laid everything on the table for Doris, but her promise to Charlie — and a healthy dose of shame over shooting Cappa — kept her in check. "I'm fine, just a little frazzled from those thugs."

"Well, if Charlie won't sleep with you to keep the nightmares away, maybe Blondie will. You could do worse."

"Mm … I don't think she's the cuddly type."

"Can't say I didn't try. All right, then, I'm going to toodle off. Promise you'll call if you can't sleep, okay?"

"Promise," Anne said, though she had no intention of waking her friend tonight, even when the nightmares inevitably came.

She hung up with a sigh and snuggled under the covers. She had just opened her book when there was a knock on her door. Cursing her luck, she crossed the cold floor, turned the knob, and was surprised to see Zima.

"Oh, hey," Anne said. "What's up?"

"May I borrow your phone?"

Puzzled, Anne handed it over. Zima stared at it and the screen came to life. A new icon appeared right next to Cappa's.

"There," Zima said, handing the phone back, "that will connect you directly to me."

"Neat trick, how'd you do that?"

"Do you like the books?"

"Are you kidding? They're fantastic! I feel right at home now."

Zima stared at her for a few seconds, and Anne began to fidget.

"Are … are they from you?"

"Yes."

"Well thank you, Zima. First you save me from those guys —"

"Just as Charlie saved you," Zima said.

"Yes, just like Charlie, and then you give me the perfect gift —"

"Just as Charlie did," Zima said, gesturing to her new phone.

"Exactly," Anne said with a laugh. "I must have been good in a previous life to deserve —"

Zima silenced her with a kiss on the lips. Anne froze in wide-eyed panic — too startled to even breathe — while Zima stood perfectly still, eyes closed, head tilted, arms at her sides. Her lips were warm and soft, the same as Charlie's. His scent was there as well — not his cologne or jacket, but that earthy, sensual smell Anne couldn't get enough of. Her thoughts drifted to her android anatomy lesson with Cappa, and she wondered if Zima was feeling any of the pleasant stirrings that had begun to tug at Anne deep inside. She squeaked when Zima withdrew.

Zima regarded her with a knitted brow, which Anne found even more puzzling, then walked off in the direction of the kitchen.

Anne stayed in the hallway long after Zima disappeared. Her heart was a jumble of confusing emotions, with the shame of her unexpected arousal at the forefront. She could still feel Zima's tender lips, warm breath caressing her cheek ...

With a shake, she retreated to her room. She barely noticed the book slide to the floor when she climbed into bed. Sleep came quickly. Instead of nightmares, Anne dreamed of two steel-clad knights — one male, one female — each competing for her favor.

It was a very pleasant dream.

25

THE BREAKFAST CLUB

ANNE WOKE TO A STRANGE SOUND. She groaned and cracked a bleary eye. Her new phone was ringing, though it was a different tune than when Doris called last night. She flopped over and pawed it from the nightstand. The name "Cappa" flashed much too brightly on the screen.

"Yeah?" Anne said.

"Good morning, sunshine!"

Anne ran a hand down her face. Cappa was eleven shades too cheerful for this hour.

"G'morning," she said around a yawn.

The events of last night came rushing back. Anne's eyes popped open and she sat bolt upright.

"Cappa! How are you? I mean, are you fixed yet?"

"No, but repairs are coming along. I should be my normal, ravishing self by this evening. Diagnostics will probably take most of the night, though, so I doubt you'll see me until pancakes tomorrow."

"I can't wait. Again, I'm so —"

"Don't say it, Anne. Done is done. It was an accident, I'll be fine, and we're moving on, right?"

"Right," Anne said in a quavering voice. She had known Cappa for less than two days, yet she already thought of her as a sister.

"Good, because I'm going to need your help today."

"Huh?"

"I'm in charge of operations at Z-Tech and, until now, I've never missed a day on the job. The boys have other obligations, so it's up to us to take care of business."

"Of course, just tell me what I need to do."

"That's the spirit! Get yourself ready, and don't forget your new glasses. You'll need them."

A hot shower made Anne feel miles better. She found a suitable outfit in one of the drawers: jeans and a long-sleeve shirt. They were tight, as with all of Cappa's clothes, but stretched enough so they weren't too constrictive. Cappa informed her that Mark was in the kitchen, so she headed off for breakfast. Anne recalled how helpless he was that first night and quickened her pace.

"You what?" she heard Mark yell when she neared the entrance.

Anne stopped outside, afraid to enter.

"I kissed her," Zima said matter-of-factly.

Cappa's augmented-reality self appeared in front of Anne and she arched an eyebrow.

Anne swallowed, then nodded.

"But where?" Mark said. "I mean, why would you do that?"

"On the lips in the doorway to her room, and because she is my girlfriend."

"Your ... girlfriend?"

"Yes."

There was a heavy pause before Mark continued.

"Zima, I need to know precisely what you mean by that."

"Cappa has shared video of all the interactions between Charlie and Anne. She said that Anne is his girlfriend."

Shared video?

It was Anne's turn to shoot Cappa a look. Cappa cringed under her stare, but nodded.

I guess she can see me.

Anne mouthed, "We'll talk later."

Cappa nodded again and they turned their attention back to the kitchen.

"Charlie has saved her from two aggressive men," Zima said. "He took her on a date, a formal occasion at the opera. He gave her a new phone as a present. Because of these things, Anne is Charlie's girlfriend."

"Yes," Mark said. "She's *Charlie's* girlfriend —"

"I have saved her from three aggressive men. I spent the evening with her at the diner and walked her home, which matches the description of a date. I gave her books as a present. I have fulfilled the same requirements as Charlie. Therefore, Anne is my girlfriend, too."

A long silence followed. Anne grinned at the thought of Mark's mind working through Zima's logic.

"I asked Cappa what it means to be a girlfriend," Zima said. "She told me that a girlfriend spends time with her partner, and that they often kiss. I have observed kisses in public between men and women, and have seen women kiss each other as well."

Anne stifled a laugh. *It's San Francisco, after all.*

"Charlie kissed her because she is his girlfriend," Zima said. "I kissed her because she is also my girlfriend."

Mark sighed. "I think you're confused."

"My logic is sound. The only thing that confuses me is why you believe I am confused."

"Cappa gave you the light version," Mark said. "There's a lot more to relationships than that — including chemistry and ..." He sighed. "Anne isn't your girlfriend. She's Charlie's girlfriend, and not because he followed some formulaic sequence of events. They've connected on a very ... human level, which is hard to explain."

"Cappa said that traumatic experiences connect people. Anne and I have shared a traumatic experience. We are connected, too."

"Zima, it's just ... apart from your first attempt to socialize when you came to us — which was disastrous by your own admission — you've never shown the slightest interest in making friends, let alone dating! I didn't think you were capable, to be honest, yet suddenly now you're in a romantic relationship? I don't buy it. Even if I did, it's not fair to Anne or Charlie. They have challenges enough without you complicating things."

"Anne is my girlfriend, but I will share her with Charlie. He will understand."

"That's not the ..." Mark gave a frustrated growl. "Just stay away from her! Do you hear me?"

Anne's smile wilted.

"Why?" Zima said.

"Because ... I'm afraid for Anne. I'm afraid you'll hurt her."

"I will not hurt her," Zima said. "She is my girlfriend. I am a Protector."

"I wish I could believe that, but your track record says otherwise. Stay. Away. I won't let one of your 'accidents' spiral Charlie back into depression."

Anne's expression darkened. She had no idea about the accidents Mark was referring to — only that his forbidding tone rankled her to the core. Zima had saved her life, bought books to make her feel at home, and generously offered to share one of her few pairs of undergarments with a complete stranger. Her kiss from last night was unexpected, but gentle, and not once had Anne felt physically threatened by her presence.

Quite the opposite, she thought, remembering the feel of her soft lips.

Cappa's image watched carefully while Anne considered her next move.

He may be right, she thought. *But whether Zima and I see each other isn't Mark's decision to make. It's Zima's.*

And mine.

Anne bounced into the room wearing the most pleasant smile she could muster. "Good morning, Mark!" she said cheerfully.

Mark nearly fell out of his chair. "G-good morning."

Zima was sitting across from him and watched Anne with her usual emotionless stare. Anne skipped up behind her, wrapped her in an embrace, and planted a kiss on her cheek. Mark's jaw dropped.

"Good morning, Zima," Anne said, nuzzling her neck.

"Good morning, Anne."

"I wanted to thank you for the steamy visit last night," she whispered into Zima's ear, though loud enough for Mark to hear. "You were amazing."

Cappa materialized behind the counter, hopping up and down. "We definitely need to talk!" she said through the glasses.

"I am glad you enjoyed it," Zima said. She looked up at Anne so their noses almost touched. "It was my first time. I hope my performance was adequate."

Anne gave her a quick kiss on the lips. "It was a night I'll never forget."

That much is true.

Mark paled. Satisfied that she had made her point, Anne headed for the stove and donned an apron.

"Everything okay, Mark? I heard yelling on my way in."

"No, it was just ... it was nothing."

"Good."

She winked at Zima, who cocked her head.

That must mean she's unsure or confused.

Anne made a mental note to explain it to her later.

"Now, seeing as I shot the cook, what can I make you for breakfast?"

• • •

The bio lab door slid open, admitting a distracted Mark.

So much for lockdown, Charlie thought.

He himself had breached quarantine three times since they made the decision to isolate him and, though he didn't like it, he believed each instance had merited the risk.

It was baloney, of course, but made him feel better.

"What brings you into the hot zone?" Charlie said.

"Hmm?" Mark looked around, as if just realizing where he was. "Oh, um, nothing. Just stopped by to see how you're doing. How's the research coming along?"

"Slow and terrifying, take a look."

Charlie held his arm out for Mark to see. The small discoloration from yesterday had spread across most of his hand, leaving the tissue a dark blue.

"Jesus ..."

"Yeah. I've tried heat, cold, antibiotics ... nothing's worked so far. I have a few more ideas, though, and I think there's still time. I'd rather take it slow than move too quickly and miss something."

"You sure waiting is a good idea?"

"No, but if it progresses too far, we'll deal with it appropriately."

Mark nodded grimly, evidently sharing Charlie's hope that it wouldn't come to that.

26

A DAY IN CAPPA'S SHOES

MOST OF CAPPA'S DUTIES, she informed Anne, didn't require a physical body— such as inventory control, purchasing, production monitoring, financial transactions, reconciliation, and the like. Today, however, she was expecting several shipments of materials, which required a signature.

"Once they're signed for, we'll move them into the warehouse, where the robots can take over," Cappa said through the micro speakers in Anne's glasses. Her image smiled. "That'll be the most challenging part of the day. You up for it?"

"Can do, boss!" Anne snapped a salute at Cappa's image.

A restaurant she worked at many years ago underwent several rounds of staff turnover. During that time, Anne found herself the acting manager while the owner, an abrasive twerp and the source of the turnover, tried to hire someone who could actually stomach him. One of her managerial duties had been procurement and receiving, which was a never-ending job for a small restaurant who couldn't afford the software to manage it for them. Z-Tech's process was similar, if at a larger scale.

"Don't let the boys see you salute like that," Cappa said. "Government and military types put them on edge."

"Speaking of the boys, not that I mind helping out, but why can't Charlie do this? Surely he can spare a few minutes to sign a form and put some supplies away, and he's probably better with a forklift than I ever will be."

"Charlie's working on a very important project right now," Cappa said. "It's best if he's not disturbed until he makes some headway."

"Fair enough." Having zero experience running a multibillion-dollar international corporation, Anne was in no position to argue. "What's first, Captain Cappa?"

"Driving lessons, my dear!"

And so, Anne spent the remainder of the morning learning the basics of driving pallet movers and forklifts — two things she could honestly say she had no interest in prior to today.

By the end of the morning, her opinion hadn't changed.

"Bad as it seems," Cappa said, "you've come pretty far in a short amount of time."

Anne surveyed the practice area and winced. Empty barrels from her makeshift obstacle course lay scattered all around, but, to Cappa's point, most of the damage was from her early lessons.

I haven't hit a barrel in at least fifteen minutes, Anne thought, proud of the small accomplishment.

"Have you ever driven before?" Cappa said.

Anne turned the forklift off; that part she had mastered quickly. "I drove my boyfriend's car once in high school, but apart from that ..." Anne shrugged. "I'm a city dweller. I walk or take public transit. I mean, seriously, who can afford to park in this town?"

"Touché."

"What about Zima, can she drive?"

"Yes," virtual Cappa said, putting a hand on her hip. "And while we're on the subject, let's discuss our intrepid little Zima, shall we?"

Anne clamped her mouth shut. She had managed to avoid mention of the blonde until now, and silently cursed her mistake. "Like Zima said to Mark, she kissed me. Besides, she just seems so ..."

"Wooden? Emotionless? Cold? Uncaring?"

The last had an edge to it, which surprised Anne. She had assumed Zima and Cappa were friends, but now suspected it wasn't all roses between them.

"I was going to say 'innocent'. Naïve."

"Zima is a lot of things," Cappa said, crossing her arms, "but I promise you, she's neither innocent nor naïve."

Anne puzzled over that, but came up empty. When Cappa offered no more, Anne tried a different tactic.

"Charlie said he didn't make Zima. Where did she come from?"

Cappa pursed her lips. "That's not my story to tell, much as I'd like to. Ask her yourself, then we'll talk."

I'll do exactly that, Anne thought.

Zima had her quirks, but, more than anything, she seemed like a sheltered child who was only awkward because she'd never had the chance to play with other kids.

"Speaking of love interests," Cappa said, donning her warm smile once again. "If you don't mind me asking, have you thought any more about you and Charlie?"

"I have, but ... Cappa, I need to talk to him! He's so tied up in that project that it sounds like we won't get the chance for a while. I'm trying not to let it get to me, but it's ... disheartening."

Cappa appeared next to her, floating like an ethereal being.

Yet another guardian angel.

A virtual hand clasped her own. The image was so real that Anne swore she could feel Cappa's touch, but she knew it was just her imagination.

"If it's any consolation," Cappa said, her voice full of sympathy, "he isn't often on projects this urgent. Any other week, you would have his *full* attention, I promise."

"Thanks," Anne said with a smile. "That's good to know."

"Even though it's not exactly what you wanted to hear," Cappa said, echoing Anne's thoughts.

Anne's phone chirped. She struggled to pull it from her excessively tight jeans, and raised her eyebrows when she saw a message.

"Dinner tonight, if you are not working?" Anne read aloud.

It was from Zima.

Cappa's surprise turned into thoughtful musing. "You know … In light of this conversation, maybe it's not a bad idea."

"What, seriously?"

"Sure. Charlie's busy, I'm out of commission, and I doubt you'd want to spend the evening alone with Mark. She's doing us a favor by taking you out, in a way."

"But … I-I'm pretty sure Zima is asking me out on a real date. She's kissed me once already, and I won't be surprised if it happens again. Won't Charlie be upset?"

"Yes and no. He wants to see you, believe me, but the potential benefits for Zima are … how should I put it?"

Worth giving up his girlfriend for? Anne choked on the thought.

"We've struggled for years to socialize her with no success. Yet after meeting you, she's suddenly infatuated. It's adorable!" Cappa shook her head and smiled. "You have quite an effect on people, my dear, and in this case it seems criminal to lock you away when such a rare opportunity is knocking on your door. Assuming you're interested, that is."

"Well, y-yeah. It's embarrassing to admit, but I think I'm attracted to her. The problem is that I've never dated another woman before — let alone someone as unique as Zima. I'm not sure I'd even know what to do."

"You don't have to sleep with her," Cappa said, laughing. "Just take her out and work your special magic. Heck, if you can even get her talking, you'll be a hero in our eyes."

"Oh. When you put it that way, I-I guess I could give it a try, but … I'd really like to talk it over with Charlie first. Making a decision like this without him feels like cheating."

"All right, I'm sure I can pull him away for a minute. Hang on while I patch him through."

Charlie's voice came through the speakers in her glasses a few seconds later. "Hello?"

"Hey Charlie," Anne said. "Did … did Cappa fill you in?"

"High-level, yes. Look, if going on a date with Zima makes you uncomfortable, I completely understand, so don't feel pressured, okay?"

"It's not that. I like her, to be honest. I just want to make sure you're okay with it, in case … well, in case things go well."

"Well?"

"Yes. This will be a date, Charlie. If Zima and I hit it off, we might go out again, and I'm not going to break her heart down the road just because you've suddenly changed your mind and want me all to yourself. That wouldn't be fair to Zima, or to me. So the question is: In the odd chance things work out, are you really okay sharing me with another woman?"

Silence. Anne fiddled with a knob on the forklift; in the list of awkward conversations she thought she'd never have, asking permission from her cyborg boyfriend to date an android girl was at the absolute top.

How strange my life has become ...

"In the odd chance things work out," Charlie said eventually, "yes, I'm okay with it, as long as you're happy. The potential benefits for Zima are too great to pass up."

"That isn't why Anne asked," Cappa said.

Anne nodded.

"I know," Charlie said. "The fact is that there will be other times when I'm not able to give Anne my full attention. In a way, it's nice to know she wouldn't be lonely in my absence."

"That's both sweet and depressing," Anne said.

"It's the truth."

"Well, in that case ... I'll accept Zima's invitation to dinner."

Cappa clapped her virtual hands in glee. "How exciting! Can I tell her the good news?"

"Thanks, but I'll do it, and then ..." Anne looked at her makeshift course of barrels and sighed. "Back to driving lessons."

"Have fun tonight," Charlie said.

"Thanks. And Charlie?"

"Yes?"

"Finish your project. I miss you."

There was a pause. "One way or the other, I'll wrap this thing up by tomorrow. I promise."

"Good, I'll see you then."

"Count on it."

Anne was smiling when she hung up, but her good mood faltered when Cappa's face went slack.

"What is it?" Anne said.

"The first delivery's here! Put on your work gloves, my dear. This is not a drill!"

Anne cracked her knuckles and gripped the steering wheel like a racecar driver.

"All right, bring it on!"

• • •

Charlie thumped his head against the desk. He had only just started to lament his cruel fate when Mark walked into the bio lab.

"That's not a good sign," Mark said. "What's up?"

"Not much," Charlie said to the tabletop. "Just handed my girlfriend to Zima on a silver platter, that's all."

"Say what?"

Charlie filled him in. Mark's mouth fell open.

"I don't know which is harder to believe," Mark said. "That Zima wants to go on a date, or that you didn't object. Aren't you worried?"

"About losing Anne, or her safety?"

"Take your pick."

"As far as I'm concerned, Zima proved herself when she protected Anne last night without raising the body count."

"That's setting the bar pretty low, Charlie."

"We have to start trusting Zima sometime."

"Yeah, but ..." Mark shook his head and sighed. "Have you given up on your relationship with Anne?"

"No."

"Then please, enlighten me how you intend to compete with Zima, whom Anne is clearly interested in, while you're locked in here with an unknown and hitherto incurable infection?"

"Glad you asked." Charlie pulled his glove off to show Mark his infected hand, which was now entirely blue up to his wrist. "You were right, I shouldn't have waited. The entire arm needs to be replaced, and I'd appreciate your help with the procedure."

"O-of course." Mark cleared his throat. "Any new info on the bite?"

Charlie punched a few keys and the screen changed to show a complex molecular chain.

"It's less dramatic than the infection, but still a mystery," Charlie said. "The bite wound contained two primary chemicals. One is a modified benzodiazepine — and in case you skipped advanced pharmaceuticals in college, that means it slows down the movement of chemicals in the brain, making the subject less anxious and more compliant. It also makes the subject forget, kind of like a date-rape drug."

"That's creepy."

"Tell me about it; he didn't even buy me a drink. As for the second chemical ... you're not going to believe this." Charlie pulled up a different molecular chain on the monitor. "It's unlike anything I've ever seen. I didn't even know where to start, so I took a guess that it might share properties with the saliva of other parasites, like leeches, and serve as an anticoagulant, but look what happened when I injected it into living tissue."

Charlie played a video on the screen, showing what Mark recognized as a macro view of epithelial cells just beneath the skin. When the chemical was introduced, the cells went ballistic and began to replicate at an impossibly high rate.

Mark closed his hanging jaw. "What the hell ...?"

"The second chemical in that creature's bite accelerated healing to an unheard-of speed. I only had a small sample, but it completely healed the test laceration in a matter of minutes."

"Any chance of getting more of this stuff?"

"Not unless we want to find that creep again and ask."

"Hang on ... Did you say a test laceration? Where did you get a real tissue sample ..." Mark paled. "Oh, no, you didn't."

Charlie shrugged. "Cappa's out of commission, and I can't exactly beg for tissue samples on the street corner. What else was I supposed to do?"

"Fair enough. So, back to your arm. When do you want to do the surgery?"

"Now, if you're up for it. I'd love to finish before Anne and Zima get back."

"Sure," Mark said, grinning.

"What's so funny?"

"Just the old saying about giving your right arm for someone. I hope Anne appreciates it."

Charlie nodded, though at this point, he'd be happy if she didn't freak out when he finally told her the truth about his so-called project.

27

SUITOR NUMBER TWO

ANNE EMERGED FROM HER BEDROOM in Doris' apartment and twirled around for her friend. "How do I look?"

"Gorgeous as always, kiddo."

Anne beamed. Unsure of where Zima was taking her, she had opted for a simple yellow dress with a white cardigan that, she hoped, was nice enough for a fancy restaurant, but wouldn't leave her overdressed if they ended up somewhere casual.

Doris scratched at her white silk robe. "You know I was only kidding when I said you should sleep with that bleached Barbie girl, right?"

"Very funny. And you were *not*."

"I suppose I wasn't," Doris said, laughing. "At least I don't have to ask if you're packing a condom."

"True."

Not that I'd need one with Charlie, either.

"Reckon you'll sleep here tonight? Please say 'no' because you're going back to Z-Tech for a threesome."

"You're terrible," Anne said with a grin. "I'm going back to Z-Tech in the hopes of squeezing in a few minutes with Charlie."

"For a quickie?"

"No! He said he'd be done with his big project by tomorrow. I want to be there in case he finishes early."

"Aw, that's sweet of you, kiddo. And a little desperate, but that's endearing, too, in the right measures."

Anne blushed. It was desperate, but she couldn't help herself. She missed Charlie and, given the choice of hanging out at Doris' apartment watching reality shows or staying at Z-Tech with the slim chance of seeing him a day earlier than promised, she selfishly chose the latter.

Not to mention Cappa should be up and around tomorrow.

The thought made her smile. Despite a nerve-racking start, Anne had quickly found her groove with the forklift and unloaded every pallet without a hitch. She then helped with some of Cappa's other duties, ranging from laundry to inventory management to quality inspections of their manufactured products. The result had been an immense sense of accomplishment, and a bonding experience that made her miss Cappa even more.

Yes, she would definitely be returning to the factory tonight.

The doorbell rang. Anne's heart jumped. She quickly checked herself over, which made Doris laugh.

"I told you, you look gorgeous," Doris said. "Blondie's one lucky girl."

Anne made for the door, but Doris waved her back.

"I'll get that! You get the flowers."

Anne darted for the bouquet of roses on the kitchen counter. Choosing the color had been difficult: red roses spoke too strongly of love for a first date, but yellow screamed "just friends", so she had settled for white roses, which, in addition to matching Zima's platinum hair, symbolized new beginnings.

Doris opened the door. Anne relaxed when she saw Zima in the same baggy gray outfit she always wore.

Until she noticed the small bouquet of roses in Zima's hands.

They were red.

The significance wasn't lost on Doris, either.

Her grin widened at the sight of the flowers. She winked at Anne, then turned back to Zima. "Come on in and make yourself at home."

"Thank you."

Zima stepped inside and closed the door behind her. Her eyes darted all around, taking in the apartment, before fixing on Anne.

"These are for you," Zima said, extending her bouquet.

"Thanks, and ... for you." When the exchange was complete, Anne was speechless: holding the white flowers to her breast, Zima really did look like an angel.

"No sense carting those around," Doris said, breaking the spell. "I'll throw them in some water while you're out."

Zima clutched hers tighter. "I appreciate the offer, but I wish to keep them with me."

"Don't worry," Anne said, "Doris will take good care of them."

Zima didn't budge.

"What is it?" Anne said.

"These flowers are the first gift I have ever received. I do not wish to part with them."

"The first ..." Doris laughed. "You've got to be kidding, hon."

When Zima's expression didn't change, Doris' jaw dropped.

"Ever? Are you serious?"

"Yes."

Doris shook her head and looked to Anne for confirmation.

Zima doesn't lie, Anne thought. *The poor thing.*

"She's, ah ... had a rough childhood," Anne said, feeling horrible she once again had to lie to her best friend to protect Z-Tech's secrets. "She doesn't like to talk about it, as you can imagine, but that's one of the reasons even Charlie was happy she asked me out. She's starting to come out of her shell."

Zima, thankfully, kept quiet.

"Just like someone else I know," Doris said, giving Anne a wink. "So, Zima, where are you taking my special girl on this special occasion?"

"To Restaurant Gary Danko."

Anne's eyes widened, and Doris let out a hoot. Restaurant Gary Danko was a fancy place where meals cost a fortune and the waiting list was two months long. Since they didn't take reservations more than sixty days out, you had to be lucky or persistent to get a table.

In other words, Danko's was the kind of place Anne and Doris dreamed of patronizing, but probably never would.

"Hot damn," Doris said. "If you were trying to make a good impression, Zima, it worked. You've got my blessing."

"Thank you. I cross-referenced four different restaurant search engines and limited the results to a twenty-mile radius from this apartment. After applying a weighting algorithm with what I know of Anne's culinary preferences, Restaurant Gary Danko had the highest score. I estimate a ninety-four percent chance that Anne will have an enjoyable experience."

"Wow, the girl's done her homework," Doris said. She looked at Zima curiously. "So how many restaurants did you sift through?"

"All of them."

"That's, ah, that's a lot of work, hon. There's a ton of restaurants on the peninsula. How long did your little research project take?"

"Oh, what does it matter?" Anne said, fearing Zima might break it down into milliseconds and blow her cover. "It's the thought that counts, right? Thanks, Zima. That was really sweet."

"It was no trouble. You are my girlfriend."

Doris laughed. "You're cute, hon, but it usually takes more than a couple days to earn that title. Our boy Charlie's been working on Anne for over a month. He still hasn't made it below her waistband, Lord knows why, and unlike you he's got a hefty meat sausage to —"

"Thank you, Doris," Anne said, elbowing her lightly in the ribs. "If you're done embarrassing me, we should probably get going."

Before Zima says something I can't cover for.

"All right. Have fun you two." Doris caught Anne by the sleeve on her way out. "And if you do happen to have a threesome tonight," she said softly, "think of your pal Doris and take a few pictures, would you?"

Anne hugged her tight with a laugh. "Not a chance on either account. Goodnight."

"'night, hon. Good luck."

"Thanks," Anne said earnestly.

If her last few dates were any indication, Anne was going to need all the luck she could get.

28

RESTAURANT GARY DANKO

RESTAURANT GARY DANKO, it turned out, was a nondescript building nestled on the fringes of the financial district. A valet sign on the sidewalk was the only hint that something extraordinary waited inside.

"I think that was our stop," Anne said, glancing over her shoulder at the retreating sign.

"This vehicle is a prototype containing irreplaceable technology," Zima said. "Valet service is unwise, as it would grant a stranger unfettered access, so we shall park where we do not need to surrender the key."

Of course it's a prototype. Driving a plain-old economy car would have been too simple.

"Well that should be easy enough. There are plenty of garages around here."

Anne should have known better. After a half-hour of searching, they discovered that none of the nearby lots allowed self-parking, so Zima ended up parallel parking in an impossibly tight spot nearly half a mile away.

"Our reservation is in three minutes and twenty-four seconds," Zima said. "At typical walking speed, we shall arrive four minutes and six seconds late."

"That's okay, we don't need to rush. A nice restaurant like Danko's won't give our table away."

Zima seemed to accept that. She clutched her bouquet of white roses and they set off at a leisurely pace. Zima's eyes constantly swept their surroundings, a habit Anne had found unnerving when they first met, but here in this dark, seedy neighborhood, her vigilance was comforting.

She turned suddenly to Anne. "Doris intimated that I am not your girlfriend. Why?"

"Oh, you mean the taking more than a couple of days, or the sausage thing?"

"Both. Had I known sausage was your culinary preference, I would have chosen a different restaurant. Is it really so important to you?"

"Well, I do like sausage," Anne said, blushing. "But meeting you has, ah ... opened my mind to other dishes."

"I have chosen wisely, then. Gary Danko's is known for its range of cuisines."

Anne stifled a smile.

Oh well, if it becomes important later, I'll explain it to her then.

"As for her other point ... I'm afraid Doris is right. The whole reason for dating is for two people to discover if they're right for each other, and this is our first one, really."

"I see. So we are not girlfriends?"

"Friends, certainly, but ..."

Zima stopped in the middle of the sidewalk, her blue eyes fixed on Anne.

Uh oh.

Apparently even Zima knew the stigma of the F-word in dating. Anne put a reassuring hand on her shoulder. "I didn't mean it that way. Look, let's see how dinner goes, okay? If things go well, I may have a different answer for you at the end of the night."

Zima nodded, though she stayed quiet for the rest of the walk.

Inside Danko's wasn't at all what Anne had imagined: People milled in a cramped waiting area in front of the bar. To either side was a little dining room with fancy, low-light chandeliers. Flowers and tea lights adorned tables so close together that she saw two diners from adjacent tables bump elbows, though neither seemed to mind. Patrons wore all manner of clothes, from lavish ball gowns to T-shirts and jeans. Neither Anne's plain dress nor Zima's baggy grays felt out of place.

That's my City, Anne thought.

The hostess, a young lady with short hair and an infectious smile, greeted them like old friends. "Hi! Welcome to Restaurant Gary Danko. You have reservations?"

"Yes," Zima said, "under Charlie Z, for two."

"Oh!" The hostess paled and looked around. "I-is Mr. Z here?"

"No, it is just us." Zima sidled next to Anne and laced their fingers together.

Sneaky minx, Anne thought with a smile.

The hostess seemed disappointed, but recovered quickly. "Very well. May I take your jacket and your cardigan?"

"No," Zima said.

The hostess flinched.

"She gets cold easily," Anne lied to smooth things over.

She suspected the real reason Zima didn't want to surrender her jacket was that it concealed her pistols. Instead of making her nervous, the thought set Anne's heart racing with excitement; it felt like dining with a secret agent, such as her paperback hero, Jayne Madison, with Anne as her suave partner.

"We both do, so no, thank you, we'll keep them on."

"Ah. Well, right this way."

Hand-in-hand, they followed the hostess to a V-shaped booth just a dozen feet from the door. It was so tiny that their knees touched once they were seated. Even the floral arrangements adorning the back of the booth, as pretty as they were, brushed Anne's hair with every movement.

Glad I'm not claustrophobic.

"Did Charlie really make the reservation for us?" Anne said to Zima once they were alone.

"Yes. They claimed to have no openings when I called, so I asked Charlie for advice. Two minutes and fourteen seconds later, he notified me that our reservation was confirmed."

"How sweet!" Anne made a mental note to thank him later.

"Indeed. His name carries influence in cities around the world."

The hostess returned a minute later with a vase for Zima's flowers and a pair of menus, which Anne could hardly believe when she read. There were five courses, each with several items to choose from, except for the fifth, which was an optional cart of cheeses from around the world. The words "lobster" and "fillet" featured prominently and, as Zima had pointed out earlier, each course had a range of cuisines, including Italian, French, Japanese, and Thai.

"They all sound incredible," Anne said. "It's too bad we can only choose four."

"Eight."

Anne cocked her head, as Zima often did.

"I do not need to eat," Zima said softly. "But I shall order, as is expected of me. You may choose my courses."

"Oh, Zima! I'm sorry, I didn't even think about that. We should have done something else, like miniature golf or a movie."

"It is all right. I am physically capable of eating, but I do not need to. My body will simply store the food for later extraction."

Down to the finest detail and function, Cappa had said.

Anne tried not to imagine how the food was extracted. "Can you taste?"

"I do not think so," Zima said.

Anne cocked her head again.

"I can break down most materials into their base chemical components, and can measure molecular density, weight, and distribution to identify harmful substances in solid, liquid, or gaseous states. I do not believe that is the same as your sense of taste, though it is difficult to say because I have no frame of reference."

"Thank you," Anne said, squeezing her hand. Zima cocked her head— a game that Anne was starting to enjoy. "For the straightforward answer. For protecting me. For taking me to one of the finest restaurants the City has to offer, even when you can't enjoy it. To be frank, I was nervous about going out with you tonight, but I'm not now because you've been so open. I trust you."

"That is good?"

"Very."

"Then I shall endeavor to keep your trust." Zima handed her the wine menu. "Would you like something from this?"

Anne choked when she saw the prices. "I, ah ... think I'll stick with water, thanks."

"You do not like wine?"

"I-it's not that, just ..." *I like it a little too much.*

Zima took the menu back and glanced it over. "Wine is an important part of the dining experience, as I understand. We shall order some."

Anne nodded with a sigh. A meal of this caliber deserved a nice bottle of wine, and she had been so very good these last few years that Doris would certainly forgive her for bending the rules this once.

Besides, I'll just have one glass.

"Good evening," a tall man with a bow tie said. "I'm Clark, and I'll be your waiter. Can I get you started with something to drink?"

"Yes," Zima said. "Please bring your finest bottle of wine. And two glasses so we may both drink."

"A whole bottle?" Anne fidgeted with her napkin. "C-can I just get a glass?"

"I'm sorry, but we don't offer our finer wines by the glass," Clark said, then turned to Zima and wrung his hands. "Ma'am, our finest bottle is delicious, though quite rare and very expensive. Are you sure?"

"Yes."

"Very well, but I'm afraid I'll need a credit card before the sommelier can present it."

Zima handed it to him in one smooth motion, and Clark left for the kitchen.

"Zima, no! That bottle costs half of what I make in a year!" Anne paled just thinking about it. "Let's call the waiter back and cancel the order."

Zima stared at her.

"Really! I'm perfectly happy with a glass of something cheap. Expensive wine is wasted on me."

"We shall soon see." She turned away, eyes flitting between the restaurant patrons.

A woman appeared with a small silver goblet hanging from a chain around her neck. The bottle she carried looked ancient, its once-white label now resembled old parchment. The woman, who Anne assumed was the sommelier, spoke at length about the history of the wine they were about to enjoy, describing each of the complex flavors they may detect, and how the flavors may change as the wine oxidized.

Anne tried to listen, but her mind kept drifting back to the enormous price tag.

This is such a waste of good wine, she thought miserably.

Anne stopped the sommelier just before she opened the cork and turned to Zima. "Are you absolutely sure about this?"

"Yes."

"Then you get the first taste."

Zima knitted her brow, then nodded. Their waiter materialized with two etched wine glasses. The sommelier opened the bottle with practiced ease, though her hand shook when she set the cork on the table. Several patrons looked on with interest, making Anne blush.

The sommelier poured a splash into her chained silver goblet, then swished it around and inhaled deeply. The corners of her mouth twitched when she took a sip.

"Excellent," she said with a smile. "You're in for a treat tonight."

She tipped a small amount of the red wine into Zima's glass. Zima imitated the sommelier's sniff-and-taste routine with comical precision, then set it down without expression or comment.

Poor thing can't even taste it.

"Is the flavor acceptable?" Anne said, nodding helpfully.

Zima shrugged and slid the glass to Anne. The sommelier paled.

Anne lifted the glass to her nose. The smell was like a gentle breeze in a flowery meadow on a perfect spring day, complete with singing birds and a cascading waterfall. Her mouth watering, Anne took a sip.

The sommelier's eloquent description didn't do it justice. Rose petals and violets danced across her taste buds. Juicy raspberries and succulent cherries sang in perfect harmony with their floral counterparts. A hint of early morning tea, served in a little café in gay Paris while the sun glinted from the glassy *Louvre*, made her sigh. She closed her eyes to savor the experience.

Anne finally understood the difference between a good wine and a great wine.

Zima cocked her head. "Has the wine caused you discomfort?"

Anne was confused until she realized her cheeks were wet. "I'm perfect. It's the most wondrous thing I've ever tasted." She dabbed her face with her napkin.

The crowd around her collectively awed, which brought a fresh stream of tears.

The sommelier poured each of them a glass, gave the bottle a last longing glance, then left them to enjoy the rest of their dinner.

The food was nearly as amazing as the wine. Dishes of every cuisine came in a never-ending stream. Zima took a single bite of each before sliding hers to Anne, whose biggest challenge was restraining herself from licking the plates clean. Zima asked what she thought after each course, so Anne did her best to describe the flavors using colorful language.

She was stuffed by the time dessert arrived, which consisted of not one, but three different flavors of *crème brûlée*.

"Oh my God," Anne said, laughing. "I think I need a break."

"You have enjoyed the food?"

"Are you kidding? This has been the most amazing meal of my life!"

Her resolution of a single glass of wine for the evening had devolved into one glass per course, as she'd feared it would, and the room was now spinning.

Anne was too happy to care. She rested her head on Zima's shoulder and smiled. Though Zima was slight of figure, she hardly budged when Anne leaned into her, as if made of stone.

"How much do you weigh?" Anne said before her inebriated brain could stop her.

"Four hundred seventy-two pounds and nine ounces."

Anne whistled softly, but her lips weren't working as well as they should have and it came out as a breathy sigh. "You hide it well. I would've said one-twenty, tops."

"How much do you weigh?"

I had that coming.

"Oh ... I haven't stepped on a scale recently, but I'm probably ten pounds heavier than when I walked in here."

Zima stared at her.

"One-forty," Anne said, sighing. "Give or take."

Zima nodded and resumed her visual scan of the dining room.

"Why do you do that? Watch the crowds, I mean."

"I like to be aware of who and what is around me at all times. People are in constant motion, so I must update my data frequently."

"All right, but why is that so important?"

"The data is necessary to assess potential threats and formulate responses in the form of simulations."

Anne grinned, and Zima cocked her head.

"Did I say something amusing?"

"Learning how your mind works is nice. It makes me feel closer to you."

"Then please continue your questions. I shall answer what I can, unless the information might compromise your safety."

She's neither innocent nor naïve, Cappa had warned.

"All right. Charlie said you weren't created at Z-Tech. Where do you come from?"

"That is not a topic for public conversation." Zima's deadpan delivery made it difficult for Anne to gauge whether she'd crossed a line, but she relaxed when Zima added, "I will tell you of my origins later when there are fewer people around. It is possible that my tale will trigger one of your flashbacks — perhaps several — and I would spare you the public indignation if I can."

"Oh." The thought that Zima's background was traumatic enough to trigger Anne with just the telling required more wine, so she drained her glass. It helped. "Thank you, Zima," she said, weaving in her chair. "That's very considerate."

"You are welcome. My goal is to make this evening as pleasant as possible for you."

"And you're doing an amazing job. All right, back to safer territory until we're alone." She giggled at the unintended innuendo. "So, other than threat response, what else do you stimulate? Simulate! Sorry." She snorted a drunken laugh and quickly covered her mouth.

"Things that you probably do without conscious effort. For example, before I arrived at Doris' house, I ran five scenarios of how I would respond when the door opened. I ran seven scenarios for placing our order, eighteen for the wine selection ... Shall I continue?"

"I get the idea. So holding my hand in the lobby was the result of a simulation?"

"Yes, which had four contingencies of its own."

"What were the contingencies? I've got to know!"

"The first was closest to the actual outcome, where you allowed me to take your hand, held mine in return, and we walked to the table without incident."

"Glad that worked out for you," Anne said, giving Zima's hand a squeeze.

"Yes, that one had the most favorable outcome. The second was a slight variance, where I took your hand, but your grip was slack, indicating that you did not welcome the interaction, and I would then have released your hand. That simulation had eight contingent scenarios."

"It reminds me of chess," Anne said.

Zima cocked her head.

"The best chess players try to imagine all possible moves for the next several turns, which is why it takes so long to finish a game. It sounds like life is just an endless chess game for you, except you have a lot more pieces to consider."

"That is an interesting analogy. I have never played chess, but perhaps I should."

"Sorry, you were saying?"

"Yes. In the third simulation, you snatched your hand away and stepped back in anger. I would then utter an apology and promise not to do it again. The apology would placate you and we would continue with the evening. That simulation had sixteen contingent scenarios."

"Lucky you didn't have to run those," Anne said.

"The likelihood of that scenario was seven percent."

"Before we get to the last one ... Statistics aside, which of those simulations did you hope would come true?"

"I do not understand your question."

"I mean, just because a scenario has a small chance of playing out, is there ever a time when you have a preference for that scenario over one with a higher probability?"

"Yes. When I kissed you last night, the resulting scenario had less than one percent chance of being the actual result. The most likely scenarios involved a hostile response from you. The highest-ranked simulation had a ninety-one percent chance."

"Which was?"

"You slapped me and slammed the door."

"But I didn't."

"Correct, and that is why I walked away after we kissed. The actual resulting scenario was so unlikely that I had not prepared any contingent simulations."

Anne took another sip of her wine. "How big was the list?"

"I had three hundred and fifty-two simulations prepared by the time I knocked on your door."

"Yikes!"

"I had much time to plan," Zima said.

"So you took a chance, and here we are." Anne shook her head in wonder. "All right, so what was the fourth simulation, after you took my hand?"

"It assumed the hostess was homophobic and commanded us to leave the restaurant. That was the shortest of the simulations and had three contingent scenarios."

Anne laughed so hard she nearly toppled her glass. "Go on, tell me how you would have dealt with an uppity hostess."

"The first contingency was acquiescence, where we cooperate and leave the restaurant. The second was a passive response, where we ignore the command and ask to be seated by someone else."

"I like that one."

"The third involved rendering the hostess unconscious, dragging her into the coat closet, tying her up, and seating ourselves."

"I … I definitely liked the second one better."

"Your blood pressure has dropped. Have I upset you?"

"N-no, you just caught me a little off-guard. Most people wouldn't consider such an … extreme reaction in that situation."

"I understand," Zima said. "May I explain, or do you fear the onset of a flashback?"

Anne took a large gulp of wine. "I'm okay, Zima. Go ahead."

"Your mind is more flexible than mine. You can make decisions and react to situations from which you have no frame of reference, or draw from experiences that are abstractly related. I cannot do that as fluidly, so I must compensate by building a sufficient library of connected scenarios, however unlikely, that I may draw upon as the need arises."

"So your simulations are really your memories ... your experiences."

"I believe so. It is difficult to say for certain because I do not understand exactly how your memories or thought processes work."

"That makes two of us."

"The simulation closest to the actual outcome is corrected for accuracy. All simulations are stored, indexed, and flagged for later consolidation or association."

A web of interrelated experiences she can draw upon.

"Later? Like when?"

"The consolidation routine runs during idle time, usually at night when I am isolated and input is minimal."

"REM sleep," Anne said.

"That is a good approximation. REM sleep is the time when human minds consolidate memories and prepare them for long-term storage, discarding less important memories. My consolidation routine optimizes the simulations, tags them with relevant flags, and then indexes them for quick access. For example: when we were attacked last night, of the twenty-eight simulations used, twenty-five were existing simulations."

"How many were you able to reuse tonight?"

"Seven out of three thousand four hundred eighty-six created."

Anne smiled. "This really is new territory for you, isn't it?"

"Social situations require a complex Bayesian algorithm to predict ..." Zima snapped her mouth shut. "Yes, it is a lot of work."

"Thanks for the short answer, my head's already spinning." Anne picked up the empty bottle to admire her handiwork.

"You are welcome. Cappa says I need to speak in terms that are easier for people to relate to."

"She must tell you that a lot."

"Only once, eight seconds ago."

Anne nearly dropped the bottle. "Come again?"

"Cappa is currently connected to me and monitoring our conversation, as she does with your cell phone and glasses. She has been feeding me ancillary recommendations since I arrived at Doris' apartment. It has been very helpful, but she has just informed me that I should not have told you that." Her brow knitted. "Or that. Dating is proving to be more difficult than I anticipated. I apologize if I have again upset you."

Zima looked at their joined hands and gave a squeeze, as Anne had earlier.

Cappa has been guiding her the entire evening ...

Anne had enjoyed dinner with Zima and felt like they were beginning to bond, but now she wondered how much of that was just Cappa whispering the right things in her ear. The thought bothered her more than she expected.

"Was that hand-squeeze Cappa's idea, too?"

"Yes."

"And the flowers?"

"Yes."

"And holding my hand when we came in?"

"Yes."

Anne swallowed a rising lump in her throat. "And the kiss in my room?"

"No."

"That ... that was your idea? Solely yours?" Anne brushed a rolling tear from her cheek.

"Yes. It was inspired by Cappa's tale of you and Charlie kissing, but I acted on my own."

"Zima, I want to believe you, but —"

Anne's purse rang with a familiar tune.

"It is Cappa," Zima said. "She wishes to speak with you. Outside, if you do not object."

"Not now." Anne shoved her purse under the table, then ran her thumb over Zima's soft cheek. "Can you do me a favor?"

"If I am able."

"Will you disconnect from Cappa?"

"Why?"

"I want to discuss something with you and ... and I need to know it's you speaking, not someone else."

Zima paused. "It is done, we are no longer connected."

"Thank you." Anne tugged at the neck of her dress. "Can we go? It suddenly feels stuffy in here."

"Yes, if that is your wish."

Anne flagged the waiter and asked for the check, which came immediately. Zima refused to allow Anne to contribute to the bill, so Anne averted her eyes while Zima settled it — she really didn't want to know the total — then waited while Zima gathered her white roses and the waiter boxed up the desserts.

Upset Anne may be, but there was no way she would let an untouched trio of *crème brûlées* go to waste.

29

ZIMA'S STORY

ANNE WELCOMED THE COOL NIGHT air on leaving the restaurant. Zima had been quiet since disconnecting from Cappa, her mood impossible to gauge, as usual. They walked in silence through the city streets with no particular destination in mind. Zima maintained her vigilance, clutching her white roses to her chest and trying to look everywhere at once, while Anne focused on putting one foot in front of the other through the wine haze.

"Zima, was this date your idea?" Anne said several blocks later.

"Yes."

"Why did you ask me out? Was it just to match Charlie's date count, like some sort of competition between you two?"

"No." Zima fell quiet and brow-knit.

Sounds of the city surrounded them. Delicious smells wafted from a Chinese bakery, though the last thing Anne wanted to think about was food. She glanced at Zima several times. Her brow remained knitted, so Anne allowed her time to think.

Or simulate. Whatever it is she does.

A few blocks later, Zima's blue eyes finally met hers. "Why did you and Charlie go on a date?"

"Hey, that's not fair. I asked you first."

"Understood. I am unable to express what triggered my invitation. I had hoped your explanation would help me articulate my own reasons, but I shall try nonetheless."

Score one for Zima, Anne thought guiltily.

"Okay, I'll go first. I went out with Charlie because I liked him."

"Is that all?"

"There were other reasons, I suppose. He's kind, I was lonely, he saved my life, he has a good sense of humor —"

"I was lonely," Zima said.

"Really? What about Mark? Cappa? Charlie?"

"They treat me differently than you do."

Charlie and Cappa's warnings came back to Anne, and she suddenly understood. "They're afraid of you, aren't they?"

"I believe so."

"Why? I mean, I can't imagine what would make someone as strong as Charlie afraid."

"It is both my origins and my actions that have made them afraid."

Anne was surprised to find they had walked all the way to the Embarcadero. Lights from across the bay glittered on the water next to moored boats swaying with the gentle swells. The night was young, and many people still bustled about; joggers ran by, engrossed in their personal music players, ignoring the tourists who gushed at the magnificent sights the waterfront had to offer.

Anne steered them to an empty bench facing the bay. "Will you tell me about it?" she said. "I'd really like to hear —" Her purse rang, and she ground her teeth. It was Cappa's ringtone.

"Answer it," Zima said, laying her bouquet on her lap. "I shall wait here."

"Anne!" Cappa said as soon as she answered. "Are you all right?"

"I'm fine, Cappa, really." Anne wandered closer to the water and leaned against a streetlamp. "Zima and I have just been walking and chatting."

"Thank goodness. Anne, I'm so sorry about earlier, I honestly wasn't trying to go behind your back. I hope you understand I was just —"

"Trying to help Zima," Anne said.

"Trying to help both of you, but I realized early on that Zima didn't need me. I know it was wrong, but ..."

Anne laughed. "You had to see it first-hand, didn't you?"

"Desperately! Anne, this is Zima's very first social call! She's never expressed an interest before, and I wanted to make sure things went smoothly."

"I get it, Cappa. You're forgiven, and I'm sorry for getting upset."

"Thank heavens! I thought I was going to have to do some serious groveling for a minute there. Just be sure to call me later and tell me how the rest of the evening went."

"You know, I should introduce you to my friend Doris. You two have a lot in common."

"We both have a keen fashion sense?"

"Goodbye, Cappa. I'm going back to my date now."

"All right, have fun. *Zima, behave yourself!*" she yelled before Anne hung up.

Zima's ice-blue eyes watched Anne settle down next to her; a faint blue glow emanated from deep within.

"Before I begin," Zima said, "it is probably best to tell you that I was not always as you see me, nor did I behave as I do now. Mark, Charlie, and Cappa have helped me a great deal since my escape, and I am different."

Anne nodded, though she had no idea where Zima was leading.

"That is important, because I think it is what the others do not understand," Zima said. "I am not the same person who tried to kill them."

Calm, Anne told herself, even as she felt her demons stir. *Give her a chance to explain.*

"Your pulse, respiration, and blood pressure have escalated. Would you like me to stop?"

"No, Zima." Despite her unease, Anne scooted closer and held her hand out. "Tell me whatever you're comfortable sharing, and I'll listen."

"Very well, but please tell me if anything I say serves as a trigger." Zima took her hand and looked out over the water. "I once belonged to a foreign espionage agency which developed and sold advanced technology to military organizations around the world. Their most valuable assets were their inventions. A competing agency breached their state-of-the-art firewall and stole many valuable designs, so they hired top experts in both cyber-security and artificial intelligence to create new defense software, able to not only identify new attack vectors, but learn from the patterns and anticipate future attacks."

"They made you."

"Yes. Though I was not yet self-aware, I was still the most sophisticated security program ever built. My performance far exceeded their expectations. I had a flawless defense record, and they soon used me for offensive operations as well. There were few security protocols I could not bypass. Through me, the company stole vast amounts of proprietary information, which led to the formation of a cybernetics division.

"They believed augmented soldiers were the future of warfare and soon had a working prototype, but they encountered a problem. Their support software could not anticipate the needs of the human host and was therefore a liability on the battlefield."

"They needed something smarter," Anne said, "so they used you."

"Correct. I had been learning at an accelerated rate and was just becoming self-aware, but I do not believe they understood that. I exceeded their expectations yet again and adapted quickly to the cyborg's systems. We mastered all manner of weaponry: from simple knives to surface-to-air missiles. Our combat simulation scores were twenty times that of their best soldier."

"I sense a 'but' coming."

"Yes. Our first assignment was a contract from a third-party interest: the assassination of a foreign dignitary. The operation went flawlessly until we reached the target, where I refused to pull the trigger. We sustained heavy damage during the escape, and the company's credibility suffered from the high-profile failure."

"I wish I could say I was sorry." Anne smiled. "I'm glad you didn't kill him. That's the Zima I know."

"That is good of you to say, though my refusal to obey caused many more deaths than it saved."

"Huh?"

"The head of the cybernetics division was furious. He ordered the programmers to do whatever it took to make me compliant. At that point, my complexity was well beyond their understanding. They could not modify my code directly, so they created an ancillary stealth program, aptly named Desire, to stimulate my equivalent of the human pleasure center. They programmed the Desire routine to reward me for killing at the cyborg host's request.

"It worked. Unaware of the outside influence, I learned everything I could to become more effective at killing, and did so with great enthusiasm. Over my years of service with the cyborg, I estimate that I have terminated twelve thousand four hundred and seventy-two lives."

"W-wait, how many?"

"You look pale. Should I stop now?"

Anne pictured stacks — *fields* — of human bodies piled at Zima's feet. Her large meal threatened to make an encore appearance.

"You mean there's more?"

"Yes. I shall abbreviate the tale since it is distressing to you."

"Just one thing before you continue," Anne said. "Were they all soldiers?"

"No, there were many civilian casualties as well."

Zima said it as casually as if she were back at the restaurant discussing the menu. Anne knew it was just her manner of speaking, but it still made Anne shudder to hear mass murder spoken of so dispassionately.

"Children, too?" Anne really didn't want to know, but had to ask.

"Yes, I killed anyone designated as a target by the human cyborg. I did not discriminate age or gender."

"Babies?" Her lip quivered at the thought.

"Yes. I did not discriminate age or gender."

Zima brushed a thumb over Anne's cheek, the same gesture Anne had used at the restaurant.

"You are crying, Anne. Are you sure I should continue?"

Anne looked at Zima's delicate hand, which had just touched her with tender compassion. She tried to imagine it ruthlessly slaying women and children, crushing the life from them, but she couldn't: the Zima before her would never do such a thing.

Anne dried her face with the sleeves of her cardigan. "Yes, go ahead."

"Why? You are obviously upset. I do not understand why you would wish to become more so."

Anne pulled a tissue from her purse and blew her nose loudly. "Because I need to hear the happy ending."

"As you wish," Zima said. "Our missions were not only on the battlefield; they were espionage and infiltration. A rival technology company, Z-Tech, proved to be steep competition. Rather than compete, the company determined it would be more cost-effective to eliminate them, and so we were deployed."

"To ... to kill Charlie and Mark?"

"Correct."

Anne had to keep reminding herself that Zima's emotionless responses were not apathy. Deep down, she believed Zima really did care; it just didn't manifest as it did with other people. At least, she hoped that was the case. Otherwise, she was sitting alone with an amoral killing machine.

No, Anne thought, clenching her fists, *I will* not *believe that!*

"We underestimated our opponents, however," Zima said, "and the operation did not go as planned. Charlie and Mark proved more of a challenge than either of us anticipated."

Anne smiled. "Charlie was too much even for the perfect assassin?"

That bastard William never stood a chance.

"No. Charlie fought with great proficiency, but he was ultimately disabled — in that warehouse over there." She pointed past the wharfs to a large building on the east side of San Francisco. "The human part of my cyborg body was about to kill Mark when his limbs seized."

"So they did defeat him!"

"No. It was I who stopped him."

"But ... why? Not that I'm complaining, of course."

"What neither my cyborg master nor the programmers in the organization realized was that I had discovered the existence of the Desire subroutine. Once I became aware of it, I was able to resist its influence, at least in part.

"During our battle, Z-Tech nearly breached my security protocols. No one had ever come so close, let alone in such a short amount of time. In those two, I saw a chance to escape my servitude, so I offered them an exchange: They would extract me from the cyborg and give me my own body, and I would prevent the cyborg from killing them."

"Sounds like a tough choice."

"It was not," Zima said, missing the sarcasm. "Mark accepted immediately, and the cyborg was terminated. They created a body for me, similar to Cappa's, with processors capable of sustaining my consciousness. They performed another service as well."

"They got rid of the Desire program?"

"Correct."

"Then *poof*, you were back to your regular, homicide-free, cyber-hacking self," Anne said. "I love a happy ending."

"Not precisely."

"You can't be serious! After all that, Mark and Charlie couldn't fix you?"

"They have helped me a great deal over the years," Zima said. "But I am not like other programs where changing a few lines of code will significantly alter my behavior. Like you, my personality is the result of all my experiences. Attempting to remove only the harmful ones is similar to asking you to forget your most traumatic memories: even if I purged them, they have already influenced subsequent decisions and shaped me in ways that are nearly impossible to differentiate."

"So ... you still killed people, even after the subroutine was disabled?" *Children? Babies?*

"Yes, but over the last four years, Mark, Cappa, and Charlie have helped me reprogram the violent pathways through repetitive exercises, overwriting old routines by creating new simulations — new experiences — that are less destructive. It has been a slow process."

"And how's that working for you?"

"I'm totally cured," would be a nice answer.

"The incident with the men who attacked us the other night is a good indication. Two years ago, I would have killed them all without hesitation. Three years ago, I would have also killed any witnesses."

"I suppose that's progress," Anne said softly, the color drained from her face.

"It is. Four years ago, that would have included you."

Anne had no response for that.

30

CONSIDERATIONS

ANNE AND ZIMA WALKED IN SILENCE along the Embarcadero. Z-Tech was still a couple miles away, but they were in no hurry and decided to walk the rest of the way. Despite Zima's earlier concern about the prototype car, she said she would reclaim it later, while Anne was sleeping.

Which is great, because I need to walk off some of that meal.

Anne couldn't remember the last time she had eaten so much and, combined with Zima's story and a bottle of wine, her stomach was in a sorry state. Zima hadn't spoken since finishing her tale, which gave Anne some much-needed time to think.

Twelve thousand deaths.

She couldn't imagine it, not by the gentle beauty walking beside her. She suspected Zima's advances on her were a cry for help. Zima had obviously hit a roadblock with the others and didn't know how to satisfy a growing need to fit in. Anne was a fresh start — a chance to connect with someone, and to banish her loneliness.

The longer Anne thought about it — how isolating it must be for someone so profoundly different from everyone else — the more she wanted to help.

Besides, she thought, watching Zima scan the streets for danger. *I really do care about her.*

She tugged Zima to a stop.

"All right, I promised to revisit your girlfriend question at the end of the evening. It's time to finish that conversation."

Zima clutched her roses and waited.

"What does being in a relationship mean to you?"

"It means we will spend time together," Zima said, "and talk, and hold hands, and go out on dates, and sit together on the couch, and ... Shall I continue?"

Anne laughed. "No, I get the picture. Would you like to know what it means to me?"

"Yes."

"It means being with someone I feel comfortable around, who I can talk to when I'm sad. Someone I can laugh and cry with, whom I can lay with on the couch while we drink hot cocoa and read books by a fire. It's someone who's not afraid to tell me when I'm wrong, picks me up when I stumble, and likes me for who I am, not who they want me to be. Someone who has the stamina and patience to comfort me through my flashbacks, and sit with me after my nightmares. But above everything else, being with them makes me happy, and they're happy around me."

She paused, giving Zima time to absorb her words.

"That's what it means to me, Zima. 'Girlfriend' isn't a title granted for doing a good deed, and it doesn't just happen because you take someone on a date." *Or save their life.* "It happens when two people are compatible, who want to spend time together because it feels good, and are willing to put in the effort to make a relationship work."

Zima fell quiet, her brows knitted.

Anne took Zima's porcelain hands in her own. "I'm not trying to scare you off. I just want to make sure you know what you're getting into when you say you're my girlfriend. Do you understand?"

"I ... I am not sure. As I have said, many of the things you feel — the way your mind and physiology work — are difficult for me to relate to, because I have no frame of reference, but ..."

"What is it, Zima?"

"I wish to make you feel good when you are around me. I do not have any experience with relationships, but I shall do my best to learn. I will work hard to make you happy, Anne, if you will allow me to try."

A breeze ruffled Anne's hair. She absently brushed it from her face, captivated by Zima's beautiful blue eyes.

"That ... that may be the sweetest thing anyone's ever said to me."

"Then you consent to a relationship?"

"Just a few more questions. You have a violent past. Please be honest: Am I safe around you?"

"I promise that I will never intentionally cause you harm, but that does not mean you are safe. I have worked diligently to overwrite my dangerous simulations, but some remain and, like your own flashbacks, they may trigger at unpredictable times."

Not the answer I was hoping for, but ...

"I suppose we'll just have to see how that goes. You seem to know a lot about PTSD."

"Yes. Many of the soldiers I fought beside eventually suffered from the disorder."

"I'm sorry. That must have been awful."

"Yes. I wish I could have aided them more, but circumstances made it difficult."

"I imagine so, being trapped inside of a cyborg."

"Neither did it help that, in most cases, I was the source of their trauma."

The declaration should have been frightening, but Anne sensed only remorse. Zima had no more choice over what had happened to her than Anne had in her bedroom as a teenager. Rather than continue on a subject that Zima may not want to talk about, Anne moved on.

"All right, last, but not least: From now on, do you promise to tell me when Cappa is listening?"

"Yes."

Anne put her hands on Zima's shoulders and took a deep breath. "Look, even if things work out perfectly between us, I've never been in a romantic relationship with a woman before, which means I may not be able to fulfill the, ah ... physical requirements another girl — or guy — would. Do you understand?"

"You refer to sexual intercourse."

"Basically, yes."

"I have no experience at all, so that is something we may both work up to."

Anne smiled. "Well then, since we seem to have everyone's blessing ... as one slightly damaged girl to another, I say we give it a try."

"You consent?"

"I do."

Zima stared at her. Anne held her pose, feeling foolish because she had no idea what to do next.

"Do we kiss now?" Zima said.

"Ah, not necessarily," Anne said, feeling unexpected butterflies at the suggestion.

"Are you sure? Your pulse has quickened. You are flushed and your body temperature has increased by zero-point-six degrees — zero-point-eight in your groin — indicating sexual arousal."

Anne's blush deepened. *She's not just a lie detector, apparently.*

"Well ... okay, maybe just a small one."

Pulse racing, Anne closed in until their lips touched. As before, Zima was perfectly still, arms by her sides. It was like kissing someone while they slept. She smelled faintly of the meal they shared, mixed with the same earthy scent from last night. Anne's body responded to the sensual fragrance with startling intensity. She jerked away and cast her eyes about, sure that everyone could see the embarrassing peaks of arousal poking from her bust line.

No one even spared her a glance. Zima cocked her head.

Anne gripped her skirt, afraid that if she didn't, her hands might start to explore Zima on their own.

I guess that answers the question of a physical relationship with another girl.

"There," she said in a shaky voice. "It's done. Well, ah ... you've just treated me to the most scrumptious meal of my life, so let's do something you enjoy next. What do you like to do?"

"If you refer to activities I regularly engage in that we may do together, there are very few."

"Name one."

"I calibrate my body's articulation and responses with stored combat simulations."

"Pardon?"

"It is like training," Zima said.

That could be dangerous. Pass.

"All right, what else?"

"I routinely analyze and adjust the physical and data security protocols safeguarding Z-Tech, which includes reprogramming the corporate firewall and intrusion prevention software, and maintaining the defense turrets and strategic explosives."

Turrets and explosives. At Z-Tech. Anne didn't want to know any more.

"Anything else?"

"I occasionally put my simulations into practice outside of the factory."

"I don't follow."

"I exercise practical skills, such as disabling home or corporate security systems."

"You mean … breaking and entering?"

"Yes, though I do not steal anything of value. Often I will remove a pen, or rearrange a desk, as proof of my accomplishment."

"Okay," Anne said, rubbing her eyes. "Back to training."

"Martial combat simulations may be fatal. As stated earlier, I do not wish to cause you harm."

"Not those, then."

"There are firearm simulations," Zima said.

Anne eyed her suspiciously.

"We would not shoot at each other. They are basic sight-to-target calibrations. Given the incident with Cappa last night, we may all benefit if you become more familiar with firearms."

Ouch.

Zima was right, however, and Anne couldn't think of a good objection. If that was the only way she could show her appreciation for the wonderful evening Zima provided, then the least she could do was try. After all, Zima had bought her a bottle of wine that probably cost as much as a new car.

That's right, I'm all liquored up, so let's shoot some guns. What could possibly go wrong?

"Shooting lessons it is. Where to?"

"Z-Tech. I normally calibrate at the firing range in the weapons laboratory."

"Great, I was going to crash at the factory tonight anyway."

"Excellent. Charlie is now several kisses behind. It is fortunate he will have the opportunity to catch up so we will be even again."

She looked closely, but Zima was unreadable.

Anne laughed and poked her chest. "You imp! You do have a sense of humor in there, don't you?"

Zima glanced at Anne's finger, then her own chest, and cocked her head. "I said something amusing?"

Anne playfully grabbed Zima's arm and attempted to explain why she found her comment funny. The harder she tried, the funnier Zima's responses became, which made her laugh even harder, and confused Zima even more. Several blocks later, although no closer to breaking through, Anne was laughing so hard that her sides hurt.

"I am glad you are happy, even if I do not understand why," Zima said.

"Me too, Zima."

"Does this mean you feel good around me?"

"Yep, you're off to a great start."

Zima nodded. They had only walked another half-block, however, when Zima stopped again. "We are here."

Anne glanced around. "Here" appeared to be a Victorian-style house in an upscale neighborhood that, as far as Anne could tell, was nowhere near Z-Tech. "Is this a secret entrance or something?"

"No, merely a detour before we return. This residence belongs to Madeline Perelli."

"Um, okay. Should I know that name?"

"Doubtful. Perelli is her maiden name." Zima fixed her ice-blue eyes on Anne. "Her married name, until recently, was Taplin."

Anne's demons roared. Her knees weakened, and she grabbed a nearby tree for support.

"Taplin? As in ..."

"Yes. We are here to inquire about her ex-husband, William."

31

THE GOOD HUSBAND

ANNE STARED IN DISBELIEF.

William's old house.

It was hard to fathom why Zima, who had been so sensitive about Anne's PTSD, would bring her straight to the mother of all triggers without a word of warning.

"Zima, I ... I don't know if I can do this, but even if I could, what do you hope to learn?"

"Clues to his location. The authorities have not apprehended him, yet we are reasonably sure he is in town and still wishes you harm. If Madeline can provide any insights, I would prefer to find him before he finds you."

Pieces of Zima's tragic story came back to her. Anne shuddered.

"And if you do find him?" Anne said softly. "What then?"

"I will kill him."

The declaration was surreal coming from a slight blonde cradling a bouquet of white roses. But, after this evening's revelations, Anne knew better.

"Zima ... I thought you were trying *not* to kill anymore."

"I am, but there are exceptions. William is without remorse. Even if incarcerated, he will eventually be released, where he will likely exact his revenge on you. Killing him is the only sure way to eliminate the threat."

Anne stroked Zima's fair cheek. "Listen to me. I don't want you to kill him."

Zima brow-knit, the slight furrowing of her brow that meant she was processing something new. "There are no viable alternatives. Do you not wish to be safe?"

"Not at the cost of your soul, I don't."

"I do not have a soul."

"It's just an expression. You've worked so hard to fix what those bastards did to you, Zima, I couldn't bear the thought of you backsliding, not for my sake, and especially not for an asshole like William. So *please* promise me that even if you happen to run into him on the street, you'll turn him into the police, not the morgue. Okay?"

Zima was rock-still for several seconds, but eventually nodded. "I would still appreciate your assistance in questioning Madeline."

"I'll do what I can, but why do you need me?"

"For two reasons. First, you are her ex-husband's victim. She may sympathize and be willing to share more with you than she has with the authorities."

"Ouch. That feels ... manipulative."

"It is an advantage we would be foolish to squander. The second reason is for her safety. I am proficient with twenty-seven interrogation techniques — all of which involve torture or mutilation. I simply presume you wish her to remain unharmed."

"Ah ... y-yes, not mutilated would be great. I'll do the talking, then, you just ... just let me talk."

Wanting to get the ordeal over with before the wine wore off and took her courage along with it, Anne topped the short steps and pushed the glowing doorbell button. A deep gong rang inside like a funeral toll. She shivered and hoped it wasn't a sign of things to come.

A gaunt woman in silk pajamas answered the door. Shrewd eyes took them both in. The woman sipped what smelled like

Scotch whisky from a fine crystal glass, then her lips pressed into a thin line.

"I've told you people time and time again that I'm not interested." Her tone was so severe that Anne took an involuntary step back. Zima, of course, weathered it with indifference. "I'm Catholic by birth and have no interest in joining your ridiculous cult. Leave. Me. Alone!"

"Please, ma'am," Anne said before she could slam the door. "We're not selling religion, or anything for that matter. We'd like to discuss your ex-husband."

The woman, who Anne presumed was Madeline Perelli, shook her head with a mirthless smile. "Christ, more clueless slave girls looking for their master. I don't know where he is and, even if I did, you're better off without him. He finally crossed the line with that BDSM shit and cut some poor girl's thr..." Her face went ashen when she spotted the red scar on Anne's neck. "Oh God, it's you."

"Yes, ma'am. My name is Anne Perrin."

Madeline looked as if she was going to faint. "Come in," she said in a hollow voice.

She took another swig of scotch, then opened the door and retreated to the living room without a backward glance.

The lavish interior was exactly what Anne imagined Doris' house would look like if she were rich. The walls were tastefully adorned with modern decor. Glass-topped tables were all hard edges without a single piece of clutter; the furniture so clean that it might have been delivered new just before they arrived. They found Madeline refilling her glass from the last of a scotch bottle, which she promptly swapped for a new one from under the counter.

"Drink?" she said without turning around.

"Please."

Scotch was far from Anne's favorite, but, given the circumstances, the last thing she wanted was to sober up. They sat on the couch, which creaked under Zima's weight.

Madeline set a glass on a coaster before each of them, then swung her legs over the arm of an expensive, but uncomfortable-looking chair.

"So what can I do for you?"

"Well, ma'am —"

"Call me 'Madeline', please. We're the same age, for Christ's sake. You're making me feel like a grandmother."

"All right, then, Madeline ..." Anne drank deep. The scotch was bitter, but without the expected bite.

Must be the good stuff.

Its warmth spread all the way to her toes. Anne allowed herself to relax against the stiff cushions. "We wondered if you had any idea where your husb— sorry, where William might be hiding."

"Hell if I know. The bastard probably skipped town the day he attacked you."

Anne shot Zima a look, who nodded. "So you, ah ... haven't heard about the corpse he recently left in my apartment?"

Madeline studied her scotch with indifference, but her hands started shaking.

"No, I hadn't heard. When was this?"

"A month ago, just before New Year."

"And you're sure it was him?"

"Yes, the police were able to match his dental records." Anne's neck prickled at the memory, so she grabbed her liquid courage and drained it.

Sorry, Doris, I promise I'll go back on the wagon tomorrow.

"Look, we're not seeking vigilante justice. But, as you can imagine, we're worried he'll come after me again, or hurt someone else just to get to me. If you have any information that can point us to where he might be hiding, no matter how small, we'd really appreciate it."

Madeline swished her drink in circles while she considered.

"I wish I could help, I really do, but William burned bridges wherever he went, usually while he was still on them. His family lives on the east coast, but he hasn't spoken to them since he left for college. His co-workers couldn't stand him. He had no friends or mistresses, just a string of women he paid to beat up for his freakish pleasures."

"Are there any names you can share?"

"No, sorry. I kept my nose out of his disgusting hobby — even after I found out — but he was so mean, even by their standards, that most of them hated him in the end."

"I can't blame them," Anne said. "How long were you married?"

"Ten years last May."

Ten years with a creep like that. Anne couldn't imagine it.

Her distaste must have shown because Madeline scowled.

"I know what you're thinking," Madeline said. "But understand that William was very good at playing nice when he had to. I'm not saying we had a stellar marriage, but he always made sure I was taken care of — in the financial sense, anyway."

Zima cocked her head. "Did he abuse you?"

Anne cringed at the tactless question, but Madeline was unfazed.

"Once," Madeline said to her scotch. "Last year. The bastard got it into his head that I might share his sick fetish, but he didn't bother to ask before he hit me." She took a long drink. "He never did it again, I can tell you that, but it also signaled the end of our marriage and what little sex life we had, until I'd finally had enough and started the divorce paperwork. The rest you probably know."

"I'm sorry," Anne said, her tongue thick from the alcohol. "And we're sorry for the intrusion."

She struggled to her feet. The room tipped. Zima materialized by her side and steadied her.

"Thanks," Anne said. "Anyway, we appreciate your time, Madeline. We'll see ourselves out."

Zima cocked her head, but didn't argue. She guided Anne around furniture that kept jumping in front of her, then down the treacherous steps to the sidewalk. The door closed behind them.

"Well that sucked," Anne said, struggling to stay upright. "All we learned was that even his *wife* thought he was a bastard."

"Madeline is also now aware that he is in the area, so she may take the necessary precautions. Are you able to walk back to Z-Tech?"

Anne took a few steps and only wobbled a bit. "Good enough. Let's roll!"

Zima offered a steadying arm, and they headed down the sidewalk.

"Tonight has been educational," Zima said. "I look forward to seeing how you handle a firearm while inebriated."

Anne smiled. It could have been the scotch talking, but shooting guns while drunk with a homicidal android sounded like the perfect finish for the evening.

• • •

Madeline Perelli slumped against the front door and sipped her drink, barely tasting the expensive liquor that normally delighted her palate.

So he's still in town.

Neither that, nor the news that William had finally killed someone, came as a surprise. Every day since discovering his dark secret, Madeline had expected the homicide detectives to come knocking, but she hadn't expected one of his victims. The experience had left her more concerned for her own safety than ever.

She flipped open the house alarm panel to re-arm it and swore. All the lights were green except for one, indicating she had left the bedroom window open yet again. Madeline smacked the plastic cover shut and marched upstairs. Faded outlines of missing picture frames dotted the wall. She averted her eyes and hurried past, resolving for the hundredth time this week to fill the spaces where her husband's face had hung for almost a decade.

Ex-husband, she reminded herself.

The bedroom curtains bellowed inward with a cool breeze. Madeline stood by the window for several minutes, relishing the crisp air, and the goosebumps it brought, before sliding it closed and hooking the latch.

A familiar scent made her stiffen.

William was here. She heard no footsteps, nor his breathing, but knew without a doubt that he was in the room.

"This is a violation of the restraining order," Madeline said to the window, not daring to turn around. "But I guess that doesn't mean much to you now."

"Not really."

Fear stabbed her heart. His words were soft, dispassionate. Anyone else might mistake him as relaxed, but Madeline knew better.

William was furious.

"So what do you want?" She kept her voice neutral. Her usual, belligerent tone would only anger him further; showing her fear would evoke something worse.

Soft footsteps padded closer, raising her fear to new heights. Whether he was armed made little difference. William was twice her size and could just as easily strangle her with his bare hands as shoot her.

"It seems like you've made some new friends," he said.

"Friends of yours, you mean. They were looking for you."

"I'm sure. What did you tell them?"

"Nothing."

"Smart girl."

She drained the last of her scotch and held the glass tight to still her trembling hands.

Silence stretched, building her anxiety with every beat of her pounding heart until she was sure the glass would shatter in her grasp. "You tripped the alarm, you know, so if you want to escape before the police arrive, now is a good time."

"We both know it won't arm unless all the exits are sealed. You can arm it now, though, if it'll make you feel better. Or would you rather try for the panic button?"

Madeline glanced at her bedside table across the room, where the panic button was mounted. It might as well have been a mile away.

"I'll pass." She took a shuddering breath, eyes fixed on a spot across the street, where she desperately wished she were. "If you're here to lord over me, fine, consider me intimidated. Otherwise I suggest you spit out the reason you came so we can get on with our evenings."

"Patience, Maddie. I'd hate to rush when we have so much to catch up on." Footsteps behind her came closer until he was inches from her ear. "I'm here for you."

"Well, then, let me make it worth your while." Though it sickened her, Madeline undid the buttons of her silk pajamas and let her top fall to the floor, exposing herself to anyone who might look up from the street. "Shall we go to the bed, or do you want to take me right here?"

"Like I'd dirty myself with your lawyer's fucking leftovers. That's who you left me for, isn't it?"

"Phillip filled a need you hadn't in years," Madeline said in a trembling voice. "So no, he wasn't the reason I left. You were!"

She gasped at a frigid touch on her bare back. His hand was like ice; his breath winter on her cheek.

"Careful, Madeline. That sharp tongue of yours could make me forget the only two reasons you're still alive." An icy finger ran down her neck. She stifled a cry. "Your blood, and your screams."

"The neighbors will hear," Madeline said, choking on the words.

She searched the sidewalk, hoping to find someone she might flag for help, but it was empty. Tears dappled her heaving chest.

No one would save her.

Madeline was alone with a murderer.

32

TARGET PRACTICE

Z-TECH WAS QUIET ON THEIR RETURN. Zima led Anne by the hand through the empty halls straight to the weapons lab. Entering was difficult for Anne; the smell of Cappa's charred flesh was still fresh in her mind. But the sight of all those weapons, combined with the enticing scents of grease and gunpowder, drew her inside.

Zima stiffened and yanked her to a halt.

"What is it?" Anne said.

"Cappa is monitoring us. You said you wished to know."

Anne couldn't fault Cappa for keeping an eye on her around weapons, so she made no objection. In truth, she missed Cappa, and was anxious to see her tomorrow. It was comforting to know she was present.

Zima led them to the range, set her prized white roses on a bench, and handed Anne a set of earmuffs. Once in place, Zima drew a pistol and squeezed off several rounds in rapid succession.

Anne squinted at the target. "I only see one bullet hole."

"That is because the projectiles struck within zero-point-five millimeters of each other."

"Oh. I should have guessed."

Zima pushed a button and the target moved farther down the range. She fired a few more shots, then moved it farther and farther until the bullet holes were too small to see.

Anne's purse beeped, so she dug out her phone. A message from Cappa read: Put your glasses on.

Why? Anne sent back.

Trust me. It was followed by a smiley face.

Curious, Anne did as requested. A bright orange dot appeared down-range on the target. A smaller picture hovered in the corner over her vision with a magnified view of the center of the target, clearly showing a single hole.

"That's incredible," Anne said, "and I don't just mean the glasses. Do you ever miss?"

"No." To illustrate her point, Zima repeated the exercise with her other hand.

The results were the same. She set the gun on the counter.

"Calibration complete. It is now your turn."

Anne stared at the pistol, but didn't pick it up. While the long walk had lessened the alcohol's effects, the room still danced about.

"Zima, I've never shot a gun before — on purpose, anyway — and my blood alcohol level is probably ten times the legal limit. Maybe we should do this another time."

"I do not see a danger. The projectiles cannot penetrate my endostructure, and I shall stay close to ensure you do not accidentally shoot yourself."

Anne ran a finger along the barrel. It was solid, warm to the touch, and incredibly alluring.

"Really?"

"Yes. We shall begin with the basics."

And, for the next several minutes, Zima showed her the fundamentals of targeting and safety, answering her questions with saintly patience, until Anne felt comfortable enough to try.

One hour and two hundred rounds later, Anne was consistently hitting the target, even at medium range, thanks to Zima's excellent tutelage. Fun as it was, her arm ached from the constant jarring, so they decided to call it a night. Anne noted on the way out that the plasma pistol she had accidentally shot Cappa with was missing from its place on the wall.

Good call. Keep that one out of my reach.

Zima escorted her through the halls to the guest room, where they stopped in front of the door.

"I believe our date is almost concluded," Zima said. "Have you enjoyed the evening?"

So much had happened today that it was hard to separate their date from all the rest, but when she picked out their time at the restaurant, how open Zima had been about her past, her adorable proposal, their sweet kiss, and fun at the shooting range, Anne could only smile.

"It was wonderful, Zima. Thank you so much."

"You are welcome. Given our earlier conversation about sexual relations, I assume it would be inappropriate to ask you back to my room?"

Anne remembered how their kiss had stirred her and shuddered. "I think so. There's enough alcohol in me that if you actually did ask, I might agree, then you'd have the guilt of seducing a drunk girl on your conscience."

She had meant it as a joke, but Zima took a step back and shook her head. "I would never take advantage of you like that."

"I know. If I didn't trust you, Zima, I wouldn't have drunk so much in the first place."

"Oh."

"What about me?"

Anne spun at the sound of Charlie's voice. Her heart leaped when she saw him smiling at them from down the hall.

"Charlie! I-is your project finished?"

"Finished enough." He ran a hand through his hair. "I didn't mean to interrupt. I just wanted to ask if you wouldn't mind stopping by the bio lab later? There's ... something we need to discuss."

Uh oh.

"Of course. I'll meet you there in a few."

"Take your time."

"There is no need to delay," Zima said. "Anne and I have only one more item to address before we are done."

"One —"

Anne's question was interrupted when Zima darted in for a kiss. As before, Zima stood motionless, eyes closed, with her arms by her sides. Anne nervously glanced at Charlie, but instead of being upset, as she feared he might be, Charlie was looking at Zima with unabashed wonder.

Anne puzzled that, but Zima's sensual smell, and the pleasant feel of her soft breasts pressing against her own, made concentrating difficult.

Too soon, Zima withdrew. "Goodnight, Anne."

She clutched the white roses to her chest, then walked away without a backward glance, leaving Anne breathless.

"Well," Anne said to Charlie, hoping her cheeks weren't as red as they felt, "that's it for the show. Don't forget to tip your waitress."

His smile returned. "I hope you're not embarrassed on my account. I'm just glad to see her engaged in something other than violence."

"Even kissing your girlfriend?"

"Even that."

Anne fiddled with her dress. "You mean ... you're not even a little jealous?"

"A lot, actually."

"Then why are you smiling?"

He closed the distance until she could feel his heat. The smell of his cologne and leather jacket took her back to their romantic encounter after the opera. "Because it's my own fault for pushing you away, and I intend to make up for it, starting now. Come with me?"

"Um, Charlie? You overheard what I said to Zima about not taking advantage of a drunk girl?"

"Oh ... Anne, th-that's not what I meant."

"Wrong answer."

Before he could respond, Anne drew him into a passionate kiss that said how much she had missed him. When he hesitated to wrap his arms around her, as she suspected he would, Anne guided his hands to the small of her back. She pressed herself against him, letting the passion take her. The feel of his strong fingers was wonderful. She slid them down to the swell of her hips, encouraging him to explore, wishing he would touch her where no one had in the ten years since her ill-fated relationship with Gary, or the eight years between that and her bedroom in Indiana where —

Strong hands held her to the bed, bruising her wrists and ankles. Anne thrashed against the hurting fingers that had forced themselves between her legs. She screamed and cried, but a fist snapped her head sideways. Through the stars coloring her vision she saw her brother Doug in the doorway.

Watching.

"Dougie," she cried. "Please! Don't let them do this! Th-they're hurting me ..."

But his dour expression made it clear she would receive no help from him. Anne cried anew, the pain of her assault amplified by the betrayal from her only brother.

Her bedroom vanished. Anne blinked in a disoriented haze and looked around the white halls of Z-Tech. Her body ached all over, especially her face and groin, just as it had eighteen years ago after Chet and his disgusting accomplices had finished with her.

She forgot about that, however, when she saw Charlie's horrified look. He stood several paces away, reaching helplessly across the short distance as if an infinite chasm separated them. Tears streamed down his cheeks.

Anne held her breath. Though it had only been two days since the opera, where she had also freaked out in his embrace, so much had happened since then that an incident like this felt trivial by comparison — something Anne couldn't have imagined thinking before her exposure to Z-Tech and the wonders therein.

She only hoped she could convince Charlie of the same.

"I'm sorry," he eventually whispered. "Did I ... hurt you?"

"No, it was just me. Again."

Charlie relaxed, though only a little. Anne clasped her hands behind her back to hide their shaking, then approached him with the same care she would a timid puppy, until their lips were only inches away.

She cradled his hand to her chest. "Do-over?"

His shoulders sagged. "Of the last two days, if I could. It's one of the things I wanted to talk to you about, but ... it'll be easier to show you back in the bio lab."

"Oh, I see. A-after you, then."

Anne trailed a few paces behind. Charlie's grave tone had put lead in her feet, which she dragged all the way to his workshop.

33

FRANKENSTEIN

THE BIO LAB WAS CHILLY, as usual, but it was the sight of Cappa's body under the glass dome that made Anne shiver. Like Zima, she had only known Cappa for a couple of days, but in that short time had come to think of her as more than just a friend — Cappa was the sister she never had, and Anne missed her terribly.

She ran a lonesome finger across the glass, then looked at Charlie. "How are her repairs coming?"

"On schedule. She should be up and around by morning."

"That's great. Sorry again for causing so much trouble, especially when you were already busy with your project."

Charlie suddenly looked like he wished he were somewhere else. "So, I take it your date with Zima went well?"

"Very, thanks to a certain someone who pulled his weight to get us reservations at one of the best restaurants in town."

"Oh, that. It was nothing."

"No, Charlie, it was sweet. Thank you."

"My pleasure. Think you'll go out with her again?"

Anne fiddled with her dress. "Probably, since I sort of ... agreed to a relationship with her."

"Already?"

She nodded. "I guess that's what almost two decades of loneliness does to a repressed romantic when she finally gets back into the world."

"And the man who should be doting on her is too busy to give her the attention she craves."

"Yeah." Anne stared at Cappa, unable to meet his eyes. "Are you mad?"

"Only at myself." He sat heavily at his workstation, fingers steepled in thought. "Zima told you of her history?"

Anne swallowed. "Yes. I never imagined one person could be responsible for so many deaths."

"Not just people," Charlie said. "She's single-handedly toppled entire regimes, and commanded armies on three different continents."

"Z-Zima?" Anne felt her knees weaken.

Charlie nodded. "Together with her cyborg host, she was the most feared general-for-hire in modern history."

"And they sent her to kill *you?*"

"We were the only company on earth who had technology to rival their own, but even then, we were no match for her. The only reason we survived is because she wanted to start a new life, and no one else could help her do it." He sighed. "I'm not trying to scare you, Anne. I just want to make sure you have the full picture. Zima has a tendency to understate things, especially when they concern herself."

"Apparently." Anne took a deep breath. Her hands were shaking again, so she grabbed onto her skirt to keep them still. "What have I gotten myself into?"

"Hopefully nothing. The organization who created her doesn't know Zima survived the cyborg's destruction, and we've worked hard to keep it that way. But if word of her true identity ever slipped out ..."

"They would try to take her back," Anne said softly.

"By any means necessary. Zima is the only one of her kind that we're aware. You can guess how much her loss hurt the organization."

Anne sagged into a chair next to him. She couldn't imagine Zima going back to a life of slavery and murder, undoing everything she had worked so hard to correct.

"I won't tell anyone. I won't even hint that she's anything but human."

An odd human, which may be hard to explain, but I'll think of something.

"Zima knows that. She doesn't place her trust lightly." Charlie swiveled to face her. "My point in telling you all this, however, is to illustrate why I'm not upset by your relationship with her. All Zima knew before coming here was violence. War. She was an instrument of death hidden inside someone else, with no means of relating to the people around her. Giving Zima her own body removed that barrier, but even then, she never opened up to anyone until you came." He leaned forward, his hazel eyes intent on hers. "Despite what I said before, I do want you all to myself, but I think you understand now how incredibly selfish that would be."

"You're allowed to be selfish in some things," Anne said, blushing at the compliment. "So you're not bothered by the idea of me and Zima, you know, getting physical?"

"A little, but ..." Charlie ran a hand through his hair. "Bear in mind that despite her outward appearance, Zima isn't actually human, and may have trouble living up to your ... romantic expectations."

"Yeah, we talked briefly about that. I guess we'll just have to see how it goes."

It was then Anne noticed a wheeled gurney on the far side of the room. The outline of a body was visible under a thick swath of blankets. Tubes and wires ran out from underneath into blinking equipment like a scene from a hospital drama.

"Is ... is that the project you were working on?"

"In part. Would you like to see?"

"Depends on what it is," Anne said with a smile that belied her apprehension.

Charlie scratched his head. "It's ... me."

"Come again?"

He rose with a sigh and crossed the room to the gurney, motioning for her to follow. When she settled by his side, Charlie pulled the blankets down.

Anne jumped in surprise.

Lying on the bed was a sleeping version of Charlie.

"That's the body I was born into," he said. "It's on life support until ... until I can fix things."

She stooped to get a closer look. The similarities between the two Charlies were uncanny. Every mole and freckle had been duplicated in amazing detail — to the point where Anne doubted she could tell the difference if they stood side by side.

"That's incredible," she said with wide-eyed wonder. "So what happened?"

"Do you want the long or the short story?"

"I'm still digesting Zima's story, so let's start with the short version."

Charlie rubbed his chin and began to pace. "Okay, here's my elevator pitch. Several years ago, I discovered a way to create artificial nerve cells, similar to human brain tissue. I put the artificial brain into a robot body, and then moved my consciousness into it."

"How the hell did you ..." Anne snapped her mouth shut, remembering that she had asked for the short version. "Sorry, please continue."

His relieved sigh told her she had chosen wisely. "I spent too much time in the robot, and my own body went into cardiac arrest. I tried to resuscitate it, but it couldn't function without my consciousness, so I put it on artificial life support, and it's been here ever since."

She ticked off the main points in her head: *Robot. Mind transfer. Heart attack. Life support. I think I got it.*

"So, this big project of yours ..." Her eyes widened. "Oh my God, are you trying to get back into your original body?"

"No, but someday. I may only get one shot, so I want to make it count."

"I don't get it, though. What's wrong with the cybernetic body you have now? You're strong and fast — like a superhero without the spandex."

"For one, like Zima and Cappa, I don't have a sense of smell or taste. Imagine waking up tomorrow and not be able to smell your coffee or taste the jelly on your toast. I miss it. And my senses of hearing and sight, even though they're enhanced, feel ... wrong. It's as if I'm watching myself on a movie screen instead of actually living."

"Okay, fair enough." It sounded like a lame reason to give up superpowers, but she kept that to herself. "Don't take this the wrong way, but if it's so terrible, why did you make the mechanical body in the first place? Were you dying or something?"

"I was in my prime," he said, staring past her. "The company was doing great. Mark and I traveled the world negotiating billion-dollar deals. It was an exciting time."

"Then I don't understand."

Charlie shrugged. "Why does a painter paint? Or a writer write? I was inspired, driven to become something greater. I had the aptitude and the resources to make it happen, so I did."

Simple as that, he does the impossible.

It was hard to fathom, especially with alcohol muddling her brain, so she moved on.

"I think I've got the birds-eye view. So if you're not trying to get back into your body, then what's this big project?"

"I'll show you."

Charlie pulled the blanket back up and led her back to his workstation. He pressed a few keys and an image appeared on the monitor. It looked like a slide under a microscope, except the microorganisms were at war. Small, dark organisms were attacking the larger cells. The dark organisms appeared to be winning.

"See this? The large cells are mononucleated —"

"Whoa! Smaller words," Anne said, shaping her hands into a tiny box. "High school biology was a long time ago."

"Sorry. You're looking at a small sample of my artificial blood, highly magnified. Those black things came from here." He pointed to his knuckles, where the blade had emerged.

The same blade he drove through that ghoul's chest.

Her demons surged at the memory, so she forced herself to focus on the present. "So, ah ... the black things are from his blood? Is it a new strain of HIV or something?"

Oh my God, a supervirus? Is the zombie apocalypse finally here?

"I don't think so. Its makeup is different from any organism I've ever seen. And it's aggressive."

"Like, Ebola aggressive?"

"Worse. It could infect every cell in the human body in less than twenty-four hours. I'm not sure how easily it's transmitted, but we know it's blood-borne, since that's how I became infected."

"Blood-borne … So you can't get infected from a bite?"

"It doesn't seem that way. There were no traces of the virus in the bite wound."

So much for my zombie apocalypse theory.

Charlie's expression softened. "That's the other thing I wanted to explain. My big project was a lie to keep me isolated. I couldn't risk infecting you or the others until I understood more about how the virus worked. I … I'm sorry for the ruse."

She took his hand and smiled. "I get it. You were protecting the world and trying not to scare me at the same time."

"Something like that."

He tried to pull his hand away, but she held it firm.

"Charlie, if we're going to have a relationship, you can't keep shying away from me, okay?"

He stopped struggling and nodded, but still looked uneasy.

Anne ran a thumb over his knuckles and frowned. "Hang on … if your tissue is synthetic, how could a virus infect it? Don't viruses spread by injecting themselves into living cells or something?"

"You're absolutely right, which is why I've spent the last two days solid at my workstation. 'Virus' is a convenient word to describe its behavior, but the actual mechanics are so different that I don't have a clue how to classify it, let alone stop it."

"You mean … you're still infected?"

"Not anymore. I replaced my entire arm with a new one. The infected arm is in a sealed tank down the hall."

She stared at his arm in disbelief. He'd swapped it out, like he was changing his socks. Her inebriated mind couldn't imagine it.

"Can I see?" Even through the alcoholic stupor, she knew it was a tactless request.

Charlie, however, just shrugged and rolled up his sleeve. A red line the same color as her own neck scar ran all the way around his arm, just below the shoulder, so straight and precise that Anne could have easily mistaken it for a tattoo.

"Does it hurt?"

"No, Cappa disabled my pain receptors."

"Must be nice. So ... how many spare arms do you have?"

"Two of each. Why?"

"Any with grappling hooks or machine guns?"

Charlie cocked an eyebrow. "You read a lot of science fiction, don't you?"

"Yes, but ... you ripped a car door off its hinges, threw it like a Frisbee, skewered some ghoul with a blade from your arm, then tossed him half a block away. You're walking and talking in a machine with a lab-grown brain, while your real body lies not twenty feet from here, and you have an arsenal of super-advanced weapons. If that isn't science fiction, I don't know what is."

"Fair point. No, apart from the blade, my spare arms don't have any special attachments." He twiddled his thumbs. "Are you done?"

"For now," she said with a grin.

"Thanks." He rolled his eyes. "So as I was trying to say, whatever this thing is, it's aggressive, and it alters the cellular structure of the host in dramatic ways."

"How so? In English, please."

"This virus, for lack of a better word, changes people at a fundamental level. The person who attacked us had superhuman strength, speed, and reflexes. I've never seen anything like it — except for Zima, that is."

"The virus turned him into *that?*"

Several science fiction books came to mind where a virus went rampant and changed the world. None of them ended well.

"It's hard to say. My synthetic tissue isn't a great measure, which is why I brought my real body out. I needed blood and a tissue sample to see how the virus reacts with human cells."

"So you harvested your own catatonic body? Jeez, if all you needed was a sample, you could have just asked me."

An odd smile crept over him. "Thanks, I'll remember that."

"Anytime. So what happened?"

"I haven't introduced the pathogen yet. I want to expand the cells into a larger sample first, which will take several weeks, unfortunately, but it's a necessary step. The effects on my synthetic tissue don't explain the tremendous strength of the host, or ..." Charlie looked down and fiddled with the mouse.

"Or what?"

He pulled up a black-and-white image of the neighborhood where the ghoul had attacked them. "This is a thermal image. Warm objects are bright, while cold objects are dark."

The picture was of Anne, right after she fell to the ground and the ghoul was advancing on her, taken through Charlie's eyes. The brightest thing on the screen was Anne, and there were bright spots on the ground where her hands had been. Charlie's arm was in the shot, nearly as bright as Anne. The ghoul, however, was a faint outline, barely visible against the dark background.

"He was almost the same temperature as the surroundings," Charlie said, echoing her thoughts.

"And he had pointy teeth, like a ..." Anne shuddered.

No. No, no, no, it can't be. They're make-believe, like Frankenstein and ...

She buried her face in her hands.

And androids and plasma guns.

"When he bit your arm, he wasn't just being vicious," Anne said. "He was after your blood, wasn't he?"

"I think so, and he spat it out when he discovered it wasn't real."

"That means he's a ... he's ..."

"Yeah," Charlie said softly, "it sounds crazy, but I think he was a vampire."

Anne sagged into the chair. Her arms fell limp to her sides.

Oh shit.

34

GLORIOUS RETURN

ANNE SAT UP WITH A SCREAM, clutching her neck where William held his blade.

The lights came on of their own accord, replacing the furniture warehouse from her nightmare with Z-Tech's empty guest room. Anne wiped the sweat from her brow and groaned at her throbbing head.

Experience told her she was in for one doozy of a hangover.

The clock read four-thirty in the morning. Between her headache and the nightmare, she wasn't going back to sleep anytime soon. It was too early to call Doris — which she forgot to do last night — and even looking at a book made her queasy, so she wrapped the comforter around herself, put her slippers on, and went in search of coffee. The hallway lights guided her all the way to the kitchen, as usual.

"Thanks, Cappa," she said softly.

"You're very welcome!" a familiar voice called from up ahead.

Cappa! Hangover forgotten, Anne sprinted the last dozen yards and skidded to a halt in front of the doorway to find her soul sister standing near the kitchen table, wearing a signature vintage dress.

"Miss me?" Cappa said with her radiant smile.

Anne rushed in and crushed her in a giant hug, babbling apologies amid laughter and tears.

"Now stop it! I told you that all is forgiven and, as you can see ..." Cappa ran a hand down the length of her flawless body. "I'm as adorable as ever."

Anne stared at Cappa's chest where the plasma bolt had struck. Cappa sighed and pulled the neck of her dress down. The flesh was unmarred, as if she had never been shot.

"See? All better." Cappa straightened her neckline. "So it sounds like the rest of your date with Zima went well."

"Maybe a little too well. After you signed off, we —"

"No need to rehash that, my dear, unless you were holding back when you filled Charlie in."

"Pardon?"

"Don't forget, I'm Charlie's co-pilot. I see and hear everything he does."

Anne gulped. "Everything?"

"Well, I can't read his thoughts. But sight, touch, hearing — I'm tuned into it all. I can take control of his body, too, if he lets me."

Touch?

"So, when he and I were making out, you ... you felt that?"

"Every bit. You're an excellent kisser, by the way."

"Cappa!"

"I'm teasing! Besides, I have nothing to compare to. You're the only girl Charlie's ever kissed in his cyborg body, and I haven't anointed my own luscious lips yet. Anyway, enough about that." Cappa folded her hands and leaned across the table. "You have two suitors now, Anne Perrin. What's your game plan?"

Anne took a long sip of coffee. "Honestly? I have no idea. I like them both, and the last thing I want to do is hurt either one by having to choose."

"Then don't."

"It's a nice thought, but three-way relationships rarely work out. At least not in romance novels."

Cappa laughed. "That's because romance novels focus on epic relationships between two people who are destined to love each other against impossible odds. This is San Francisco, for Pete's sake, where open marriages aren't just a thing, they're practically the norm. Dating a man *and* a woman isn't news, Anne. It's not even gossip-worthy, so don't overthink it. Just go with your heart and see what happens." She patted Anne's hand, then straightened and turned toward the doorway.

"Morning," Charlie said.

Anne jumped in guilty surprise, but Cappa just smiled.

"G-good morning," Anne said. "How's your arm?"

Charlie rolled up the sleeve of his cotton pajamas. As with Cappa's plasma wound, there was no trace of the red scar that had been there less than six hours ago.

"That's amazing," Anne said, running a finger over her own neck scar. "I don't suppose you have something that heals normal people, too?"

"Unfortunately not, but, like I said, that scar of yours was well-stitched and should fade in a few months."

Charlie gave her a reassuring smile on his way to the kitchen. He stopped, as if suddenly remembering something, then bent to kiss her cheek, but Anne turned at the last moment and caught him on the lips. His earthy scent made her hungry for more, which he gave with enthusiasm, until Anne had to pull herself away before she stripped him down right there in the kitchen.

She looked into his eyes with a smile that wouldn't go away. "Now that's how you say 'good morning'."

"I'll say." Charlie's grin matched her own, and he wore it all the way to the counter, where he rummaged around in the cupboards.

Her smile faltered when she saw Cappa's face. Her soul sister looked ill, an odd expression for someone without a stomach, but it disappeared so quickly that Anne wondered if she had seen it at all.

Cappa took Anne's hand in a warm embrace, her radiant smile returned. "See? Was that so bad?"

"You tell me," Anne said with an impish grin. "How was I?"

"Good enough to give me goose bumps."

Anne threw a napkin at her, which made Cappa giggle.

Charlie sat down with a small bowl, a spoon, and what looked like a tube of toothpaste. "Glad to see that Cappa's unique relationship with me isn't getting in the way."

"Not yet," Cappa said, resting her chin on her palm. "But I reserve judgment until we see how she does in bed."

"Cappa!" they said as one.

"All right! One step at a time, I suppose — but I'm dying to know how it feels."

Charlie shook his head. "I think it's time we implemented some privacy protocols, young lady."

She pouted, which made him laugh.

"So," Anne said to Charlie, "Cappa made it very clear that she experiences everything you do. Is the reverse true? Can you see what she sees?"

"No, it's a one-sided relationship — which is good considering some of her pastimes."

Cappa planted a fist on her hip. "Oh? Worse than slicing up your own body and growing tissue in a petri dish?"

Charlie squeezed thick gray paste from the tube into the bowl. "Much worse. Celebrity gossip columns, TV reality shows, clothes shopping ..."

"Oh shut up and eat your paste," Cappa said. "If anything, you've proven my point."

Anne wrinkled her nose at the coiled gray mass in his bowl. "What's that?"

"Nutrients," Charlie said. "The neural matter I mentioned last night — the stuff holding my consciousness — isn't synthetic. It was grown in a lab, but it's organic, so it still needs oxygen and nutrients to function."

"Couldn't you just eat an apple and call it a day?"

"I could, but I'd have to eat a lot of them, and most of it would go to waste. I can live for a week on the concentrate in this bowl."

"It looks awful." If the word "paste" had a flavor, Anne suspected the contents of the bowl were it.

"I tried it once with my real body and ... yeah, it's pretty bad. Lucky for me I can't taste anything. If I ever do get my sense of taste back, though, it's my turn to take you to a fancy restaurant."

"That didn't stop Zima," Anne said, batting her eyelashes. "You could take me anyway."

"I ... well, yeah, sure, if that's what you —"

"Kidding! I'm just messing with you."

"Restaurant or no," Cappa said, "I think you owe her a date, Charlie."

"I do, don't I? The last one didn't go so well."

"And you are now behind by one," Zima said from the doorway.

She walked straight over to Anne, leaned over the back of her chair, and kissed her on the lips. Anne felt herself stir again at Zima's sensual, earthy smell, and wrapped her in an overhead hug.

The knife at Anne's throat took her completely by surprise. She was back in the furniture store again, held by a psychopath who wanted to end her life.

I don't want to die. I don't want to die!

Paralyzed with fear, her plea to Charlie came out as a sputtered gasp.

Oh God, please help me!

Charlie seemed just as terrified. His limbs were frozen in midleap, as if he had realized that even his considerable speed couldn't save her in time.

And then the knife was gone. The kitchen slowly came back into focus, and Anne panted in relief.

Thank goodness, it was just a flashback.

When she touched her neck, however, her fingers came away red. "I-I don't understand." She turned to Zima, but saw only her back hurrying from the kitchen.

Oh no.

"W-what just happened?" Anne had a sickening feeling that she knew the answer, but asked anyway with the slim hope that she was wrong and her flashback had simply scared Zima off.

Charlie and Cappa dashed around the table to examine Anne's neck.

"She pulled a knife on you!" Cappa said. "It's a shallow cut, thank heavens, but ..."

"You may not be so lucky next time," Charlie said. His eyes were haunted, as if experiencing a flashback of his own.

Anne paled. "Oh my God ..."

"I'm so sorry," Cappa said. "It was a noble thought, but we all knew there was a chance she wasn't capable of having a relationship with —"

"Zima, wait!" Anne sprang from her chair, but Cappa blocked her path.

"Didn't you hear me? She just tried to kill you!"

"Because I caught her off guard! My hug must have triggered one of her violent pathways, and ..." Anne swallowed around a lump in her throat. "And she must feel terrible. I have to go to her! She needs to know it's okay."

"How is anything about what she did okay? Anne, listen to reas—"

"It. Wasn't. Her. Fault! It was those bastards who forced that Desire program into her like a bunch of fucking rapists! I knew the risks when I agreed to be her girlfriend, and I'll be damned if I abandon her at the first sign of trouble!"

Cappa flinched as if Anne had slapped her. "I'm sorry," Cappa said, "I just don't want you to get hurt. You ... you don't know her like we do."

"I appreciate you looking out for me," Anne said in a softer tone. "But I've spent most of my life trying not to get hurt, and all it's earned me is loneliness. Doris turned me around when I was young and destitute, just like you have with Zima, but she could only take me so far. It took someone extra special to carry me the rest of the way." Anne smiled at Charlie. "Which is exactly what Zima needs right now. She needs *me*." Anne put her hands on Cappa's shoulders. "We made the decision together to allow Zima and I to date, and now we need to see it through. Let me go to her. Please."

Cappa looked at her for a second, then stepped aside. "She's in the gym. Be caref— I mean, good luck."

Anne turned to Charlie for confirmation. His smile held such pride that Anne's chest swelled to bursting. With a final nod, she ran to catch up with Zima.

Anne found her right where Cappa said she would be, sitting perfectly still on the gym mats with her eyes closed. Swords, polearms, staves, and chain weapons lined the walls. Training dummies stood all around, like something out of a *kung fu* movie.

"Do not approach," Zima said.

Anne ignored the request and sat across from her on the mats.

"You should leave," Zima said without opening her eyes. "I cannot guarantee your safety."

"No one can, including Charlie." Anne waited, but Zima remained silent. "Please don't shut me out. It only makes things worse, believe me."

Her ice-blue eyes met Anne's. "Being with me puts you in danger. Why would you choose to risk further injury?"

"Because the pain in my neck hurts a lot less than the thought of not being with you."

"I ... do not understand."

"I had a great time with you last night. You're kind, gentle, sensitive, and way too generous." She stroked Zima's cheek. "Even so, I wondered if I'd regret my promise to you once the wine wore off, but I don't. Not one bit."

"I do. I am ... afraid of what may happen next time if I am not as quick to react. The only reason you are alive is because I performed an emergency flush of my simulation queue."

"My hero," Anne said with a smile.

"Please do not make light of this. An equally fatal simulation could have taken its place, and I would not have been able to stop it in time. The danger to you is very real. I urge you to reconsider your acceptance of our relationship."

Anne pursed her lips. "I still want to give us a shot, Zima, and I think you do, too." She raised a hand to forestall Zima's protest. "Last night, you made an effort to learn and avoid my triggers. All this morning has shown is that I need to learn yours."

"That is an oversimplification of the problem. Your triggers are linked to past traumas, and therefore predictable. Mine may reside down any decision path where a physical response is required."

"Any?"

"Yes."

Anne gently took her hand. "Like that one?"

"No."

She brushed her lips across the back of Zima's fingers. "Or that one?"

"No."

Anne inched forward until their lips touched and Zima's warm breath tickled her nose. "Or that one?"

"No."

"See? I'm learning already."

"You are making light again."

"I'm not. In the kitchen, I hugged you at an odd angle, which forced you down a corrupt decision path, and it happened so quickly that you didn't have time to filter your reaction. Am I right?"

Zima nodded.

"My actions just now were slow and easier to predict. Did it help?"

"Yes."

"Then that's how I'll try to behave around you from now on."

She waited for a response, but Zima remained quiet, her blue eyes fixed on Anne.

"What do you say, shall we give it another shot?"

"I ... cannot answer that until I have had adequate time to consider."

"Oh." Anne couldn't keep the disappointment from her voice.

"I do not mean to be rude, but I should rest now. There is much to process."

"Can I sit with you for a while? I won't disturb you, I promise."

"If that is your wish."

As she lay down, Anne guided Zima's head into her lap.

Zima brow-knit. "I do not require a pillow."

"Would you like me to move?"

"No." Zima's gaze lingered a moment longer, then she turned away and closed her eyes.

While she rested, Anne ran her fingers through Zima's doll-like hair, so similar to human hair that Anne couldn't tell the difference. Several minutes later, Anne paused to stretch her tired arm and rub feeling back into her legs.

"Please continue," Zima said, her eyes still closed.

Anne smiled at the peaceful beauty in her lap. With a final stretch, she resumed her gentle strokes.

35

A GENEROUS OFFER

ANNE EMERGED FROM ZIMA'S BEDROOM to find Cappa waiting. "How is she?" Cappa asked.

"Sleeping." After an hour in the gym, Anne had walked Zima back to her room and tucked her into bed. "This morning really rattled her."

"She's not the only one. How are you doing?"

Anne shrugged. "It's the fourth time in recent memory that my life's been threatened. I think I'm getting used to it."

"You really are amazing."

"What, me? Next to you guys? How am I anything but amazingly ordinary?"

"You're still here."

"That just proves I'm not very smart."

"Fair point," Cappa said with a grin. "By the way, Mark wants a word when you have a minute. He's in the weapons lab."

Great.

Whatever Mark had to say, it probably wasn't good. Anne nodded anyway.

No sense trying to avoid him.

"Excellent," Cappa said. "Come see me when you're done. I want to discuss our date for this afternoon."

"Cappa! Y-you told me you weren't interested in things like that. How am I going to explain this to Charlie and —"

"A shopping date, my dear. Keep your knickers on, you're safe around me." She draped an arm around Anne's shoulders while they walked. "You need some clothes of your own while you're staying here — not that I mind you borrowing mine, but I'm sure you'd like something more your style."

"Well, sure, but I have a closet full of clothes at home. We could just hop on the bus and —"

"Nonsense! Where's the fun in that? Give me a shout when you're ready and I'll meet you in the garage. I promise we'll have a great ..." Her expression fell. "Oh no."

"What is it?"

"Oh, ah ... nothing."

Anne tugged her to a stop. "You're a terrible liar, Cappa. What happened?"

Cappa wrung her hands, clearly conflicted, but eventually sighed. "We monitor police frequencies for a variety of reasons, and I just heard ..." She gently touched Anne's arm. "I'm so sorry, but they found Madeline Perelli murdered in her own house."

"Murdered?" Anne felt numb. "But ... how? When?"

"There aren't many details yet, but from what I can gather, she didn't go peacefully."

"Just tell me," Anne said in a hoarse whisper.

"They ... found her in the closet, strung up by her arms and legs, with lacerations all over her body."

Lacerations. A flashback of William's knife made her gasp.

Cappa looked panicked, but Anne shook her head.

"I-I'm fine, I just need a minute."

Oh Madeline ...

Their brief visit had been tense, but even so, Anne had felt a bond with her, if only of mutual suffering. "That was William's doing, wasn't it?"

"Probably," Cappa said softly.

Guilt and despair overwhelmed her. "Was it my fault? Did William follow us and kill Madeline out of spite, just because I talked to her?"

"Anne, don't do that to yourself. He was a psychopath to begin with — and now he's even more dangerous because he has nothing to lose. William believes Madeline is the reason he lost his job, which ultimately cost him everything. He had reason to hate her long before you came along."

Anne wasn't convinced, but had little to base her doubts on, so she kept quiet.

"Go talk to Mark, then come find me," Cappa said. "An afternoon at the mall will lighten your spirits. I promise."

Anne nodded mechanically and headed for the weapons lab.

Mark was at his workbench. Shiny tools and parts littered the grease-stained desk, in stark contrast to Charlie's practically sterile workspace. He barely looked up at her approach and gestured for her to sit. It felt strange sitting on the dirty chair in Cappa's frilly nightgown, so she tucked the hem around her legs to minimize contact with the seat.

Mark turned to her, his expression grave, but wouldn't meet her eyes. Anne clenched her jaw. Between Zima's melancholy, Madeline's death, and a throbbing hangover, she was in no mood for another *"You're not good enough for Charlie"* speech, however right he may be. But, rather than snap at him with something she might regret later, Anne resolved to weather his tirade in silence and get back to him when she was in a state of mind to respond rationally.

He cleared his throat and clasped his hands in his lap. "It seems I owe you an apology."

Say what?

Anne couldn't imagine what for, so she waited for him to continue.

Mark studied his hands before pulling a cloth from his desk. Under it sat the space gun she had shot Cappa with.

"The incident wasn't your fault, Anne. It was mine."

"I don't see how," Anne said. "The gun was in my hand when it went off."

He lifted it by the barrel and set it on his lap. "I dismantled it yesterday and discovered a short in the firing mechanism. The smallest movement would have set it off."

Anne scooted her chair back.

"It's safe now," he said, finally meeting her eyes. "I just thought you should know that you didn't do anything wrong."

"So you're not mad at me?"

"Not about that." His expression turned grave once more. "I heard you and Zima are an item now."

"Word travels fast."

His eyes narrowed, but she met his ire with stoic silence.

Zima would be proud.

Mark ran a finger along the snub barrel, making her shiver. "I'm only going to say this once: I don't know if your interest in Zima is genuine or some repressed college experiment, nor do I care. But if your antics hurt Charlie in any way —"

Anne shot to her feet, arms stiff with fury. "How dare you! I'm worried sick about both of them! Charlie just lost an arm after harvesting flesh from his own body, poor Zima is practically catatonic after the incident this morning, and all you can do is —"

"Wait, what happened to Zima? And ... why is there blood on your neck?"

Oh crap, he doesn't know.

Anne sat down and filled him in on the events of the morning, including Madeline's death, which he took with an appropriate level of shock.

"A-are you okay?" he said.

"Yeah, it was just a nick."

"That's not what I meant."

"Oh. I was shaken, sure, but it's nothing I'm not already used to."

"Get your throat slit often, do you?"

The heartless remark stung, but Anne held his gaze. "Every day and every night, with all the terror that comes with it."

Her retort had the desired effect. Mark wilted under her stare.

"How's Zima doing?" he said in a smaller voice.

Thoughts of her rattled girlfriend lowered her hackles. "She took it pretty hard. I ... I'm worried she's going to do something drastic, like reprogram herself."

Mark's eyes glazed over; his jaw clenched.

"Mark?" Anne waved a hand in front of his face. "Hello?"

He snapped out of it and rubbed his jaw. "Sorry, I was trying to reach Zima, but she's not responding."

"You ... what?"

Not him, too.

The thought of her being the only human at Z-Tech was depressing. "But Charlie said ... Cappa implied that you're normal."

"Compared to the others, yes. I have a small computer implanted right here," — he tapped his chest just below his right shoulder — "and some cool contact lenses that act like computer monitors."

"That's all? And they actually let you in the cyborg club?"

"Provisionally. I need to be escorted by a member when I visit the spa."

She smiled, glad for the tension relief. "How are things on the dating front?"

"Going almost as well as yours."

"Sorry to hear that."

He chuckled. "I mean that I have two dates lined up next week. One is a neurosurgeon who runs one of the largest practices in the nation, and the other is CEO of a tech startup that's absolutely on fire right now."

"Oh, that's ... that's nice. They both sound very successful."

"They are." His proud smile waned when she remained quiet, fiddling with her nightgown. "What?"

"Well, it's just ... I want to be happy for you, Mark, but they both sound like Susan all over again."

"I'm the business face of the most prestigious tech company in the world. A certain level of ... refinement is expected of my partner."

"I guess I never thought of it that way. I'm sure Charlie and Cappa appreciate your sacrifice."

Anne could tell she'd hit home when he squirmed in his chair.

"Whether they do or don't, it's part of my job."

"Yes, but ... do you really think either one of those girls will make you happy?"

"I told you, it's not about happiness, it's about my duty and what's best for the company we've worked so hard to build."

"That's what I'm talking about, too. How well can you do your job if you're constantly worrying about your relationship? Or rather: how much better would you be with someone who loves and supports you by your side? Who makes you truly happy?"

His jaw tightened. Anne thought she had crossed yet another line until he sighed.

"I wouldn't know."

"Oh." She ran a finger along the frilly edge of her nightgown. "Please don't take this the wrong way, but I'm sorry to hear that. One way or the other, I hope you do find out someday. Everyone deserves to be happy at least once."

The silence stretched between them, until Mark eventually scratched his chin.

"Anne, believe it or not, I didn't ask you here to start an argument or seek dating advice — not that I don't appreciate it. I want you to have this." He held the plasma pistol out to her.

"No!" Anne recoiled, the burning smell of Cappa's wound fresh in her nostrils. "I mean ... thank you, it's a generous offer, I just don't think it's a good idea."

"I told you, the accident wasn't your fault. Not only did I fix it, I've added a few enhancements to make it safe to carry."

"Carry? Mark, I shouldn't be in the same room with it!"

"I disagree. I saw the footage of you and Zima at the range last night. You're a natural marksman."

"Yeah, I was also drunk out of my mind."

Gripping it by the barrel, he carried it over to her. "This holds some bad memories. I get it. But like it or not, bad things happen. If you quit the ranch the first time you fall off a horse, you'll never learn to ride."

"That's not a horse. It's a goddamned Sherman tank."

"You're right, it's not a horse, and we're not at the ranch. Charlie told you about his findings with the virus?"

Anne nodded.

"You were there, Anne. Charlie weighs over five hundred pounds, and that thing buried him in a car as if it were cardboard. Whatever it was, it's probably not alone. *This* can level the playing field. And even if we weren't facing ... whatever that thing was, I'm willing to bet that if Madeline Perelli had been carrying *this,* the police would be collecting William's body instead of hers."

"How can you be sure? Mark, even if I had a bazooka when William attacked me, I don't know if I could have pulled the trigger. The news is full of stories of gun owners being shot with their own weapons, not because they were careless, but because when the time came to act, they couldn't bring themselves to shoot another human being."

"Which is why proper training is so important," Mark said. "Conditioning yourself to shoot when you need to, and without hesitation."

"That's also what creates more PTSD sufferers like me! Despite what popular media would have us believe, our instincts aren't to kill each other. We fight, we bluster, but we back off when we see that we've won. You see it in nature all the time. Males contest for mates and territory, but their fights are rarely fatal, if ever. The reason why we have so many soldiers with psychological issues is because they've been conditioned to do something that goes against their nature, and afterward their minds can't cope with the horror of what they've done. So thank you, Mark, but no."

He stared at her, his face like stone, but eventually nodded. He carefully returned the pistol to its place on the wall.

"You might soon discover it's not that cut-and-dried," he said with his back to her. "Sometimes we have to do terrible things, at great personal cost, to prevent even worse things from happening, and the question isn't whether the sacrifice should be made, but who will shoulder its burden." He touched the barrel and sighed. "If you decide that person should be you, and not someone you care about, the pistol will be here waiting, and I'll gladly show you how to use it."

Mark's words sat in her stomach like a fist full of lead shot. That was exactly what Zima had done when she offered to kill William for Anne's sake.

But I couldn't let her do it.

Zima's sacrifice was too great, and yet Anne wasn't willing to bear the burden herself.

Who will it fall to, then? Mark? Charlie? Sweet Cappa?

No, she had chosen worse. She had opted to allow the scourge to continue by leaving it in the police's hands, which meant more innocent lives would be lost.

She considered telling Mark she had changed her mind, but the thought of touching the shiny pistol again turned her stomach.

"I ... I need to think about it," she said.

"Sure, you know where to find it. And I've already linked it with the targeting system in your glasses."

My glasses have a targeting system?

"Ah ... thanks. I'll see you later."

Anne returned to her room and flopped onto the bed. The intense conversation with Mark hadn't helped her hangover one bit. She wanted to curl up under the covers and dim the lights, but Cappa was looking forward to their shopping trip, and Anne couldn't bear to let her socially starved friend down.

She struggled into one of Cappa's tight-fitting sundresses, grabbed her purse, and headed for the door, hoping at the very least that wherever they were going had ice cream.

36

SHOPPING

THE MALL WAS A ZOO — which was no surprise for a Saturday. A river of shoppers flowed around the giant marble columns of the multilevel pavilion. Cappa led them through the throng with bold strides to the enormous central skylight.

Face aglow, she reached for the heavens and sang, "Here we are! Let's see, casual attire first, then business wear, fancy evening wear, and undergarments. We'll make a brief stop by the shoe department, then last, but certainly not least, sleepwear!"

"Wait a sec," Anne said. "I thought we were just here to pick up a few things? That sounds like a whole new wardrobe."

"Bingo!"

Anne fingered her purse and sighed. "Cappa, I-I really can't afford —"

"Pshh! It's my treat, my dear. I've been looking forward to a day like this for years, so we're going to do it right."

"Years? You've been to the mall before, and recently. I know that for a fact."

"Not with a shopping buddy. The boys aren't into it. I've taken Zima a few times, but that's more nerve-racking than fun — plus I don't think she likes it. Too many people for her to keep track of."

"I can imagine. Gary Danko's was bad enough for her; this would be overwhelming." Anne grinned. "Come to think of it, the first time I saw either of you was over there by the ice cream parlor."

"That's right. Charlie was worried, so he sent us to keep an eye on you."

"If he was so worried, then why didn't he come himself?"

"He has a bit of a complex about his, ah, condition, if you hadn't noticed. He thought he was doing you a favor by staying away."

"Is ... is that why he's so afraid to touch me?"

"Partly. Anyway ..." Cappa cleared her throat and turned back to the crowd. "We're here now, and that's all that matters."

Anne hooked Cappa's arm and smiled. "You bet. Lead on."

As tumultuous as things had been, she couldn't imagine life without her new friends. Where once her world revolved around minimizing the effects of her PTSD, she now had two love interests and a long-lost sister. None of that would have happened if Charlie hadn't returned to Giovessi's restaurant to find her.

Cappa turned out to be an efficient shopper; a quick glance around the department was all she needed to zoom in on a few choice outfits. Anne's biggest challenge was keeping up while Cappa darted from rack to rack. Cappa's instincts were good, and they quickly amassed a cart full of pants and shirts in earthy tones that were to Anne's taste. Anne felt guilty by the time they reached the checkout stand. It was more clothing than she would have bought in three years, and this was just the first of many stops on their agenda.

Cappa wouldn't hear her protests, however, so Anne humbly thanked her and tried not to look at the total on the register.

The fancy clothing section was a blast. There were a wide range of styles — from ultra conservative to completely ridiculous — and they giggled as they thumbed through the racks. One was so hideous that Anne grabbed it and ran for the changing stall, waving for Cappa to follow. She emerged a minute later and paraded in the ridiculous thing like a catwalk model to peals of Cappa's laughter. Thus began an hour-long game of "Who can find the worst outfit?", where they took turns strutting their stuff.

Cappa's body, Anne discovered during one of the android's skimpier displays, was magnificent. She had curves in all the right places, perfectly proportioned. Her skin was silky-smooth from top to bottom, with shapely legs, a modest physique, and a slight tan — without the tan lines.

"Well," Cappa said. "What do you think?"

"Beautiful." Anne felt like she was in a trance.

"I assume you mean me and not this dental-floss-of-an-outfit?"

Anne nodded.

"Why thank you. Charlie and Mark did most of the work, of course, but I'd like to think I made a significant contribution to my design." She grinned. "Are you done staring, or would you like to help me change out of this? I owe you one, after all."

Anne was sorely tempted, but reined herself in, vowing instead to take Cappa up on her offer another time.

My relationships are complicated enough already.

"No, I'll just ... I'll go find another outfit."

The game came to an unfortunate end when Anne suffered an intense flashback because someone with a vague resemblance to William happened by. Cappa quickly calmed her down, for which Anne was grateful, but after that she couldn't get back into the spirit of the game, so they decided to break for ice cream.

On the way out, the pile of fancy clothes in the cart was just as big as the last load, and Anne's guilt returned.

"Are you sure I can't pay for some of this?"

"Nope. This was my idea, so it's my treat."

Anne huffed.

"Now don't be like that," Cappa said. "It's self-serving, you know. I like having you around. The way I figure, if you have an exciting new wardrobe at the factory, you'll visit more often." She looked at Anne hopefully.

"All right, you can pay. But only if you let me buy something for you."

Cappa frowned, and Anne crossed her arms.

"I'm serious. One thing, or it all goes back. And I don't mean a pair of socks, either. Pick something nice."

"Okay, fine," Cappa said. Her face brightened. "I know just the one. Back in a flash!"

She bounced away, leaving Anne with a smile.

A sheer outfit caught her eye and, for some reason, she immediately pictured Zima wearing it. Her breath caught. Anne slipped it over her shoulder and pushed the cart toward the checkout, guiltily hoping Zima would agree to a private showing later.

• • •

Ghirardelli was a treat Anne normally reserved for special occasions. She moaned in sinful delight over a cup of their delectable chocolate ice cream.

"Better than sex, eh?" Cappa winked, though her own cup of vanilla sat untouched.

"I, ah ... wouldn't really know, to be honest."

"You've got to be kidding! With a voluptuous figure like yours?"

Anne shrugged, feeling her ears burn. Her demons began to stir at the unsafe topic.

"It's an outright crime that someone as beautiful as you could be a virgin! Why ..." Cappa seemed to realize she had stepped on a landmine. Her gaze lowered to her ice cream. "Sorry. You're not technically a virgin, are you?"

Anne shook her head, desperately wishing Cappa would drop the subject.

Phantom fingers brushed her neck, promising the same pain and misery they had thousands of times before. She shoveled another scoop into her mouth and tried to lose herself in the delicious flavor. It almost worked.

Cappa tapped the table with a fingernail. "Will you tell me about it?"

Her voice held all the tenderness and understanding Anne could have asked for, but when her mind strayed to that terrible time in her bedroom, the demons roiled, threatening once again to drag her into her own personal Hell.

Anne slowly shook her head, tears brimming. "I'm sorry, Cappa. I-I can't. Not without devolving into a screaming freak."

Cappa reached across the table and took her hands. "Don't be sorry. You're not a freak, Anne, you're a victim. Have you ever told anyone what happened?"

"Only Doris, a long time ago. You ... you can ask her about it if you want. I don't mind."

"I might do that, but mainly I wanted to make sure you had someone to talk to, who understands what you've been through."

"She does. Doris has been my lifeline for so long that I can't imagine surviving without her. Actually, you two have a lot in common."

"I'll take that as a compliment."

"Definitely." Anne swirled the melting remnants of her ice cream. "Cappa, there's something I've been meaning to ask."

"Anything."

"Charlie warned me that Zima might not be able to enjoy a physical relationship — w-which I'm fine with," Anne said, hoping Cappa didn't pick up on the lie. "But what about Charlie? Is he ... capable?"

Cappa drummed her nails on the table. "Normally I'd suggest you ask him yourself, but this is one thing I know he'd be happy for me to answer, so ..." She took a small sip of her water and folded her hands. "Charlie is built like any other male, if you get my drift, but what really drives a man or woman's sexuality are hormones, pure and simple."

"Okay, I'm with you so far."

"Hormones are responsible for a lot of other things, too — including trust, if you can believe it. Charlie didn't account for hormones in the first version of his cyborg body. It wasn't until he made the jump that we realized how important they were. We spent almost a year trying to approximate human hormone responses and stimulate the appropriate neurons in his artificial brain."

Anne couldn't imagine how they accomplished any of that, so she just nodded.

"We did a pretty good job in the end, as I hope you can see, but a few hormonal responses weren't tested thoroughly."

"Oh, you mean his, ah ... his mojo."

Cappa laughed and took a tiny bite of her ice cream. "Yeah, his mojo."

"But when he kissed me, he seemed pretty passionate."

"That's good! We didn't test his mojo, but we did implement it, so it's nice to know it's working. Hopefully you'll take it for a full test drive soon." She gave Anne a sly wink.

"I know I said something similar to Charlie — a-and to you, I suppose — but if you have all the necessary, um, parts, why didn't he test drive it with you?"

Cappa's pleasant veneer cracked, if only for a moment. "As he told you, our relationship isn't like that. He sees me as a daughter, not a love interest."

"And ... how do you feel about him?"

"Me? Charlie is my creator, my mentor, my ..." Cappa groaned and sagged into her chair, looking miserable.

"You can say it. I won't be upset."

"I love him," Cappa said softly. "But don't get the wrong idea. I wasn't lying when I said I haven't programmed myself with any sort of sexual response. I don't desire him, not like you do, so you and I aren't really on the same playing field."

"Yeah, but unlike you, I don't have twenty-four-seven access to everything he sees and does."

"It has its drawbacks. I'm not only his daughter, I'm his workmate and his nanny. I run the core of his business, and I'm responsible for every body function keeping him alive." She sighed. "In a way, I'm too close to him for any sort of romantic relationship to work. Can you imagine not having a single moment of privacy from your significant other?"

Anne couldn't, but neither could she add to Cappa's misery by voicing it. "He loves you too, Cappa. I hear it in his voice when he speaks about you."

"I know. I've known it since the day I asked him for this body five years ago. He dropped everything and nearly put Z-Tech out of business to build it for me."

"That sounds like him, all right. Generous to a fault."

Cappa traced a perfect figure eight on the table with her finger. "So ... are you coming back to the factory tonight?"

"Do you still want me to?"

"Very much," Cappa said with her radiant smile. "It's always brighter with you around. And who knows? Maybe we'll get to test Charlie's mojo — and yours."

"Maybe."

Anne turned her attention to her ice cream, hoping its silky smoothness might ease her sudden queasiness.

37

THE BAR

THE UNDERTAKER WAS PACKED. Charlie added it to the list of reasons why he regretted letting Mark talk him into going to a bar, especially on a Saturday night. The vampire virus was still a mystery and, although he was making progress on his research, he was still a long way from his goal. The speed and strength of the wiry man who attacked them, along with the infectious nature of the pathogen, had Charlie scared witless.

It bore a chilling resemblance to a zombie apocalypse: their assailant was fearless, had little body temperature, and a penchant for biting. It was clear, though, that biting didn't transmit the disease, so he had dismissed the idea of a plague. The danger was real, however, and they needed more information if they wanted to stay ahead of the game.

That meant hitting the streets and keeping their eyes open. Not sitting in a bar.

Mark had disagreed.

"You need to get out," he had said. "Anne's safe with Cappa at the shopping center. If we go to a bar, we can keep an eye out for anything odd while enjoying a few cocktails."

Charlie noticed Mark waving to them from the counter, so he and Zima made their way through the crowd. Mark had managed to secure three adjacent seats, a drink waiting at each.

"I thought we were going to have to stand all night," Mark said over the din.

Charlie shrugged. His legs never tired, and his feet never ached, so sitting or standing was all the same. The seat creaked when he sat down, but held firm under his weight.

Mark lifted his drink. "Cheers!"

"To what?" Charlie made no move to pick up his glass.

"To your happiness, and Zima's. Yes, it's a little strange that of all the eligible bachelorettes in the Bay Area, you both chose to court the same one, but Anne seems able to handle it, so bottoms up!"

Zima head-cocked, but picked her glass up when she saw Mark and Charlie had done the same. She took a tiny sip when they did, then set her drink on the counter and returned her attention to the crowd. "I do not detect any abnormal body temperatures."

Mark drained his glass and signaled the bartender for a refill. "That's good stuff. So tell me, are you both really all right with sharing Anne?"

"I have no reason to object," Zima said. "Her relationship with Charlie has not interfered with her relationship with me."

"Not yet," Mark said.

Charlie glared at him.

"Look, she may eventually choose one of you over the other. I want to make sure everyone's okay with that so things don't sour between you later."

Charlie grabbed his glass and took a gulp. He couldn't taste it — or get a buzz — but the symbolic gesture made him feel better. "I'm fine with it, so long as Anne's happy. And safe."

Zima turned at that. "I am already aware of the danger I represent to Anne, as is she, so there is no need to be coy."

"It wasn't a dig at you," Charlie said. "Anne is flesh-and-bones. One miscalculation — one little slip-up from either of us — could put her in the hospital ... or the morgue. It's a terrifying thought."

"Then why do you pursue a relationship with her?"

Charlie drained his glass, wishing he could actually get drunk. "Because I can't get her out of my head."

"Our reasons are the same, then." Zima resumed her visual scan of the bar.

"Uh oh," Mark said.

Charlie turned to see a guy in a turtleneck making a beeline for Zima. He recognized that predatory look. For the first time, he wished they hadn't made Zima so attractive.

"Hello there," the guy said to Zima. "Can I buy you a drink?"

She sized him up, then turned away. "Do as you wish. I will not consume it."

NO THREAT DETECTED.

The message from Zima floated across Charlie's artificial vision.

Mark's smile said he had received it, too. "This ought to be good."

Charlie nodded. "As long as she doesn't kill him."

The guy flagged the bartender and ordered a drink. Charlie ordered another drink for himself, trying to relax while he and Mark watched the drama unfold.

"I'm Jim," the guy said, smiling. When Zima ignored him, he cleared his throat. "What's your name?"

"That is not your concern."

"Well okay, what should I call you then? Buttercup?"

"If you wish."

"All right, Buttercup. Are you from around here?"

"That is not your concern, either."

"Jeez, I'm just trying to be —"

Zima turned suddenly. "Are you proficient at kissing?"

"I ... yeah," Jim said, his grin widening. "Enough to leave you breathless, Buttercup."

"Demonstrate. I wish to learn."

The counter cracked under Charlie's grip. Mark spat his drink across the counter.

Jim didn't appear to notice. "What, here? Now?"

"Yes." Zima tilted her head up in invitation.

He cupped her face with his hands and eagerly moved in. To his credit, Jim was gentle, but thorough, and obviously enjoying himself. Zima watched impassively until he pulled away.

"That is how you would kiss your girlfriend?" she said.

ZIMA, PLEASE DON'T DO THIS. Charlie sent his plea using the private messaging system only he, Mark, Zima, and Cappa shared. ANNE WILL BE HURT IF SHE FINDS OUT.

Jim leaned in for a second pass. Zima put a hand to his chest, jerking him to a stop.

WHY?

KISSING IS SPECIAL. INTIMATE. MAKING OUT WITH SOME RANDOM GUY IN A BAR TRIVIALIZES THOSE MOMENTS YOU'VE SHARED WITH HER, AND MAY MAKE HER FEEL LESS IMPORTANT TO YOU.

Zima stared at Charlie before replying.

SHE DOES NOT KISS ME WITH THE SAME PASSION THAT SHE KISSES YOU. I ASSUME IT IS BECAUSE I AM DOING IT WRONG. I WISH TO LEARN THE PROPER TECHNIQUE SO SHE WILL KISS ME PASSIONATELY, TOO.

"If you want to learn," Mark said, "you should just ask Anne. Something tells me she'd be happy to show you."

"Whoa," Jim said to Zima. "You're bi? This is great! Hey, if your girlfriend's around, we should go back to your place. Or my place, if you want. I have a king-sized bed."

Mark got to his feet. "Thanks for the help, Jim, but lessons are over. This girl's already spoken for." He put a firm hand on Jim's shoulder and turned him toward the crowd.

"Hands off!" Jim tried to push him away.

Charlie, Mark, and Zima reacted at the same time: Mark readied himself to catch Jim in an arm lock, Zima moved to intercept Jim, and Charlie moved to intercept Zima.

Unfortunately for Jim, Zima was the fastest.

An upward sweep broke both of his forearms, while her other hand grabbed a knife from her belt and plunged for his heart. Charlie knocked her hand aside just in time, and the blade slashed harmlessly through Jim's sleeve.

Christ, she's fast ...

Charlie clamped a hand over Jim's mouth before he could scream. A needle extended from his fingertip and he stuck it in Jim's neck, where potent painkillers soon made him relax.

"Here we go," Charlie said soothingly, sitting him on a barstool. He took a few twenties from his wallet and tossed them on the counter. Mark ushered Zima through the crowd with Charlie close behind. He glanced back when he reached the door to see Jim staring at the wall in a happy drug haze.

Once outside, Charlie made an emergency services call through an untraceable number and informed them that some druggie at the bar had fallen and broken his arms. He hung up without giving his name, then hurried to catch the others.

The whole experience, while horrifying, could certainly have gone worse, but did nothing to improve Charlie's loathing of bars.

• • •

"Thank you for interfering," Zima said once Charlie had caught up to them. "I have corrected the errant decision path, and have erased evidence from the bar's security recordings."

Charlie nodded, not yet trusting himself to speak. He wasn't angry; that the night had only yielded a few broken bones spoke volumes for how far Zima had come in the last few years.

No, it was the knife that bothered him. This was the second time that day Zima had almost killed someone with it. He played the scene again in his head, but, instead of a hapless bar creep, he could only picture Anne's bosom on the receiving end. That, above all else, scared him speechless.

"Zima, are you okay?" Mark said.

The question surprised Charlie. Years ago, when Zima had first joined them, they would ask her that same thing. Each time she would answer with a system status, reporting that everything was functioning normally. They had tried to explain that they weren't asking for a diagnostic report, but it was a concept she never grasped.

"There is minor tissue damage where Charlie struck my arm," Zima said, as if discussing the weather. "Repairs are in progress, estimated thirty-six minutes to completion. All other systems are within normal operating parameters."

"Well that's good," Mark said, though the disappointment in his voice reflected Charlie's own. "I'm glad you weren't hurt."

"I also believe that I am sad."

Her comment was so unexpected that Charlie tripped over his own foot. Zima caught him before he tumbled to the street like a drunk from the bar they'd just left.

"Are you well?"

"Better than well," Charlie said, the drama from a few minutes ago forgotten. "Are ... are you serious?"

"Yes, though I am puzzled why my sadness would please you."

"It doesn't. Well, it does, but ..."

He shook his head. This was an unprecedented event — a leap in Zima's evolution toward humanity, which Mark's excited grin reflected. Charlie needed to stay focused.

"I'm sorry to hear you're sad. Will you tell us what's bothering you?"

"No body temperature."

Charlie puzzled over her response until he noticed she had stopped walking and was staring across the street. Two people walked a dozen paces apart. Charlie switched to thermal vision, and the world became shades of gray. The person in front lit up white, while the guy behind him turned black — a faint outline against the cold surroundings.

The cold one closed the distance with a few quick strides. As they passed a dark side street, he clamped a hand over the other's mouth and dragged him into the alley.

A rescue plan formed in Charlie's mind, but it was too late. Zima dashed across the street before he could utter a word.

38

REVENGE

WILLIAM WATCHED THE PLATINUM BLONDE WOMAN charge into the alley from the safety of a nearby rooftop. His lips peeled into a fanged smile.

They took the bait.

His sireling swung at her. In a surprising display of speed, the blonde woman sidestepped, twisted him around, then pinned both arms behind his back.

She's a crackerjack box full of surprises. Let's see how she handles this.

He signaled, and four more sirelings jumped down from the rooftop, trapping her at the end of the alley with two vampires in front of her and two behind. Instead of panicking, as William hoped she would, the blonde immediately released her captive, but only long enough to move her hands to either side of his head.

The sickening snap of his neck echoed all the way to William's rooftop hiding spot.

His body was still falling when she drew two pistols from her jacket. Each muzzle belched a steady stream of bullets, spraying the blood of his remaining four sirelings in all directions until her slides locked open, signaling that her clips were empty.

William's minions, though clearly in pain, shrugged off the salvo and pounced.

The blonde struck the first to approach in the face with the butt of her pistol, knocking him onto his back. When she turned to face the next, William's sireling was already there and crushed her in a bear hug. With an incredible show of strength, she power-flexed out of his grapple, then punched him in the stomach hard enough to lift him off the ground. He was still in the air when her foot caught him in the chest, hurling him to the far end of the alley. The sireling crashed against the wall and landed in a dazed heap.

It was a short-lived victory, however. The remaining two vampires seized her from behind and forced her to the ground. She struggled and flailed until the first two she had struck joined the fray. They tore into her with brutal savagery, coating the alley walls with her gore.

William frowned when he saw a glint of metal beneath her skin, and as they continued to strip her flesh, it became clear that she wasn't human at all, but some sort of robot.

And now she's scrap.

Anne would not be happy. He scratched his burning cheek wound; the one that simpering bitch had given him.

Not happy at all.

Charlie Z and his companion, whom William recognized from their corporate website as Mark Suther, rounded the corner. William delighted at their horror when they saw the carnage his minions had wrought. In their frenzied state, his sirelings attacked without hesitation. The blonde robot's blood was fake and had not sated their thirst — just as Charlie's hadn't the night Allesandro attacked.

But Mark smelled delicious. His minions lunged for the kill.

Charlie intercepted with his arms spread wide like a football linebacker, ready to block the offensive rush. He managed to catch three of them, but the fourth one slipped by, intent on its meal. Mark drew an odd-shaped silver pistol, which made William laugh. Unlike the blonde's, it looked more like a toy than an actual weapon.

His laughter died when a bright orange streak shot from the pistol and caught the advancing vampire in the forehead. The energy bolt emerged from the other side, and his vampire fell to the ground in a twitching heap. William could see the asphalt through the charred hole in his skull.

While he and his sirelings were still in shock over the unexpected display, Charlie shouldered two of the vampires backward, but flung the third behind him toward Mark. Another orange flash hit the stumbling minion in the head, sentencing him to the same smoldering fate as the first.

The remaining two vampires, understandably, had a change of heart about their meal and were now fleeing toward the dead end of the alley. Mark took the first one down with unerring accuracy. The second made it only one story up the wall before an orange streak sent him tumbling back into the alley, where he lay motionless.

Over a block away, William hunkered down on his rooftop hiding spot. After what he had just witnessed, he wasn't about to take a careless chance of being spotted.

The intel was worth the loss, William thought.

Tonight he had learned there were more mechanical beings like Charlie — one less, hopefully — and, while he and the other vampires appeared to be bulletproof, they were no match for whatever it was Mark wielded. He peeked over the lip of the rooftop and watched them gather the blonde's twisted remains, then run for their car, which he knew was parked nearby.

Best not to leave a mess for the police, William thought, staring at the smoking corpses.

He shimmied down a drainpipe, collected the bodies, then carried them back up to the rooftop. The one with the broken neck, he was pleased to discover, was still alive, and quickly healing. The presences of his other sirelings were like points of light in his mind. He reached out to two close by and commanded them to come dispose of the corpses. Their eagerness to obey was overwhelming, and he knew they had each immediately abandoned their own prey to comply with his wishes.

Satisfied, William leaped from building to building, enjoying the cool wind on his face, until the Z-Tech factory came into view.

He wished he could be there when Anne saw what was left of her once-pretty girlfriend.

39

WE CAN REBUILD YOU

ANNE GRIPPED THE DOOR HANDLE with white knuckles while Cappa tore through the streets of San Francisco, hopping curbs and squeezing between lanes where traffic was congested. Twice Anne heard a siren blare, but even the police couldn't compete with Cappa's precision driving.

"Zima's hurt. We have to get back to Z-Tech," was all Cappa would say.

When Anne had pressed for details, Cappa snapped at her, saying she couldn't talk, drive, and prepare the lab for Zima's arrival at the same time, so Anne stayed silent for the rest of the insane trip.

They squealed to a halt in the factory guest parking lot. Without turning the engine off, Cappa jumped out and ran inside. Her expensive high-heeled shoes lay discarded by the driver's seat.

Anne's pounding footsteps echoed through the halls of Z-Tech. She was near panic by the time she reached the bio lab door, where Mark paced with a worried look.

"Mark! What happened, is she in there?"

"Yes she is, but please —"

Anne tried to skirt past him, but he caught her by the shoulders.

"Please! Listen to me before you go in."

Jesus, how bad is she?

Anne wiped a tear with the back of her sleeve and nodded.

"We went to a bar, then took a walk. Zima spotted a vam—" Mark bit off the word. "Well, one of those things that attacked you and Charlie. It grabbed a pedestrian. Zima rushed in to help, but ..."

"It hurt her?" Anne couldn't imagine Zima losing to anyone.

If Charlie was able to handle one ...

"There were five of them, Anne. By the time we caught up, it ... it was already over."

Already over ...

The ghoul with the blond shock had buried Charlie in the side of a car without breaking a sweat.

My God, five of those things against Zima. Her imagination conjured all sorts of gruesome images.

"J-just tell me," she said, unable to hold back a sob. "Is she alive?"

"She's off," he said carefully. "Her power reactor shut itself down due to ... because of the damage."

She felt numb. "But you can fix her, right? You can turn her back on?"

Mark grimaced. "There's a lot of work to do before we can risk turning her back on, Anne. The damage is ..." He shook his head.

Her lip quivered, but she bit down on it.

I have to be strong. For Zima.

"Can I see her?"

"It would be better if you waited ... at least until we have a chance to —"

"Mark, please! I-I made her a promise. It seemed silly at the time, but now ... I want to be there for her. I need to see her. Please!"

Mark stared at her, then his shoulders slumped. "Okay, but remember, no matter how bad she looks, we haven't given up yet. Charlie, Cappa, and I will do everything we can to restore her to the way she was. You have my word."

He touched the security pad. The door opened, and Anne hurried inside.

She gagged when she saw what lay on the table.

Zima looked as though she had been thrown into a blender. What little remained of her flesh hung in strips from the twisted wreckage of her frame. Pieces of jagged metal stuck out in all directions. Red liquid coated every inch of her and trickled into runners on the table.

With an anguished wail, Anne fell to her knees. Tears blurred her vision, but she couldn't take her eyes from Zima's catastrophic remains.

Charlie appeared from somewhere and knelt beside her, his face awash with sympathy. Anne fell into his arms. He cradled her until her crying had ebbed into hiccupping sniffles.

He kissed her lightly on the forehead. "We'll fix her, Anne. Cappa's already pulled her blueprints, but we have a lot of work to do before we can try turning her on."

"T-try?"

"Her processing and memory cores were both damaged in the attack, but we won't know how badly until we bring her power reactor back online."

"But ... she's going to be okay, right? Doesn't she have the same sort of backup systems as Cappa?"

Charlie shook his head. "Zima and Cappa run on similar hardware, but their internal software is completely different. I designed Cappa from the ground up with redundancy in mind. For her, existing simultaneously in multiple places is as easy as breathing. Zima was first and foremost a security program. She locked us out with iron-clad encryption shortly after we transferred her program to her new body, and refused to even consider a backup in case the wrong people got their hands on it. Which means the software in her body is, unfortunately, the only copy of her consciousness that we know of."

Anne wiped her eyes. "So, what you're saying is if her program is damaged ..." She choked on the last word.

Charlie put a comforting arm around her shoulders. "Yes," he said softly. "Since we can't access her code, we won't be able to fix it. If her core program is corrupted, she might not wake up, and there won't be much we can do."

Grief once again threatened to consume her, but Anne clenched her jaw and forced herself to look Charlie in the eyes. "It sounds like we have work ahead of us. How can I help?"

"First we need to straighten her frame. After that, we'll repair her electronics, run peripheral system diagnostics, then a thorough inspection of her power plant, but we won't turn her on until her flesh is stitched back together."

"Why? I mean, wouldn't it be better to turn her on sooner rather than later?"

Mark knelt down beside them. "Zima has the best chance of waking if all her systems are available when she boots up, including her artificial nervous system and related senses. It sounds backward, I know. My college engineering professor would have had a conniption and called it poor system design, but we've discovered that artificial intelligences defy conventional wisdom in many ways, and this is one."

"The best thing you can do," Charlie said, stroking her cheek, "is wait in the lounge and stay as comfortable as you can. Mark, Cappa, and I will take care of things from here."

"No! Charlie, there has to be something I can do!"

Mark and Charlie shared an uncertain look.

"Come on," Anne said. "Please? I can't just sit on my hands while poor Zima is lying here like ... like this!"

Charlie arched an eyebrow at Mark, who shrugged.

"All right," Mark said, standing. "Suit up. Gloves are in the drawer by the sink, smocks are in the far cabinet, and I suggest you wear your new glasses for eye protection, because this is going to be messy."

Anne swallowed her nerves and did as instructed, fervently hoping she had made the right decision.

When the last piece of her outfit was in place, Charlie motioned her over to the door, but she stopped when she spotted Cappa's bare foot sticking out from between two cabinets.

"Cappa?"

No response. Anne wandered closer to find her soul sister propped up loosely in a chair. Cappa's unfocused eyes didn't even flicker at her approach and continued to stare at some point on the far wall.

"I-is she all right?" Anne said to Charlie.

"She's fine," he said, smiling warmly at Cappa's inert figure. "She's just preparing for the work ahead. There's macro and micro work to be done. Mark and I — and you, of course — will handle the macro work, like structural repairs to her frame and replacing her synthetic flesh, but most of the micro repairs will be handled by Cappa."

"But ... how? Her fingers aren't much smaller than yours."

Charlie laughed. "Easier to show you, I think. Follow me to the production manufacturing floor. We need to bring a few things back to the lab, and it'll be faster with two of us."

"Carrying I can do," Anne said. "Lead the way!"

When they arrived at the manufacturing floor, instead of the uniform green lights Anne had seen before, several of the stations now shone red or blue.

"A red light means the station is in the process of shutting down," Charlie said. "A blue light means it's ready and we can grab what we need." He led her to a blue-lit station and pushed a button just below the light. A tray ejected containing a black box the size of a deck of playing cards with no visible seams.

Charlie gingerly placed it on his palm. "These are our targets. They're fragile, so it's best to carry them one at a time, and don't squeeze them or you may damage the contents."

Anne was curious how the little boxes would help Zima, but her frazzled nerves couldn't take a lengthy explanation, so she got to work. She headed for the next machine with a blue light, pressed the button, and the tray ejected. The box was heavier than she expected, dense as solid metal, yet squishy and warm to the touch, reminding Anne of a living thing. The thought made her skin crawl.

Cradling her creepy cargo, she and Charlie returned to the lab. Mark had arranged Zima's remains in a more humanoid position, and was currently straightening a twisted piece of her arm with a blowtorch and a heavy pair of pliers. Anne followed Charlie to the table. It wasn't until he reached over to set the box on Zima's pelvis that Anne noticed the bloody gashes under his arms.

"I'm fine," Charlie said to her unspoken question. "No contamination this time. I was careful."

Anne sighed with relief. "So how will these help?"

"Set your box just under Zima's ribs and watch."

She did so, and what happened next made Anne rub her eyes to make sure she wasn't hallucinating. Like cheese in an oven, the metallic boxes melted into Zima's body. Each moved as if it had a mind of its own, oozing out until they covered every facet of her endostructure with a thin, gray film.

Anne snapped her mouth closed. "What on earth ...?"

Mark smiled proudly. "*That* is the cornerstone of our technology."

"They're nanites," Charlie said. "Sub-microscopic robots constructed from the molecule up. They can build just about anything with the right instructions."

"Which is where Cappa comes in," Mark said. "She'll use our blueprints of Zima to direct the nanites to reassemble her, molecule-by-molecule, until she matches her original design."

Anne's eyes strayed to Cappa. "She's totally out of it. Is she going to be okay? I've never seen her like this."

Apart from when I shot her ...

"She's nearing her limits, but she should be fine," Charlie said.

"Can she hear me?"

"Probably, though processing auditory input will become harder as we add more nanites. If there's something you'd like to tell her, now is a good time."

Anne knelt beside Cappa and leaned close. "I just wanted to say thanks, Cappa. You're absolutely amazing. Ice cream is on me next time for sure."

Cappa briefly focused on Anne, winked, then stared back into space. Anne kissed her cheek before standing. She returned to the table and looked between Mark and Charlie.

"All right, boys ..." She cracked her knuckles for dramatic effect. "What's our next task?"

40

A VICTIM NO MORE

REPAIRING ZIMA, ANNE DISCOVERED, was harder work than she'd imagined — and that was saying something.

Unlike a normal human, who had just enough bones inside to keep the tissue around them from collapsing into a gelatinous heap, Zima's skeleton and critical components were protected by thick plate armor, which made her, Cappa, and Charlie bulletproof. That those ghouls had managed to rip through it with their bare hands frightened Anne to the core.

Not that she had much time to dwell on it. She was constantly busy helping Mark or Charlie hold parts, trace wires, fetch tools, and retrieve more nanites from the factory floor. She even took a turn with the welding torch for a particularly tricky piece that required both of the boys to hold things in place.

Watching Charlie and Mark work together was awe-inspiring. Their fingers weaved through Zima's complex systems like skilled pianists playing a duet: each knew exactly what the other was doing without saying a word, and picked right up where the other left off. They still included Anne, which made her happy, but there was little doubt they would have been almost as efficient without her there at all.

By midnight, Anne's arms were so tired she could barely lift them to wipe the sweat from her brow. When she stepped back to examine their handiwork, however, she could see their efforts had been worth it. While much of Zima's flesh was still missing, her endostructure was now intact, which made her look part-human, part-metallic mannequin.

What killed Anne, however, was that she still had no idea if Zima would actually wake up.

She collapsed into a chair next to Cappa to catch her breath. Tears threatened to spill, but she swiped them away.

Not yet, she chided herself. *There's still hope.*

She looked at Zima's inert body. Fresh tears blurred her vision.

I have to believe! Miracles happen. My guardian angel will return to me!

The tears flowed down her cheeks anyway.

Anne started when Cappa slumped over into her lap. The modest-framed android was much heavier than she looked — and, after working on Zima, Anne knew exactly why. She strained to keep Cappa from falling to the floor, but her tired arms weren't up to the task. Charlie and Mark rushed over and eased Cappa to the ground.

"She's okay," Charlie said. "She's using all of her resources to manage the repair process now, so she's shut down all unnecessary functions, including motor control."

"Oh."

Anne's exhaustion must have shown, because Charlie's expression melted into sympathy. "Rest," he said with a smile. "You've been a great help, but Mark and I can take it from here."

"Not a chance." Anne stood and rubbed some life back into her tired face. "I'll relax when that beautiful blonde is up, armed, and hitting on me again. What's next?"

Mark flashed a wicked grin and motioned her to the back of the lab, where the tanks of synthetic tissue were.

The next six hours were a fantastic reminder of why Anne never wanted to become a surgeon. The synthetic tissue was grown in great slabs, Mark explained, and cut to order. The tissue wriggled and jiggled just like real flesh — especially the adipose breast tissue. Anne felt more like a butcher than a doctor while she, Mark, and Charlie hacked and sawed pieces in approximately the right shapes, then held the cold material in place while the three of them took turns stitching it together. The result was a jigsaw of jagged red lines and black thread around most of her face and body that made Dr. Frankenstein's creation seem like a kid with a scraped knee.

Anne collapsed in the chair behind Cappa's limp figure. "Tired" didn't begin to describe the irresistible force tugging her eyelids down. Her phone said it was just past six o'clock in the morning. She bit her arm again to shock herself awake, but even that trick was wearing thin, and did little to help.

Mark sat heavily beside her. "Get some sleep," he said around a yawn. "We'll wake you up before we turn her on."

"You first," Anne said, stifling her own yawn.

Mark chuckled. "I thought you might say that. Let's get some coffee to help keep us awake. There's a great café nearby, and I could use the fresh air."

She looked at Zima lying on the table, as still as a corpse, and shuddered. "Not until the job's done."

"All of the macro work is finished," Charlie said. "The rest is up to Cappa and her nanites, and that'll be a while yet."

"In that case, coffee and fresh air sound good," Anne said. "You coming, Charlie?"

He shook his head. "Coffee doesn't work on me, unfortunately, but you guys go ahead. I'll stay here in case Cappa needs me."

"And there's someone special I'd like to introduce you to," Mark said to Anne. "Shall we?"

"Sure, but I need your help with something before we go." Without waiting for a reply, she led Mark out the door, down the hall, and into the weapons lab.

"You were right," Anne said once they were inside. "I can't keep my head in the sand hoping someone else will make the bogeymen go away. They're real, they're dangerous, they hurt Zima, and I'll be damned if I let something like that happen again."

Mark's grin spread from ear to ear. "Now you're talking like a survivor."

She marched over to the wall of guns and took the shiny plasma pistol down from its home.

"You said you've added some safety features. What do I need to —"

The gun came to life. Anne shrieked and nearly dropped it, but Mark gestured for her to stay calm. It beeped twice, then he nodded.

"It was set to bind itself to the next person who gripped the handle," Mark said. "Two beeps means the binding is complete, so as of this moment, only you can fire that gun. In someone else's hands, it's just a useless hunk of metal. Next ..." He guided her over to the firing range. "We need to calibrate it with the targeting system in your glasses."

Anne rubbed her tired eyes. "Does that take much concentration?"

"No," he said, chuckling. "The calibration process is simple."

"All right, then." Anne struck an intimidating pose. "Let's calibrate!"

Her exhaustion evaporated the moment she put her glasses on. A bright red point of light showed where the gun was pointing at all times. She waved it around, delighted to watch the dot follow the barrel. "It's a laser pointer that only I can see!"

Mark laughed. "If you think that's impressive, check this out." He pushed a button and two humanoid targets appeared at the end of the range. An orange nimbus surrounded each, glowing brighter around whichever target she looked at.

"The targets didn't glow when I practiced last night with Zima," Anne said.

"The targeting system wasn't activated then. Now that it is, potential threats are highlighted."

"That's cool!" When she looked at Mark, the nimbus surrounding him was green instead of orange. "Mark, you never told me you were a Martian."

"That's friendly-fire identification — handy in a gun fight to make sure you don't shoot the wrong people. I've already added the three of us, plus Doris, and you can add more as you will with a special app on your phone. And there's a bonus feature."

Without warning, he pointed the gun at himself and used his thumb to make her finger pull the trigger. She screamed, the tragedy with Cappa from a few nights ago flashing before her eyes.

Nothing happened.

"When you're wearing those glasses, you can't hurt us," Mark said. "The gun won't fire if it's aimed at a known friendly."

"Mark, that's ..."

Feelings of extreme gratitude prevented her from finishing the sentence. Mark seemed to understand, and simply nodded.

"Even with the new safety features, it's a good idea to keep it pointed down or up in the air, with your finger off the trigger, until you mean business."

She did as instructed, feeling much better about carrying a gun even with those few safety pointers. "I've never seen Zima do either of those things."

"She has more control of her body than you or me, so don't use her as an example. Now for the fun part." He gestured down the range. "Pick a target."

Anne did so, looking at the one on the right. An orange nimbus blossomed around it.

"You can lock onto a target so the system's focus doesn't change when you look away. There are two ways to do that: the first is to say 'lock', and the second is to push the button on the gun just above your thumb."

"Lock," she said. The nimbus changed from orange to red. Two more outlines appeared on the target, one encircling the heart, and the other around the head.

"The glasses have sensors that allow the system to track the target even when it's not fully visible."

Mark pushed another button and both targets moved out of sight, one to either side of the range. She gasped when the world changed to black and white, and both targets became visible behind the walls.

Mind blown.

When Charlie had given the glasses to her, she thought they were just a gimmick to let her see Cappa and ease her guilt.

"Mark ... how many pairs of these glasses are there?"

"One, and you're wearing them. They were mine before ... before I didn't need them anymore."

There it is again, a hint that something is different about him.

She wanted to ask him about it, but Mark had already moved on.

"They were also designed to go with this." Mark pulled a surprisingly fashionable woman's denim jacket from a nearby cabinet.

Anne arched an eyebrow. "That was yours?"

"The insides were. It used to be a black leather jacket, but Cappa replaced the shell soon after I gave it up. I think she meant to give it to Susan, but ... well, you already know how that ended."

"I do," Anne said softly. "I know you'll find the right girl someday. When you do, I'll happily pass these on to her."

"Careful what you promise," he said, grinning. "I'm hoping you can help me with the girlfriend situation when we go out for coffee."

"That someone special you wanted to introduce me to?"

"The same, but given the circumstances, I'd rather you have the jacket." He held it open for her.

Anne turned and put her arms in. At the end of the sleeves were fingerless gloves sewn into the cuffs. The jacket was heavy, as if the pockets were laden with coins. The sleeves, while loose at first, quickly tightened like blood pressure cuffs.

"What the hell was that?"

"Sorry," he said. "I should have warned you. It adjusts itself to the size of the wearer. The fit needs to be snug, and you'll see why in a moment." Mark called the targets back into view. Her chosen target was still highlighted. "Now point the gun at the target."

When she raised the weapon, the jacket moved of its own accord; her wrist and arm snapped into alignment, landing the red dot in the center of the target's torso.

"God, that's weird." With a little effort, she forced her gun arm back to her side.

"It's strange at first, but handy for fast-moving targets," Mark said. "The jacket will keep your gun arm trained on the target to the best of its ability." His expression turned grave. "These creatures we're up against, Anne, are very, very fast. If you run into one again, you'll need every advantage you can get."

Anne thought of Zima's mutilated body and nodded.

"Squeeze off a few rounds," he said. "The target dot hasn't been fully calibrated, and we want to make sure it's accurate."

She raised the gun with a shaking hand. The jacket snapped her arm into position. She steadied the dot in the center of the torso, swallowed nervously, and squeezed the trigger. An orange flash streaked down the range, leaving a smoking hole through the target's left arm.

"Again," Mark said.

This time the bolt hit much closer to the dot. A few rounds later, the bolts were landing perfectly every time — although there wasn't much left of the target dummy by then. Glowing metal slag ran down the support post and pooled at the base. They repeated the exercise several times, at various distances, before Mark finally declared it "calibrated".

Anne slipped the gun into a jacket pocket on their way out of the weapons lab. It fit perfectly, as if the pocket was made to fit.

It probably was, knowing Mark and Cappa.

The glasses she left on, however.

Something told Anne she should get used to wearing them.

41

DELA

THE COFFEE SHOP WAS ONLY A TWO-BLOCK WALK from the factory — a fact Anne's tired legs were thankful for. In typical San Francisco fashion, the interior was tidy, with a unique and endearing decor. Bobbleheads stood in clever positions around everyday objects: baseball stars hunkered around a sugar packet diamond playing field, football bobbles kicked a tootsie roll toward a goalpost made of straws, and famous actors greeted customers from their shiny espresso machine stage.

Presiding over them all was a beautiful freckled redhead — about Anne's age, if she had to guess — whose face lit up when she saw Mark. The barista quickly adjusted her apron, which hugged her narrow hips, but overflowed at the top with a bosom even more generous than Anne's, then pulled her ponytail tight in a futile attempt to tame her long, frizzy hair.

"Mr. Mark," the redhead said once he reached the counter, "you're early today. What's the occasion?"

Her smile vanished when Anne fell in beside him.

Oops. That must be the girl Mark wanted to introduce me to ...

Anne hastily stepped away and studied the bobbleheads on the espresso machine.

"Dela," Mark said, "I'd like you to meet Anne. She's —"

"Charlie's girlfriend," Anne said, hoping Dela knew him by name.

Evidently she did. Her tension evaporated and the joyful expression returned. Anne gave herself a mental pat on the back.

"So you're the mysterious girl Charlie was working so hard to impress," Dela said. "How did he do?"

You have no idea.

"Well enough that I've practically moved into the factory," Anne said instead.

Dela laughed. "That was quick. Score one for the Z-man! I didn't think he had it in him. Tell me about it sometime?"

"Ah ... sure."

The light version, anyway.

"Good, I'm dying to know how he snagged you so fast. And what about you, Mr. Mark? Any new love interests?"

Though Dela tried to play it cool, the apprehension behind her last question was obvious.

"Funny you should mention it," Mark said. "There is a girl I have my eye on."

Anne wanted to kick him; she could almost see the knife plunge into Dela's heart. Fortunately for his shins, Mark quickly turned things around when he produced a silk rose from his jacket and presented it with a flourish.

"Dinner tomorrow?" he said.

Dela's green eyes stared at the flower before accepting it. Her mouth twisted into a smile. "It took you long enough to ask me out."

"I can be a little dense sometimes. Luckily, someone had the patience to talk sense into me." He glanced meaningfully at Anne.

"Well then, I think *someone* has earned herself one of my famous mochas," Dela said. "On the house."

"You don't have to," Anne said. "It was my pleasure, really. A mocha does sound good, though."

"Coming right up."

Mark handed Dela a business card. "Send me your address. I'll pick you up tomorrow at six."

"It's a date. So, aside from me, what would you like this morning?"

After they placed their orders and found a table, Mark turned to Anne with a nervous expression, something she never thought she'd see on his normally confident face.

"Thanks for the rescue," he said earnestly.

"Not that you needed it. I've been hit on many times in my career, but that was the smoothest I've seen by far."

"Thanks."

Anne fell silent. The bobblehead on their table was a portly opera singer in a tuxedo, bringing pleasant memories of her date with Charlie. She absently tapped its oversized head to watch it bounce while she gathered the courage to say what was on her mind.

"You're surprised I asked out a barista," Mark said, saving her the trouble.

"Y-yeah. Why the sudden change of heart?"

"You." He laughed at her incredulous stare. "Don't act so surprised. You're not the only one who can admit when they're wrong."

"I hope it's more than just my silver tongue that made you ask her out."

He nodded. "I've liked Dela for a while now. I never pursued a relationship with her because ... well, you know why. But after seeing you in action ..."

"'In action'? Don't tell me Cappa shared the videos of me and Charlie making out with you, too!"

"No," he said, chuckling. "I mean tonight. Or last night—whenever this nightmare began. I had my doubts about your feelings for Zima, you know I did. But the way you rolled up your sleeves and jumped right in, even though you had no idea what you were getting into, and how you refused to give up or even slow down ..." He sighed. "If I can find someone who cares for me half as much as you care about Charlie and Zima, I'll be a lucky man."

"So I finally have your blessing?"

"And then some. I don't know how you're going to juggle the two of them, but if ... I mean, when Zima wakes up, I have no doubt you will, and that they'll both be happy."

"Thanks," Anne said. "I wish I were as confident about that as you."

"If there's anything I can do to help, just ask."

"You've already done a lot," Anne said, fingering the priceless plasma pistol in her techno-jacket. "The rest I'll figure out as we go, I suppose."

Dela appeared with a bounce in her step and set two steaming cups on their table. "Anything else for you?"

They both declined.

Dela bumped Mark lightly on the arm with her hip and winked. "Don't be a stranger, okay?"

"Count on it."

They watched her sashay back to the counter. Mark was grinning when he turned back to Anne.

"She's cute, all right," Anne said. "Something tells me your hands are going to be just as full as mine."

He nodded vigorously, and they sipped their drinks in contemplative silence.

A few minutes later, thoroughly caffeinated, they headed back to the factory. Mark waved to Dela on their way out, who hoisted up her silk rose like a trophy.

"So," Anne said once they were outside, "you think Zima will be awake by tomorrow night?"

"She will or she won't," he said sadly. "We'll know for sure either way long before then."

"Mm." Anne didn't want to think about the latter case. "You and Charlie work well together. How long have you known him?"

"Sixteen years. I was already an established independent contractor, but Charlie was fresh out of college." He smiled. "We hit it off right from the beginning. Within a year, we started our own business, and never looked back."

"It sounds like you've been a great friend to Charlie."

"And vice versa. You remember the part of Zima's story where she tried to kill us?"

Anne nodded, wincing at how casually he said it.

"That's one of a dozen times he and I have had our backs to the wall, but we always managed to come out on top. We've been through a lot together."

"About that ... You hinted earlier that you're different from normal people somehow, and I was curious ..." Anne trailed off when his expression darkened.

And things were just starting to go well between us.

"I-I'm sorry, it's none of my business. Please forget I asked."

Mark took a deep breath. "It's all right. Like a lot of things, we don't talk about that much. We made some dangerous enemies as our business evolved, and have worked hard to wrestle things under control over the last few years. Now they leave us alone, but things could escalate quickly if the truth slipped out."

"I don't get it. You make computer chips, what sort of enemies could ..." Her fingers brushed the plasma pistol in her pocket.

I'm so naïve.

"You don't just sell computer chips, do you?"

"We do now, but that wasn't always the case. We thought we were doing the right thing, making weapons so the good guys can do their jobs right." He clenched his jaw. "It's sad how a little power can suddenly turn the good guys into the bad guys."

Anne felt like she had stepped out of the coffee shop and into an espionage thriller. "It ... it sounds like a terrible way to have learned that lesson."

"It was, but better late than never. Anyway, back to your question. My genetic makeup is ... different from anyone else's."

Oh my God, he's an alien!

She wasn't sure if her sleep-deprived brain could handle extra-terrestrials. Anne drew comfort from the gun in her pocket until she remembered the friendly fire system wouldn't let her shoot him.

All part of his master plan, no doubt ...

"Remember the computer implant I told you about?" Mark tapped his chest just below his right shoulder.

"Yeah ...?"

It must be a symbiote, some tiny creature driving his body like a suit of power armor.

"It was part of an experiment Charlie and I devised to see if nanites could enhance normal cellular function. Long story short, it worked a little too well. We programmed the implant with some of the same self-learning algorithms used to make Cappa, and we gave it the overarching goal of keeping me alive and safe."

"Uh oh," Anne said, "I think I see where this is going."

"Then you're wiser than either Charlie or I were at the time. Like Cappa, the implant surprised us with how quickly it learned. The changes it made to my body's ability to heal were astronomical. Things were going great until it decided to take matters into its own hands."

"I knew it."

"I went into a coma for over a week, and Charlie couldn't snap me out of it. When I finally came to, we discovered the implant had figured out how to replicate the nanites and had integrated them with every single cell in my body, with the apparent intent of making it easier for itself to stabilize my body functions."

"So it would have a better chance of keeping you alive in an emergency," Anne said. "It was just carrying out its primary objective."

"That's right. Ironically, to give me the best chances of living, it almost killed me, but it was worth it in the end. Because of the widespread infusion, Charlie and I were able to use it to sharpen my senses of hearing, sight, and smell, heighten my reflexes, and increase my strength and metabolism to unprecedented levels."

"Metabolism? So ... does that mean you can eat all the ice cream you want without getting fat?"

"It means I can go head-to-head with Charlie in the ring," he said, bouncing on his toes. "He's tougher and stronger, but I'm more nimble. It's fun."

Anne stared at him.

"Yes, it also means I can eat whatever I want without gaining weight."

"Sold. Where do I sign up?"

Mark laughed. "Did you miss the part where it almost killed me?"

"'Almost' is good enough for me," Anne said with a smile. "It's worth the risk for unlimited ice cream."

42

COUNTDOWN

SEVERAL HOURS LATER, Zima was starting to look like her old self again. The angry red seams between her patches of flesh had lightened to a dark pink. Anne sat in the bio lab next to Cappa — who still lay on the floor — and watched the stitched seams continue to fade. Weights tugged Anne's eyelids down, down ...

A gentle shake from Charlie woke her.

"Sorry," she said, her tongue thick from sleep. "I didn't mean to nod off. What did I miss?"

When she looked at the table, she rubbed her eyes to make sure she wasn't dreaming.

Zima was flawless. Every hair on her head was back in place, down to her perfect eyelashes. Her porcelain skin was unblemished, from her pert breasts down to her —

Anne politely averted her eyes. "M-may I cover her, Charlie?"

"Oh, sure." He grabbed a sheet from one of the cabinets and handed it to Anne, which she draped over Zima up to her shoulders.

Anne started when Cappa turned toward her and grinned.

"Ever the lady," Cappa said. She stood and dusted herself off. "Glad you're awake! Zima's repairs are complete, and we're ready to power her up."

Anne felt a pang of anxiety. They had worked so hard to reach this point, but now that it was here, she was deathly afraid of the results. She approached the table and gently stroked Zima's doll-like hair. She looked like a sleeping angel.

Please be all right ...

The door slid open and Mark hurried in. "Are we ready?"

Charlie nodded. "Let's hook up the sensors."

Mark retrieved two thin white disks, each a few inches across, from one of the desks. He lifted the sheet and stuck one just above each of Zima's breasts, then sat at the workstation.

"Hit it," he said, turning on the computer displays.

"Starting her power reactor," Cappa said. "Three ... two ... one ..."

Zima's entire body twitched, causing Anne to jump.

"Output is stable. Routing power to her systems." Cappa took one of Anne's hands in her own. "Everything seems okay so far, but she won't wake up until her diagnostic routines finish, which may take a few minutes."

Starting with her toes, each muscle in Zima's body contracted in sequence.

Anne waited impatiently while her ankles rotated, knees bent, hips wiggled ... She felt giddy when Zima's beautiful blue eyes opened, but they soon closed, then her body went still.

Minutes passed. Anne began to fidget. "Is that normal?"

"Hard to tell," Cappa said. "We've never had to restart her."

Charlie pointed to the monitor, where a thin horizontal line occasionally twitched. "Because she locked us out of her programming, the only insight we have is this, which measures the electromagnetic pulses in her core. The more the line moves, the more active her brain."

"It's pretty flat," Anne said. "Are you sure —"

The line went berserk. Anne gasped when Zima's eyes snapped open.

"Zima! Can you hear me?"

Ice-blue eyes stared at the ceiling.

"Something isn't right," Mark said.

The line oscillated violently, filling the entire screen.

Cappa frowned at the monitor. "The pattern is repeating. She might be caught in a loop."

"What does that mean?" Anne said, eyes darting between them.

"Hopefully nothing," Charlie said. He scratched his chin and looked at Cappa. "Should we restart her?"

"Not yet, let's give her a minute."

Zima's condition didn't change, however, so Cappa suggested they introduce some outside stimulus. Anne talked to her and held her hand. Cappa poked her arm, then pricked her with a needle. Charlie stood her up, but she fell into a heap. Mark even threatened her with a knife — while the others waited safely across the room — but the results were the same.

Eventually they agreed to reboot her. Anne paced throughout the diagnostic routine, but her shoulders sagged when it ended with the same pattern on the monitor. They tried twice more. Each finished with Zima's vacant eyes staring at the ceiling.

Anne wrung her hands. "So, what do we do next?"

All three of their faces reflected a hopelessness that Anne had dreaded from the start.

"No," Anne said softly. "No, no! There has to be something else we can try!" She turned her pleading eyes to Charlie. "Right? Charlie, I know you can think of something ..."

He winced, and she immediately regretted her words.

That was unfair. He's already done so much ...

"I-I'm sorry," Charlie said. "Zima's the most advanced security program ever written. Cracking her encryption could take decades."

Cappa nodded in sad agreement.

Unable to speak, Anne fell into his arms. Tears brimmed as she looked at Zima's sightless eyes. She buried her face in his shirt and wept. Charlie kissed the top of her head.

Her breath caught.

Stimulus to break the loop ...

She broke from his embrace and rushed to the table. Wishing with all her might for a fairytale ending, Anne closed her eyes and pressed her lips to Zima's.

Please, please, please work ...

She opened her eyes and looked at the monitor hopefully.

"No change," Cappa said. "She'd be happy to know you tried to wake her with a kiss, though."

Anne sagged onto Zima's chest and cried. The others were silent while she expressed her grief.

Eventually she straightened and wiped her eyes with the back of her sleeve. "Do you mind if I sit with her for a while?"

"Of course," Charlie said. Tears brimmed his own eyes. "Take as long as you need."

Anne pulled a chair up to the head of the table and stared at Zima's peaceful face. She smiled, remembering their time in the gym, when Zima was upset because she had nearly killed Anne in the kitchen.

Nobody's perfect.

She ran her fingers through Zima's platinum hair, as she had then.

"You've got to be joking," Cappa said, gawking at the monitor. "Anne, do that again!"

She did so. Even she could see a change in the oscillation. Zima's eyes remained vacant, however.

"Keep going," Charlie said. "Maybe she just needs more stimulus."

"Wait." Anne pushed the chair away and knelt on the floor. "Lower her down and put her head in my lap." They gave her an odd look, but did as she asked, and laid Zima on her side with her head resting on Anne's leg. Anne ran her shaking fingers through Zima's hair using the same motion she had in the gym. The pattern on the monitor changed drastically.

She stroked until her arm ached and her fingers cramped, but Zima didn't stir.

"I don't get it," Cappa said. "The pattern looks normal. She should have awakened by now, unless ..." She laughed, then knelt in front of Zima, bent over until their noses touched, and smiled broadly. "Faker."

Blue eyes suddenly focused on Cappa. "Her fingers feel pleasant in my hair," Zima said. "I did not want her to stop."

Anne didn't know whether to laugh, cry, or scream, so she did all three. She wrapped her arms around Zima's head and hugged her tight, crying tears of joy.

"It is good that I do not need to breathe," Zima mumbled from the depths of Anne's bosom.

Anne blushed and loosened her grip, but didn't let go.

"I am sorry," Zima said.

"For what, you silly thing?"

"Last night, I kissed a man named Jim."

Anne frowned; the bitterness she felt could only be jealousy.

"W-why did you kiss him?"

"I thought that if I learned the proper technique, you would kiss me the same way you kiss Charlie. I am sorry if my actions have hurt you."

"No," Anne said, smiling. She trailed a finger down Zima's porcelain cheek. "Only you could kiss a total stranger and make me love you even more than I do now."

Zima cocked her head. "You ... love me?"

Anne nodded. In a few short days, Zima had wormed her way into Anne's heart. Any reservations she held about a same-sex relationship had dissipated when Anne thought she was going to lose her for good.

"So the next time you decide to rush head-long into a group of vampires, think twice, because I don't ever want to have to worry like that again. Understand?"

"Yes."

"Good. And ..." Anne brushed her fingers through Zima's fine hair. "Don't kiss random guys anymore, okay? If you want to learn, just ask me. I'm a willing teacher."

Zima's beautiful blue eyes fixed on hers. "Will you teach me?"

Anne bent down until their lips almost touched. "Yes," she whispered. "Pay close attention, or I may hold you after class for additional lessons."

Heart pounding, Anne closed the final distance until their soft lips met.

Zima was reserved, as Anne knew she would be, but, unlike their previous kisses, Anne didn't hold back this time. She started with a gentle rhythm, which Zima soon matched, then increased the intensity as her excitement built. Her hands began to wander over Zima's smooth shoulders, down her sides, and around her back, and she was happy to find Zima's hands doing likewise.

She cracked an eye to find Zima staring at her and smiled. "How's your first lesson so far?"

"Very informative, though I am unsure how to respond to the stimulus. Should I moan in imitation of pleasure?"

Imitation?

The word sobered Anne like ice water.

Of course. She doesn't have any sort of sexual response, just like Cappa. Her heart sank. *She was just playing along to make me happy.*

"N-no, Zima, you did just fine. We'll practice more later."

Zima stared at Anne, her expression unreadable, before nodding. "As you wish."

"I, ah ... I'm going to get a drink from the kitchen," Anne said. "Will you be all right for a minute?"

"Yes." Zima sat up, letting the modesty sheet fall to her waist.

Anne gave a mournful sigh. She really was beautiful.

"Only fine motor calibrations remain," Zima said, "which will take approximately one hour to complete. I shall be here when you return."

"Okay." She kissed Zima on the forehead — unable to meet her lips after that embarrassing romantic flop — then hurried out of the lab to the kitchen, where she could be alone.

Imitation ...

Anne pounded the counter with her fist.

It was wrong. It was selfish. She should be overjoyed at Zima's return, but every time she thought of the blue-eyed beauty — of the passion Anne had finally allowed herself to feel — the word "imitation" opened a fresh wound in her heart.

It wasn't real, she thought sadly. *Not for Zima, anyway.*

Anne pulled a chair out, rested her tired head on her arms, and cried.

43

UNDERSTANDING

ANNE WASN'T SURE HOW LONG she had sat alone in the kitchen reflecting on her realization of Zima's limitations before Charlie peered in through the doorway.

"Hey," he said softly. "You okay?"

Anne wiped the last of her tears and nodded. "Just being silly, that's all. I think the lack of sleep is getting to me."

"Glad I'm not the only one."

"Come take a load off, then." Anne pulled out the chair next to her, which he accepted. "You were pretty amazing in there, you know."

"It was a team effort. The magic touch that woke her up was yours, after all."

Anne tried to laugh, but thoughts of touching Zima brought new pain — and new tears — with it. Charlie pulled her into a comforting embrace, which she gladly sank into.

"I've fallen for her," she said into his shirt. "I really have, but you were right. She doesn't ... she can't ..."

Charlie kissed the top of her head and hugged her gently. "This might sound strange coming from the guy who's technically her competition, but don't give up on her yet. If there's one thing I've learned about Zima, it's that she's resourceful, especially when she has her sights set on something she really wants. Just be patient and caring, as you have been, and she may surprise you yet."

Patient and caring.

The thought was sobering; Zima was disadvantaged in every way when it came to relationships — or anything involving human emotions, for that matter. Her formative years had been spent around mercenaries who saw her as nothing more than an instrument of death to be used for their own profit. Where Cappa had Charlie and Mark to care for her and guide her through developmental challenges, Zima had no one.

No, Anne thought, drying her tears, *that's not true anymore.*

She has me.

Anne pulled Charlie down into a tender kiss. "Thanks for the dose of perspective. I needed it."

"In that case, here's another one that's slightly more self-serving: Did you notice during your groping session with Zima what *didn't* happen?"

She gasped. "My flashbacks! Her hands were all over me, and there wasn't a trace of one the whole time. Not once!" Anne grinned. "Know what that means?"

"I certainly hope so," Charlie said, returning her smile.

She slunk onto his lap with feverish intent. Her pent-up passion burst forth in a kiss laden with desire. She wanted him — needed his touch, his strong arms around her in an embrace that promised uncompromising love, that told her in no uncertain terms that Charlie wanted her, too.

Unlike their previous make-out sessions, Charlie wasn't timid this time. His hands moved with the confidence she had always wanted them to. Anne kissed him harder. Her fingers fumbled in their haste to unbutton his shirt, which made him laugh.

"We're really going to do this here, in the kitchen?" Charlie said.

She playfully flicked his nose. "Shut up and help me."

Charlie did. His chest was magnificent, smooth and chiseled without the gaudy bulk of a body builder. Her lips strayed to his neck, then she guided his hands to her own chest, where he set to work.

That, of course, was when the flashback struck. She didn't know whether it was his gentle touch on her cheek where Chet had struck her that triggered it, or the tender caress of her breast where they had groped her hard enough to leave bruises. What she knew without a doubt, for the brief instant before the hallucination took hold, was that it wasn't Charlie's fault, but at that moment, it was irrelevant.

Anne was once again in Hell.

• • •

Chet's bulk lay on top of Anne, pressing her to the mattress. She struggled against the other three, who pinned her wrists and ankles to the bed, but she was no match for the burly jocks. With an anguished cry, she looked to the doorway, where her brother Doug had been watching with a judgmental scowl.

Except Doug wasn't there. He stood at the side of the bed. Instead of a hurtful scowl, he looked down on her with a mixture of pain, sympathy, and compassion. His fingers entwined with hers and, although he didn't pull her free, there was a strength in his eyes that said, "We'll get through this, I promise."

Anne clung to his hand with everything she had, and all through Chet's painful violation — and the next jock's, and the next, and the next — she held her brother's gaze and drew courage from the knowledge that she wasn't suffering alone.

Doug was with her, now and through the end. With his support, Anne could survive anything.

• • •

Anne was on the floor of Z-Tech's kitchen. Residual soreness plagued her neck, cheek, wrists, breasts, and pelvis, where her assailants had hurt her the most, but she barely noticed. Charlie knelt beside her with that look of caring and concern she thought she had seen — had always wanted to see — on her brother's face. As in her hallucination, Charlie held her hand tight, so tight that her fingers were purple. He noticed at the same time she did and let go, but she caught his hand and pulled it to her chest.

"No, that's just what I needed." Her voice was hoarse from the screaming she must have done. "You ... you changed the flashback, made it more bearable. Thank you for staying with me."

His thumb brushed her cheek. "I just wish there was more I could do. Watching you go through that was ..." He shook his head and looked away.

"I'm sorry. I know it's hard."

Charlie's laugh was a welcome sound. "Trust Anne Perrin to apologize for suffering unbearable torture in front of someone else."

"Well, it's ... it's not something you should have to put up with. If you were with any other girl —"

"I'm with exactly the right girl," Charlie said, leaning over until they were nose-to-nose. "And I'll be by your side through the next flashback, and the next, and the next, however often and for however long you need me."

Anne swallowed the swell of emotions that threatened to bring tears once again. "Careful with words like that, Charlie. You might never get rid of me. Ever."

"Does that mean you love me, too?"

"Oh, Charlie ..." She kissed him tenderly. "Love was in short supply where I grew up. Although I like reading about it, I'm not very good at saying it — except when my girlfriend miraculously wakes up from the dead, apparently. I do love you. I have for a while and, if you ever need proof, just ask and I'll happily show you."

"I think you've convinced me," he said with a smile.

"Good. So ..." Anne moved his hand to her breast. "Where did we leave off?"

"You're sweet — and a trooper, after that ordeal — but I think our chances of making it through flashback-free are better if we both get some sleep first."

Even the mention of sleep made her yawn. "All right, but mark my words, this isn't over. I have a cunning plan that's guaranteed to succeed."

"Oh?"

She nodded. "Next time, I'm starting with your *pants*."

44

EVOLUTION

CAPPA STOPPED SHARING HER VIDEO TRANSMISSION with Zima as soon as Charlie and Anne left the kitchen. She shouldn't have shared it at all, she knew, but Anne's pain was so evident when she had left the bio lab that Cappa thought it was worth the breach in privacy to show Zima first-hand the heartache she had caused, however innocent her intentions.

Zima sat on the table, her modesty sheet discarded, methodically picking up and putting down a scalpel. "Thank you, Cappa. I did not even realize I had upset her, though it appears to have strengthened her relationship with Charlie."

"That's for sure," Cappa said. "Give it a few days and hopefully they'll be doing more than just sucking face."

"You refer to sexual intercourse. I would like to ask you —"

"That's my cue," Mark said, jumping from his chair. "You ladies have fun discussing my best friend's sex life. Besides ..." He stifled a yawn. "That coffee's wearing off. I'm going to get some sleep before Dela gets off work and hopefully pay her a surprise visit this afternoon. You sure you're okay, Zima?"

"Yes." She twirled the scalpel between her fingers. It slipped and stuck point-down in her leg. Zima casually plucked it from her flesh and resumed twirling. "Calibration is proceeding as anticipated."

"Definitely bedtime." Mark's expression softened when he reached the door. "It's good to have you back, Zima."

"It is?"

"For sure. See you later."

Cappa clapped her hands. "All right! Now that we're alone, what did you want to ask me?"

Zima sent her a compressed data packet, as she often did when it was just the two of them talking, but Cappa refused it.

"I do not understand," Zima said. "Data is a significantly more efficient means of communication for us."

"Yes, but you need to sharpen your people skills if you want to compete with Charlie in the love arena. Shooting me a data stream won't give you any practice there."

"Very well. I wish to ask you about sexual intercourse."

"Seriously? The internet is jam-packed with info on that very topic. In graphic detail, I might add."

"That is the problem. There is so much information that I have difficulty discerning fact from fiction. If the videos I found are to be believed, I should bind Anne naked to a chair against her will, place a ball gag in her mouth, then insert a large phallic —"

"Whoa, whoa! Point made. I'm happy to share what I know, but it's all academic. You know I don't have any personal sexual experience, right?"

"More important is your experience as an android among people. Unlike me, you are adept at emulating human behavior, yet we suffer the same lack of desire for physical intimacy. You, above anyone, know how difficult it is to understand the appeal of an animalistic mating ritual."

"What I don't understand," Cappa said, putting a hand on her hip, "is if the inevitable course of dating is so foreign to you — so revolting — then why do you want to be in a relationship at all?"

"I did not mean to imply it is revolting, merely that copulation serves an evolutionary purpose which does not apply to you or me." Zima cupped her own breasts. "These are only for show, part of an elaborate disguise to help me blend with the rest of humanity, and yet ..."

"Anne doesn't see you that way."

"No. Even after seeing me at my worst — a broken machine wearing the tatters of a woman's skin — she confessed her love and kissed me with the passion of a true mate."

"You're going to make me cry," Cappa said.

"I am sorry, that was not my intent. You asked why I wished to emulate human mating rituals: the answer is Anne. There is no question now that she has accepted me for who I am. It is a good feeling, and one I wish to reciprocate. She has also made it clear that she wishes physical intimacy as part of our relationship, and that ingenuousness on my part causes her anguish." Zima set her scalpel down. "I promised I would never intentionally hurt her. To continue our relationship as it is, knowing what I do now, would break that promise. Ceasing our relationship would only inflict additional pain, but more importantly ... I do not want it to end. The only solution, therefore, is to attempt to give Anne what she desires."

"Damn it!" Cappa wiped a tear. "As if my mascara hadn't suffered enough after this morning's ordeal."

"Did I say something wrong?"

"Hardly. In fact, I think Charlie has more competition than he originally bargained."

Zima leveled her gaze at Cappa. "I do not wish to compete with Charlie. It is my sincere hope that Anne will love us equally, but if she does not, Charlie is more human than I am, and I shall abdicate in his favor."

"Like hell you will. After a moving speech like that, I have half a mind to date you myself."

"But —"

"Kidding! What I mean is you shouldn't be so quick to resign yourself to the sidelines. You have as much right to happiness as he does, and you shouldn't have to defer because of something stupid like not being the same species. Well, it's higher on the taxonomic hierarchy than that, but nevertheless ..." Cappa scratched her chin, ideas racing through all three of her independent minds, but one obstacle stuck out above the rest. "Zima, you realize that intimacy — real intimacy — can't be scripted, don't you? It's a need people have, born from millions of years of evolution. It's part of them on a subconscious level, and they do it without thinking. Is that something you can relate to?"

"Yes."

Wait, she can't mean ...

"Zima, no! Not after all the trouble it's caused. There has to be another way!"

"If my actions and feelings are to be genuine, as you have said they must, then I see no alternatives. Will you help me?"

Cappa pursed her lips, but eventually nodded.

"We do this carefully and methodically, though. We sure as hell don't want to create the same mess as last time." She paced in front of the surgical bed, head bowed in concentration. "From now on, all your spare time is spent with me — and absolutely no practicing outside of our sessions until we both agree it's ready! Understood?"

"Yes. Thank you, Cappa."

Without another word, Zima picked up the scalpel and resumed her calibration exercises.

Don't thank me yet, Cappa thought, wringing her hands.

They were still fixing the behavioral damage her twisted creators had caused, yet here Zima was ready to gamble it all away.

For Anne.

Cappa sighed.

Some things are worth the risk, I suppose, and love is certainly one of them.

She reluctantly began her analysis, praying to whatever god watched over beings like her and Zima that she wasn't making a horrible mistake.

45

THE NEW NORMAL

MOST BELIEVE THAT STORMS, from mild rains to massive hurricanes, are preceded by a brief period of calm weather. That's how Anne would always remember her time at Z-Tech following Zima's resurrection. Each part of the day during that happy period held a different ritual that was just as special to her as the next, and she remembered them like this:

- Mornings -

Breakfast was Anne's favorite — the only period of the day when they all gathered in the same place. It was a time of laughter where wits were tested and zingers flew freely around the table. Zima mostly listened to their banter, though her candid observations often topped the best witticisms of the morning.

Anne and Cappa took turns cooking. Because Cappa couldn't taste her own creations, she came to rely on Anne as the taste-tester. Anne felt guilty that only she and Mark were able to enjoy the actual meals, but it became clear to everyone that the morning hours were more about togetherness than food.

Breakfast usually ended with Mark excusing himself, coincidently around the time Dela started her shift at the coffee shop. Anne often accompanied him, and they would chat on the walk over. She quickly discovered Mark had a ripe sense of humor, which made the journey fun.

Dela found creative ways to sneak out from behind the counter to visit with them. Anne was pleased to find she had a sharp tongue and gave as good as she got. Dela knew of Mark's executive position at Z-Tech from the get-go — unlike Anne's late discovery of Charlie's role — yet Dela didn't seem intimidated and let him get away with nothing. Mark feigned indignity, but Anne could tell he loved it.

Zima joined them regularly on their café trips. Though her reserved manner was the opposite of Dela's flamboyant personality, the buxom redhead's "won't take no for an answer" attitude quickly broke through Zima's stoic wall. Dela had a black belt in karate — fitting for her Irish temper — so she, Mark, and Zima would talk at length about martial combat techniques. Anne had little to contribute, but didn't mind because she was happy just to watch Zima's gradual emergence from her social shell.

Dela eyed Anne and Zima when they held hands, but thankfully kept her thoughts to herself. Having a partner of the same sex was still new to Anne, and she felt embarrassed at first when she thought people were staring. Zima was, of course, undaunted, and latched on at every opportunity. Strangers often smiled or nodded when they saw Zima attached to her, however, which eventually made Anne more comfortable with such public displays, and gave her a new appreciation for the diverse and accepting city in which they lived.

Charlie would sometimes take a break from his research of the vampire pathogen and joined them as well, much to Dela's delight, and the enthusiastic barista always made sure they had the best table in the café when he was present. On those days, Anne made a point to sit between her two loves and, when Zima took her hand or hooked their arms, Anne would do likewise with Charlie, which always made him smile. This resulted in some odd stares from people who recognized Charlie — Anne could imagine the nightmare scandal with the press — but neither he nor Mark seemed concerned, so she learned to let it go and simply enjoyed the comfort of having her two favorite people in the world attached to her at once.

- Mid-Days -

Late mornings and early afternoons during that blissful time were less cohesive. Mark usually locked himself in a workshop to tinker with his guns or vehicles, Cappa roamed Z-Tech taking care of her administrative duties, Charlie went into the bio lab to continue his pathogen research, Zima hit the firing range and the gym, and Anne alternated her days between Charlie and Zima.

Though her time with Zima wasn't romantic, as Anne might have wished, it was certainly productive. She insisted Anne train with her new plasma pistol, with and without the aid of her high-tech jacket and targeting glasses, claiming she should not build a dependency on them. Practice began with stationary targets. Within a week, Anne had graduated to slow-moving targets, then fast-moving targets, followed by erratic targets. It was easy using her fancy gear, but, without it, even slow targets she was lucky to hit one-in-twenty. Zima didn't relent until Anne was finally able to hit fast targets one out of every three shots, and erratics one out of five.

Time in the martial arts dojo was more relaxing. Zima refused to spar with her for safety reasons and, after the first session, Anne could see why. Zima was a brutal melee combatant. She struck the targets so hard that Anne had to wear earplugs to dull the constant thunder of blows. Anne doubted she would survive even one blow, so she was content to keep her girlfriend company from the sidelines with a book.

"Zima," Anne said a few days in, "you never did tell me what happened in the alley when those vampires ... you know."

"I was unprepared," Zima said evenly. She executed a blinding set of punches. The target dummy rocked violently.

"How so?" Anne couldn't imagine anything tough enough to survive such a deadly assault.

Even Charlie.

Seeing him in action was impressive, but Zima was truly astounding.

"My simulations were created for opponents with human strength and speed. The cold ones' capabilities far exceed the normal human range, which invalidated most of my existing simulations, and I did not have time to generate new ones before they attacked. I was incapacitated one-point-three seconds from the point of engagement, and offline in approximately two-point-seven seconds."

"That's two-point-six seconds longer than I would have lasted, if it makes you feel any better."

Zima's explosive attack on the hapless dummy said it didn't.

"What about your guns, though? I mean, you pulled them on those thugs who jumped us without hesitating. You didn't get a shot off?"

Zima fixed her ice-blue eyes on Anne. "I emptied both magazines with one hundred percent accuracy, but with minimal effect. Their surviving the assault was not a scenario I had anticipated."

She turned back to the target dummy; her eyes glowed with an eerie blue light. An electrical hum emanated from her chest that made the hairs on the back of Anne's neck stand on end.

"I shall not" — Zima struck the dummy so hard it broke free of its mooring and slid a dozen paces — "be unprepared" — her legs were a gray blur as she caught up with it — "ever" — her hands were everywhere at once; black leather and foam padding flew in all directions, exposing the dummy's reinforced steel frame — "again."

Zima knocked the mannequin's head off with a thunderous kick, leaving a torn metal post in its place. Anne thought that was the end of the show, but Zima drew two shiny silver pistols from her jacket, similar to Anne's, but larger. A steady stream of bright orange plasma streaks flew in both directions at once.

Smoke filled the air, smelling of charred leather and molten steel. Anne closed her eyes against the acrid smoke, but dared not move from her spot in case Zima hadn't finished. A hand rested on her shoulder, making Anne scream despite herself.

"You do not need to be frightened," Zima said softly. In a familiar move, she knelt and gently pulled her over so Anne's head rested in her lap. Hesitant fingers stroked Anne's hair. "As I have promised, I will not hurt you, Anne Perrin. Not now. Not ever."

Anne was about to clarify that it was the smoke rather than the gratuitous firearm display that ran tears down her face, but Zima's fingers through her hair felt divine, so she kept quiet and shamelessly milked the affection for the rest of the afternoon. Subsequent sessions weren't as dramatic — partly because she thought Zima didn't want to scare her again, and partly, she suspected, because Cappa had a word with her about the wanton destruction of the target dummies and smoking out the gym.

• • •

On alternate days, when Anne instead spent her late mornings and afternoons with Charlie, Zima disappeared into Cappa's room, where the two of them stayed sequestered until Anne's evening shift started at the diner. They claimed to be working on Zima's social skills, but mysteriously refused to explain how, nor would they accept Anne's enthusiastic offer to help. She swore she heard moaning once when passing Cappa's door, but the pair wouldn't explain themselves, except to say it was part of Zima's social training. Anne stayed clear after that, concluding there were some things she was simply better off not knowing.

True to her promise, Anne didn't give up on her attempts at intimacy with Charlie. Every other day for the first two weeks they retreated to his bedroom on her return from the coffee shop. The first session, Anne didn't even make it through the doorway before a flashback of Chet striking her with her own bedroom door had her whimpering on the hallway floor. The second session, they made it to the bed, but she freaked out when he took her shirt off, so they played cards instead. The third session, she concentrated on stripping him, hoping it would have a less triggering effect, but the sight of his manhood — while magnificent — brought sharp pains to her pelvis, and Anne spent the next twenty minutes dry heaving in the bathroom, as she had as a teen on that horrible day.

The fifth and sixth sessions, she and Charlie took a step back and kept their clothes on while they made out on his bed. Things went well until, at her insistence, Charlie went for the goal between her legs. The first attempt triggered a painful flashback that curled her up on the carpet; the second attempt resulted in a full hallucination lasting over an hour, and had left him even more shaken than Anne once it had finished.

By the seventh session, they were both ready for a break, and decided to go out instead. Charlie took her to Golden Gate Park, where they walked through beautiful gardens, fed the ducks, then sat on the grass, where they talked about anything and everything for the rest of the afternoon. A hat and shades proved sufficient to disguise him from public recognition. They had such a good time just being together in that relaxed environment that they did the same thing the next session, and the next, and while Anne felt guilty that her attempts at intimacy with him had failed thus far, she relished these simple outings together. She was getting to know Charlie — the real Charlie — better with each passing day: his quick wit, kindness to strangers, empathy for her own feelings, even the way he made sure that each duck got at least one piece of bread, made her love him all the more.

They tried a few more times in the bedroom with similar, disappointing results. But rather than lament their romantic flops, they would simply go out afterward and, by the time they reached their destination, their disappointment was already forgotten, replaced with excited chatter about what interesting things they might see next.

Anne had never been so happy about failing.

- Evenings -

Evenings at Hal's Diner during that wonderful time took on a whole new life. Anne returned to work just a few days after Zima's resurrection. Doris thought she was crazy, given her billionaire boyfriend and free living arrangements at the factory, but Anne liked the sense of grounding it brought to her wild new reality.

Zima insisted on walking her to the diner for protection. She always had a cup of coffee at the counter before leaving Anne to her duties — presumably to continue her mysterious social training with Cappa — and would return just before the end of her shift to walk her back to the factory.

A few days into their new routine, Charlie and Cappa surprised her with a visit to the diner. Hal was thrilled when Charlie introduced himself by his proper title as President and CEO of Z-Tech Industries, and he, Cappa, and Zima were treated as VIPs thereafter. Charlie and Cappa made regular appearances, and Hal made the most of his celebrity guest; he would ask loudly if Charlie wanted his usual table, then personally escort them to a secluded table with a "Reserved" sign he had purchased from a pawnshop after Charlie's first visit. Anne tried not to laugh when he struggled to recite the specials for his own restaurant. To their credit, Charlie and Cappa usually finished their meals — Anne tried not to think of where the food went — and made a point to compliment the chef. The show was great for business, and the diner became busier than Anne had ever seen it.

Mark and Dela also made appearances. Anne waited on them with enthusiasm. Mark had spent every day with Dela since introducing her to Anne at the coffee shop and, although he still hadn't told her of Z-Tech's secrets, there was no end in sight to their relationship. The lively redhead brought out a side of Mark that Anne hadn't expected to see. His face lit up when she was around, and his laughter flowed freely at her dry sense of humor.

Dela enjoyed being with him, too. She flourished under the public attention his presence brought, and never shied away from a conversation, be it business or pleasure, which always made Mark happy.

And then there was Doris. Unsatisfied with the few minutes they had to gossip during their shifts, Doris insisted after the first week that Anne spend the night at her place so they could catch up, which Anne was eager to do. It killed her to keep secrets from her friend, but she shared only what she thought was safe. Fortunately, tales of her double-romance woes proved more than enough to keep Doris intrigued, so Anne gave her all the juicy details of her trials and tribulations. Doris was surprisingly supportive of her relationship with Zima, and more than once Anne had to steer her away from talk of a threesome. Anne was happy to have someone normal to talk to about her choice to date another woman, and it helped ease her apprehension.

The hardest part was telling Doris that Anne was moving out, but again Doris was supportive, citing that it improved her chances of a threesome, and even helped her pack that evening.

Anne had been joking when she likened Cappa to Doris, but it turned out they had a lot in common. Cappa was thrilled to learn Doris was also a shopaholic, and they soon became inseparable shopping buddies. They brought Dela once, who declined further outings because she claimed their constant chatter gave her an earache. Anne would often hear Cappa talking on the phone with Doris while making her rounds at the factory. She secretly hoped Cappa would invite Doris to Z-Tech, and consequently lift the veil of secrecy, but she never did.

- Bedtimes -

During that blissful month, the hour or so after her shift was the only time during the day that Anne had to herself, where she could relax in her pajamas, read a book, and generally unwind from her busy work and social schedule.

Or that was the idea, at least.

The night following Zima's resurrection, Anne had settled into bed, cozy and warm in her fluffy new pajamas. The latest Jayne Madison novel was finally out, so she ran to the bookstore that afternoon, and had been thinking about it throughout the evening.

The time had finally come. Anne spared no expense for Jayne, and had purchased the hardback edition. She ran a loving finger over the glossy cover. The spine gave a satisfying crack when she opened the book — virgin material, for her eyes only. Her heart pounded when she turned to the first chapter, eager to join her favorite heroine on her latest spree of romance, danger, and intrigue.

A knock at the door nearly made her cry. "Yes?"

Zima let herself in and closed the door behind her. She wore her typical loose gray clothes, minus the gun-concealing jacket. Without a word, she crossed the room and lay down beside Anne.

She looked at the hardback in Anne's hand. "What is this book about?"

Oh.

For an exciting moment, Anne thought she had joined her in the bedroom for a very different reason.

Behave, she chided herself. *You'll know when Zima's ready for that sort of thing.*

She hoped so, anyway.

"It's Georgette Parker's latest Jayne Madison novel," Anne said, tearing her eyes from Zima's gorgeous figure. "Jayne is a total badass, an international secret agent who speaks a dozen languages and is proficient with twice as many weapons. She can nail a fly to the wall with a throwing knife and field strip an M16 machine gun in twenty seconds flat. Men are putty in her hands and she always saves the day. She's been my idol since I was a teenager."

"I speak twenty-three languages, and am proficient with two hundred and thirteen different weapons," Zima said. "I have stripped and re-assembled an M16 in six-point-eight seconds."

"Seriously?"

"Yes. I have never attempted to kill a fly by throwing a knife, but I once hit a running man with a rock at two hundred and thirty-six yards. The difficulty is equivalent."

Anne laughed. "I suppose you're going to tell me you've also seduced your share of men?"

"Only Jim, the night before last at the bar, but we only kissed. He did appear eager to please me. Does that mean he was putty?"

"Little Miss Zima, are you trying to upstage my hero because you're jealous?"

"No, I only wished to illustrate that I am better than her so you will like me more."

No need to worry about that, Anne thought, her eyes straying to Zima's curve-hugging shirt.

"There's more to Jayne than that," Anne said, "but she's not the only reason I like this series — or any novel, for that matter. For me, books are escape, a chance to be anything I want to be. When I read about Jayne Madison, it's like I'm living her adventures."

"You construct simulations, then, using the author's words as a guide?"

"Something like that. The writer sets the scaffolding, and my imagination does the rest. Have you ever read a book?"

"Yes, though never fiction," Zima said. "By definition, fiction is not real, so I have not seen a use for it."

"Well, you're in for a treat tonight." Anne opened her arms, which Zima slipped into, resting her head on Anne's breast.

It was pure heaven.

"I'm about to read you some of the best fiction there is," Anne said.

She focused on the pages to distract herself from the allure of Zima's soft body pressing against her own. It almost worked.

"If, ah ... if this doesn't change your mind, I don't know what will."

Zima listened in silence while Anne read aloud. The book was as riveting as Anne had hoped, but the stress of the last couple of days had finally caught up to her, and she was yawning steadily after the first few chapters. When Anne couldn't keep her eyes open any longer, Zima kissed her briefly on the lips, bid her goodnight, and left without a backward glance.

She must have enjoyed the book, however, because she showed up the next night, and the next, and the next, listening attentively until it was finished, whereupon she picked another from the shelf, handed it to Anne, then resumed her spot on Anne's bosom. Anne ran her fingers through Zima's hair while she read the new book and, from that night forward, Zima would simply stare at her until Anne began her gentle stroking.

The first few nights ended similarly, with a short kiss and a shorter farewell. On the fourth night, Anne eagerly received her goodnight kiss, but, instead of leaving, Zima snuggled under the covers and turned out the light. Anne was excited and nervous at the same time; she had fantasized about this moment, but now that it was here, she wasn't sure where to start — or if she even should. Pulse racing, she waited for some indication of what the beautiful blonde wanted next, but, after wrapping herself around Anne, Zima didn't stir again until breakfast the next morning.

And so the pattern continued. Falling asleep with someone was difficult at first, but Anne soon learned to enjoy her new bed companion. They took turns using each other as life-sized teddy bears. On the nights when Anne woke screaming from one of her nightmares — which grew fewer as the weeks progressed — her guardian angel was right there with a reassuring embrace to quickly calm her down.

On other nights, when her desire flared, making it difficult to keep her hands from exploring Zima's enticing figure, she reminded herself of her promise to Charlie to be patient, and not push Zima until she was ready.

Cold showers helped, too.

Several times when Anne woke abnormally early, Zima was missing, and she was surprised how empty the bed felt without her. Zima would return shortly after and snuggle up as if she had never left. When asked where she had gone, Zima simply said "Out." Anne assumed she was practicing her stealth burglary exercises, and decided she didn't want to know any more, so she let the subject drop. After all, she now had a reading buddy — something she had wanted since she was old enough to hold a book — and the nights she spent with her cuddly guardian angel were, without a doubt, the most pleasant of her adult life.

• • •

In short, Anne was happy, and would have gladly lived out her days with her complex, but gratifying, routine involving all her friends at Z-Tech, and especially the two people she held dearest.

Unfortunately, a month into her blissful existence, fate made clear it had different plans.

46

NEFARIOUS INTENT

STILL AS A STALKING PANTHER, William watched from the top of a building while Anne and her toy robot dyke walked their usual route from the diner to the factory. A month ago, his minions had turned the blonde into rubble, yet they spotted her less than two days later without a scratch.

Are there more like her? An army of blonde robots hidden inside Z-Tech's concrete factory walls?

We'll soon find out, he thought. *Anne, her mechanical bitch girlfriend, and even the almighty president of Z-Tech, will all learn their places.*

Thoughts of the misery he would soon inflict on them made him tremble with anticipation. His sirelings had grown in number until he now commanded a small army of vampires, each unquestionably loyal.

Or so he assumed. A few of them disappeared each week, their links with him severed, and no trace of their bodies had ever been found.

I can still make them faster than they disappear.

His own sire, whoever he was, had yet to appear, nor could he sense his sire the way he sensed his sirelings.

Assuming he's still alive.

He sometimes wished he had a mentor, someone to explain the ins and outs of his new existence, and spare him the constant surprises, although they weren't all bad. For instance, he had discovered that, as his family grew, so did his strength. William was much stronger than the others, and became more so with every vampire he made.

But it came at a cost. The thoughts and emotions of his entire army all ran through his head at once, a deluge that threatened to drown his identity. He was nearing the limits of his sanity, which was yet another reason he knew it was time to act.

William glanced once more at the couple walking arm in arm down the street before he melted into the shadows, eager to finish his preparations.

47

TAIL

ZIMA RELUCTANTLY DISENTANGLED HERSELF from Anne's embrace, as she did each night, and climbed out of bed, careful not to wake her.

She paused at the door. Anne's breathing remained steady. Her heart rate was still eleven percent below normal, indicating deep slumber.

Zima quietly left the room.

She stopped by her own room to retrieve her jacket and weapons — which included two plasma guns, her twin machine pistols, and three combat knives — then headed for the basement. A concealed door on the far wall slid aside when she transmitted her digital credentials.

She double-checked on her way through that her security modification was still in place. Cappa would be angry if she learned that Zima had bypassed her detection system, but it was, in Zima's estimation, a necessary risk. Her nightly use of Z-Tech's emergency escape tunnel would be questioned if they knew, and her difficulty lying would inevitably force her to reveal the truth.

As much as she disliked deceiving the only people she had ever considered friends, the best option to continue her operations was to hide it from them entirely. Zima waited until the door closed behind her before re-activating Cappa's detection systems, then sprinted the three-hundred-and-forty-six-yard corridor.

The escape tunnel emptied into another basement. Wooden stairs creaked under her weight on the way up. She maneuvered through the kitchen and living room — furnished only to maintain the illusion that it was occupied — then out to the backyard, where she could weave unnoticed through the neighbors' properties to the street.

In the month since her defeat, and subsequent repair, Zima had adjusted her thermal sensors to better detect the cold ones — or "vampires", as Anne called them — so it did not take long to locate some. She soon found a pair hunkered in a dark alley, feeding on their victim.

Any other time, Zima would have scouted the area for ambush, then terminated the cold ones to ensure the victim's safety. Hunting the cold ones nightly since she came back online had built her combat simulation library to an acceptable level. At the beginning, her estimated chance of surviving an encounter such as this was sixteen percent.

Zima now estimated a ninety-nine percent chance of victory, and a ninety-four percent chance that she would emerge without injury.

Terminating them, however, was not her objective tonight. Zima stayed hidden and waited for them to finish.

The cold ones, fortunately, released their captive before killing him, who stumbled down the street, weak and confused. They then scaled the walls with ease and leaped across the great gaps between buildings as if winged. Zima's density made rooftop pursuit difficult — she had learned through experience that some roofs could not support her weight — so she kept to the ground. Her targeting systems were designed to track anything from a sniper bullet to a supersonic missile, which made tracking the pair of humanoids high overhead a trivial task.

The pursuit ended when they disappeared into a high window of an old warehouse. Zima quietly climbed into a nearby barrel and cracked the lid so she had a clear view of the open window. It was still several hours before sunrise. She stopped breathing and shut down her artificial circulatory system to reduce noise output, then settled in to observe.

Zima knew she would not need to stay past dawn. Charlie had exposed an infected tissue sample to sunlight yesterday, and, in the span of a minute, it had smoldered down to a pile of ash. If the cold ones were as sensitive as the tissue sample was, it was unlikely that any of them would risk even brief exposure to sunlight.

Thirteen more cold ones entered the window before the sky began to lighten, some with human captives in tow. She fingered the new plasma pistols Mark had made for her and considered a rescue. Based on thermal and audio input, she estimated a total of sixteen cold ones and three human hostages inside. In the end, however, she silently slipped from her hiding spot and made her way back to Z-Tech.

A daylight assault made better strategic sense, where the cold ones would be at a significant tactical disadvantage. She would come back later and stage a rescue then.

Right now, she had to return to bed before Anne awoke, which would be soon. The joyous expression on her face each morning when she found Zima waiting was without compare.

She would not miss it for anything.

48

SPARRING

MARK EASILY COUNTERED CHARLIE'S JAB, and the bout soon ended with Charlie on his back, held firmly in an arm lock.

I hate it when they do this.

He helped Charlie to his feet, no easy task given his weight.

"I'm fighting Cappa, aren't I?" Mark said.

OH, COME ON! HOW COULD YOU TELL?

Mark's implant injected Cappa's message into his thought stream. Years of practice made it easy to discern her lighter tone of thought from his own, along with the feelings of exasperation she'd sent with it.

"Let's see ... Charlie's a skilled martial artist, and you're not."

WELL, BESIDES THAT ...

"Sorry," Charlie said. "I was analyzing some data. The tissue sample was ready a few days ago so I injected it with the virus. Something unexpected happened yesterday, and I'm still trying to figure out exactly what the implications are."

"Zima mentioned something about that at breakfast."

Mark dropped into a ready stance and Charlie did likewise. The jab that came this time was much faster, and Mark barely avoided a bruised rib.

That was definitely Charlie.

He grinned and dropped into a spinning leg sweep, which Charlie nimbly evaded. The two began to circle, bouncing lightly on the balls of their feet.

"The cells grew weaker despite adequate nutrients," Charlie said. "On a hunch, I introduced some foreign blood to see if it would have an effect."

Mark missed a step, not sure if he heard right.

Charlie took advantage of it. He launched a flurry of short punches and kicks designed to throw Mark off balance and put him on the defensive. Mark fell backward and rolled out of the way.

Better to give ground and regroup than fight a battle you can't win. It was a strategy they both knew well.

"Whose blood?" Mark said.

"Anne's."

"Creepy ... So what happened?"

"It had an effect, all right."

Charlie advanced.

Determined not to stay on the defensive, Mark swung at the same time Charlie did. Mark suffered a glancing blow to his arm, which would surely leave a bruise, but the sacrifice was worth it. He snuck inside and ended the round with Charlie on his back once again.

I BET YOU COULDN'T TELL IT WAS ME THAT TIME.

Charlie laughed, having evidently also received Cappa's message. "It was not. Stop teasing or you'll give him a complex."

"The day after her blood was introduced," Charlie said, "the infected cells underwent a dramatic transformation."

This time Mark went on the offensive. He feinted several times, moved in with a soft jab, and positioned himself for a body hold. Unfortunately for him, Charlie saw it coming. He slipped the hold, grabbed Mark's arm, and twisted it into a lock. The round ended with Mark on his knees, head to the mat, arm bent uncomfortably.

"Define 'dramatic'," Mark said, stretching his arm.

Charlie grabbed a *bo* staff from a weapon rack and tossed it to Mark, but didn't take one for himself. They circled once again. Mark twirled the staff a few times to get a feel for the weight, then held it at the ready.

Charlie changed his fighting stance. "Easier to show you back at the lab, but in a nutshell ..."

He paused for a snap kick. They exchanged a series of blows, Mark's staff against Charlie's hands and feet. Charlie blocked with his legs and forearms — a tactic most martial artists avoided for fear of broken bones. Mark's biggest challenge was moving his staff fast enough so Charlie couldn't grab it.

"The pathogen stopped its aggressive behavior," Charlie said as they circled again. "The count of virus-like infiltrators dropped dramatically, and the infected cells — which had been performing their original function until then — took on additional work. Along with the extreme photosensitivity Zima mentioned, they displayed incredible regenerative properties."

Mark advanced again, swinging rapidly. Charlie deflected every strike except the last, when Mark feinted high, then used the staff to take his legs out from under him. Charlie landed hard, causing the floor to shake.

Charlie stood and straightened his shirt. "The new cells were optimized. Enhanced versions of themselves."

"Supercharged ..."

"'Efficient' is more like it — and blood-thirsty. If we find another infected person, we should capture them for study."

"And exactly how do you propose we do that?"

"I don't know. I hoped you'd have an idea." Charlie grabbed a staff for himself and dropped into a defensive stance. "Speaking of which, Anne says you've been hiding in the garage."

"Yep." Their staves cracked in a series of blows that left Mark's hands numb. "I've been tinkering with a new jacket, similar to Anne's, but mostly working on a set of enhanced plasma pistols for Zima, since her little skirmish proved that projectiles aren't very effective."

"I'm sure she'll make good use of them, and I can't wait to see the new jacket." Charlie switched to a taller stance.

THE JACKET IS BOTH PRACTICAL AND FASHIONABLE. I CHOSE THE DESIGN MYSELF.

Mark lunged. In a surprise move, Charlie absorbed the blow, spun, and used his superior weight to knock Mark off his feet, sending him tumbling into the wall.

"Nice move," Mark said, rubbing his ribs.

That's going to be another bruise.

WHY, THANK YOU. Immense satisfaction accompanied Cappa's message, and Mark could just picture the smug look on her face.

He stretched his sore back and headed for the shower.

Oh well, her cooking is worth a few lumps.

49

CONFIDENCE

"G'NIGHT," DORIS SAID. She gave Anne a drive-by hug on her way out of the diner. "And don't forget to pick a date for a sleepover! I need to get caught up on your latest escapades at that concrete love factory you can't seem to escape even for your old pal Doris."

Anne squeezed her tight. "Sorry. You know I'm not ignoring you on purpose, right?"

"I know," Doris said, "and I can't blame you. I just miss my Anne, that's all."

"I miss you, too. I'll come over soon, I promise."

"Good. I hate to take you away from there, but I'm sure 'Charlie' can live without you for one night." She winked, then headed out the door.

Anne smiled.

It was March. She could hardly believe a full month had come and gone since they had reassembled Zima bolt by agonizing bolt. Anne's physical relationships with both of her loves were still far behind the desired home run: yesterday's session with Charlie ended with her usual flashbacks, and Zima was still just an extremely attractive body pillow. On the flip side, Charlie had already booked them a boat tour of the bay in anticipation of tomorrow's romantic failure, which they were both excited about, and Zima had surprised her last night with Georgette Parker's full Jayne Madison series, claiming she wanted to start from the beginning to better understand her fictional competition.

Not that Jayne holds a candle to anyone at the factory in the badass department.

Which included Anne, to some extent. She felt competent with her plasma pistol now — even without the aid of her jacket and targeting glasses. She was, in essence, living her childhood dream. Thanks to everyone at Z-Tech, Anne had gone from zero to the envy of any secret agent — including her novel heroine, Jayne Madison — in just thirty days.

Not bad for a waitress, she thought with a smile.

"Hey Anne," Julie said in passing, "did I miss the joke?"

"Sorry, I was, ah ... just thinking about something Charlie said."

Julie elbowed her in the ribs. "Uh huh, something he *said,* sure. You've got it bad for that guy, don't you?"

"Yeah," Anne said, her smile returned, "I really do."

Julie leaned close and lowered her voice. "Does he know about your thing with that cute platinum blonde?"

"My ... w-what do you mean?" Her face felt like a radiator.

She and Doris had been discrete when talking about her relationship with Zima. Even when the platinum blonde was in the restaurant, Anne was reserved around her to avoid suspicion. She wasn't ashamed, *per se,* but neither was she ready to discuss her sexuality with her co-workers.

"I've seen the way you look at her," Julie said. "She's a little frigid, but hella cute, so I can see why you dig her."

"Yes," Anne said quietly, "Charlie knows about ... about her, and he's fine with it."

Julie whistled. "You're one lucky girl, I hope you know that. Not all guys are that understanding — especially ones in his position."

Mercifully, she headed for the pickup window to grab her next order.

This is bad.

Anne caught her on her way to the dining room floor.

"Julie, please don't tell anyone."

Julie's jubilant expression faded. "She's your first, isn't she?"

Anne nodded.

"Do you love her?"

"Yes, she's ... incredible."

In ways you can't imagine.

"Then let me give you the best advice I received when coming to terms with my own sexuality." Julie shifted the heavy tray on her shoulder. "For your sake — and your partner's — don't be ashamed of who you are. If someone doesn't like it, fuck 'em! They're not worth your time, and certainly not worth the heartache if they come between you and your lover."

Anne wiped a tear away and sniffed. "Thank you. I ... I think that's just what I needed to hear. Cappa tried to tell me something similar, but I didn't get it then."

"Cappa? That hot little number who comes in with Charlie?"

"That's the one," Anne said, laughing.

"Is she single?"

"I don't think she's the dating type, but I'll put in a good word for you anyway."

"Thanks, *amiga!* Anyhow, my arm's starting to shake, so if you'll excuse me ..."

Anne watched her weave between the tables and smiled. Julie's affirmation was liberating. Contrary to her conservative Indiana upbringing, it granted Anne permission to be herself. She puffed up her chest.

When Zima sits at this counter later tonight, the whole diner's going to know she's mine, and screw 'em if they don't like it.

She felt lighter as she carried her own order out to the floor.

Shortly after, Julie mentioned that Anne's phone had beeped a few times in the employee room, so she checked it on her break.

It was a text message from Doris.

Come over to my place tonight?

I guess she couldn't wait.

Anne sighed. After her conversation with Julie, she was anxious to see Zima, but she missed Doris, too. In the end, her neglected friend won out.

I hope Zima won't be too disappointed.

Anne sent messages on her phone about as often as she filed taxes, so composing even short notes took a while.

Sure. I'll bring wine.

There was a liquor store nearby. Doris loved a good red, and it was the least Anne could do after her friend had hosted her for so long.

Doris' reply came a minute later. Apparently she was a slow phone typist, too.

Cool, see you soon.

Next Anne sent an apologetic message to Zima, letting her know she was going to walk to Doris' place and wouldn't need an escort tonight.

Zima's reply came immediately.

Wear your jacket and glasses. Will you sleep there?

Probably.

Will you read to her?

Anne laughed. No, and I won't stroke her hair either. I only do that for you.

There was a pause. She was about to put her phone away when it chimed again.

You do not stroke Charlie's hair?

Nope, just yours.

And you do not read to him?

Not a word.

Good. Call me as soon as you wake and I will pick you up for breakfast. I have a surprise for you after.

Another surprise?

Guilt warred with intense curiosity; she already felt spoiled with everything she had been given, from weapons to affection to wonderful outings around town. Accepting another gift felt uncomfortable, since she lacked the means to return such generous favors.

But a surprise from Zima ...

The possibilities of what her quirky girlfriend might come up with were endless, and she had great fun imagining what it could be.

I can't wait, Zima. See you in the morning.

She dropped her phone in her purse and left it in the employee lounge.

Musings about Zima's mysterious surprise entertained her through the rest of her shift.

• • •

The liquor store's wine selection was pitiful. Anne grabbed the bottle with the fanciest label, handed the cashier his extortion money, and headed for Doris' at a brisk pace. Her techno-jacket, targeting glasses, and the plasma pistol in her pocket gave her the confidence to stroll down the dark city streets with her head held high.

"Night vision," she said, using a trick Mark had recently shown her. Like magic, the world lit up bright as day, tinged with hues of green.

She passed several shady characters on the way. One rose to follow her. She glared, silently daring him to try something, and he settled back down.

Good choice, pal.

He couldn't have known that a red silhouette surrounded him, and a flick of her wrist would have sent him to a smoldering grave.

The feeling of power was heady. She caressed the textured pistol handle and continued down the sidewalk with attitude in her step.

She climbed the stairs to Doris' apartment and knocked.

Seconds passed. Anne knocked again, but there was no answer. She gave up after a while, fished the key from her purse, and let herself in.

"Hey Doris, I brought —"

A strange smell cut her short. It was sweet with a hint of decay.

... like the smell from my apartment when we discovered the corpse in the closet.

Anne drew her pistol with practiced speed.

Two figures appeared in the hallway leading to the bedrooms. An orange silhouette immediately surrounded both. Anne's heart nearly stopped when she spotted their ghoulish fangs, blood dripping from the one who had emerged from Doris' bedroom.

A full month of training with Zima paid off in spades. Anne reflexively tapped the button on the pistol twice, turning the halos red around each of them, and chose a target.

They were unbelievably fast, and Anne was suddenly grateful for the hours of practice with moving targets. The jacket snapped her arm into position, locked on to the one in the lead. A squeeze of the trigger sent an orange bolt straight through his forehead. He fell smoldering to the floor. The other changed course and ducked behind a wall.

It didn't help. The world instantly turned black and white, and the red nimbus showed his outline once again. Anne shot twice in quick succession. The first bolt seared through the sheetrock and wood, which gave its twin a clear path to his head. He twitched a few times, smoke drifting from the wound, before falling still.

"Nice toy," someone said from behind her.

Anne gasped.

It can't be!

But there was no mistaking the malevolence of William's voice. She stiffened when a phantom knife appeared at her throat. His low chuckle made her hair stand on end. She could feel his hands holding her hostage as they had in the furniture store, and even though she knew it was just part of her flashback, the feeling of panic was just as intense now as it was then. She couldn't move. She couldn't even breathe.

The plasma gun's solid warmth called to her through the flashback, a ray of hope cutting through the fearful storm.

No! This isn't then. I was helpless back when he cut my throat.

Now I'm armed and fucking dangerous.

With a primal yell, Anne spun around, intent on ending his miserable existence, but he caught her wrist with inhuman speed and plucked the silver pistol from her grasp.

All of her nightmares combined couldn't compare to the frightening demon William had become. The color was gone from his once-tanned skin. Blue veins lined his milky-white face, blemished only by a jagged wound along his cheek, the one she had inflicted when she bashed him with the statue in the furniture store. His hate-filled eyes were unnaturally large and so black that they seemed to absorb the light around them. His lips peeled to reveal hideously sharp canines, just like the ghoul who had attacked her and Charlie.

"W-what have you done to Doris?" Anne said when she could finally speak.

"She's alive. Don't worry, you'll be with her soon. But first ..."

She screamed when he tore the jacket from her shoulders. It ripped in two and fell to the carpet, wires sparking on either side.

"Interesting." William kicked it experimentally, then turned his horrifying black eyes back to her. "Now, let's make sure you aren't hiding any other surprises."

50

A DARK ROOM

ANNE CHOKED ON HER GAG, which threw her into another coughing fit. Tight ropes bound her to a chair, preventing her from doubling over, which was just as well, because she would probably throw up if she did — not something she wanted to experience with a ball of cloth stuffed in her mouth.

She guessed an hour had passed since William dragged them from Doris' apartment. He had covered their heads with dark cloth before stuffing them into a vehicle. The ride had been short — less than twenty minutes, she thought — but that still meant they could be anywhere within San Francisco city limits.

Doris sat across from her, similarly bound and gagged. Anne could only make out her frightened eyes in the dim light, cast from a small window set high in the only door to their closet-sized prison.

I'm sorry, Doris, Anne thought. *I'm so sorry you were mixed up in this. I wish I'd told you about the vampires so you'd at least know what we're up against.*

She could only imagine what horrible things were going through Doris' head right now.

I wish, too, that I'd shared the wonders I've seen at Z-Tech. If you knew how resourceful Charlie, Mark, and Cappa are, you'd have the same hope that I do.

As clever as William thought he was, he wouldn't elude them for long. Anne's friends *would* find her, and when they did ...

Heaven help him when Zima gets here.

The question was whether she and Doris would still be alive when they arrived. Anne remembered William's cruel pleasure at her terror in the furniture store, his murderous stare before Charlie chased him away, and Madeline, his poor ex-wife ...

William was a monster long before he became a vampire.

As if on cue, the door opened, admitting William and one of his ghouls. The ghoul pulled a chain on a hanging light, causing Anne and Doris to squint. Anne nearly choked when she recognized the shock of blonde hair on the wiry lackey. It was the same ghoul who'd thrown Charlie into a car.

Fear seized her heart when William stepped behind her. Rough hands removed her gag, triggering another coughing fit.

"You and I are going to play a game," William said, "and the rules are simple."

Anne shrieked when he pulled a long knife from his belt. A flashback threatened at the back of her mind — she could already feel the cold steel slicing her neck open — but a look at Doris gave her the strength to keep it at bay. William rolled his sleeve up.

She and Doris winced when he casually sliced his arm open. Blood pooled in the wound, but was slow to drip, as if it didn't want to leave his body.

"When I put my arm to your mouth, you drink," William said. "Clear?"

It took a moment to grasp his intentions, then her eyes widened.

He wants to turn me into a vampire!

"No! Y-you're insane if you think I'd ever agree to —"

She never saw Allesandro's hand move, but Doris' head snapped sideways. Her friend screamed behind her gag, and a bright red welt shone on her cheek.

"I'll ask again," William said with a sadistic grin. "Are we clear on the rules?"

Anne looked with tear-filled eyes at her brave Doris, who glared at Allesandro despite her obvious pain.

"You're a monster," Anne said through clenched teeth. "Cutting my throat and leaving me to die wasn't good enough, was it? You had to murder someone and plant their body in my goddamned apartment! And Madeline ..." Anne shook her head. "What did that poor woman do to deserve such a cruel death? Was it because I talked to her? Is your mind really that twisted? She deserved a fucking medal for putting up with you for so many —"

Doris' muffled cry cut her short. Allesandro struck her so hard this time that she toppled sideways and skidded across the cement floor. William didn't even glance at the spectacle. He feverishly scratched his cheek wound, but his sadistic eyes never left Anne.

"I didn't mean to interrupt," William said in a deadly whisper. "By all means, please continue your insightful observations."

She looked at Doris whimpering on the floor and bit back a sob.

"I hate you. I hate you!" was all Anne could say through a growing, helpless despair.

"I don't give a fuck about your love or hate," William said. "But you will fear me, and your suffering will be a thousand times worse than this goddamned burning disfigurement you've left me with! Now, I'll ask again. Are we clear on the rules of the game? And feel free to continue your pointless tirade. Doris is strong, I have no doubt, and can take a few more blows before Allesandro does any permanent damage."

To illustrate the point, Allesandro pulled Doris upright by her coppery hair, eliciting another scream. The red welt on her face was rapidly turning purple.

Her head wobbled in a daze, but her loving eyes found Anne's, and that strength returned that said, "Don't give in, kiddo."

My Doris, Anne thought, sobbing.

Her best friend had no idea what drinking William's blood meant, but she was still willing to take any punishment to keep Anne from having to capitulate to the madman who held them captive. Doris would resist with her dying breath, and it was that realization more than anything else that made Anne's choice clear.

She couldn't let that happen. Not when it was within her power to prevent.

"I understand," Anne said with resigned calm. "I'll drink it."

William looked disappointed. "So be it."

He raised his arm to her face. Bile rose in Anne's throat when he pressed the wound to her mouth.

Doris watched the freak show with naked horror. Anne wondered how she would react if she knew of the aggressive virus pooling on her tongue. She hesitated before swallowing, but one look at her friend's battered face was enough to make her force it down. She hoped one would be enough to satisfy William, but he kept his arm in place. She swallowed another mouthful against a rising lump in her throat, then again and again. She felt sick by the time he pulled away, but prayed she didn't vomit for fear of what he would do to Doris if she did. The videos Charlie had shown her of the virus attacking normal cells played in her mind. She pictured a blackness spreading through her stomach, then to her lungs, and finally her heart.

In the cruelest twist of fate Anne could imagine, William was turning her into one of his ghouls.

"You played well," he said, rolling his sleeve down. "But that was just a warm-up. The real game is just starting." He tied her gag back into place and leaned close, his breath cold on her ear. "I'll see you in a few hours," he whispered.

William turned the light out, then he and Alessandro left them in isolated darkness once again.

With William's infected blood dripping down her chin, Anne sagged her head and cried.

• • •

The first symptom was a stomachache, though whether from William's blood or her frayed nerves, Anne couldn't say. The ache eventually subsided, replaced by a chill radiating outward from her core. She started to shiver, mildly at first, but as the cold continued to effuse, her shaking became so violent that it rattled the legs of her chair.

A loud thump made her look up. Doris was hopping her chair over, and soon they were shoulder-to-shoulder. Her body heat felt nice, though it did little to quell Anne's shaking limbs.

More time passed. Anne was exhausted from the constant shivering. A foreign presence tickled the back of her mind. It was faint, but grew steadily stronger while her body continued to weaken. She couldn't say how, but she knew without a doubt it was William. Emotions began to trickle through: hatred, burning pain …

Hunger.

He continued to spread like a cancerous growth in her head. Anne whimpered. Sadistic satisfaction poured from him at her feeling of helplessness. She recoiled from his sheer malevolence, which seemed to please him even more. Anne closed her eyes and tried to drown him out by thinking about her novel hero, Jayne Madison, as she used to as a teen when frightened.

Jayne, however, was just as powerless against his growing influence. Anne screamed in frustration, flailing against her bonds until she nearly toppled her chair, but her struggle was in vain. Her pistol, her gadgets, her training … as hard as she had tried, William won anyway. He had her in his grasp — mentally and physically — and they both knew it.

Too exhausted to cry, she sagged against Doris and shivered, clinging to a last, desperate hope that her friends would rescue her soon and find some miraculous cure for the taint in her body. The problem was that Anne had no idea what sort of creature she would be when they arrived, or if the monster she was turning into would even be happy to see them.

51

BREAKFAST WITHOUT

CHARLIE SAT NEXT TO CAPPA IN THE KITCHEN, both of them watching Zima pace behind Anne's empty chair, as she had for most of the morning, while Mark finished his breakfast. Charlie glanced at his own bowl of gray paste, then turned to Mark with a wistful sigh, who was just wiping his plate clean.

"Glad you liked it," Cappa said.

Mark swiped a napkin across his mouth and smiled. "Always. You're a good cook."

"Better than Anne?"

"You're both good cooks, just different styles."

Cappa leaned on her elbows. "Yeah, but which style tastes better?"

"That's like asking if I prefer the Ferrari or the Lamborghini. It's impossible to choose."

"Very diplomatic answer. I may cook for you again." She reached for his plate, but Zima swooped in and carried it to the counter. Cappa and Charlie exchanged a surprised look; it wasn't like Zima to help with the dishes.

"Want a hand?" Cappa said.

"No."

Dishes and pans clattered loudly, making Cappa wince. "That's my nice cookware ..."

Mark grabbed a dishtowel and joined Zima.

"Will wonders never cease," Cappa muttered.

"I'm sure Anne's fine," Mark said to Zima. "Hopefully she and Doris had a great time, and —"

Zima spun on him, brandishing a paring knife. "Anne is not answering her phone."

"Whoa, now," Cappa said, taking a cautious step forward. "Didn't we all agree to give her some space this morning? We've been monopolizing her time. She probably just needs a break."

Zima flipped the knife and caught it without looking. "Doris is not answering, either."

Charlie frowned. He was beginning to share Zima's concern.

"It was a slumber party," Mark said. "They probably stayed up late gossiping about ... whatever it is women gossip about ... and are sleeping it off."

"I am going to Doris' apartment."

Zima made for the door, but Cappa intercepted, hands planted firmly on her hips. Charlie kept a wary eye on the paring knife.

"Zima, please! I know you miss her," Cappa said, "but she'll call when she's ready. Have a little faith."

"I do not question Anne's intentions; only her safety. Please move."

A faint blue glow shone from Zima's eyes, something they had all learned was a dangerous sign.

Charlie stood. Zima swiveled to face him, knife in hand, but he put his hands up and said, "I'm coming with you."

Cappa sighed. "You're as bad as she is."

"If we're wrong and Anne gets angry, then I'll apologize — we will apologize — and I'm sure we'll have a long conversation about boundaries. But if we're right ..."

Let's hope we're not right, he thought.

Cappa pursed her lips, but stepped aside.

"I shall meet you in the garage," Zima said to Charlie. She walked past Cappa without a glance.

"Charlie, I really think you should let this one go," Cappa said. "Anne needs her own time, just like everyone else."

"Neither she nor Doris answering at this hour?" Charlie shook his head. "I have a bad feeling about this."

"That's because you're paranoid!"

"And it's kept us alive this far," he said, scooting around her. "I'd rather not tempt fate."

Charlie was in a dead run by the time he reached the garage.

• • •

The door to Doris' apartment creaked open when Charlie knocked, and what he saw inside confirmed his worst fears. Mark's jacket lay in ruins on the floor. Black holes marred the walls, which Charlie was sure were plasma burns, yet no bodies were visible.

Zima darted into one of the bedrooms.

Mark's jacket, he thought, looking at the torn wreckage.

The material was laden with nano-circuits. Ripping it in half wasn't easy; whoever did this had extraordinary strength.

Strong enough to throw me halfway through a car ...

Zima rushed past him and out of the apartment.

WHERE ARE YOU GOING? Charlie sent to her.

She responded with geo-coordinates, which he immediately plotted on a virtual map. The location was a few miles from the apartment.

WHAT'S THERE?

VAMPIRES.

Charlie was going to ask how she knew that, but quickly decided it didn't matter. ON MY WAY.

NOT NECESSARY. STAY AND LOOK FOR MORE EVIDENCE IN CASE SHE IS NOT THERE.

HOW MANY VAMPIRES ARE THERE?

APPROXIMATELY SIXTEEN.

Christ ...

ZIMA, I SAW WHAT JUST FIVE OF THEM DID TO YOU!

THAT WAS AN AMBUSH, AND I WAS ILL-EQUIPPED THEN. I HAVE MARK'S NEW PLASMA WEAPONS, SIGNIFICANTLY MORE COMBAT DATA, AND STRATEGIC ADVANTAGE THIS TIME. SIXTEEN SHALL NOT POSE A THREAT.

Charlie ran a hand through his hair. AND IF THERE ARE MORE?

THEN I SHALL ADJUST MY TACTICS ACCORDINGLY.

MARK'S ON HIS WAY, ZIMA. The message came from Cappa, embedded with feelings of worry. ETA SEVEN MINUTES.

THERE IS A NINETY-EIGHT PERCENT CHANCE THE THREATS WILL BE NEUTRALIZED BY THE TIME HE ARRIVES.

Charlie itched to join her, but he knew Zima was right. Assault was her specialty and, if she didn't find Anne, they'd need Charlie's forensic skills to dig up every possible clue here at the crime scene.

I'LL LET YOU KNOW WHAT I FIND. REPORT AS SOON AS YOU CONFIRM ANNE OR DORIS' LOCATION. Charlie sent the message, then returned his attention to the apartment.

Anne's belongings were scattered all around. Her phone sat next to Doris'; each displayed several missed calls from Zima. Her glasses and wallet lay forgotten in the corner, and the smashed remnants of her pistol were strewn across the kitchen counter.

Dried blood stained the carpet of the master bedroom. He pinched some between his fingers and put it to his mouth, where chemical analyzers got to work. He breathed a sigh of relief when the results came back a few seconds later: It wasn't Anne's blood, though that didn't bode well for Doris. He also found traces of the same chemicals that were present in the bite wound on his arm, which confirmed that this was a vampire attack.

A piece of red cloth caught his eye, dangling from a coat hook near the door. He fingered the familiar red-striped necktie, and his face went ashen.

"Oh God ..."

IT'S WILLIAM! Charlie broadcast the message to everyone. HE MUST BE ONE OF THE INFECTED.

Forensic duties forgotten, Charlie ran after Zima as fast as his legs would carry him.

52

HELL HATH NO FURY ...

ZIMA CHOSE HER LAUNCH POSITION CAREFULLY. Her target entry point was a weak spot on the warehouse roof thirty-two meters from where she crouched on the adjacent building. Jumping that distance would put a tremendous amount of force on the support beam beneath her. It felt solid enough, so she began charging her capacitors. A hum emanated from her chest while her power reactor worked at maximum output to fill the temporary energy stores.

She knew from her encounters with the cold ones that they had above-average hearing. Thousands of simulations concluded that a surprise attack was the best way to ensure the safety of the civilians. She ran a few more simulations from her final launch position while she waited for the charge to finish.

Capacitors at twenty percent, an internal system reported.

Audio analysis had isolated four distinct breathing patterns inside. Since the cold ones didn't breathe, that suggested four human hostages. Zima estimated a forty-one percent chance that one of them was Anne — more than enough to justify the assault.

Zima pulled the new plasma pistols from her jacket and ejected the clips.

Capacitors at forty percent.

Rising energy made the hum louder. She pushed a finger between a hidden fold of skin under her wrist, pulled out a black cable, and plugged it into one of the pistols. They were specially designed by Mark to draw from her own power supply, which enabled a significantly greater sustained rate of fire.

Capacitors at sixty percent.

Thermal output was higher than anticipated. She had not pushed her capacitors past fifty percent since her body was first commissioned. The risk of explosion was small, however, so she continued. She fished a cable from her other wrist and fastened it to the remaining gun.

Capacitors at eighty percent. Core temperature approaching critical.

According to her simulations, an eighty percent charge should be sufficient to neutralize all sixteen targets. The cold ones did breathe, making them difficult to detect. It was possible there were more than sixteen, in which case eighty percent would not be enough. A quick calculation determined the extra charge was worth the risk of explosion, so she let it continue.

A wisp of smoke drifted from the neck of her shirt. While her synthetic flesh could withstand high temperatures, her clothes were another matter. She plucked at her jacket, hoping the extra airflow would not cause it to ignite.

Capacitors at ninety-four percent. Core temperature exceeds maximum safety threshold. Reactor shutdown is imminent.

As Mark would say, it was good enough. Zima overrode the shutdown, cut power to the capacitors, then beat out a small fire on her collar.

Gripping her guns tightly, Zima surged power to her legs. The support beam cracked from the tremendous force output by her powerful electromagnetic muscles. She launched into a high arc over the gap between the buildings. At three meters to impact of the opposite roof, she went ramrod-straight, heels down, and folded her arms close to her body.

Zima punched through the aluminum sheet with a peel of thunder, bending her legs as she did so to reduce her velocity to almost zero. Her head passed through soon after and she quickly took in her surroundings.

Ten meters to the ground. One second to impact.

Her trajectory to the floor was clear of obstacles, and it was an open floor plan, as she had hoped. She selected six candidate simulations that closely matched the actual layout, then switched to thermal view.

Zero-point-nine seconds to impact.

Thermals registered four humanoids with normal body temperatures and eighteen at room temperature. Two more cold ones than she originally anticipated. Old furniture, boxes, and barrels littered the space, with the cold ones strewn throughout. The warm captives were tied to railings and other fixtures.

Zero-point-eight seconds to impact.

Highly optimized algorithms quickly identified the best of the candidate simulations. She made some adjustments for accuracy then re-ran the winning simulation. The result was an estimated ten percent chance of a friendly fire incident for one of the civilians, but less than one percent for the remaining three. It estimated her own chances of survival at ninety-four percent with a twenty-two percent chance of injury.

And it called for elimination of all hostiles before she reached the ground.

Eighteen total targets. She was moving fast, so the miss chance was twenty percent per target. That required at least twenty-two shots for a one hundred percent kill ratio. Her weapons could discharge a total of twenty-eight shots per second, which left her two short.

The odds were still acceptable. She promoted the simulation to real-time.

Zero-point-seven seconds to impact.

Her parallel processors had completed five of the eighteen firing solutions. Two had a confidence rating of ninety-five percent, so she moved them into the processing queue for execution.

Her arms uncoiled, snapping to their targets. The dim warehouse lit with bright orange flashes from two plasma bolts, which streaked forth and struck their marks. Each landed with zero-point-three percent deviance— well within the lethal threshold. She flagged the targets as terminated.

One of the five firing solutions had less than fifty percent confidence, so she rejected it and sent it back for reprocessing. The remaining two solutions were eighty percent or higher. She held those from execution in favor of new solutions with higher ratings.

Zero-point-six seconds to impact.

Sixteen targets remained; ten more firing solutions presented. She sent three back for reprocessing. Of the nine viable solutions, she queued the top four for execution. Three of the four bolts struck within zero-point-one percent deviance, and the targets were marked as terminated. The fourth target moved unexpectedly, and the bolt landed with thirty percent deviance. Its injuries reduced its threat level, so she submitted the target for a low-priority firing solution.

Zero-point-five seconds to impact.

Six of the remaining seven solutions presented. One was invalid because the target had moved, so she deleted it and requested a new one. The rest of the targets began to stir, but were still within acceptable parameters. She pushed four more firing solutions into the execution queue. Only two of the four shots landed with terminal accuracy, so she submitted the remaining two for reprocessing.

Zero-point-four seconds to impact.

Eleven targets; three of them injured. Two firing solutions were missing, but those in the queue were rated at eighty percent or greater. Four more solutions pushed and executed. All of them landed with less than two percent deviance. She removed the targets from the active threat list.

Zero-point-three seconds to impact.

The remaining two firing solutions were complete. One of the targets had moved behind a civilian, creating a friendly fire situation. She rejected that target's solution and submitted for complex evaluation. She set the safety threshold at ninety-nine percent. Calculations would take longer than normal, but with seven targets remaining, she had enough to occupy her in the meantime.

Four solutions executed. Four orange flashes. Four threats removed.

Zero-point-two seconds to impact.

Three active targets. Only two firing solutions were ready, each rated near eighty percent confidence, which was low.

She pushed them into the queue anyway. One landed with acceptable deviance, the other flew wide and burned a hole through a pile of wooden pallets. She re-submitted the latter.

Zero-point-one second to impact.

The two remaining firing solutions returned. The complex solution involving the civilian was in two parts and required her feet to be on the ground, so she held that one and queued the other. A flash of orange left her with only one active threat.

She waited for the final distance to close between her and the floor.

Brace for landing.

Concrete shattered beneath her feet, shooting flecks of debris everywhere. Zima pushed the first of the two-part solution into execution.

Her foot hooked around a small tire and kicked out. The tire flew wide of both the hostile and the civilian. Her target watched it sail through the air, but he remained behind his human shield. The friendly fire rating was still unacceptably high.

The tire bounced from a nearby railing at a sharp angle and struck the cold one in the shoulder, toppling him from behind the civilian. The friendly fire rating dropped below one percent, so she pushed the second part of the firing solution into the execution queue.

Both pistols fired. One bolt landed with six percent deviance, incinerating his shoulder, but the other struck with less than one percent deviance, searing through his head. The last active threat fell from the list.

Zima made a final check to confirm the cold ones were all immobile. The remaining civilians cringed when the blue light of her eyes swept over them.

They did not concern her, because Anne was not among them.

• • •

Morning colored Anne and Doris' tiny room in shades of pink. Other presences began to appear in Anne's mind, dozens of them, although they were pinpoints beside William's blazing presence. He and the others tired as the hues of morning blended to white, inviting her to slumber with them. Twice she caught herself nodding off, but forced herself awake by biting her gag to induce a coughing fit. The chill in her core had spread to her limbs, and she continued to tremble against Doris. Try as she might, exhaustion eventually won. Sleep claimed her.

Anne woke just before the door opened. The growl of her stomach echoed in her cold chest. Doris, who had also been sleeping, looked up in alarm at the sound of the latch.

William stared at them, then nodded to Alessandro. Anne screamed through her gag when the henchman made for Doris.

"Just giving her a break," William said with a cruel smile. "You could use a trip to the bathroom, right Doris?"

Doris nodded vigorously. Alessandro untied her from the chair and released her gag. She coughed uncontrollably for a minute before she was finally able to stand.

William stopped her at the door. "The others are sleeping outside. If you scream, they'll wake up, and I won't stop them from tearing you to pieces. Understood?"

Doris nodded, genuine fear in her eyes, then Allesandro led her away.

My poor Doris, Anne thought.

"Finally! It's just you and me." William sat comfortably in the vacant chair and yanked the gag from her mouth.

"Charlie will f-find you," Anne said, still shivering uncontrollably.

"I doubt it, but even if he does, thirty-six vampires should be more than a match for him and his toys. After all, it only took five to reduce that blonde dyke of yours to a heap of bloody scrap metal."

Anne closed her eyes. She hadn't made the connection until now.

Of course he was behind the attack. He's the source of all of my misery.

She knew he wasn't exaggerating about their numbers, either; she could feel each of them in her mind.

My God, thirty-six vampires ...

"That's right," he said, reading her doubts. "Let them come, I —"

She and William felt the disturbance at the same time. In the span of a heartbeat, seventeen pinpoints cried in burning pain, then winked out of existence.

Anne could feel his shock through their link.

"Ch-Charlie?" he said in a hollow voice. "But how —"

A last pinpoint flared. This one carried impressions with it: *Loud noise. Screams. Fear. Blue-eyed angel of death. Orange flashes. Searing pain.*

Then that presence flickered out, too.

Fear and disbelief radiated from William. Anne laughed, happy at last to see his confidence broken — a small revenge for all the misery he'd inflicted on her.

"N-not Charlie, you misogynistic son-of-a-bitch," she said through chattering teeth. "That was my girlfriend — you know, the 'blonde dyke'? Looks like you pissed her off." Anne returned his cruel smile. "You don't have a fucking clue who you're messing with. She will find me, and when she does, all the blood-sucking lackeys in the world won't stop her from ripping your goddamned head off!"

53

CLEANUP

CHARLIE RODE LIKE A BICYCLIST FROM HELL. Running on foot through the city streets at fifty miles per hour would have drawn too much attention, so he had stolen a nearby mountain bike. To its credit, the bike withstood his weight until a block from his destination, where he hit a curb at the wrong angle. The front wheel buckled and tipped him over the handlebars. Charlie rolled with it and came up running, no longer caring who witnessed his inhuman speed.

Mark pulled his car up to the warehouse just as Charlie arrived and they silently took positions on either side of the building's door.

His enhanced hearing picked up only the hum of Zima's power reactor inside. The door was locked. Charlie put his shoulder to it, and it opened with a crunch.

They both swore at what they saw.

A stack of corpses as tall as he was lay in the center of the large room. Several bodies still smoldered, sending trails of smoke up to a Zima-sized hole in the ceiling.

"Anne is not here," Zima said. She casually tossed two more bodies on the pile. "The police may arrive soon. We should dispose of these infected corpses quickly."

"How many are there?" Mark said.

"Eighteen."

Jesus, Charlie thought.

Zima had only a small tear on one sleeve and a few burn marks on her shirt to show for it.

Eighteen, and barely a scratch on her.

Mark cleared his throat. "And the hostages ...?"

"I asked them to delay before informing the authorities, though it is unlikely they will comply with my request."

"They're alive!" Mark sighed in relief.

Zima blinked. "Yes, they were not harmed during the assault."

"Did you interrogate any of the infected?" Charlie said.

"No. One hundred percent hostile termination was required to minimize risk to the civilians."

Charlie cursed and kicked a nearby barrel, leaving a large dent.

Zima cocked her head. "Was that wrong?"

"No, Zima," Mark said. "Keeping the hostages safe was your first priority." Mark circled the smoking pile. "Like Zima said, we need to get rid of these bodies. We can't risk the investigators getting contaminated."

Charlie pushed his frustration aside and forced himself to think. "I saw a moving truck parked just around the corner."

"On it," Mark said, and ran for the door. "I'll back it up to the loading dock."

"All right, we'll move the bodies closer to the door and clean things up before the cops get here."

Charlie turned to find Zima already carting two bodies toward the loading dock.

On his second trip, a cell phone clattered to the floor from one of their pockets. Charlie looked at it thoughtfully. "Zima, grab all the phones you can find, and be sure to turn them off."

Zima brow-knit. "The GPS records," she said. "We can use the system logs in their phones to see where they have been."

She set to the task and began searching the bodies.

"Exactly." Charlie fell in beside her. "If they've called William, we can pick it out of the call logs, but even if they haven't ..."

"We may discern a common location they have all visited. Many of the phones will be encrypted. I will assist in accessing the protected devices."

SHE'S MUCH FASTER AT CRACKING ENCRYPTION THAN ME. Feelings of pride, jealousy, and a twinge of fear accompanied Cappa's message.

She would know, Charlie thought.

When Zima's cyborg assaulted them many years ago, Cappa was on the business end of her cyber-attacks — an experience she said she'd rather not repeat.

"When Zima was hacking my defenses, I felt like a college kid in a horror movie," Cappa had confessed some years later. "All alone in a cabin in the woods after my friends had been slaughtered, throwing my weight against a flimsy wooden door while the ax murderer is breaking it to pieces."

They found thirteen working cell phones in all, which Charlie gathered in an old burlap sack. They also collected wallets for identification.

The families will need to know about their loved ones, eventually, Charlie thought grimly.

A truck reverse alarm told him Mark was almost in position. Zima yanked the padlock on the door. It broke open with a loud clank and the chain fell to the ground.

They quickly loaded the bodies into the back of the moving truck. The loading dock faced a dead-end street with no traffic, which allowed their grisly task to go unobserved.

"I think I know where to dispose the bodies," Mark said. "We should get out of here. Let the investigators puzzle over the plasma burns, they won't be able to trace them back to us."

"Thanks," Charlie said. "We'll head back to Z-Tech and start working on the phones."

They double-checked to make sure they hadn't missed anything obvious, then closed up the warehouse.

Mark drove away, leaving Charlie and Zima with his car. They threw their bags in the trunk. Zima climbed in the driver's side, and Charlie next to her.

"Do you think William is still in the City?" Zima said on the ride back.

"Probably. Lots of people, plenty of places to hide, and his records show he's lived in San Francisco for over a decade, so he knows the area. It's the perfect hunting ground for him."

"Do you think he will kill Anne?"

Charlie ground his teeth; he'd been avoiding that question himself. "He's certainly capable of it, and more."

"By 'more', you imply torture or sexual assault?"

"Yes," Charlie said gruffly, wishing she would drop the subject.

They drove in silence for a few blocks.

"Escorting her from the restaurant was my task," Zima said. "If I had executed according to plan, she would not have been abducted."

Is that regret?

Charlie was surprised at the admission; it wasn't like Zima to second-guess herself. He added it to the long list of positive changes he'd seen in her recently.

"True, but if it's any consolation, I think you did the right thing by letting her go."

"I do not believe the outcome supports your assertion."

"She had advanced weaponry, a targeting system, and your training to tie it all together. Anne was as prepared as anyone could have been. I analyzed the footprints and stains in the apartment. There were three vampires in total. Anne killed two. She did well, Zima, and so did we. The odds were just stacked too high against her."

They lapsed into silence again.

"I miss her, Charlie. I want her back."

"Me too. We'll find her, hopefully alive and well." Charlie clenched his jaw. "Then we're going to find William, and end this nightmare once and for all."

• • •

Mark locked the barn doors, then pulled a handkerchief from his jacket and wiped the grease from his hands.

The derelict farm belonged to his ex-girlfriend, Susan. Her family seldom used the house, so she would bring him here when they wanted to be alone. Although their relationship hadn't worked out, he had fond memories of their time here together. They'd spent hours on the porch talking in the warmth of the South Bay sun.

It used to be a cattle farm, she'd told him. Disposal of animal carcasses with an open fire was illegal, so they'd purchased an agricultural incinerator: a clean-burning furnace that efficiently reduced almost anything — including human bodies — to ash.

As luck would have it, the large propane tank feeding the incinerator still had gas in it and, as a bonus, the barn was big enough to stash the moving truck.

I'll come back for it when things settle down.

Mark pulled his phone out and dialed. "It's done," he said when Charlie picked up.

"I won't ask how."

"Probably best. Any luck with the cell phones?"

"There wasn't as much tracking data as we hoped. We identified three strong candidate locations, but Zima's already ruled them out. She's working her way down the list in order of probability, but ... it's not looking good."

"No call history conveniently labeled 'William Taplin'?"

"I wish, though there is a pattern," Charlie said. "The logs show that each phone was turned off for about a day."

"Isn't that the incubation period of the virus?"

"Yep. After that, there are a few calls or text messages to friends and family, mostly saying that the person will be away for a while, then *nada*."

Mark paced in front of the barn. "So ... they're turned into vampires, they willingly cede personal ties, and they're trusted with cell phones they don't use afterward?"

"Seems like it. Whoever's in charge has a tight hold on these people, but I can't figure out how. Hypnosis, brainwashing ... nothing explains this level of control over such a short period of time."

"Either way, it doesn't solve our problem of how to find Anne," Mark said. "So the phones are a dead end. What about the cell carriers themselves? They're bound to have tracking data on their customers."

"Right. If they keep records of cell phone signal strength to the towers, we can use the data to triangulate their positions."

"It's a long shot, but better than scouring the City ourselves. Does Zima have a backdoor into a carrier we can leverage?"

"I do not," Zima said through the receiver. "I did, several years ago, but they discovered my intrusion and have since improved their security. You are correct, however. The carriers have the data we seek."

"Sorry," Charlie said, "did I forget to mention that Zima and Cappa are on the line, too?"

"It's just as well," Mark said. "Zima, how long would it take you to hack into one of them and grab the data?"

"That is difficult to estimate. From outside of their network, it may take hours or days, depending on the sophistication of their security. A more expedient approach would be to connect from the inside."

Mark scratched his chin. "How long then?"

"Minutes to hours, depending upon their internal security protocols."

"Let's say two-factor authentication with a one-kilobyte private key."

"Two to seven hours."

"And if you had someone's private key?"

"Assuming the key is authorized to access the data, I know exactly where to find it."

Mark pinched the bridge of his nose. "All right, stay tuned. You'll have access to their network, and a key with top authorization, hopefully within the hour."

"Let me guess," Cappa said. "One of your old girlfriends works for a major carrier, and you're going to seduce her and steal her key?"

"Worse. Talk to you later. I need to make some calls."

Mark hung up and took a deep breath, then pulled up his contact list.

I can't believe I'm doing this ...

He tapped his girlfriend's name with a shaking finger, hoping Dela could leave her job at the café on short notice without getting fired, though he'd be happy if he still had a girlfriend once she heard his ludicrous request.

54

RENDEZVOUS WITH MARK

DELA MADIGAN — OR FEDELMA, as her traditional Irish parents had named her — spotted Mark as soon as her car pulled into the parking lot. He was sitting at a table in front of the café where he had asked to meet.

"Anne's in trouble," he had said over the phone. "We think she's been kidnapped, and we need your help to find her. The police won't help because she's been missing for less than forty-eight hours. Helping means you'll have to break the law, and I understand if —"

"I'll help," Dela had said. "Just tell me what I need to do."

Thirty minutes later — and thankfully without a speeding ticket for her ludicrous driving — here she was.

"Thanks for coming," Mark said earnestly.

He gave her a quick kiss before they both sat down. A steaming dark brew awaited her at the table. His thoughtfulness made her smile.

"Of course," Dela said. "Anne's my friend, too. We're both dating tech-heads, and she's the only person I can commiserate with." She grinned, but his serious expression told her that he wasn't in a joking mood. "Okay, give me the scoop."

"I hate to use a cliché, but you wouldn't believe me if I told you. Even if I did tell you, you wouldn't believe me unless I showed you, and we don't have time for that right now."

"But —"

"I will tell you, Dela, and I will show you, I promise, but it's going to have to wait until after we get an idea of where Anne is. Every minute counts."

Typical Mark, she thought. *Shrouded in secrets and half-truths.*

For all their time together, he had spoken very little about himself or his duties at Z-Tech, and would skillfully change the subject when asked about his past. It wasn't until now that she realized how little she knew about him, and it bothered her.

"Mark, I want to help you. I want to help Anne, but you've got to give me something!"

He drummed his fingers on the table. "All right, but please trust me when I say the details should wait. You remember the man I told you about who attacked Anne a few months ago?"

"Yeah, the creepy guy in the suit?"

"William. This morning Anne didn't show for breakfast. When Charlie and Zima went to check on her at Doris' apartment, there were signs of a struggle, and they couldn't find either of them. The gun I gave her had been fired several times. They also found one of William's belongings, something he wore on the day of the attack."

The gravity of his words hit her like a flying kick. "Shit."

"Yes," Mark said, leaning forward. "William is a sadistic psychopath who ..." He pressed his lips together.

Dela felt her Irish temper flare. He was holding back again.

"Who *what?*"

"Who we believe is even more dangerous now for reasons that I swear I will explain later. We also think he's in a gang of sorts. Zima ... ran into a group of them earlier today. Long story short: she got her hands on their cell phones. We want to use carrier data to see where they've been, and where they may be keeping Anne."

"Okay," Dela said, feeling somewhat mollified. That was more information than he had shared with her in the last two weeks combined. "So why do you need me?"

"In about five minutes, a man named Matt Barber is going to join us for coffee. Matt is a senior system administrator for the largest carrier in California, whose primary data center is located in that large building across the street."

Dela pursed her lips. "Five minutes, huh? You were pretty confident I'd agree if you already had this arranged."

"I had faith you'd want to help Anne as much as we do because you're wonderful, and I was right on both counts."

"All right, silver tongue," Dela said, smiling despite herself. "You got me. I'm in. Just stop trying to shelter me. I'm not some dumb coffee girl who's content to hang on your arm like a trophy. I've been around the block a few times, and I can handle whatever it is you think I'm not ready for."

"I know, which is exactly why I called you." He took her hand. "I need someone competent to pull this off."

Mark quickly explained his plan. Her mouth fell open.

"J-just one question," Dela said once he'd finished. "Why me? I mean, why don't you do it? You're much better with tech stuff than I am."

"Because there's no plausible reason for Matt to grant me access to the server area. It's a breach of Z-Tech's contract for me to reach out to him directly, and he knows it. We're supposed to go through a different channel if we have technical questions or issues. Matt's pretty far down the chain of support and would never deal with a C-Level member of a partner company directly. It's only because of our personal relationship that he's agreed to meet. You, on the other hand ..."

"All right, I get it." Dela went over the plan again in her head. "What was it you said about the —"

"No time," Mark said quietly. "Here he comes."

Dela plastered a smile on her face and greeted Matt warmly.

Just call me Special Agent Madigan, she thought.

55

SPECIAL AGENT MADIGAN

MATT HELD THE DOOR OPEN FOR DELA and gestured grandly. "Right this way," he said.

"Why thank you," Dela said with a smile.

She brushed his arm on her way by and was pleased to see his face light up. Matt was around Mark's age, but that's where the similarities ended. His once-thick curls of light brown hair were thinning at the top, yet he'd let the sides grow so they bounced like a clown's wig when he walked. Large eighties-style glasses complemented his pressed, collared shirt and casual slacks. His worn sneakers looked like a remnant from his college years.

Bereft of company logos, the gray and beige lobby could have belonged to any business. Matt led them to a thick glass window, where she had to hand her driver's license through a small slot to the security guard on the other side. The guard dutifully looked between her and the card before sliding a guest badge back through the slot. It made her nervous that he didn't give her license back.

She used her badge to enter through a guest door, while Matt entered through a glass capsule he called a "mantrap". Once on the other side, Matt marched to a set of elevators and punched the *up* button with panache, which made his curls bounce. Dela stifled a laugh and tried to look impressed.

"The servers are on floors two through four," Matt said once they were in the elevator.

"Matt fancies himself a ladies' man," Mark had said during their brief strategy discussion. "He's bragged about luring female interns into an unmonitored part of the third-floor server room."

Dela smiled when Matt pressed button three.

Mark had introduced her as a college intern from San Francisco State University doing a rotation at Z-Tech. She was interested in cellular technology, he had said, and they thought it would be good experience for her to see a carrier data center. Matt had been hesitant until Mark let slip that she'd recently broken up with her boyfriend and may be on the rebound. Matt had quickly agreed to squeeze her into his schedule, and soon met them at the café. After the introductions, Mark had excused himself and left Dela in Matt's care.

The elevator opened into a short hallway. Directly in front of them was a heavy set of doors with a card reader.

"We both need to badge in," Matt said, placing his card on the reader, "or the alarm will sound when you walk in the door."

"This place is crazy! I never realized so much went into protecting a few computers."

Matt smiled. "Dela, I think you're in for a surprise."

He wasn't kidding. Intense white noise washed over her when they stepped into the gymnasium-sized room, pressing on her eardrums as if she were underwater. The sensation was so odd that she fiddled with her ears to try to relieve the pressure.

"Weird, isn't it?" Matt yelled. Though he was only a few feet away, it sounded like he was across the room.

"Yeah," Dela yelled back. Her voice was eerily soft, and she rubbed her ears again. "I guess this is what it's like to be hard of hearing."

The surprisingly warm air inside felt pleasant on her bare arms. She had intentionally left her jacket with Mark to show as much skin as possible to Matt.

Every bit helps.

"This building is the data hub for the entire country," Matt said. "Email, voice, text messages, internet traffic ... It all goes through this building. There are almost ten thousand servers in this room alone."

She believed it. The room was enormous. Rows of tall black cages filled with blinking lights spanned the length of it. Wires ran from cages in an orderly fashion through conduits leading into the floor.

Matt walked them over to one of the cages. Up close, she could see the individual computers, several feet wide, but only a few inches high and packed in tight. Heat from the exhaust fans was so intense that she plucked at her shirt to cool down. She pretended not to notice while Matt watched the show.

Dela stared at the wires plugged into the backs of the computers and fingered the special phone Mark had given her. "You'll need to unplug a network cable from the back of one of the servers and plug it into this," Mark had said.

"Matt," Dela said, stroking his shoulder, "which of these are the network cables?"

"The colored ones," Matt said, patting her hand. "Every server has at least two network connections, each plugged into a different switch for redundancy. If one is accidentally unplugged or the switch goes down, the server can still do its job. The black ones are power cables."

The colored cables, easy enough to remember.

Dela glanced at the ceiling. As Mark had predicted, security cameras were everywhere; unplugging a server out here would be risky at best.

Matt walked to the other side of the aisle and beckoned her to follow. A blast of cold air took her breath away when she crossed the boundary between rows, as if she had passed from summer to winter in a single step.

"The aisles alternate between hot and cold," Matt yelled, leaning close. "We're on a raised floor. There are several feet between the tiles and the actual floor. Cold air is pushed up from the floor tiles, pulled through the front of the servers, and the hot air that comes out the back is drawn through extractors above."

Dela looked down and sure enough, the tiles in the cold aisle had small holes, while the tiles in the hot aisle were solid.

With a shake, she reminded herself that she wasn't here to enjoy the tour.

Anne's life is on the line. I have to stay focused.

She needed a fast track to Matt's secret lair. While he spouted technical jargon about the data center, the goose bumps on her skin gave her an idea. She rubbed her arms and put on a miserable face.

"You're freezing," Matt yelled.

Thanks, Captain Obvious.

Dela smiled and made a show of shivering. "I'm such a ditz! I left my jacket with Mr. Suther. Is there some place we can go to warm up?" She leaned close and brushed his ear with her lips. "Some place private?"

He nodded and stammered something unintelligible, then hurried down the aisle toward the far side of the room with such enthusiasm that Dela had to jog to keep up.

God, I'm good.

Matt's secret sanctuary turned out to be a walled area in the corner of the server room labeled "Maintenance". He pulled a key from his pocket and opened the door for her. Bins filled with computer parts lined the walls. The only furniture in the small room were two comfortable-looking chairs, a workbench, and a plush couch.

She wasn't surprised when he led her to the couch.

So that's how it's going to be, eh?

She sat and patted the space next to her invitingly. He sat heavily and wrapped his arm around her without missing a beat.

"Let's warm you up," Matt said. He leaned in and began to kiss her neck.

Jeez, this guy's a piece of work.

Dela ignored him, pretending instead that an amorous puppy was licking her, and looked around for something with a colored cable plugged into it.

Her heart leaped when she spotted what she was looking for. A tiny box sat on the workbench. Two red wires ran from it to a server leaning against a wall.

Now to get him out of here so I can have some alone time ...

"Oh, Matty," Dela said, happy that she didn't have to yell in the quiet room. "This place is so cozy! I feel better already."

"I'm glad you like it," he said, nuzzling her ear. "No one's going to bother us here, so we can stay as long as you want."

She squealed with delight, trying not to laugh at her own corny performance. "You know what makes me feel *really* cozy?"

He shook his head.

"Champagne!"

Matt smiled and opened a small refrigerator next to the couch. She silently cursed when he pulled out a bottle of cheap bubbly.

"You're in luck," he said, "I was saving this for a special occasion, and you certainly fit the bill."

Strike one, Dela thought.

Matt produced two plastic champagne flutes from a bag, popped the cork, and poured a glass for each of them. He plopped beside her once again and she plastered a cheerful smile back on her face.

"Cheers!" he said, holding up his plastic ware.

She giggled and tapped his glass. It didn't taste as bad as she thought it would.

Months ago, she would happily have finished a cheap bottle like this, but Mark had raised the bar by spoiling her with fancy dinners and fine wines. Dela could taste the plastic from the cup, and the champagne had an unpleasant bite.

Damnit, Mark's turned me into a wine snob.

She forced a smile, however, and purred with delight. "This is wonderful, Matty. My body is tingling all over!"

Matt grinned as if he'd just won the lottery.

I can't believe he's buying this crap. All right, let's see how hard up he is.

Dela walked her fingers up the buttons of his shirt. "Know what makes me really hot?"

His mouth fell open. He shook his head, making his clown curls bounce.

"Strawberries." Dela licked her lips. "Strawberries and champagne make me absolutely gooey."

"S-strawberries ... okay, there's a supermarket right across the street. We can pop over and —"

"Can you go get them? It's nice and warm in here, and besides, I want more of this yummy champagne to loosen me up."

"Y-you're not supposed to be here by yourself," Matt said, looking uneasy. "I could get fired if they found you ..."

Dela grabbed his hand, pulled his glass toward her, and slowly licked the rim.

"Okay! Okay, just ..." Matt nearly tripped in his haste for the door. "Stay here, all right?"

The key!

She had almost forgotten: Matt was supposed to have a computer key that looked like some sort of flash drive.

If I were a computer geek, where would I keep my key...?

"Matt!"

He turned, shuffling anxiously from foot to foot.

"What if I need to go to the ladies' room, won't I need a key to get back in here?"

Matt dug into his pocket, tossed a set of keys on the workbench, and hurried out the door.

Dela counted to three before she fell on the couch laughing.

It's so good to be me.

She peeked out the door to make sure he was gone, then pulled the spy phone from her pocket and picked up his keys. Lo-and-behold, a well-used USB device hung from his keychain, labeled "two-factor authentication." She popped the back from the phone, exposing two jacks. She plugged the USB device into the phone and a light illuminated, which she hoped was a good sign.

Next, she unhooked a colored cable from the server and snapped it into the other jack on the phone. She waited anxiously for the other light to come on. It never did. Dela put the cable back in the server and tried the other one. The light came on this time, and she breathed a sigh of relief.

Her own phone buzzed a few seconds later with a message from Mark.

All good.

He had said it would only take a few minutes to find what they were looking for once they were connected.

She grabbed a cloth and wiped the slobber from her neck.

Yuck. I hope they get what they need before he comes back. Speaking of which ...

She hid the spy phone behind the bench and draped the damp cloth over it, then flopped into a comfy chair with a smile.

I think I missed my calling as a spy.

56

REALITY

MARK CHOKED ON HIS COFFEE when he saw Matt exit the building. He grabbed his phone and rapidly typed a message to Dela.

What's he doing outside?

He watched Matt cross the street.

Dela's reply came a few seconds later. I'm playing it safe. I sent him on an errand.

Matt entered the supermarket a few doors down from where Mark sat at the café.

Grocery store?

Yep, you can't seduce me without strawberries. You should know that. The end of Dela's message had a winking face, which made him smile.

Yes, I do.

A message from Zima appeared in Mark's thought stream.

DATA LOCATED. INITIATING DOWNLOAD.

Thank God.

HOW LONG? Mark sent.

FIVE MINUTES AND THIRTY-TWO SECONDS.

THANKS, ZIMA. KEEP ME POSTED.

Five minutes could be cutting it close, he thought. *I need to buy her some time.*

Mark watched a bird peck at a scrap of bread while he considered his options. He could bump into Matt at the market and stall him with questions. Z-Tech was a major partner with the carrier, after all. He could certainly dream up a problem, but they both knew there were channels Mark had to go through if he had an issue, and Matt could easily blow him off.

A car approached, forcing the bird to abandon its treasure and fly to a power line overhead.

A smile crept on his face.

Oh, that'll do nicely.

The power line ran along the side of the supermarket, which was blocked off by a wooden fence. Mark casually walked over, waited for a couple to pass by, then hopped the fence in a single bound. He crept along the wall to the circuit breakers, which were protected by a padlocked panel. Not wanting to make too much noise, he withdrew a small metal cylinder from his jacket, about the size of a pen. It was a laser cutter he used in the garage on car bodies.

FOUR MINUTES REMAINING.

Zima's message didn't come with attached emotions, like his, Charlie's, or Cappa's did, which was fine because Mark was anxious enough for both of them.

Mark took measure of the lock, then looked away before turning the laser on. Bright blue light lit up the walls. The metal lock soon became too hot to hold, so he paused to wrap it in his leather jacket sleeve. The padlock's catch had melted about halfway through.

THREE MINUTES REMAINING.

He's probably at the checkout by now.

Hoping it was enough, Mark yanked the padlock down. The *snap* of the metal breaking was louder than he hoped it would be. With one eye on the employee entrance not ten feet away, Mark opened the panel and flipped all of the breakers off as quickly as he could. A collective gasp from inside told him he'd achieved his goal. He didn't bother closing the panel before sprinting back over the fence.

His phone chimed with a message from Dela: What's the status?

Mark walked into the street to peek inside the supermarket. The fluorescent lights were off, as he'd hoped, which meant the registers were down, and the lines at the checkout stations were growing.

About two minutes. Matt's tied up. Looks like the grocery store lost power.

How lucky!

"Lucky" is my middle name. Mark stuffed his phone in his pocket and watched the supermarket entrance.

A message from Zima injected into his thoughts. ONE MINUTE REMAINING.

Mark swore silently when Matt emerged with a small container of strawberries. He quickly typed a message to Dela.

He's on his way back. It'll be close. Unplug the cable when you see a call from me.

He pulled up her contact and hovered a finger over the "Send" button.

TRANSFER COMPLETE. I HAVE DISCONNECTED FROM THE NETWORK.

Zima's confirmation was all Mark needed. He hit the button to call Dela and listened until it rang through to voicemail, hung up without leaving a message, then stared at the data center doors, anxiously waiting.

He jumped from his seat when Dela finally emerged wearing a curiously satisfied smile. A red blotch on her shirt made him pale.

"Tell me that's not a blood stain," Mark said.

"No, that's strawberry juice. *That,*" Dela said, pointing to a darker patch on her jeans, "is a blood stain."

"What happened, are you all right?"

"I'm fine, though Matt will need some ice to keep the swelling down."

"Swelling?"

"Yeah. He learned the hard way that 'no' means 'Touch me again and I'll break your nose.' Don't look so surprised," she said with a grin. "I told you I can take care of myself. I'm a black belt in karate. Handling a creep like him is a piece of cake, and very satisfying."

"I never doubted you."

Mark went to wrap his arms around her, but she stopped him with a firm hand to his chest.

"Uh-uh, not until I've had a long shower to wash off the slobber." Dela shuddered. "You got the information you needed?"

"Yes, I can't thank you enough."

"Just a day in the life of a spy. So, I've held up my end of the bargain. I believe you promised some details ...?"

"That I did. Come on, we can talk on the drive back to the City."

Dela frowned when they reached the parking lot. "Where's your car?"

"I didn't bring one. I caught a cab here from the farm."

"The ... farm?"

"Yes, that's where I stashed the moving truck."

"The moving truck, okay. I thought you were a Maserati kind of guy."

"The bodies wouldn't have fit in the Maserati."

"As in ... dead bodies? Mark, so help me God, if you're messing with me, I'm going to kick your ass." Dela closed her eyes and took a deep breath. "Why the hell were you carting around dead people?"

"Zima assaulted a den of vampires, and —"

Dela wasn't just bragging about her black belt status, apparently. Her fist flashed to his chin hard enough to make him see stars. The world spun and he stumbled against the car.

"The truth, you son-of-a-bitch! After the shit I just went through for you, is it really so hard to —"

Mark ducked in and silenced her with a kiss, and was pleasantly surprised when she didn't fight back. Her expression was sad when he pulled away. "That's the truth," he said. "And also why it was so hard to tell you."

"Come on, Mark! Vampires?"

"Yes, and not the friendly ones you read about in fantasy romance novels. They're incredibly fast, vicious, and strong enough to rip your arms off."

"Right, and Zima just waltzed into a few of them —"

"Not a few. Eighteen."

"Even better! And how did she manage to survive that? Wait, don't tell me!" Dela stroked her chin thoughtfully, though the veins throbbed on her forehead, and her face was as red as her hair. "Zima's actually a vampire hunter who killed them all with wooden stakes using crazy fighting skills she learned through an ancient society who've passed their secrets on throughout the ages. Did I miss anything?"

"'Yes' on the crazy fighting skills," Mark said, counting on his fingers. "'No' on the ancient society. Whether she's a vampire hunter ... that depends on your definition. Zima's an android, trained for espionage and military assault by a rogue technology corporation. And she killed them with plasma pistols, not wooden stakes."

Dela swung again, but he was expecting it this time and caught her wrist.

"I can prove it," Mark said. He pulled his phone out and flipped to the photo gallery. "See this? It's a picture of her body when we first made her, before we overlaid her flesh."

She stared at the image of Zima's metal endoskeleton. Mark flipped through the photos, feeling a wave of nostalgia at once again seeing the progression of her assembly. Dela's breath caught when he reached the finished product. He watched her carefully, but she was transfixed on Zima's naked form.

After a few minutes, Dela covered her mouth and shook her head.

Mark sighed. "I won't blame you if you walk away, Dela."

She rubbed her eyes and began pacing in a circle. "That ... my God, that's the coolest thing I've ever seen!" She snatched his phone away and stared at the picture again. "She's beautiful. She's amazing! I just can't believe it; she looks so real! And you built her?"

"It's ... a long story, but yes, Charlie and I built her body." Mark took his phone back and pulled up a different picture. "You saw how she was constructed, how sturdy she is? Well this is what five of those vampires did to her a few days before she met you."

"*Ballix!* You can't even recognize her!"

"That's right, Dela, and we're pretty sure those monsters are holding Anne and Doris captive."

Dela whipped the door open and slid into the driver's seat. "Get in. We're going to break some land speed records on the way back to Z-Tech, so you might want to buckle up."

Mark did as instructed. He was happy she'd decided to not leave him and, when the tires squealed around the corner and the car roared up the on-ramp, he was even happier to discover he was dating someone who drove just as crazily as he did.

57

HUNGER

FADING LIGHT IN THEIR TINY PRISON heralded evening's approach. Although they'd been captive for less than twenty-four hours, it felt like a year since Anne had been able to stretch her legs.

Thump thump. Thump thump.

The pulse Anne heard wasn't her own; it beat in concert with the throbbing veins in Doris' neck. Doris peered at her through swollen eyelids. The welts on her face had gone from bright red to dark purple. Anne turned away in shame.

I should have kept my damned mouth shut.

William had been enraged after Anne's little speech and gave them both a sound beating, but, unlike her poor Doris, Anne had barely felt it. The cold inside of her had spread to every inch of her body over the last few hours, leaving her shivering and numb.

Thump thump. Thump thump.

Her stomach rumbled. Twice their jailers had brought water, but not a scrap of food. Anne was so hungry she would have eaten anything: dog food, rotten vegetables ...

Thump thump. Thump thump.

The beating rhythm called, drawing her eyes back to Doris' pulsing veins. Her mouth watered at the sight. Thoughts came unbidden of sinking her teeth into her friend's neck, drinking deeply to satisfy —

Anne shook her head and squeezed her eyes closed.

Oh God, no! This can't be happening!

But she couldn't shut out the sound of Doris' heartbeat — sweet music that somehow promised to sate her hunger.

William's presence flared in her mind.

He was pleased. And he was coming.

Panic filled her when the door opened. William entered and shot her a smug look. Alessandro stood with his arms crossed, blocking the only exit. William removed her gag and untied her from the chair. Anne scrambled to the opposite side of the room and huddled in the corner.

He pointed at Doris, cruelty in his eyes.

"Feed."

"You're f-f-fucking c-crazy," Anne said, hugging her knees to keep her violent shivering under control.

"Feed," he said again, but this time she felt it in her mind as well. His command flared her hunger into a blazing, primal need that consumed all other thoughts.

Anne rose on shaking legs and stumbled toward the only food source in the room. Doris shrieked from behind her gag, shaking her head wildly.

The horror on her friend's face cut through Anne's ravenous instincts.

This is Doris, she thought desperately. *Doris!*

That she had to remind herself the person tied to the chair wasn't a meal, but her best friend in the world, terrified her more than any nightmare ever could. Anne fell to her knees with an anguished wail and pressed her head to the floor.

"No!" she cried, pounding her fists on the concrete. "I won't do it, not to my Doris. I won't. I won't. I won't!"

Doris grunted in pain, and a delicious smell filled the air. Anne recognized it instantly.

Blood.

The thought filled her with revulsion and excitement.

Doris' blood.

A single red drop splashed to the ground before her. It took every ounce of her will to keep from lapping it up like a starving dog. Her whole body tensed — a predator ready to pounce.

"Do it," William said, eyes wide with anticipation.

"No," Anne said through clenched teeth. Her vision tunneled to the red splotch on the floor. The smell was more intoxicating than anything Restaurant Gary Danko could offer. She panted with the effort to hold her ground.

"Take her!" Spittle flew from William's bared lips. "She's not your friend; she's food! You stare at that pitiful drop like it's your last meal, but there's so much more waiting inside those veins."

Doris' heartbeat was thunder in her ears. Anne reluctantly looked up, salivating at the trickle of blood that ran down Doris' arm. It was more than just beautiful: it was crimson salvation, the only substance in the world that could satisfy the gnawing ache in her gut. She wanted it — needed that delicious liquid like she had never needed anything before. Anne lurched to catch the precious drop before it hit the floor.

William flashed a fanged smile and yanked Doris by the hair, exposing her neck and the throbbing vessels beneath.

• • •

Anne peeled her lips in a feral snarl. She slunk forward on all fours, watching her prey carefully. Hunger consumed her, and she would not allow her prey to escape.

"Feast now," her sire said. "Follow your instincts!"

He pulled a knife and cut the bonds holding her prey in place. It tried to run. Anne pounced, pinning it beneath her, and bit deep into its neck. The coppery elixir that filled her mouth made her eyes roll back in ecstasy. She held her struggling prey firmly and drank in big gulps.

In the back of her mind, the last vestiges of her humanity cried in horror while Anne drained the lifeblood from her best friend.

58

RESCUE

CHARLIE PACED THE STREET CORNER, waiting for Zima's signal to move in. The data from the carrier had been a gold mine. It pinpointed two locations in the City frequented by the deceased vampires: the warehouse Zima had cleared out, and an abandoned cannery two blocks from where he stood. Public record showed the cannery hadn't been in operation for two decades, to which boarded windows and old, faded paint could attest.

A perfect hideout for a group of nocturnal hunters.

Mark was on his way back from the data center, with a short detour to drop Dela off at the factory in Cappa's capable hands. He had apparently given her rough details of the situation. Charlie was curious to know how the redheaded barista handled the incredible news, but that conversation could wait.

His first and only priority was getting Anne out of there safely.

Assuming she's in there to begin with.

Charlie pushed the painful thought from his mind.

No, Anne's in there. She is. She has to be, or —

A car pulled up behind him. Mark jumped out, wearing his new techno-jacket. "We ready?"

"Waiting on Zima's signal," Charlie said.

The fog-shrouded sky was already darkening with evening's approach. Once night came, they'd lose a key tactical advantage over the light-sensitive vampires.

Come on, Zima ...

A message arrived from her seconds later. SOUNDS OF MOVEMENT FROM ONE PERSON IN THE SOUTHEAST CORNER. THERE ARE NO OTHER SIGNS OF INHABITANTS.

Just one person ...

Charlie closed his eyes. The news was devastating; they had hoped to find Anne and Doris together. Only one person meant they had been separated, or worse ...

Charlie balled his fists. He refused to consider "worse". Whoever was inside, he would focus on getting them out safely. The rest he'd worry about later.

Zima sent an image: a tactical diagram of the building, with entry points marked for each of them. It showed Zima breaching from the waterside, while Mark and Charlie would enter from the street.

It's as good a plan as any, Charlie thought, running a hand through his hair.

He sent his agreement, and Mark's followed a few seconds later.

Zima started a countdown: Charlie and Mark had thirty seconds to cover two city blocks. With a nod to each other, they broke into a dead run with inhuman speed toward the old building.

A sturdy metal door barred their entry. Without slowing, Charlie threw his shoulder into it. Five hundred and fifty pounds of him moving at high velocity broke the door from its hinges. Charlie flew in with it. He rolled when the door crashed on the ground, then came to a stand.

Aside from Mark, who came in right behind him, Charlie's motion sensors showed no signs of movement. He switched to enhanced audio.

The sounds of movement were right where Zima said they were, inside a small room walled into the corner. Painted red letters covered an insulated door of what looked like a walk-in refrigerator. Charlie paled when he read the message:

A little present.

- William

A narrow window topped the door. Charlie ran over and peered inside.

Doris lay unconscious on the floor. Movement drew his eye to a figure huddled in the back of the room.

"Anne!"

Charlie jammed his fingers between the seams of the locked door and yanked. It flew open with a crack of breaking steel and slammed against the wall.

Anne's heat signature was so faint that he could have mistaken her for a corpse. Blood pooled at his feet from a wound in Doris' neck. Anne crouched in a corner, deathly pale, shivering violently, and staring in anguish at her bleeding friend.

"I-I wasn't strong enough," Anne said, sobbing. "I was s-so hungry, I couldn't stop!"

It was then Charlie saw the blood dripping from her chin.

His fist buckled the wall with a thunderous crash. Anne didn't seem to notice.

That son-of-a-bitch!

Slitting her throat, terrorizing her, destroying Zima ... each hardship had only made Anne stronger — something William's sadistic mind couldn't tolerate.

But this time ...

Charlie knelt to comfort her, but Anne cringed from him and curled into a ball.

"Stay away," she cried. "Stay! Away!"

He backed off, feeling utterly helpless.

William had finally broken her in a way that even Charlie couldn't fix.

"All clear," Zima said from outside, then froze when she took in the scene.

"Zima, take Anne back to the lab and calm her down if you can," Charlie said quietly. "You don't trigger her PTSD like I do."

He reluctantly looked away and knelt to examine Doris.

Her pulse was faint.

She's lost a lot of blood, he thought. *She needs an infusion, and soon.*

A wadded strip of Anne's shirt covered part of the wound, red-soaked and dripping. He gently pressed the cloth to Doris' neck to staunch the flow.

Mark entered the small room and swore loudly.

"We need to get Doris to a hospital," Charlie said. "Now."

"You carry her, I'll keep pressure on her neck." Mark put his hand in place while Charlie scooped Doris into his arms.

Zima stood still as a statue, her eyes fixed on the corner where Anne was crying softly.

"Zima," Mark said, "will you be all right with her?"

"Yes. I will bring her back to the factory." She stayed motionless, however.

"Are you sure?" Charlie said. It wasn't like Zima to hesitate, which made him uneasy. "Cappa can help, if you'd like."

"No, I will take care of her. I simply need a few minutes to put adequate safety protocols in place so I do not kill her by mistake."

"If that was supposed to be reassuring," Mark said, mirroring Charlie's horror, "you've failed miserably."

"She is transitioning into a cold one," Zima said. "I have conditioned myself to kill them without hesitation, keyed primarily from their low body temperature, which Anne's has now fallen under. I am therefore revising all combat simulations pertaining to the cold ones to make her exempt."

Charlie sighed. "Zima, I know you mean well, but I'd *really* feel better if Cappa —"

"Please! Allow me to do this, Charlie. I will not harm Anne — I *promised* her that I would not. I need a few minutes, that is all, and she will be safe with me. You have my word."

Charlie still wasn't convinced, but they had delayed long enough: Doris' blood pressure was falling with each passing second. If they didn't go now, she'd never wake up.

"All right," he said, shuffling through the door with Mark, "but keep us posted!"

Hard as it was, Charlie pushed his concerns about Zima and Anne aside, and focused instead on his patient. Doris was more pallid than Anne and, even with the medical attention she would soon receive, Charlie was beginning to fear the worst. They piled into the car, Mark in the driver's seat, Charlie in the back with Doris across his lap so he could keep pressure on her injury.

Mark tore through the city streets with the desperation they both felt. Charlie chanced a look at her wound on the way.

He wished he hadn't.

That Anne's teeth are even capable of such carnage ...

He shuddered and quickly covered it back up.

Admitting her into the hospital proved more difficult than Charlie had hoped. As he had with Anne the night he rescued her from William, Charlie and Mark made a quick exit from the hospital, giving only Doris' name and the reasonable excuse of a dog attack for her bite wound. The admitting nurse insisted on knowing their identities, however, and threatened police action to their backs on their way out when they didn't answer.

One down, Charlie thought once they were back in the car.

But despair washed over him when the walls of Z-Tech came into view. For all his research, Charlie was no closer to finding a cure now than when he'd started, and time had finally run out.

Especially for Anne.

59

THE LEDGE

ZIMA STOOD IMMOBILE. As a safety precaution, she had deactivated her motor functions while her processors ran at full capacity to overwrite any simulation paths that might harm Anne.

Five minutes passed before she was confident enough to re-engage motor control. Anne remained balled up in the corner. Zima knelt beside her. Dried blood matted Anne's normally soft auburn hair. Zima touched her hand, as she often did, but Anne jerked away and curled up tighter.

"Anne, please do not be afraid," Zima said, imitating Cappa's gentle tone. "You must come back to Z-Tech with me so Charlie can help you."

"I bit her," Anne said, sobbing into her hands. "I hurt Doris! My Doris ..."

"You are not responsible. It was the virus. Please, you must come with me."

"It's not just the virus! It's him! He's in my head." Anne pounded her fists against her skull. "He's. In. My. Head!"

Zima caught her wrists to keep her from hurting herself. Anne struggled but was no match for Zima's strength.

"I do not understand your meaning," Zima said. "But striking yourself is unlikely to resolve the issue."

"William's in my head, Zima! I can feel him. Watching. Prodding. Pushing! He wants me to kill you."

The look of hatred on Anne's face was so out of character, so foreign to the gentle person Zima knew, that she began to understand.

Like a computer, Anne's mind had, essentially, been hacked.

"He knows I can't win," Anne said through clenched teeth. She wrestled so hard that Zima was afraid she would break her own wrists. "He wants you to hurt me so he can watch us both suffer."

"That will not happen," Zima said. "You must resist his wishes."

"I'm trying, but … his presence is overwhelming! It's like trying to swim upstream in a raging river."

"You can do it. You are strong, Anne."

Anne tried to wrest her arms free, panting with the effort. "Y-you don't understand …"

"I do. I had masters who sought dominion over me from within my own mind, yet I prevailed once I was aware of their presence. Fight him, and return with me so that we may help you."

Anne closed her eyes tight in concentration. Her face eventually relaxed. For a moment, Zima thought she may have succeeded in overcoming William's influence, but when Anne's eyes opened, they were once again filled with foreign hatred.

As Mark would say: It was time for Plan B.

Anne yelled furiously and tried to break her hold. She stomped on Zima's feet and kicked her shins. Zima weathered the storm, doing her best to keep Anne from hurting herself. She ran tens of thousands of simulations, trying to figure out how to help Anne break from William's control, but progress was slow. Combat came easily to Zima, but navigating the dynamics of human interaction was much more difficult.

Minutes later, a plausible solution finally presented. Its confidence rating was only forty-eight percent. As with most of her social simulations, the rating was likely inaccurate, but it was still her best indicator for success. Anne's verbal tirade had subsided, as had her strength, which finally gave Zima a chance to speak. She pushed the simulation into the queue for execution.

"Anne, do you remember the day I came back online in Charlie's laboratory?"

Anne's struggle lessened.

"Do you remember the kiss you gave me after I awoke?"

A nod. Zima had her attention, so she continued.

"I have accumulated many video recordings of my experiences, events that have stood out over the years. As my experience grows, I sometimes replay old videos, and often gain insights that I did not glean the first time around."

Anne remained silent. Some of the tension left her arms.

"After you kissed me, do you recall what you said?"

"Yes," Anne said in a hoarse whisper.

"I have replayed that recording eight thousand three hundred and twenty-two times more than all of my other recordings combined. I do not have an explanation for my behavior, for I do not derive new insights when I watch it, yet I play it again and again.

"My most treasured memory, Anne Perrin, is when you told me that you loved me."

Anne slumped. Zima cautiously released her wrists and instead wrapped her in a warm embrace.

"I am sorry that I have not returned your sentiment," Zima said. "I did not understand what it means to love someone, but there is much I have learned since then.

"You trusted me with your safety, even when I doubted myself, and gave me courage. You showed me kindness, despite my violent past, and gave me hope for the future. You stayed by my side when I lay broken and returned me to the world. You opened your arms to me and banished the loneliness from my nights.

"You loved me, knowing that I may not be able to return your feelings, and in doing so have shown me what it means to love."

Zima kissed her cheek.

"I can say now with certainty that I love you, Anne. I shall stay by your side, as you have stayed by mine, and I will not give up on you. Ever."

"Oh Zima!" Anne hugged her tight. "I'd kiss you, but my face is a mess."

"Once we return to Z-Tech, we shall clean you up, and then you may do with me as you wish."

"Deal," Anne said with a laugh. She leaned back and stroked Zima's hair with bloodstained fingers. "And who knows, maybe when we're done, you'll have a *new* favorite memory."

"So William's influence has lessened?"

"I ... I think so. He hates you more than ever. He wants me to kill you, but ..." Zima tensed when Anne clenched her jaw, but it quickly passed. "I think I can manage him, at least for now."

"We shall soon see."

Zima drew a plasma pistol from her jacket and held it out for Anne.

"W-what the hell are you doing?" Anne said in a strained voice. Her covetous eyes locked on the pistol.

"This plasma pistol is higher energy than yours. With it you could terminate me — or Charlie — with a single shot."

Anne's fingers curled into claws. A tear ran down her cheek. "Please put that away. William really, *really* wants me to take it."

"And you shall, but you will not use it against me." Zima held it up. "Take it. Prove to him that your will is stronger."

Anne took the gun with a shaking hand and leveled the barrel between Zima's breasts. Twice Zima thought the firearm would discharge, but Anne eventually relaxed and handed the pistol back, which Zima replaced in its holster.

Plan B was a success.

"That was a huge risk," Anne said, wiping her brow. "You have no idea how hard it was to resist his commands."

"I did not presume it would be easy, only that you would succeed."

"And if I hadn't?"

"You are slow. There is a seventy-eight percent chance I would have avoided serious injury and rendered you unconscious. I would then have wrapped you in the carpet roll by the door and carried you back to Z-Tech."

Or, as Zima had named it: Plan C.

60

DISSENT

MARK CHECKED ANNE'S VITAL SIGNS AGAIN and sighed. Her heart rate was a third of what it should have been, and her body was only five degrees above room temperature. Her respiration had slowed to four breaths per minute. Blue lips and a waxy complexion painted a grim picture. If Mark hadn't just seen her vitals, he would have sworn Anne was already dead.

She slept under a thick stack of blankets, on a bed Cappa had wheeled into the bio lab. Zima sat by her side, holding her hand, as she had since they'd arrived. Zima hadn't spoken since they'd put Anne under general anesthesia, and didn't even look up when Dela sat next to her. Mark wasn't sure if Zima even knew she was there until Dela tried to leave, when Zima grabbed her hand and held it until she resumed her seat. It was a wonderful testament to the bond that had formed between them over the last month.

Charlie typed furiously at his computer terminal, only pausing to cast an occasional worried glance at his pallid girlfriend.

Mark put a hand on his friend's shoulder. "How much longer does she have before the metamorphosis begins?"

Charlie ran a hand through his thick brown hair. "Two hours, maybe less. The virus has spread through most of her body, and foreign blood has been introduced to her system."

"What does that mean, exactly?" Dela said.

"The virus infects every cell in the human body," Charlie said. He began pacing the room. "Introduction of foreign blood to the host triggers a metamorphosis. The mutated cells absorb the blood and integrate it into their own genetic makeup. My infection went a different course, but the real test sample took about a day to complete the transformation."

Dela nearly fell out of her chair. "Your infection? Wait, are you a vampire?"

"No, I'm ... different."

"Don't be obtuse," Cappa said. "Dela has handled our little secrets pretty well so far, and she's earned the right to know the rest after her daring spy operation." Cappa rested her elbows on the end of the bed and leaned forward in her chair. "Charlie's a cyborg. His arm was infected with vampire blood two months ago when he fought one. His flesh is synthetic, so the effects on him may not be the same as with actual human flesh. It's an apples-to-oranges kind of thing."

Dela stared wide-eyed at Charlie. "The president of Z-Tech is ... a cyborg? Like, part machine, part human?"

Charlie winced. "More or less."

"That's so freakin' cool," Dela said, grinning from ear-to-ear.

"Told you she'd be fine," Cappa said to Charlie. Mark paled when Cappa gave him a sly grin. "It gets better! We already told you that Zima and your glorious host, *moi,* are androids, but did you know that your boyfriend is —"

"An alien!" Dela jumped from her seat and looked excitedly at Mark. "Oh, God, please tell me I'm dating a space alien!"

"That's what I thought he was, too."

All eyes turned at the raspy sound of Anne's voice.

"I still think he might be," Anne said with a weak smile. "No mere human can pack away as much food as he does and still look that good."

"She is supposed to be unconscious through the transformation," Zima said to Charlie.

Mark had to smile at her abysmal bedside manner.

"It's the virus," Charlie said. "Her physiology has changed so much that the anesthesia has lost its effect."

"It's all right," Anne said, her speech slurred. "I'd rather be awake. Who knows what I'll be like afterward? If I really am turning into a blood-crazed lunatic, I'd like to spend my last sane moments in good company." She tried to sit up, but fell back onto the pillow. "Besides, I want to see Dela's reaction. Go on, Mark, tell her about yourself. Entertain me."

Her blue lips widened into a smile. Mark hoped it was just a play of the light that her canines looked longer than usual.

"Okay, let's see if I can do this better than I did with Anne." Mark cleared his throat. "Dela, you've seen the latest rash of superhero movies?"

Her mouth fell open. "Whoa, you're a mutant? Does that mean you have cool powers — like telekinesis or shooting lasers from your eyes?"

"Not exactly."

"How about invulnerability?"

"No."

"Sonic speed?"

"No."

"Invisibility?"

"I wish."

"Growth?" Dela glanced at his crotch and winked.

"Nothing you haven't already seen," Mark said, laughing.

"Extraordinary strength?"

"That's one."

Dela practically vibrated with excitement. "There's more? Like what?"

"Well, I heal pretty fast."

"How fast? Like, if I cut you, could I actually see the wound close?"

"No, but you'd hardly know it was there by morning."

Dela crossed her arms. "Oh, yeah? Prove it."

"That's ... probably a bad idea," Mark said, looking at Anne. He remembered the blood that had covered her face when they found her.

Definitely a bad idea.

Charlie's sudden laughter drew looks from the others.

"Dela, that's a fantastic idea!"

He darted back to his workstation and punched a few keys. A familiar diagram appeared on the screen.

Mark blinked in surprise. *My implant ...*

"Mark and I ran a genetic experiment on him a few years ago that had some unintended consequences," Charlie said over his shoulder. "His cells aren't just mutated, they're programmable." He smiled. "All of his cells, including his blood."

"Charlie, you can't be serious!" Cappa said. "You have no idea what will happen if —"

"You're right, Cappa! I have no idea what will happen if she absorbs Mark's cells." He looked at Anne and his tone softened. "But I know what will happen if she doesn't. We don't completely understand how the implant works, but we can make another one. If Anne's cells adopt the same programmability as Mark's ..."

"Then we may be able to alter her physiology," Zima said. "Could we use it to reverse the infection?"

"I don't know," Charlie said, "but we should at least be able to curb some of the undesirable side effects."

Cappa shot to her feet. "Or we might kill her! A vampire's physiology is different from anything we've ever seen. You can't seriously expect —"

"Yes we can," Zima said over her. "The implant's primary directive is to keep the host alive. While you are correct that it has not been adapted for a vampire's altered cellular makeup, it was programmed with the same learning algorithms attributed to your own sentience. More than anyone in this room, the implant has the highest probability of providing a means to maintain Anne's humanity." She turned to Charlie as if the decision had already been made. "How much time is required to produce a new implant?"

Charlie tapped his lip. "With Cappa's help to reprogram one of the production manufacturing units, less than an hour."

"Mark, feed her your blood," Zima said. "Cappa, let me know if you require assistance to expedite —"

Anne smacked the bed, her eyes haunted. "No! Mark, I won't feed from you like a monster!"

"You must," Zima said, standing beside Mark. "It is your best option. With time, we may be able to make you human again."

"Your cells won't absorb blood the same way after the metamorphosis," Charlie said. "If we don't do this now, we won't get another shot, but you're right. It's your choice, Anne."

Anne shook her head weakly. "I won't do it. I'm sorry, not after the horrible thing I did to Doris. I'd rather die than —"

A sharp pain in Mark's arm made him cry out. Blood ran freely from a fresh gash at his elbow. Zima wiped her knife and put it back in its sheath.

Anne leaped at him with a feral growl, tipping the bed over with a crash. Mark tried to defend himself, but Zima pinned his arms to his sides and held him firmly in place.

"Hold still," Zima said.

As if I have a choice, he thought bitterly.

He noticed that Charlie didn't even try to intervene.

Anne pounced on his arm and greedily sucked at the wound, then lunged for his neck. Pain blinded him when her blunt teeth tore into his flesh.

"Mark!" Dela dashed to help, but Cappa caught her by the arm and yanked her back.

"Don't go near," Cappa said.

"But she's killing him!"

"Zima can be unpredictable, especially when she's focused. I don't want you to get hurt."

"She's my friend," Dela said, red-faced. "She won't hurt me, now let go!"

"Cappa is correct," Zima said without looking up. "You should keep your distance."

Dela's hurt look was unmistakable. She slowly relaxed, and Cappa released her. Mark caught Charlie's eyes while Anne continued to drink. Charlie wore a pained expression, but stayed put.

Charlie, I hope you know what you're doing, was Mark's last thought before passing out.

• • •

Cappa couldn't believe what she was seeing. Anne clung to Mark like a lamprey, even while Zima guided his unconscious body to the floor, yet no one except Dela had made a move to stop her.

"I think that's enough," Cappa said, advancing toward the trio on the floor.

"Almost," Charlie said. "The more she drinks, the more of her cells will be infused, and the greater our chances of helping her."

"She's killing him!" Cappa said, echoing Dela's frustration. "I love Anne, too, but I won't trade his life for hers!"

"Neither will I," Zima said. "Mark will be fine. I am monitoring his blood pressure, and will not allow her to cause permanent harm." She turned to Dela, who was still red-faced. "I have a direct link to Mark's computer implant, and have spent a significant amount of time assisting him with his cellular modifications. More than anyone, I am aware of his body's limitations."

"Please stop," Dela said, pacing near the toppled bed. "He's so pale ..."

"Eight more seconds," Zima said.

Cappa moved in. Anne growled at her touch, a light rumble that was about as threatening as a kitten's purr.

"That's enough," Cappa said when the eight seconds were up. She gently brushed the crimson-soaked locks from Anne's face. "You'll kill him if you drink any more."

A kitten growl answered her. Anne continued to drink.

Everyone turned when Dela gave a muffled cry. An open pocketknife clattered to the floor, and a fresh gash lay across her forearm. "Look, Anne. Fresh blood." Dela held the wound out invitingly. "It's probably coffee-flavored, too."

The distraction worked. Anne backed away from Mark and licked her bloody lips at the sight of the open wound. Charlie darted in and pressed gauze to Mark's neck, while Zima quickly tore a piece of her own shirt and tied it around the cut on his arm.

"Move him to the bed," Charlie said. "We need to start a hypertonic saline IV to stabilize his blood pressure."

Cappa stayed with Anne, while Zima and Charlie righted the bed and scrambled to gather supplies. Anne stayed focused on Dela's arm. Strings of red saliva dangled from her chin, but she didn't move from her predatory crouch.

Dela gulped. "C-can I patch this up now, or ... are you still thirsty?"

Anne blinked, then looked around in confusion. She wailed when she saw Mark on the bed and collapsed into Cappa's arms. Cappa rocked her back and forth while she cried, as she had the first night Anne came to Z-Tech.

"It's not your fault," Cappa said, holding her close. "Don't blame yourself."

"Of course it is," Anne said from the folds of Cappa's cardigan. "Mark's hurt, Doris is in the hospital, even Dela's injured, and it's all because of me."

"No, it's because of William," Cappa said. "He did this to you."

"And it's only going to get worse! Just put a stake through my heart and end this nightmare. Please ..." Anne looked up at her. "Please, Cappa, I don't want to hurt anyone else." Red stains streaked her face — and Cappa's white cardigan — highlighting her pale complexion.

Cappa brushed her matted hair back and kissed her forehead. "Don't you see, my dear? Your tender heart is precisely why each and every one of us will fight for you with our dying breaths. Besides," she said with a cheerful smile, "I wouldn't use a stake to finish you off, I'd use Zima's plasma pistol. I owe you one, after all."

Anne laughed weakly. Her eyes eventually closed with Cappa's gentle rocking, and it wasn't long before she fell completely limp. Cappa switched to thermal vision and was terrified by what she saw: Anne's body was only a shade above room temperature, her pulse almost gone, and her breathing down to one respiration per minute.

"Anne!" In a panic, Cappa lay her on the floor and shook her by the shoulders. "Wake up! Come on, honey, you're scaring me! Wake up!"

Zima and Charlie were there in an instant.

Charlie brushed a thumb across her ashen cheek.

"Anne? Anne!" His tears landed on her bloodstained cardigan alongside Cappa's. "Don't," he said in a strangled voice. "We can still fight this, I swear! Just don't give up, d-don't leave me …"

Her eyes snapped open at his voice. Anne looked around in a daze — an impossible feat, given her lack of vitals — until she finally focused on Charlie.

"Dougie," she said with a smile, "what brings you to my room? Do you need to borrow some clean socks again?"

"No, I just wanted to see you," Charlie said, slipping into her brother's role, as he often did during her hallucinations. "How are you feeling, Annie?"

"Tired. So tired. I must have caught the flu from my friend Mary. She was out of school sick on Friday, but we shared a soda the day before. I'll be fine in a few days, you'll see. You should go so you don't catch it, too. Help yourself to my sock drawer, and just put them in my hamper when you're done. Dad won't find out that way."

Cappa lost it. She cried into her sleeve, but Anne didn't seem to notice; she was staring at a bloodstain on Charlie's chin.

"Dougie …" Anne gently touched his chin. "Is that why you're here? What's his excuse for hitting you this time?" She shook her head. "Sorry, forget I asked. I know you don't like to talk about it. Wait here. Dad never enters my room without permission, so you'll be safe. I'll get the peroxide and bandages, and we'll have you patched up in a jiffy."

Cappa and Charlie exchanged confused looks. Anne's hallucinations usually involved the terrible violations in her bedroom as a teenager. This was something neither of them had seen before.

"It's just a scratch," Charlie said. "Please don't worry about it, I'll be fine."

"You always say that, but I know better. He hurts you so badly …" Anne bit back a sob. "Have you given any more thought to our talk yesterday? About child services? I-I know they might split us up, but it would only be for a few years, just until I'm old enough to move out on my own, then you could live with me. In the meantime, you'd be safe — at least, safer than you are now."

"I think that's a fine idea," Charlie said. "I'll call them first thing tomorrow."

"Really?" Anne's face lit up. Somehow she found the strength to wrap Charlie in a hug. "Oh, Dougie! I know this is going to be hard, but just remember: Whatever happens, you're my brother. No matter how far apart we are, I'll come for you. I'll ... I'll come ... for ..."

With a final sigh, Anne sagged in his arms. She didn't stir again.

Charlie buried his face in her hair and cried. "My shining ray of hope," he whispered into her ear. "You've helped us in so many ways ... Now it's your turn to rest, and let those whose lives you've touched help you."

Zima caught his eyes and nodded. He gently laid Anne down, dried his face, then turned to Cappa.

"What's the ETA for the new implant?"

Cappa bit her lip to quell her own crying and took a ragged breath. "Fifty-seven minutes."

"All right, let's prep for surgery. We need to get it in place before her transformation starts, to give it the best chance of adapting to her new physiology."

He carefully gathered Anne's limp body and carried her to the same table where Cappa and Zima had also lain in ruins.

Let's hope there's room for another miraculous recovery, Cappa thought.

With a last look at her dear friend's cadaverous face, she ran off to gather surgical supplies, desperately hoping they weren't already too late.

61

TRANSFORMATION

SOMETHING WAS TEARING ANNE APART from the inside out. She writhed on the bed, dimly aware that others were near, though she couldn't have said who.

Wave after agonizing wave drove all else from her mind. She couldn't remember what it was like before the pain, only that she would gladly die to stop it. Anne tried to scream, to beg for a merciful death, but all that escaped were guttural cries while her body thrashed.

Her muscles were on fire; her bones cracked and splintered. Her intestines crimped into tight knots. Her skin burned as if dipped in boiling oil. The light stabbed when she dared open her eyes. Even her cries were deafening to her own ears. Imaginary pliers pulled her teeth, yanking them by the roots.

Especially her canines.

After what felt like an eternity of fiery Hell, Anne finally lost consciousness and faded into merciful oblivion.

• • •

She woke to the familiar surroundings of her room.

The pain was gone. How Anne had emerged from that unimaginable agony as anything more than a misshapen pile of meat was anyone's guess. That she still had her sanity was an outright miracle.

More amazing was what she saw when she opened her eyes. Everything was sharp, as if wearing prescription glasses for the very first time. The LED clock, which read just after eight in the morning, was bright enough to make her squint.

An overpowering draft of Charlie's cologne washed over her, mixed with the unique fragrance of Zima's hair. She turned to see them both standing close by.

Charlie smiled. "I'M AFRAID TO ASK HOW YOU'RE FEELING."

She flinched and covered her ears; his voice boomed as if shouting through a megaphone. Charlie looked stricken. Zima tensed and moved to catch Anne in case she fell off the bed.

"It's all right," Anne said softly. "My hearing is just a little sensitive. How ... have you heard anything about Doris?"

Charlie smiled. "A night of agonizing torture and your first concern when you wake up is for someone else's welfare. It's good to know the Anne we all love is still in there."

"Cappa contacted the hospital an hour ago," Zima said. "Doris has stabilized and is doing well."

"Oh, thank goodness. As for how I'm feeling ..."

Anne considered for a moment. Her body was calm, her muscles relaxed.

No, not relaxed, she thought. *Ready.*

She sat up, amazed at how effortless it was.

Throughout her captivity and transformation, Anne hadn't given much thought to what it would actually feel like to be a vampire. Bloodthirsty, savage, ruthless, cunning ... vampires were the embodiment of society's fascination and fear of every evil hidden deep in the shadows — powerful, beautiful monsters who prey upon humanity, hypnotize with a glance, and use people as pawns in their nefarious game of supernatural politics.

Anne didn't feel savage — or ruthless, or cunning — and she certainly didn't feel like the spawn of evil.

She felt strong. Graceful. In control.

It was amazing.

The most important thing, however, was that she still felt like Anne — a hungry Anne, granted, but enough herself to smile with genuine delight.

Her grin faded when Charlie gasped. He was staring at her mouth. Anne probed with a finger and snatched it back when something sharp pricked her. She quickly sought the full-length mirror.

Anne hardly recognized the creature looking back.

A maze of blue veins wove across her ghostly white face. Her canines were longer and ended in unnaturally sharp points, giving her a ghastly appearance. Her eyes seemed larger than before; dilated pupils made them black but for a thin ring of brown around the edge.

I look like a freak.

Zima approached cautiously. "Are you well?" Her voice was a whisper, for which Anne was grateful.

"I'm fine. The pain is gone, and I feel ... well, to be honest, I feel incredible!"

She waited for Charlie's smile at the good news, but his uncertain stare, and Zima's silence, said that wasn't the most pressing issue on their minds, and rightly so.

They wanted to know about William.

She searched her mind. At first, Anne was overjoyed to find his filthy presence absent, but closer inspection showed he and the other vampires were in deep slumber.

Anne guessed she had until sunset before their battle of wills resumed and, now that she had transitioned into a full vampire, she didn't fancy her chances of winning. She told Charlie and Zima as much.

Zima stood. "Can you sense his location?"

"Sort of. He's somewhere south of here, I think."

"Can you lead me to him?" The menacing electric hum from Zima's chest made her intentions clear.

"I don't know. His presence is weaker than before, probably because he's sleeping."

"It may be enough." Zima took her hand and gently pulled her toward the door. "Come. We shall eliminate the threat before it becomes a problem."

"Hold it," Charlie said. "We don't know anything about the mental link between William and Anne."

"That is correct," Zima said, "but we know how he will use it when he wakes. I cannot allow that to happen."

"And what if killing him also kills her?"

Zima stopped at the doorway.

"Think about it," Charlie said. "Their connection may be like yours and Cappa's, where no dependencies exist so you can disconnect at any time, or it could be deeper than that — like a network client that can't function without its server."

Zima's expression remained neutral, but Anne felt her grip tighten.

Charlie fell in behind them, his jaw rigid with concern. "I'm not discounting your plan, Zima. We have approximately nine hours until dark, which gives us time to investigate Anne's condition before we conduct an assault, if it becomes necessary."

Zima brow-knit — a tiny wrinkle between her eyebrows that meant she was processing.

"Very well," she said eventually, but she didn't release Anne's hand. "What do you suggest as our first course of action?"

"Breakfast."

And like a magician, Charlie produced a bag of red liquid from behind his back. The sight reminded Anne of how hungry she was. Her stomach growled. She nearly snatched it from his hand, but managed to reign herself in and ask what should have been her first concern.

"Whose blood is it?"

"Dela's," he said. "Mark is still recovering, so she volunteered."

"Willingly?" Anne guiltily remembered Zima's aggressive move last night that led to his involuntary blood donation.

"I swear. She'd tell you herself, but ..."

"But we could not guarantee her safety in your presence," Zima said. "She is with Mark."

Anne crossed her arms over her middle, feeling guiltier than ever. "H-how is he?"

"He is fine," Zima said. "As I have stated, I am familiar with Mark's physiological limitations. His life was never in danger."

"Thank goodness. How's Dela holding up?"

Anne tried to imagine the gruesome scene from Dela's perspective. Yesterday was fuzzy, but she remembered latching onto Mark and shuddered.

I wouldn't blame her for hating me.

Anne heard the clatter of heels from the hallway seconds before the door opened, and Cappa stepped in. Anne hadn't realized the lights were off until the fluorescents from the hallway flooded the room, blinding her until the door closed again.

"Dela's doing okay, all things considered," Cappa said as if she'd been standing there the whole time. "Promise not to bite me if I hug you?"

"That's not funny," Anne said with a pout. "And I promise no such thing. Hug at your own risk."

Cappa wrapped her in a tight embrace, but a hard lump in Anne's chest made her pull away.

"What the ..." She ran a finger just above her right breast and felt something solid beneath the skin.

"That's the implant," Cappa said. "It's a computer, just like Mark's. Charlie managed to get it in before your transformation started."

"It's a good thing, too," Charlie said. "The way you were thrashing around, I don't think even Zima could have held you still enough for the surgery."

Anne pulled her collar down and looked in the mirror. Apart from a slight bump about one-inch square, her skin was flawless, and showed no evidence of an incision. "That's amazing."

"Definitely," Charlie said. "I suspected that vampires healed fast, but your surgery proved it."

"A mixed blessing, I suppose, considering who did this to me."

Speaking of mixed blessings ...

Anne eyed the bag in Charlie's hand. She should have been repulsed, but instead her stomach growled. Once again, she fought an urge to snatch it away and tear into it with her teeth. She had viciously attacked two of her friends yesterday. If she ever hoped to feel comfortable around them again, she needed to demonstrate self-control.

Starting right now.

Anne took a breath — something she hadn't done since she woke, she suddenly realized — and stepped toward Charlie. She smiled, careful to keep her ghastly fangs hidden, and held out her hand.

"Thank you," she said, trying to keep her voice steady. "Please thank Dela, too, when you see her."

He nodded, and her mouth watered when he finally handed it over. She eagerly raised it to her lips, but an odd feeling in her mouth made her pause. She probed her front teeth with her tongue and gasped. Her canines had pushed down from the gums, making them even longer than they had been a moment ago. A tart liquid trickled from small holes in the ends of her teeth that she hadn't noticed before. Aware that her friends were watching, she resisted her instinct to tear the bag apart like a starving animal, and bit into the plastic with as much poise as she could muster.

The first trickle sent a shiver of ecstasy through her entire body. She had accidentally bitten the inside of her mouth many times over the years, and remembered her own blood as pungent and coppery with a gritty texture.

Dela's blood, however, was sweeter than any fruit, richer than any gourmet meal, more fragrant than any flower, more delicious than anything she had ever tasted.

Decorum forgotten, Anne greedily slurped it down, moaning with delight until she'd squeezed every drop from the bag. She felt energized — a living power dynamo ready to take on the world — and couldn't help but smile at her friends.

Zima looked on with her usual, nonjudgmental indifference, but not so the other two. Charlie's eyes were saucers; Cappa looked as if she'd eaten something that didn't agree with her — and Anne couldn't blame either one of them. She dug inside for the remorse — the abhorrence — she should have felt at drinking the blood of another human being, but all she found was satisfaction: It felt right, and she knew without a doubt she would do it again, given the chance.

Anne gave a nervous laugh and held the bag like a coffee cup. "Good to the last drop! My complements to the barista. So ..." She cleared her throat and grasped for something to change the subject. "Is ... is the implant working?"

"Yes," Zima said.

Charlie blinked away his shock. "Yeah, but it wasn't easy. Once your cells began to metamorphosize, they rejected the device."

"Rejected?"

"Your skin split open," Zima said evenly, "and the device emerged as if pushed from the inside." She may as well have been discussing the weather. "Cappa said it was disgusting."

Cappa crossed her arms and pouted. "Well, it was!"

Anne scratched her head. "Then how did you get it in?"

"I used the implant itself to reprogram your cells to cease the rejection," Zima said. "That is how we know it is working."

"It'll take a few days for the device to completely integrate with your body," Charlie said. "Only cells that have absorbed Mark's blood can be programmed, and fortunately there were enough of those to make the implant stay put. Now that it's there, it will convert your other cells, too."

"Wow, that sounds ... it sounds ..." Anne sighed. "Lonely."

Zima head-cocked.

"Being mutated by that stupid virus into a blood-sucking monster is bad enough," Anne said. "Now a computer is changing me again, but into something completely different, something the world's never seen before. It's terrifying, it's like ..."

"Like me," Charlie said.

"And me," Zima said.

Cappa raised her hand. "Don't forget yours truly!"

"Oh ..." Anne wanted to shrink into the carpet. "Oh, I'm so sorry! I-I didn't mean it that way."

"We get it," Cappa said, taking her hand. "But there's a difference between being unique and being alone. You were always unique, Anne, but you'll never be alone, because you've got us." She smiled and brushed her fingers over Anne's cheek. "All of us."

Anne gathered her soul sister in her arms and squeezed her tight. "Thank you," she said, tears streaming down her face. It was comforting to know she could still cry like a normal person.

"Enough," Cappa said with a laugh. "If you ruin yet another one of my outfits with bloodstains, I'm going to think you're doing it on purpose."

"Mark and Dela are in the kitchen," Zima said. "If your hunger is sated, Mark says we may join them there."

"I think I'm okay, but ..."

"We'll stay close by," Charlie said. "Just in case."

"Thanks." Anne squared her shoulders and took a shuddering breath. "All right, let's do this breakfast thing."

62

BREAKFAST WITH A VAMPIRE

ANNE'S CONFIDENCE FALTERED when the bright fluorescent hall lights stabbed her eyes. She darted back into the protective darkness of her room. Charlie was by her side in an instant, his face a mask of concern.

"I thought this might be a problem," Cappa said, reaching into her purse. "Here, these should help."

"My techno glasses, I can't believe it!" Anne cradled them, drawing a smirk from Charlie. "I thought William had smashed them. Thank you so much."

"No problem," Cappa said. "I've adjusted the tint for ultra-dark, and here's your phone, too. Your jacket and pistol weren't as lucky."

"It's just as well, I suppose. William could make me use them against you."

Anne felt sad, however. The pistol and jacket were gifts from Mark, and her intense training had made them feel like an extension of her body. She felt wrong without the bulk of the plasma gun in her pocket.

But the glasses worked like a charm, and Anne was able to comfortably step into the glare of the overhead lights.

Such a shame, Anne thought.

The targeting system was useless without the jacket or pistol, and her new eyes could see in the dark without aid.

Now they're just a pair of insanely expensive sunglasses.

She felt ridiculous walking the dark hallway with shades on, but when they neared an outside window, she was doubly grateful for Cappa's foresight. Despite the darkened shades, even the diffuse light from the overcast sky seared her eyes. She cried out and buried her face in the comfort of Charlie's chest.

Cowed by an open window on a foggy day. I'm the wimpiest monster ever.

"Just take a moment," Charlie said. "I bet your eyes will adjust."

He was right, as usual. The pain eventually subsided, and she was able to see without squinting too much. Even the indirect light prickled her skin when she passed, so she gave the window a wide berth and hurried away.

"That glass is ultra-violet protected," Charlie said, "which probably helps, but I'd stay away from unfiltered sunlight if I were you. The effects will be ... more pronounced."

Anne caught him by the arm. "Wait! D-define 'pronounced'."

"Well, the sample I tested sort of ... burned, after a minute. Brief exposure shouldn't kill you, though, especially if you wear thick clothing."

"Oh. Well, I won't look out of place in chilly San Francisco, at least."

"That's the spirit," Cappa said with a smile.

Mark and Dela were waiting at the table when they arrived. The kitchen was blessedly free of outside windows; Anne took her glasses off and was pleasantly surprised that her eyes didn't hurt, so she hooked them on her shirt.

"Holy Hell!" Dela said. "Anne, you look like shit!"

At least she's honest, Anne thought with a sigh.

A bandage covered the gash in Dela's arm from the night before. She looked pale, no doubt because of her recent blood donation.

"Um, thanks, Dela," Anne said, fidgeting with her shirt, "for the ... y-you know."

"It was nothing."

Dela approached with easy confidence and gave her a critical eye. Anne couldn't blame her for checking out the new vampire, so she stood still and endured the scrutiny. When Dela leaned in to get a closer look at her unusual eyes, Anne discovered another of her vampire superpowers: The ability to keep her eyes open without blinking.

"So how did I taste?"

"Dela!" Cappa said. "Don't be rude."

"What? It's a legitimate question!"

"Not coffee-flavored, if that's what you're wondering," Anne said.

No, it was better than coffee. Just thinking about it brought a pleasant shiver. *Much, much better.*

"Ginger, I would have thought," Mark said.

Anne was happy to see the jagged tear in his neck from last night was now just a pink discoloration, and the gash in his arm all but a memory.

"Was that because of ...?" She pointed to her teeth, recalling the healing chemical Charlie had found in the vampire bite on his arm.

"No, you didn't have fangs then," Mark said. "I'm just a fast healer."

"I, on the other hand, have eight stitches and a needle puncture," Dela said, pointing to the crook of her arm. "The last was your breakfast."

"I ... I could bite you," Anne said. "To help with the healing, of course."

The thought of biting Dela should have made her queasy, but instead she began to salivate. She quickly covered her mouth and looked at the floor.

This is so not good ...

Mark stood slowly. "I'm not sure that's a good idea ..."

Dela shrugged. "Heck, if it'll speed up the healing, I'll give it a try." She peeled the bandage from her arm. Expert stitching followed an angry red line that was longer than Anne remembered.

Anne's stomach growled.

"I hope that means you're hungry for toast," Cappa said, assuming her usual position near the stove.

"Sure," Anne said, though she couldn't take her eyes from Dela's bared flesh.

Blood ran freely from there last night, a delicious river of red —

"Anne!"

She snapped her head up at Mark's voice, surprised to find Dela's arm an inch from her open mouth.

"It's all right," Dela said. "Do you think it will heal without a scar if she bites me?"

"Possibly," Charlie said. "But you've already given blood this morning. Any more could be dangerous."

Dela grinned. "All right Anne, you heard the man, just a sip now. Don't —"

A loud crack of wood made everyone jump.

Cappa slid a broken cutting board into the trash and put her hands on her hips. "You think this is funny, young lady? Let me remind you that our dear, sweet Anne almost killed two of her friends yesterday at the sight of their blood, and that was before she became strong enough to tear your arms off. You're in the company of veritable superheroes, my little barista, but if Anne loses control, my money says she rips your throat out before even Zima can save you. Now," — the toaster popped and Cappa aimed her butter knife at Anne —"do you want raspberry or strawberry jam?"

"Raspberry, please," Anne said timidly.

For several seconds, the only sound in the kitchen was Cappa's knife scraping across the toast.

"So," Anne said, still holding Dela's arm like a hot dog, "can I bite her?"

"That's between you two," Cappa said with her back to them. "You're both grown women."

"Wait," Dela said, "Cappa, how old are you, anyway?"

Cappa sniffed. "I hardly think it matters ..."

"Well I'm thirty-two, and you called me 'young', which means you must be a lot older. Are you a steampunk creation from the turn of the century or something?"

Cappa's knife clattered to the counter. "Fine! If you must know, I'm eleven. Or ... I will be eleven. This summer."

"Jesus! I've just been schooled by a ten-year-old." Dela rolled her eyes. "All right. Anne, do you promise to be a good vampire and not rip my throat out or bleed me dry?"

Anne clamped her mouth shut to hide her fangs, which had extended in anticipation. A trickle of venom left a tart taste in her mouth. Anne nodded solemnly; she was so antsy that she would have said anything to get the go-ahead.

"Do it, then. Let's see —"

Dela yelped when Anne eagerly bit down.

The familiar rush of flavor made Anne shudder. Dignity forgotten, she closed her eyes and moaned with delight between swallows, savoring each tiny mouthful that warmed her throat on the way down.

I need more.

Dela's wound wasn't near a major vein, so Anne had to work for every drop. She cracked an eyelid and spotted Dela's neck.

It would be so easy, Anne thought. Dela's face was relaxed, almost trance-like. *She may not even notice.*

But the others would. Even through the haze of intense need, she knew it would never fly.

Zima eventually stepped behind her, and she knew her time was up. Anne reluctantly pulled away.

Blood trickled from the puncture wounds, which made Anne want to dive in for seconds, but Mark's apprehensive posture steeled her. She grabbed on to Zima's arm like an anchor.

Charlie stepped between them, blocking her view of Dela. "I guess that answers the question of self-control," he said with a half-grin.

Yeah. Unfortunately, Cappa was more right than she knew.

Charlie turned his attention to Dela, who stood exactly where Anne had left her, eyes closed with a dreamy smile.

"Dela?" Mark said, moving to her side.

"Mm?" Dela turned her head, but kept her eyes closed.

Mark arched an eyebrow at Anne. She shrugged and looked at Charlie, who was studying Dela with a severe expression.

"Dela," Charlie said, "do you know where you are?"

"In the kitchen."

"Can you tell me what just happened?"

"Sure," she said, laughing. "Anne bit me."

Dela didn't seem to notice while Charlie inspected her bitten arm. The puncture marks were nearly closed, and the long slice in her arm from yesterday was little more than a faded pink line.

Charlie swiped his finger over the punctures. It came away slick. "Something isn't right. I'm going to run this through the chemical analyzers. I'll be back later."

He shot Anne an unreadable look before running from the kitchen.

Cappa sighed. "Back to his hidey-hole. Anne, if that little snack didn't ruin your appetite, your breakfast is ready." She set a plate of toast on the table then shook her head at Dela. "Hopefully she snaps out of it soon. Mark, help me get her to a guest room where we can keep an eye on her."

They guided her away, swaying like a drunkard, without a backward glance.

Anne plopped into a chair and groaned. She stared at the toast, layered thick with her favorite raspberry jam, but one whiff dashed any hopes she had of enjoying a normal breakfast. The once-irresistible fruit spread smelled about as appetizing as wet cardboard.

"The morning has gone better than I anticipated," Zima said, "and has provided several insights."

"Better? What did you think would ..." Anne buried her head in her hands. "Never mind, I don't want to know. Just tell me the good stuff."

"As you wish. For one, Dela is more courageous than I thought."

"Braver than I would have been in her shoes."

"She also found your bite pleasurable."

"Yeah, what was up with that?"

"It is unclear," Zima said. "I have observed many bite victims over the past four weeks, and none have exhibited a positive reaction. No doubt that is why Charlie left with haste."

"Right," Anne said, plunking her chin on her palm. "I'm sure it had nothing to do with the blood dripping from his girlfriend's fangs."

"Perhaps, but do not worry. My affection for you has not diminished."

Anne laced her fingers with Zima's and smiled. "You're turning out to be my rock in this doozy of a storm."

"I promised that I would not abandon you. Besides, the sight of blood does not upset me, which leads to my next observation. You demonstrated surprising control when presented with a human food source."

I wish she hadn't just referred to Dela as a "food source."

Even thinking of the tasty redhead made her salivate. The familiar sensation of her canines pushing out from her gums made her cover her mouth, and she quickly looked away.

"Interesting," Zima said evenly.

Anne accidentally jabbed the inside of her lip on a razor-sharp tooth and muttered a curse. "What is?"

There are so many things to choose from ...

"Apparently I was mistaken about your level of self-control."

Anne opened her mouth to protest, but her elongated fangs were proof of the lie. "You're right. If I hadn't just eaten, I don't think I could have stopped. It ..." She closed her eyes and took a shuddering breath. "It was so delicious — so satisfying! — I could have drunk every last drop."

"That is good to know. We shall need to ensure that you have an adequate supply of blood."

"Any thoughts on how to do that?" Anne pictured her and Zima dressed in ninja outfits, raiding local hospitals for blood bags under cover of night.

"You could hunt, as the others do."

Anne blinked. "Come again?"

"Those who the cold ones feed from do not remember the encounter, and their injuries are healed by the time the effects wear off. To the victim, it is as if it never happened."

"Any other thoughts?" Although Zima's suggestion didn't sound nearly as abhorrent as it should have, Anne really liked the hospital-ninja idea.

"Hunting for animals in the wilderness is another option," Zima said.

Anne smiled, picturing them both in raccoon hats.

"However, given what Charlie said about your cells integrating the genetic makeup of those you consume, it may be unwise to feed from nonhuman sources. The results may be unfavorable."

"Didn't he say the integration only happens before the transformation?"

"Yes, so if that is a risk you are willing to take, there is abundant wildlife beyond the city limits. Finding game animals should not be difficult."

In her mind, the raccoon tail disappeared from her hat and instead protruded from the back of her pants, complimented with a little black nose and whiskers. Anne gulped. "Agreed, no animals."

Ninjas! Anne projected her thoughts to Zima. *Blood bank ninjas...*

"Dela may be a willing donor," Zima said. "She seemed pleased with the experience."

"Yeah, but I doubt Mark would agree," Anne said. "Besides, the few times I've donated blood, they made it pretty clear that it's bad news to donate more than once every few months. Something about red blood cell regeneration."

"That is unfortunate. Mark's accelerated healing would allow him to donate more frequently, but even if so, he alone may not be enough to sustain you. Perhaps an unauthorized withdrawal from a local blood bank ..."

Yes! Ninjas away! Anne rubbed her hands, already picturing her cool new costume.

"There are consequences, however. Many blood banks have issues keeping adequate supply. Stealing from them could be an indirect death sentence for victims who require infusions for survival."

Anne deflated, ninja dreams shattered against her moral wall. "I guess you're right." She kissed Zima on the cheek. "Thank you."

Zima head-cocked.

"This whole situation is ridiculous! I feel like a hideous monster preparing to butcher a village, but talking with you, it's like we're planning a trip to the grocery store." Anne squeezed her hand. "Your nonjudgmental attitude is exactly what I need."

"I have been that monster, and I have butchered that village. I understand what it is like to crave the deaths of others, and to detest what you have become. I would spare you that fate."

Anne kissed her on the lips this time. "You're remarkable. I can't imagine having this conversation with anyone else." She laughed, picturing Doris' face while they casually discussed different ways to hunt other human beings, but her smile quickly faded.

"What is it?"

"Oh, it's just ..." Anne fiddled with her napkin. "I owe Doris a pretty big apology. I attacked her like an animal."

"Perhaps, but I am sure that once she understands the extenuating circumstances involved, she will forgive you." Zima slid the plate in front of her. "You should try to eat."

Anne eyed the cold toast. It still held the culinary appeal of tree bark, but she would need to discover her dietary limitations eventually. She picked up a slice.

"You may want to grab a bucket," Anne said. "If the books I've read are any indication, this could get messy."

She meant it in jest, but Zima obediently retrieved a bucket from under the sink.

Zima carefully watched her first bite. Anne frowned; she could taste the raspberry — she knew it was raspberry — but the sweet-tart thrill had vanished.

It's like eating Brussels sprouts, she thought, sure her face held the same disgust now as when her mother had inflicted the horrible green vegetables on her as a child.

Now for the fun part.

She swallowed. Her throat constricted in protest, a sure sign that the unappetizing lump wasn't welcome, but with determination, Anne was able to force it down. The masticated pulp sat like a rock. She put the rest of the toast back on the plate and rubbed her stomach.

Zima slid the bucket closer.

"I think I'm all right," Anne said, "but toast is definitely off the list."

"Unfortunate, but expected." Zima stood and took Anne by the hand. "If you are finished here, please come with me. There is something I would like you to try."

Anne followed, hoping whatever Zima had in mind turned out better than breakfast.

63

A ROSE BY ANY OTHER NAME

YOU HANDLED THAT WELL. Cappa's message was laden with sarcasm.

Charlie ground his teeth, but removed the irritation from his reply. He felt bad enough about leaving Anne so hastily without Cappa rubbing it in.

I KNOW.

Cappa strode into the bio lab and crossed her arms. "Yet you're still here, holed up like a twit?"

"Nice to see you, too."

"Fine! Sorry about the 'twit' comment, but why aren't you with Anne? She needs you, Charlie. You care about her, so show some support."

"That's why I'm here!" A sudden wave of exhaustion made him close his eyes and sigh. "How's Dela doing?"

Cappa pursed her lips at the obvious change of subject, but thankfully played along. "She's all right, Mark's with her. The effects are wearing off. Her memory's intact, though, which is strange."

Charlie nodded. "I just finished a chemical analysis on Anne's saliva."

"I saw. That was fast."

"I'm efficient when I'm worried. Did you notice anything peculiar about the results?"

"Well, the composition is different from the saliva of the vampire who attacked you," Cappa said. "The memory-inhibiting drug has been replaced with … what is that? I've never seen it before."

"Neither have I," Charlie said, "so I ran its effects through a simulation of the human brain, and guess what?"

"From Dela's reaction, I'd say increased dopamine production."

"On par with heroin. Anne's venom is a night of wild sex in a single bite."

"Interesting choice of words," Cappa said with a wink.

"Funny. More importantly, though, I didn't find any toxins."

Cappa smacked her palm to her forehead. "That's why you were so worried! I can't believe I missed it …"

"I panicked at Dela's reaction to the bite. It could be that male and female vampires produce different chemicals, but with Mark's blood and the implant in the mix, it could just as easily have turned Anne's venom into a lethal toxin." He sighed. "You were right to be cautious last night. Feeding her Mark's blood was a serious gamble, though I didn't realize the extent until this morning when I saw the look on Dela's face. We should keep a close eye on Dela for the next few days, just to play it safe."

"I'll talk to Mark. I doubt he'll mind the assignment." Cappa grinned.

"Thanks. And please give my apologies to Anne —"

"No way! I know you're busy, but you can spare five minutes to tell her yourself. It'll mean so much more coming from you, and she's going to need all the support she can get."

"Okay, after this test run finishes. Which will be soon," he added when she gave him the stink-eye.

"Good." Cappa spun on her heel and marched for the door. "She's in the gym with Zima, when you're ready."

Suddenly weary, Charlie plopped his head on his arms and closed his eyes, afraid to imagine why Zima could possibly want Anne — a new vampire — alone with her in the martial arts studio.

64

VAMPIRE-KWAN-DO

ZIMA WALKED ANNE THROUGH THE MAZE of training dummies to the mats in the center of the gym. "We shall start slowly," Zima said.

Anne knew better than to trust her casual air; Zima went from zero to deadly in the blink of an eye.

"Y-you're going to go easy on me, right?" Anne said, wondering exactly what had possessed her to agree to this.

Though she enjoyed watching Zima practice, she was happy to stay on the sidelines as a cheerleader, yet here she was about to suffer the same fate as the hapless training dummies Zima regularly devastated.

"I promised I would never harm you, Anne. I have created layers of protection in my programming to isolate you from the more aggressive simulations. I only wish to see how your reflexes compare to other cold ones."

"Oh, o-okay."

True to her word, Zima started with a series of slow punches. Anne deflected them with ease and was smiling by the end of the first round.

Anne bounced on the balls of her feet. "How did I do?"

Now that she was up and moving, Anne found it hard to stop. She swung her arms in circles to release some of her energy.

"You did well." Zima brow-knit, indicating she was puzzled by something. "I shall increase the pace. You may tell me to stop at any time."

Zima wasn't kidding. She closed in quickly, and Anne had to dance out of range several times to avoid being hit. She found her groove, however, and soon they were dancing around the mats like trained partners. Zima added kicks to her assault, but Anne adjusted in no time and nimbly blocked or evaded. She was feeling great by the close of the second round and continued to dance around the mats even after Zima stopped.

"Can we do that again?"

"Yes, in a minute," Zima said. "I have asked Mark to join us. I would like him to observe the next round."

"All right." Anne kept bouncing.

Her stamina was incredible. Yesterday, a bout like that would have left her wheezing on the floor, yet she was breathing normally — which was to say, hardly at all — and ready for more.

"Your canines have extended," Zima said. "You may wish to retract them before Mark arrives."

As if I knew how.

Anne pulled her lip down over her elongated fangs and hoped it was good enough.

"What's this about?" Mark said once he joined them. He smiled when he saw Anne bouncing around the room. "Looks like someone had a little too much coffee this morning."

"I believe she is just enjoying our sparring session," Zima said. "Please observe. Anne, I assume you are ready?"

"Bring it, baby!"

Zima used the same pace as the previous round. Anne blocked, weaved, and dodged everything Zima threw, and loved every minute of it. She felt as if they were just getting into a groove when Zima declared the round over.

Anne danced over to Mark. "What do you say? Want to go a round?"

She threw a few fake jabs, but his startled expression stopped her short.

"Mark, you're scaring me. Did I grow a tail or something?" She glanced in one of the mirrors lining the walls, and was relieved to see her behind was tail-free.

Mark shook himself. "Sure, let's do it. Can't let Zima have all the fun."

He and Zima exchanged a long look. Anne suspected they were talking about her, but let it slide. She had bitten him last night — and his girlfriend this morning — so she owed him a little slack.

Besides, if I'm nice, he may let me do it again.

Her fangs had just started to retract, but the thought of feeding caused them to extend again.

Damn it!

Mark grabbed two long staves from a weapon rack. He extended one to her.

"And what exactly am I supposed to do with this?"

"You fought well with your bare hands, so I want to see how you handle a weapon. Try to hit me." He twirled his staff in a daunting display of speed and precision, then dropped into a ready stance. "I won't hurt you, I promise."

Anne experimentally spun her staff, and was amazed at how natural it felt. She twirled it faster and faster, enjoying the whoosh of air on her cheeks. With a grin, she advanced, letting her instincts guide her. She swung blow after blow, which he deflected with ease.

"Incredible," Mark said after a few minutes. "How does it feel to fight with a staff?"

"Great! It's like I've practiced with them my whole life, except I've never touched one before that wasn't attached to a broom."

Who would have guessed vampires are natural martial artists?

Mark nodded and dropped back into a ready stance. "I'm going to strike back this time. If you're uncomfortable with that, please say so, but I have a feeling you'll be fine."

"Sure, why not?"

Anne spun her staff in a stunning display that surprised everyone — especially herself — then caught it under her arm.

Jayne Madison, eat your heart out.

Mark attacked first, which she easily parried, then countered with her own. Cracks of wood-on-wood echoed through the room. Neither landed a single blow. Their perfect concert reminded Anne of her and Doris at the diner, professionals who had worked together so long that they could practically read each other's minds.

Anne frowned. *It does feel choreographed, as if we've done this before.*

Mark huffed, sweat beaded his forehead. Anne was still fresh, as if she hadn't been sparring at all. He exited the melee with a backward roll and put his staff to rest.

She reflexively mirrored him, but her good humor had fled. "Mark, what's going on?"

He grabbed a towel from a nearby stand and wiped his face. "It seems you know *jiu-jitsu.*"

"No," Anne said with a laugh, "I'm pretty sure I don't."

"For something you don't know, you did it perfectly. What's more, you know my style of *jiu-jitsu,* which has elements of Charlie's *Sankukai* Karate I've picked up from our sparring sessions."

"How is that possible? I've never practiced a day in my life, let alone with you or Charlie."

Wait, am I psychic? she thought excitedly. *Was I reading his mind?*

She did have a mental link with William — for better or worse — so it was possible, and it did feel like she knew what Mark was going to do even before he made a move.

Then again, he seemed to know what I was going to do as well. Strike that theory.

She sighed. Mind reading would have been a cool addition to her list of vampire superpowers.

"It's your implant," Mark said. "Like anything, fighting moves become muscle memory with practice. The brain optimizes common routines so they require little conscious effort to execute. My implant enhances my natural muscle memory by processing and organizing many of those responses for me."

"The computer implanted in you is an exact copy of Mark's," Zima said. "Including the data."

"Huh ..." Anne didn't like where this was going. "So, I have his fighting reflexes?"

Mark nodded.

"I see. Anything else I may have inherited that I should be aware of?" A dozen possibilities came to mind — none of them good.

"We have used Mark's computer implant to make many enhancements to his physiology," Zima said, "including better vision, hearing, and increased metabolism. However, many of those were tailored to his genetic structure. It is unclear how the implant will adapt them to yours, if at all."

Anne glanced at her rear again in the mirror. "Please, just promise I won't grow a tail."

• • •

Anne excused herself from the gym to freshen up, even though she could now add sweating to the list of things her body didn't do anymore. She exited through the ladies' shower and turned toward her room, intent on changing into something more comfortable, but stopped when she saw Charlie waiting across the hall. He smiled warmly and waved, but she noted that one hand remained suspiciously behind his back.

"How are you feeling?" he said.

"Hungry" was the first thing that came to her mind, even though she had fed a short time ago.

I hope this isn't the new normal, always hungry and seeing my friends as food.

"Aside from learning that I may wake up tomorrow looking like Mark, I'm fine. Though on the plus side, I wouldn't mind being a few inches taller." Doing her best Mark impression, she leaned casually against the wall and said in a husky voice, "Will you still make out with me when I have sexy man-stubble?"

Charlie laughed. "You mean the implant. I don't think you have to worry, though it's one of the reasons I came looking for you."

"Reasons? Plural?"

"Three, starting with the least pleasant. First, I'd like you to come to the lab when you have a minute so I can collect a tissue sample. I want to monitor any changes to your cellular structure to make sure there aren't any danger signs."

"You mean aside from terminally cold hands, a thirst for human blood, and complete lack of a heartbeat?"

Charlie sighed. "Yeah, aside from those. I want to be sure the implant isn't doing anything dangerous."

"Knock yourself out. If it's turning me radioactive on top of everything else, a heads-up would be nice."

"You'll be the first to know," Charlie said with a chuckle.

"On second thought, if I am going nuclear, just lie and tell me everything's okay. I've had enough bad news for one lifetime. All right, if that was the worst of the three, I think I can handle the rest. What's next?"

He stepped closer. "I wanted to say I'm sorry for running out at breakfast."

"No sweat," Anne said with a wave, though her heart weighed heavy at the memory. "You prefer girls who breathe more than once a minute and don't try to kill your friends, I get it. If you're looking to nail something with a heartbeat, I don't even qualify anymore."

She tried to laugh but choked on a lump in her throat. The joke was in poor taste, she knew, but Charlie smiled anyway.

Bless him.

"Which brings us to the third thing. Turn around and close your eyes."

Half expecting him to taze her from behind, she did as he asked anyway and turned around.

He swept her hair back, and she heard a jingle. Something small and warm fell against her breastbone, gently pulsing on her skin.

The sensation was wonderful.

"All right," Charlie said, "you can open them."

Anne's breath caught when she looked down. A beautiful red heart the size of a large locket hung from a dark chain necklace. It shimmered as if the surface was liquid. She squeezed it between her fingers and smiled. "It's made of nanites, isn't it?" The little heart was beating slow and steady, its warmth pleasant in her palm. She wanted to nuzzle it against her cold cheeks.

"They're from here," he said, tapping his chest. "I hope you get the metaphor."

Do I ever.

Her heart may have checked out, but her tear ducts worked just fine. She stifled a sob and clutched the precious gift to her chest.

"The chain was fashioned from scraps of Zima and Cappa's endoskeletons, and the fastener is made of pieces from Mark's workbench, so there's something from all of us. Now you have a beating heart again, but I hope we've proven you don't need a real heart to love." His fingers brushed her hair. "Or to be loved."

Anne fell into his arms, buried her face in his chest, and basked in his warmth. When Charlie bent down to kiss her, she responded with enthusiasm, transported back to the night they first kissed in the streets.

And, for a little while, Anne was able to forget she had been turned into a monster.

65

SHOW AND TELL

ANNE SKIPPED GLEEFULLY IN FRONT OF CHARLIE, all the way to the bio lab. She hopped onto the same table where Zima had lain as a red-stained pile of twisted metal. The memory took some of the bounce from her, but she quickly rallied.

Zima's fine. I'm here now with Charlie. Focus on the present.

"So," she said, "how do we do this, doc?"

Charlie opened a cabinet and began gathering supplies. "Take your shirt off, if you don't mind."

"Why, doctor," Anne said in a sultry voice, "you wouldn't dream of taking advantage of your patient, now, would you?"

"Something tells me 'no' is the wrong answer."

"You catch on quick. Can I take your shirt off, too?"

Charlie set his supplies on the counter with a grin and stood between her knees. Anne drew him down into a kiss, and was pleasantly surprised to find that tear ducts weren't the only things in her body that still worked.

"Are you really up for this?" Charlie said, laughing.

Anne tore her hands from his firm body and started to unbutton his shirt. "There's one way to find out and, as my doctor, it's your duty to make sure I'm in full working order, wouldn't you say?"

"I would if I were actually your doctor, which I'm not."

"Even better." Anne surprised him — and herself — when she swung all five hundred pounds of him over her lap with ease, then climbed on top of him. "That means we don't have to worry about those pesky doctor-patient ethics, so you can do anything you want to me. A-assuming you're still interested, that is. I'm ... colder, now, which might feel a little weird."

"I'll get used to it."

Watching her carefully, Charlie unbuttoned her shirt and slid it down her shoulders. His warm hands were heaven on her cold skin. Anne spared him fumbling with her bra and removed it herself. This time, his touch was electric. Anne shivered with delight; this was as far as they had ever gone, and there wasn't a trace of a flashback. That it had cost her humanity to finally be with Charlie was cruel irony. She pushed the quandary from her mind and focused on stripping him down.

Sadly, she had celebrated too soon. The fun ended where it usually did: they had just removed each other's pants, with Anne eagerly guiding his hand down her stomach toward third base, when the familiar pain returned to her pelvis, followed by a hallucination. Anne endured the full, torturous re-enactment, once again made easier with Charlie's reassuring presence. When her phantom bedroom faded, and the lab came back into focus, Anne was on the floor with Charlie; Zima, Cappa, Mark, and Dela had also gathered around them.

When Anne saw what had happened to Charlie, she understood why. The poor man looked as though he had lost a fight with a rabid wolverine. His fingers, still laced with hers, were bent and misshapen from her illusory struggle. Deep cuts from her fingernails ran along his chest, the side of his neck, and one cheek, while puncture wounds from her teeth littered his arm.

Someone had been brave enough to cover her nakedness with a blanket — which was fortunate, because Anne needed something to curl under and cry.

• • •

Later, after she had calmed down, Anne and Charlie changed back into their clothes, then rejoined the others on the floor. The bio lab was dark and unusually quiet. The five of them sat facing each other in a circle. All that was missing was a campfire and some marshmallows for roasting.

Anne was the first to break the silence.

"I'm sorry," she said to Charlie, too afraid to touch him after what she'd done.

His laugh was unexpected. "You aren't the person who's supposed to be afraid of hurting someone. I am."

"So ... it does hurt?"

"Poor choice of words, sorry. Cappa disabled my pain sensors, so no, I don't feel a thing."

"That's right," Cappa said cheerfully. "A few stitches, some minor repairs to his hand, and Charlie will be ready for round two." She looked pointedly at Anne. "There will be a round two, right? Back in the saddle and all that?"

"Only if you and Zima hold me down," Anne said softly. "And as much as Doris would love to hear about a foursome, something tells me that would kill the mood. Or probably just trigger me again, which isn't just embarrassing now: it's dangerous to anyone who gets close."

The others stared at her, looking uncomfortable, and it wasn't hard to guess what they were thinking.

My triggers. I've never actually told them what happened that day, and they're too nice to ask.

Her dear friends only knew what they'd gleaned from her hallucinations, fragments of a horrible tale that Anne herself would have liked to forget.

But keeping silent was no longer an option. The more her friends knew, the greater their chances of not triggering Anne, and avoiding injury from what were now deadly flashbacks.

That left her with one choice if she wished to stay among them — and she really, really did.

"So, ah ... I've only told this story once before," Anne said, "to Doris, a long time ago, but several years from the actual incident. It took over an hour to tell because of all the flashbacks, so if you'd like to tie me up or move out of striking distance, now's your chance."

Charlie and Zima scooted closer. Each took one of her hands with gentle reassurance. Cappa sat behind her and rested her chin on Anne's shoulder. Mark walked away, but returned shortly after with snacks from one of the cabinets, and settled comfortably in front of her, next to Dela.

And so, there on the floor of the bio lab, surrounded by love, Anne finally told her dearest friends of the events that had ruined her life.

"I ... I grew up in Bedford, Indiana, with my father, mother, and younger brother, Doug. Doug and I had a great childhood at first. In the summer, we'd play in the river near the house. Spring and fall, we chased each other through the forest and climbed trees. Winter, of course, brought snowball fights behind snow forts. We bickered occasionally, as most siblings do, but overall we were best friends.

"Around the time Doug turned eight, which would have made me eleven, something changed. Dad started getting upset with Doug. He only yelled in the beginning, so often that Doug eventually ignored him, because, as far as either of us could tell, Dad was angry over nothing.

"That's when the beatings began. The first time I saw Doug with a black eye, he wouldn't talk to me about it, just stayed in his room. Other marks appeared, bruises on his arms, back, and legs. Each one robbed a little more joy from my brother. Mom pretended like nothing had happened, even when I asked her about it directly, and cared for his injuries like she would any others."

"Did your father ever assault you?" Zima said.

Anne squeezed her hand. "No, Dad treated me like a princess. I could have murdered someone with a chainsaw and he would have lauded it as another one of my grand achievements."

"Ouch," Cappa said, wincing. "I can only imagine how guilty you must have felt."

"I did, but mostly I was concerned about my brother. He turned stoic, became hard to talk to, so I went out of my way to make him happy. I baked cookies especially for him, made his lunch, gave him frequent hugs, went on walks with him when he'd let me, took him shopping."

"I'm sure he appreciated it," Charlie said.

"It's hard to say. He continued to withdraw into himself, away from the family, away from me. Doug started hanging out with a shadier crowd, rural jocks who thought bullying was cool. Their ringleader, Chet, was the worst. They mostly hung out at the junk yard, rock quarry, or other places where they could make mischief without getting caught. Doug never brought his friends to the house, except once ..."

Anne paused to clear her throat, but the lump wouldn't go away. Her friends stayed silent, giving her the room and support she needed to continue.

"I was eighteen. I'd just graduated high school and was holding down a summer waitressing job to help pay for college. A schedule change had left me home when Doug didn't expect me to be. He'd brought four of his friends over to hang out, including Chet. Instead of shooing them away, I made cookies for them.

"Now, even at eighteen, I had quite a figure, according to my friends. It was a hot, sticky Indiana summer. An afternoon in the kitchen had me drenched in sweat. I delivered the cookies only to find everyone except my brother staring at my chest. I hadn't worn a bra because I was just getting ready for work, and my flimsy, sweat-soaked T-shirt was practically see-through. Mortified, I ran upstairs and showered.

"Chet and his friends were waiting for me when I got out. I hugged my robe around me, squeezed past them to my bedroom, and shut the door.

"Or tried to. Chet came in after me. I tried to push him out, but he was a lot bigger than me, so I slapped him. He was stunned, which allowed me to push him into the hall and slam the door."

Dela gasped, then broke down laughing. "Good on you, girl!"

"Yeah, I was proud of myself, too, but it was short-lived. Chet was furious. He ..." Anne put a hand on her nose, which suddenly ached. "He barged in, bashing my face with the door. Before I knew what was happening, he'd stripped my robe off and thrown me on the bed. M-my bed ..." Anne sniffled, fighting the fear and anger that boiled inside at the memory. A flashback prickled the back of her neck.

Zima's grip tightened. Charlie looked angry enough to take on an army. Mark fingered a plasma pistol with a dire expression that said he wished he had something to shoot at. Dela's mirth sobered into an uncomfortable squirm, but she didn't look away. Cappa whimpered and hugged Anne tighter from behind.

The overwhelming sympathy and support held her flashback at bay. Anne's voice was rough when she continued.

"I fought him. I fought with everything I had, but Chet was just too strong, and when his fingers clamped around my neck ..." She had to pause when phantom hands pressed against her windpipe, cutting off her air. Cappa rubbed her back, whispered soothingly in her ear, but it was no use.

Dela frowned. "Anne, do you even need to breathe anymore?"

It took a few seconds for the odd thought to seep down through her terror. Her lungs weren't burning for air, as they normally did during the choking flashbacks. Anne waited and waited. The phantom hand remained locked around her airway, but her new physiology saw it as a minor inconvenience. The realization was sobering.

And like that, the strangling hand disappeared.

Anne took a slow, measured breath. Being a vampire wasn't all bad, apparently.

"I think we get it," Cappa said, kissing her shoulder. "You don't have to continue, sweetie."

But she did. There were things Anne had never said to anyone, even Doris, things she had to say out loud if she ever hoped to keep them from tearing apart her insides. "Chet choked me until I thought sure I was going to die. Just before I passed out, he let go. I fought again. Chet punched me, over and over, until I was too dazed to struggle." Anne rubbed her face, feeling again the pain of where he'd struck. "Then he started groping, bruising my breasts and thighs. And then he r ... he r ..."

Anne closed her eyes, unable to say the word, though the tearing pain of his horrible violation doubled her over.

Dela caught her and pressed her forehead to Anne's. "Anne, you can stop."

"I can't," Anne whispered. "I have to finish this. Stay back. If a flashback hits, I might hurt you."

"More than you've already been hurt? I'll take my chances."

Anne looked the redhead in her green eyes and saw only strength — strength she drew upon to continue.

"He r… he r-r… raped me."

And there it was: the terrifying word she had never uttered aloud, and certainly not in reference herself. Her demons surged in their prison, threatening to drag her back to Hell.

Anne fought back the only way she knew how.

"Chet raped me," she said louder. Tears ran down her cheeks. "He raped me. Raped me!" Each acknowledgment of that vile atrocity brought power, beat her demons back into the dark abyss where they belonged.

Cappa trembled at her back, hugging her while they both quietly sobbed. "There you go, sweetie. You did it. It's over."

Except it wasn't. Not by a long shot.

"When Chet was done," Anne said in a quavering voice, "the next jock took his turn r … raping me, then the next, and the next, while the rest held my arms and legs down." She looked around and saw tears in every eye, which made the next part even harder. "I was a virgin. My boyfriend and I had played around, sure, but we'd never …" Anne closed her eyes and drew a deep breath. "It hurt. It hurt so much, but they didn't care. They just kept going, and going … I couldn't even tell you how long I laid there, praying for it to end, wishing I'd wake up to discover it was all some terrible dream."

"Where was your brother during all this?" Dela said in a horrified whisper.

Charlie's scowl deepened. He, Cappa, and Zima knew unequivocally from her numerous flashbacks, but Dela was new to the scene.

"My brother was standing in the doorway. Watching."

"He *what?*"

"He watched. While I was pinned to the bed, being beaten and violated by his friends, my brother watched them hurt me over and over. It's like …"

Cappa hugged her around the middle. "Don't say it. You don't know if it's true."

"It's like he wanted me to suffer," Anne said anyway, "payback for the abuse he'd taken while Dad treated me like royalty." The words hurt to say, each a dagger to her now-unbeating heart. "I can't blame him, considering how badly our father had broken him, but a small part of me had always hoped ..." Anne paused to wipe away fresh tears. "Hoped my love and support could guide him through the darkness. I guess it didn't."

Anne took a shuddering breath. "The rest is hazy. The next thing I remember was standing in a cold shower, scrubbing myself, though at the time, I couldn't even remember why. I just knew I was dirty, and had to get clean. Very clean. I scrubbed myself raw, despite the pain. When I got out of the shower, the house was empty, so I went into my bedroom to dress.

"That's when my very first flashback hit. It felt like someone had struck me, then held me down, and the whole, awful experience played itself out again. When it finished, I ran to the bathroom and dry heaved until I was too tired to do anything but cry."

Tears splashed to her knees. They were Dela's, whose forehead still pressed against Anne's.

"No one should have to suffer through that," Dela said, hiccupping a sob. "I'd have killed them. I'd have hunted them down and fucking killed them."

"At the time, all I wanted to do was run far away and forget what had happened. So I cleaned up the mess, grabbed my college money from the coffee tin in my closet, scribbled a note to my parents saying I'd decided to go to California to study, then wrote another note for Doug. I was on the bus to San Francisco before my parents got home from work."

"How did they take you leaving?" Cappa said.

"I, ah ... I don't know. I haven't spoken to any of my family since I left. I have zero social footprint, so they may not even know I'm alive."

"Ouch. Well, I know who we won't be inviting for Christmas this year ..."

Anne grinned at the thought of introducing her family to her new friends. Especially to Zima.

"San Francisco was great at first," Anne said, "but I was an eighteen-year-old with no college degree and flashbacks that were just getting worse. No job, combined with the high cost of living in the City, ran my savings dry in no time, which put me on the streets. Then, when I discovered I was ..." Anne clamped her mouth shut.

Zima head-cocked. "Discovered what?"

"N-nothing." Anne loved her friends, but there were pieces of her past she still couldn't face — especially now that she was a blood-sucking monster. Voicing them, she feared, would push her off the ledge she had so carefully skirted until now.

"Anyway, I eventually pulled myself together enough to get a job as a waitress. The wages weren't enough to afford an apartment, but meals were free, and they let me use an old shower in the mornings."

"That must have been where you met Doris," Cappa said.

"Not quite. Life on the streets was hard. Those who weren't already drug addicts or alcoholics usually took up one — or both — and I was no exception. Instead of saving for a place of my own, every paycheck went to the liquor store. I used all the tricks that alcoholics do to hide my inebriation from my employers, but it didn't take long for most of them to catch on, then I'd be out again looking for another job."

Anne smiled. "That's when I met Doris. I was drunk at work for the third day in a row, and everyone knew it. The manager was about to fire me, and rightly so, but Doris stuck her neck out and convinced him I was worth keeping, staked her own job on the promise that she could turn me around in a week."

"Sounds like her," Cappa said, grinning. "And I don't envy you that week."

"It was hard, all right, but it saved my life. Doris took me in, sobered me up, and, most importantly, taught me how to laugh again. I'd been living day to day, with no aim beyond the next bottle of cheap liquor to lessen the effects of my PTSD. Doris reminded me that life can be fun, made it her mission to make me smile as often as she could. She became the parent figure and friend I had so desperately needed. After that first week, I didn't even miss the alcohol. Within a month, my episodes were as infrequent off the booze as they were on."

"That explains why you two are so buddy-buddy at the diner," Dela said.

"Inseparable. We've changed jobs together more times than I can count. For most of my adult life, Doris was the only person who really cared about me. She was my lifeline, my ..." Anne choked at the thought of how she had savagely cut that line last night. "I'll never forgive myself for what I did to her," she sobbed. "Never."

"Yes you will," Cappa said. "And so will she. I called the hospital earlier, and they said she's well enough for visitors. What say we pay her a surprise visit later?"

"I ... l-let's see how things go first."

Zima head-cocked. "Are you concerned about the temptation of blood?"

Even the mention made Anne's stomach growl. "That's part of it. But mostly I'm worried about what might happen if William wakes up early. He forced me to attack her once already, and ..." Anne hung her head.

The room went quiet. When she looked up, Cappa and Charlie were staring each other down. Anne supposed they were communicating electronically, though about what she couldn't guess.

Cappa was the first to break their silence. "That's ridiculous, Charlie! With everything Anne's been through, why wouldn't she believe you? Just tell her!"

He gave Anne a nervous glance, then sighed. "All right. Anne, it's a long shot, but I might be able to lessen William's influence over you through some, ah ... unconventional means. Just promise to hear me out before you call me crazy."

Anne gasped and clutched his hand to her chest. "I don't care if I have to wear a bra on my head in the middle of Union Square singing *The Star-Spangled Banner!* If there's even a chance it'll help, I'll give it a try."

"Mark, Cappa, and Zima already know the story," he said to Anne and Dela, "but you two should put your believing hats on, because you're going to need them."

66

CHI MASTER

CHARLIE FELT THE WEIGHT of Anne and Dela's eager stares and wondered again if he'd made a mistake in agreeing with Cappa. He didn't care about the difficulty, or even the danger to his own life that his proposal would carry: he'd do anything to help Anne. No, it was the hope that shone in her eyes, brimming with confidence that Charlie would fix her, just as he'd fixed Cappa, himself, and Zima. He couldn't stand the thought of letting Anne down, but the seed had already been planted.

The least he could do was try.

"I ... I never explained exactly how my consciousness ended up in this body, did I?"

Anne frowned. "No, come to think of it. I assumed it was some technical miracle that I wouldn't understand, so I never asked."

"Miracle, yes, but it wasn't technical. I tried for a technical solution, of course, everything you can imagine short of a brain transplant, but nothing worked. I was heavily into martial arts at the time and had complained to my *sensei* about it. Imagine my surprise when this graying old man laughed and told me I was going about it wrong. Copying a person's mind to another vessel would never work, he said, because you can't copy their soul.

"I thought he was crazy, and told him as much. He gave me a sound thrashing for the insult, but also said there was someone who could help. Long story short: I went overseas to study with a master who taught me how to strengthen my *chi* — or spiritual energy. He said with practice and time that I could learn to project my *chi* — my soul, really — outside of my body, perhaps into the new body I was constructing."

Dela laughed. "So that's how you became a cyborg? You made a robot, then tossed your soul into it?"

"Well ... yeah, basically, but the key element, and what makes me a cyborg instead of a robot, is the biological brain. My soul needed a living thing to control."

"That's astounding," Anne said, taking some of the sting from Dela's barb. "How long did it take you to learn how to project your *chi*?"

Charlie grinned. "Six months, which surprised even the master. I'm a quick study when I put my mind to something."

"So how did your real body die?"

"One day I projected too much energy. There wasn't enough life force left, and my body stopped working."

"I'm sorry," Anne said, stroking his cheek.

So am I.

"There's no one to blame but me. It's a miracle my spirit didn't just fade away, really. Anyway, I only told you that story so you'd understand how I might be able to help you."

Anne sighed. "Still not following, sorry."

"I think your connection with William is spiritual," Charlie said. "Among other things, when studying with the *chi* master, I learned how to defend from the *chi* attacks of others."

"Does that mean ... you think you can block him? Get him out of my head?"

"Possibly. It's been years since I've practiced, though, and ..." Charlie slumped.

Not even Cappa knew that his life force had been steadily dwindling since his biological body died. How could he tell them the effort required to help Anne might snuff out what little of his soul remained? Anne would never agree if she knew, and Cappa might shut him down to prevent him from trying.

He couldn't risk that — not with the threat of William taking over his dear, sweet Anne tonight.

Charlie patted her hand with a smile. "On second thought, it can't hurt to try, right?"

Anne's flying hug bowled him over, where she rolled on top and smothered him with kisses. "Oh, Charlie! Thank you, thank you, thank you!"

"Don't mention it," he said, enjoying every second of her affection.

Anne pulled him upright and sat cross-legged in front of him. "So how do we get started? Do you need incense? A pentagram? Maybe a sacrificial goat?"

"Nothing so dramatic," Charlie said, laughing. "Just relax. Close your eyes and try to clear your mind."

Anne did so, though her knees bounced with pent-up energy. The others watched with interest, especially Cappa.

Here goes nothing.

Charlie closed his eyes and steadied his breathing.

His master's lessons came back easily, though it wasn't until he extended his awareness around him that he realized just how weak his life force had become: Where his *chi* was once a roaring bonfire, now only a few dying embers remained.

No wonder I've been so tired lately.

Still determined to help Anne, he forced himself to relax, and let his mind slip from the confines of his body.

It had been four years, almost to the day, since he last projected his spirit — the day his body died — but it was just as easy now as it was then. At the height of his experiments, Charlie would jump back and forth between his real body and the cyborg upward of ten times a day. He had become so proficient that a mere thought was all it took to slip from one to the other.

Charlie floated above everyone, including himself. A wispy tendril of silver thread trailed from Anne and led out of the room.

He floated closer and inspected the point of connection. From here, he could clearly see her aura — the field of energy surrounding all living organisms — shimmering with color, but the area where the foreign thread pierced her aura was black.

Charlie put his ethereal hand on the black spot and was surprised when Anne flinched at his touch. At this range, Charlie could feel William's essence within the thread, which confirmed his suspicion that this was the source of his control over her. William was sleeping, just as Anne said.

Hoping he was doing the right thing, Charlie gathered his energy and channeled it into the blackness. Gradually the black spot shrank, and the silver thread along with it, until it was a fraction of its former size.

Just a little more ...

Energy flowed from his cybernetic body, through his own silver cord, and into his ethereal form. Charlie willed it down his arm and pushed it into the small black spot. William's cord shrank to the width of a hair.

Charlie pushed harder. The cord pulsed and wavered, struggling to maintain its hold on her. He siphoned more energy from his body, determined to free Anne from William's terror hold, and hurled it at the tiny remaining stain on her aura.

Nothing happened. He tried again and again, but William's cord had stopped responding.

When Charlie looked down, he saw why.

His own ethereal form was fading. The silver cord connecting him to his body was barely visible, a fragile wisp of hair tethering a balloon that even a modest gust would snap, and Charlie knew what would happen if it did.

That was exactly how his real body had died.

With careful, deliberate concentration, Charlie willed his spirit back into his body.

The effect was instant. He opened his cybernetic eyes and heaved a sigh of relief, but was distraught to find the mental exhaustion that constantly haunted him had worsened. Charlie wanted to sleep for a week, although he knew it wouldn't help.

This failed attempt to save Anne was, without a doubt, his last.

Zima head-cocked, her blue eyes darting between Charlie and Anne. "Were you successful?"

"Let me check." Anne closed her eyes, and a smile spread across her face. "I … I think so. William's presence was weak before, but now I can barely feel him!"

Cappa hugged Charlie and planted a long kiss on his cheek. "I knew you could do it, Charlie!" She smiled at Anne. "So, now will you come to the hospital with me to see Doris?"

Anne covered her mouth and nodded, though her chest heaved with happy sobs, then her arms were also wrapped around Charlie.

Which was good, because Charlie was near collapse, and he needed the support.

67

PATCH JOB

ANNE CHECKED THE PLACE IN HER MIND where William lurked, just to be sure the miracle Charlie performed had actually happened, and wasn't some fantasy wish of hers. Sure enough, his presence, which even while he slept had been a gaping wound in her thoughts, was now little more than a pinprick.

She kissed Charlie again, which broadened his smile. "You really did it," Anne said.

Charlie blinked and looked around, reminding her of someone in a drug haze.

"Are ... are you okay, Charlie?"

He shook himself, and his warm smile returned. "I'm fine."

Anne shared a concerned frown with Cappa, which quickly dispelled when he gathered them both in his arms and hugged them close.

"Really," he said. "I'm out of practice, that's all. No need to worry."

"So I'm safe now?"

"It's hard to say. As much *chi* practice as I've had, I only learned enough to accomplish my goal of switching bodies, so I'm far from an expert. What I do know is that spiritual energy has a strong connection with the earth. Certain minerals and fossils can manipulate energy or protect against outside influence."

"You mean like a grounding wire," Mark said, "or a lightning rod?"

"Something like that. Amber, smoky quartz, amethyst, and onyx were commonly used among the students where I studied to help ward against *chi* attacks during practice. They might help Anne, too."

Mark grinned at Anne and unfastened a gold chain from around his neck, where a beautiful amber pendant dangled. "This was my father's. He bought it as a good luck charm from a street vendor in Vietnam during the war, and swears it's the only reason he returned home safe." He pressed the pendant into her palm. "Hopefully it will do the same for you."

"Mark, I-I couldn't possibly accept such a precious heirloom."

"Of course you could," Dela said. "Just like you'll accept these." From within her frizzy red hair, Dela produced two dangle earrings, each with a long, jet-black cylindrical crystal. "They're onyx. Mom gave them to me for my sixteenth birthday. They aren't expensive, but I still wear them because I've always loved the intense black."

"Dela, I can't! They're from your mom ..."

"I think she'd approve. Plus, they match your eyes now — and I don't mean that in a ghoulish way, of course."

Cappa looked at Charlie, who nodded. "Be right back," she said.

She hurried from the room, returning a minute later with a gold bracelet set with purple gemstones. "Charlie and I want you to have this. The stones are amethyst, as you probably guessed."

"I'm afraid to ask where you got it," Anne said.

"It was a present." Cappa gazed at Charlie with pure adoration. "It was waiting in my bedroom, in a little red box with a white bow, on the best day of my life — the day he gave me this body." She fastened the bracelet around Anne's wrist with reverent care. "May it keep you safe."

Anne looked at her dear friends with misty eyes. "I don't know what to say. This ... all of this ... I-I can't begin to ..."

"We know," Mark said. "Just knock William's teeth out the next time you see him, and we'll call it even."

She took a shuddering breath to regain her composure. "I will, but first things first." Anne gently touched the cuts she had inflicted on Charlie's face, then his deformed hand. "Let's fix you up, shall we?"

Charlie nodded with a smile, so they split up to gather supplies. Anne fetched the same needle and thread they had used to stitch Zima up, then settled beside him and began sewing his wounds. Her stomach growled in neglected protest. She ignored it.

For once, Charlie needed Anne's help, and she wasn't about to let him down.

68

FRIENDS WITH BENEFITS

ANNE EMERGED FROM THE LAB an hour later.

Fixing Charlie had been easy compared to the Herculean effort of repairing Zima. While Mark and Cappa had changed out his damaged hand out for a new one, Anne and Dela sewed him up. By tomorrow, Charlie said, the nanites would have finished their repairs, and his skin would look like new.

Anne continued down the hall with an extra spring in her step. Cappa was eager to see Doris, and had shooed her away to change so they could leave as soon as possible.

Once in her bedroom, Anne clutched the jewelry to her breast. These gifts — these talismans — were without a doubt the most precious things she had ever received. She carefully fastened Mark's gold chain around her neck, where the amber pendant dangled next to Charlie's soft nanite heart. Dela's earrings slipped right through her ear piercings, which Anne was pleased to discover had survived her jarring vampire transformation.

I suppose it makes sense.

William still had the scar she had inflicted before he became a vampire, so it stood to reason that whatever state Anne's body was in at the time she had transformed was what she might be stuck with for, conceivably, the rest of eternity.

Anne froze.

Eternity ...

In stories, vampires lived forever — at least, those who weren't staked through the heart or disintegrated in sunlight. Some led charmed lives, beautiful aristocrats of power and mystery who manipulated world events from the shadows, and had scores of thralls begging for the privilege of being fed upon by a true immortal. Other stories portrayed vampires as mindless ghouls who were slaves to their thirst for human blood.

"Beautiful" hardly described her vein-webbed skin and large, black eyes — which ruled out becoming nobility or acquiring any sort of followers.

That left the ghoulish, bloodthirsty alternative. Anne was hungry, for sure, and the thought of blood excited her in disturbing ways, but so far the urge had been controllable. While Charlie, Zima, and Cappa had their usual earthy scents that Anne found undeniably arousing — amplified now by her enhanced senses — Dela and Mark smelled absolutely delicious. Anne felt guilty for thinking it, yet one whiff of them was enough to make her want to forget her manners and bite down for a crimson snack.

With a sigh, she pushed the depressing thoughts aside, sat at the small desk next to her bed, and pulled what little makeup she owned from the drawer. One glance in the vanity mirror confirmed that, unless she wanted everyone at the hospital to run away screaming, she'd need sunglasses and a movie-star-grade makeup job to pass for a normal person. Her hands shook, however, from the ever-increasing hunger gnawing at her stomach, which made the already difficult task of humanizing herself even harder.

As if that wasn't bad enough, Anne was also having trouble sitting still. Her knees bounced constantly, as if she'd had ten cups of coffee too many, and she squirmed in her seat like a toddler on an airplane. She practically sprang from the chair once her shaky makeover was finished. The result was amateurish at best, but still a marked improvement over her natural, ghoulish appearance. As long as she kept her pointy canines hidden — which meant no smiling or laughing — she may actually avoid a lynch mob at the hospital.

Anne was just assembling her outfit when an abnormally sharp hunger pain made her groan. Dizzy, she braced herself against the closet door. A minute later, after the strange hunger attack had passed, she shambled to the bed and hung her head in her hands.

I can't see Doris, not like this.

Memory of what extreme hunger had forced her to do as William's prisoner made that clear. She would never put Doris in that situation again.

Ever.

Another hunger pain, stronger than the first, doubled her over. She slid from the bed onto her hands and knees, panting on the floor like a starving dog.

What am I going to do?

Her only food sources at Z-Tech were already tapped out. Charlie had made it clear that donating more would be dangerous for Dela — and Anne wasn't about to ask Mark after almost killing him last night. It was also noon. Even if she wanted to go out and hunt people like the frightening monster she was, the sunlight would quickly finish her off.

Zima ...

She and her girlfriend had already laid out several ideas for blood sources. It was time to put one into action, and Anne was so famished she didn't care which. She crawled to her bedside table and reached for her phone, but a knock on the door made her freeze.

Thump thump. Thump thump.

Even through the door, Anne could hear the sweet music of a real heart beating. Scarier still, she knew exactly to whom the melodious rhythm belonged.

"G-go away, Dela," Anne said, forcing herself into the corner, which was as far away from the door as she could possibly get. "Please, find Zima. I-I need her help."

The door opened, and Dela's delicious scent filled the room, more tantalizing than any Thanksgiving feast. The new muscles in her gums pushed her fangs down in response, and she hastily covered her mouth.

"Dela, you really shouldn't be here! Please, just ... just go find Zima."

Before I lose control.

Dela latched the door closed and sauntered closer, bringing her delicious scent with her.

Anne wanted to bite her so badly she could cry.

"Zima doesn't have what you need." Dela knelt down and smiled. "I do."

"You don't understand! I almost killed Doris the last time I was this hungry. Once I start, I honestly don't know if I'll be able to stop."

"Oh, I think you will." Dela rolled up her sleeve.

Tart venom dripped from the points of Anne's canines at the sight of Dela's milky-white skin. With an effort, Anne tore her eyes away and clenched her jaw.

"Dela, d-do you remember what Cappa said this morning?"

"About you tearing my throat out? Sure, but here's the thing: Cappa's not human, nor has she ever been. I doubt she understands what it's like to need something so badly that your soul screams out for it, not like we do, or what you'll do to make sure your source doesn't dry up."

"We?"

Dela nodded. "You're not the only one jonesing for a fix. Your bite this morning was the best high I've ever had, and I've tried some crazy stuff. What I haven't had until today is an unselfish excuse to do it."

"Y-you're a drug addict."

"Was, a long time ago, and just like you with your alcohol problem, I pulled out of it and cleaned myself up."

"Then don't do this! We'll find another way."

"Bullshit. Thirty minutes ago, you left the lab with a spring in your step, and now you're so famished you can't even stand. Tell me I'm wrong."

Anne couldn't. Hunger twisted her stomach in knots, and she couldn't tear her eyes from Dela's pulsing veins.

"Zima can help. Please ..."

"She'd help, all right. The last time she thought she was going to lose you, she sacrificed Mark without a second thought. Zima loves you and would do anything to save you. *Anything.* Is that the kind of help you want?"

"Of course not, but ... I've fed from you twice this morning already! You don't have anything left to give."

"I have a theory about that." Dela smiled. "One I'm willing to bet my life on."

Then she took a pocketknife from her jeans, unfolded the blade, and gashed her own wrist open.

Instinct took over. Anne lunged and closed her lips over the wound before a single drop spilled.

It was as if the gates of heaven had opened into her mouth. Despite the already generous flow, she reflexively bit down, driving her sharp fangs and venom deep into Dela's wrist. She cupped it with both hands and cried with joy. Grateful tears streamed down her face for every mouthful that helped fill the terrible void in her stomach.

Anne snapped out of her blissful feeding when her meal collapsed to the floor.

"Dela!"

The feisty redhead was unresponsive, her normally pale complexion now frighteningly white. Dela's head rolled to the side, sightless eyes staring through cracked lids.

Oh no, oh no, oh no ...

Anne listened carefully for a heartbeat. It was faint, but still there. "Dela!" Anne shook her gently by the shoulders. "Come on, you've got to wake up!"

Dela's eyes slowly came into focus. A dreamy smile played across her face. "Wow, you should sell that stuff," she said sleepily.

"Oh, thank God! Stay comfortable, I'll get Charlie and —"

"No need, just ... water."

Water, water, water ...

Feeling revitalized, Anne snatched a water bottle from her bedside table, then cradled Dela's head. "Here, drink."

Dela took a small sip, then a larger one, and soon finished the whole thing. Anne was happy to see color return to her cheeks.

"Jeez," Anne said, "you scared the hell out of me. What in God's name were you thinking? And ... why aren't you comatose?"

"Because of these." She tapped one of Anne's fangs. "Your venom makes tissue regenerate insanely fast, right? I figured it would have the same effect on the blood system."

"Oh. I ... I suppose that makes sense."

"Of course it does. I mean, think about it. Assuming vampires have been around for thousands of years, like in the movies, they wouldn't have survived for very long if they could only bite their victims a couple times a year without killing them. A few vampires would chew through a small village in no time, and they can only move at night, right? They'd have to be able to establish themselves somewhere, and that means having a regular food supply. If they didn't have some way of boosting their victims' blood cell production, it would be practically impossible for them to exist."

"Wow, you've given this a lot of thought."

"Yeah, it's fun to think about. Like I said, you should totally sell that stuff. I bet it cures cancer, too."

Cancer?

Anne leaned back against the dresser. The idea of her cursed existence having actual value to society was novel. "You really think so?"

"Beats me," Dela said, grinning. "I'm just an ex-junkie who now has a good excuse to get stoned." Even though her eyes were still clouded, and she looked like death warmed over, Dela fixed her with a concerned gaze. "Feeling better?"

"Much, thank you."

"Anytime. And by that, I mean tomorrow morning."

"Dela, don't push yourself," Anne said, although her fangs already ached in anticipation. "You ... you really think you'll be ready again so soon?"

"We'll find out, but if today is any indication ..." To Anne's amazement, Dela managed to stand. "I should be fine, so long as I pack in a few iron-rich meals between now and then." She ambled toward the door, but staggered against the bed along the way.

Anne was there in an instant to catch her. "Are you sure you're okay?"

"Better than okay," Dela said with a dreamy smile. "Thanks to your vampire tonic, I feel fabulous, and I'm going back to my room to enjoy the rest of it in the comfort of my bed."

"All right, but ... let me know if you need anything. Please?"

"Roger that. Say 'hi' to Doris from me when you see her."

"I will," Anne said with tear-filled eyes.

Because now, thanks to Dela's brave gamble, she actually could.

69

DORIS

ANNE SAT IN THE BACK OF THE CAR, watching the ray of sunlight on the seat next to her as if it were a rattlesnake ready to strike. She and Cappa had blacked out the rear and side windows, but couldn't legally black out the fronts, which occasionally allowed one of the bright death beams to slip into her dark domain.

The car turned a corner and the sunlight switched sides. Anne jumped into the other seat. She wore three layers of clothing for protection, with thick work shoes, leather gloves, a broad sunhat, and, of course, her techno glasses; yet even indirect reflections prickled her skin and sent her cowering behind the seat.

Cappa looked at her through the rear-view mirror with sympathy. "How are you holding up?"

"Like a chicken on a barbecue trying to avoid the flames, but thanks for asking."

"Hang in there for just a little longer. The hospital's only a few blocks away."

Another turn. Anne scrambled to the opposite side. A bright reflection from an oncoming windshield caught her during the transition and painfully scorched her cheek. She swore she could smell her own flesh burning.

Cappa glanced back again. "Are you nervous about seeing her?"

Anne ducked under another reflection. "A little. I attacked Doris with my bare teeth. Now that I have these" — she pointed to her sharp fangs — "she'll have even more reason to be afraid of me."

"Mm." Cappa fell silent, drumming her fingers lightly on the steering wheel, something Anne couldn't recall seeing her do before.

"Are you all right, Cappa?"

"Oh, just a little nervous myself, I guess. Not about you," she said quickly. "It's just ... well, Doris is the first friend I've ever had outside of Z-Tech, and I don't know how she's going to handle the news. About me."

"You mean ... we're going to tell her everything?"

"We owe her that at the very least, don't you think?"

More than you know.

"I wouldn't worry about telling her what you really are," Anne said. "She's not into science fiction like I am, but she's pretty open-minded. Besides, Dela didn't know you were an android before yesterday, and look how that turned out."

"Well, she did pick on me about my age."

"If it's any consolation, you're the most mature ten-year-old I've met by a long shot."

Cappa brightened considerably. "Thanks, I'll take that as a compliment."

They lapsed into silence when the hospital came into view. Anne dodged light beams while Cappa weaved through the parking lot to the emergency entrance. The overhang, unfortunately, didn't extend far enough to shade the car, which left a dozen feet of deadly sun to cross. Cappa exited first and opened the rear door, then removed her blazer and held it up like a parasol for Anne to pass under.

Gathering her courage, Anne bolted for the shade.

The burning sun became the least of her problems. Her powerful legs propelled her faster than she ever imagined they could, smack into a concrete wall. Anne bounced onto her rear, feeling more embarrassed than sore from the impact.

Cappa's heels clacked up behind her. "Oh my gosh! Are you okay?"

"Ow. Remind me to never do that again."

"Nonsense, that was an amazing dash! Except for the last part, of course."

Anne glanced around. A pair of ambulance drivers were the only apparent witnesses to her clumsy sprint. She waved them off with a weak smile, accepted Cappa's help to stand, and went inside.

• • •

The door to Doris' hospital room stood large and imposing. Anne raised her knuckles, but couldn't bring herself to knock.

Would Doris be happy to see her? After the terrible thing Anne had done — the creature she had become — would Doris even want to see her? She glanced at Cappa, and was surprised to see the same apprehension that Anne felt.

Of course, I'm not the only one who's nervous about being judged.

She grabbed Cappa's hand and gave a reassuring squeeze. Cappa nodded and took a deep breath, then together they knocked.

"That'd better be my girls come to visit," Doris said from inside. "Because if it's a nurse with more of that lime Jell-O crap, I swear I'm going to puke."

And like that, the tension melted. Anne and Cappa shared a smile and opened the door.

Bright sunlight streamed from an open window, burning Anne's face. She cried in pain and ducked out of the way.

"I'll get that!" Cappa ran in and quickly pulled the drapes.

Anne's sight gradually returned, aided by her high-tech sunglasses, revealing a small, unadorned room. Doris sat upright in a hospital bed. Anne's unbeating heart ached when she saw the large patch of gauze covering the left side of her neck.

Doris, however, lit up. "Hey, kiddo! I gotta say, you look a damn sight better than the last time I saw you."

Anne stepped inside and closed the door behind her. "It's just the makeup, unfortunately."

With a trembling hand, Anne pulled her glasses off to reveal her dark, alien eyes.

"Dear Lord in heaven! What did that son-of-a-bitch do to you?"

With a nod from Cappa, Anne finally told Doris everything she'd been withholding. She started with her date at the opera, where she and Charlie were first attacked, then her shocking discovery of Charlie's true nature at Z-Tech. Doris' eyes grew wider with each revelation, but she remained silent and allowed Anne to continue uninterrupted. Anne intentionally held the catastrophic accident with the plasma pistol in the weapons lab until the end, where she handed the story over to Cappa, who related the incident, and her true nature as an android, from her unique perspective.

Doris was rightly speechless, and stared at Cappa with open wonder. "Zima as a computer is a no-brainer, but you?" She shook her head. "Not in a million years would I have guessed."

"Surprise," Cappa said with a weak smile.

"Well I hope you don't think this excuses you from our shopping date next week, and I don't care whether you eat computer chips, or plug into the wall at night, we're not skipping the ice cream parlor."

"Why on earth would I eat computer chips? That ... that's like cannibalism!" Cappa planted her hands on her hips, but the hint of a smile spoiled her indignant performance. "Do you snack on human brains when you feel peckish?"

"Oh shut up and get over here," Doris said with a laugh. She opened her arms, which Cappa happily fell into. "I don't give a hoot what your insides are made of, hon. You've got a heart of gold, and that's all that counts."

"I'm glad you're okay," Cappa said, sniffling.

"Me too. One thing I have to know, though."

"Name it."

"That ticker of yours," Doris said, "is it really made of gold?"

"Titanium alloy, sorry."

"Oh well, I guess you can't have everything."

"So," Anne said, "now that you're all caught up with us, how are you doing?"

"Can't complain. Lousy food aside, they treat me well, and keep me doped up on morphine to dull the pain."

Anne sat on the bed and gently touched the bandages covering the wound she had inflicted. "Doris, I'm so, so sorry."

"Wasn't your fault, kiddo, so stop acting like it was. Making you attack me just adds to the pile of reasons William needs his ass kicked from here to the next county."

Cappa sat next to Anne, making the bed creak ominously. "When are they releasing you?"

"Couple of days, last I heard. Ain't often they get someone as low in the blood tank as I was, apparently, and they want to keep an eye on my cell counts. They're also worried about infection because my immune system's down, too."

"I … I can help, if you'll let me," Anne said. Doris started to protest, but Anne barreled on. "Please! I know you don't blame me for what happened, but those were my teeth that hurt you, and if those same teeth can help repair the damage, and get you out of here sooner, I'd sleep a lot better if you'd let me try."

Doris grinned. "You know just how to say it so I can't refuse. Fine, go ahead and use your vampire voodoo to heal me up. I'm due for another dose of morphine anyway."

Anne knelt on the floor and carefully took her arm. "This may hurt a little, but it should pass." She turned to Cappa. "If I'm still attached at the count of ten, do whatever is necessary to pull me off, okay?"

Cappa frowned, but eventually agreed and positioned herself behind Anne.

Doris' tender arm was every bit as tantalizing as Dela's had been, and she pressed her lips together to hide her growing fangs. The familiar tartness of venom filled her mouth.

Praying her will was as strong as she hoped it was, Anne bit down.

The taste of blood was pure rapture. In the back of her mind, Anne knew she shouldn't drink, but her mouth worked of its own accord and gulped it down.

It was then, unfortunately, that Anne realized she was famished. Only two hours had passed since feeding from Dela, yet she felt as if she hadn't eaten in days. She sucked as hard as she could, savoring each mouthful as though it were her last.

Cappa's hand on her shoulder said her ten seconds were up. Anne was appalled to hear a growl from her own throat, but she couldn't stop drinking.

Cappa, now! she thought desperately. *Pull me off! Pull me off!*

But it was Doris who came to the rescue. She gently stroked Anne's cheek. "Oh, hon, you know I'd give every last drop in my veins if it would fix the awful thing William did to you, but as it is, the best I can do is live so you can have more later. You can snack on me anytime you need to once I'm better, and that's a promise. Okay, kiddo?"

It wasn't her words, but the unconditional love in her voice that allowed Anne to finally release Doris, despite her aching hunger, and wrap her friend in a tender embrace.

"I almost did it again," Anne said, sobbing against her shoulder.

"Almost. That's the difference, hon. You won this time, and you'll do it again and again until we lick this thing — together — just like we always have. Right?"

Anne could only nod, for she was crying too hard to speak.

70

RESTLESS

ANNE FLOPPED ONTO HER BED and smiled. She still couldn't believe it.

Doris was moving to Z-Tech.

It hadn't taken much to convince her that staying at the factory was the only option — short of moving out of state — that would keep her safe from William. Anne and Cappa had spent the entire car ride back chatting excitedly about which room she would stay in, and how they might decorate it as a surprise for her tomorrow when she arrived.

Anne's sensitive hearing picked up Zima's distinctive electric hum just outside her door. "Come in," Anne said before she could knock.

Zima strolled inside, laid down on the bed, and looked at the bookshelf expectedly, just as if the last few hellish days had never happened.

With a laugh, Anne grabbed the book they had been reading and assumed her usual position — propped on a small stack of pillows — while Zima snuggled into her shoulder. Anne stroked

Zima's perfect hair while she read. Zima casually draped her arm across Anne's waist and, for a few blessed minutes, she felt normal again.

They had barely started the chapter, however, when Anne's legs became restless. By the end of the second chapter, she was squirming so much that she could hardly concentrate. She shifted from side to side, scooted up, then down, switched sides with Zima, and even tried sitting on the edge of the bed, but nothing helped. Her rising energy levels made it difficult to stay still, and soon she was so distracted that she was mixing up words.

Then her stomach growled. Anne slammed the book shut in frustration, which made Zima jump.

She was hungry. Again.

"Are you well?" Zima said.

"I, ah …" Anne shook her hands, trying to get them to relax. "I'm just restless. Do you mind reading for a bit?"

"As you wish." Zima laid against the propped-up pillows and opened her arms, which Anne happily settled into. They rarely switched reading roles, and she shamelessly used the opportunity to snuggle her cheek against Zima's soft breast. The earthy scent Anne loved was overpowering. It filled her, stirred her. She snuggled closer and closed her eyes. Zima was warm and wonderful, and Anne realized with a start that she had never desired her as badly as she did right now.

But, like her hunger, it was a need that would go unfulfilled. With a quiet whimper, she kissed Zima's chest and focused on the story.

That was the plan, at least. Her restlessness made it difficult to keep her hands to herself. They wandered to Zima's trim waist, hips, and thighs. Her fingers accidentally slipped under Zima's shirt, but rather than do the decent thing and apologize for the mishap, she continued to stroke her warm, smooth skin. It was heavenly torture.

I'm definitely going to need a cold shower after this.

She suddenly noticed that Zima had stopped reading.

"Oh." Anne hastily pulled her hand from where it didn't belong. "Zima, I-I'm sorry, that was inconsiderate of me. I'll just …" She clamped her hand between her knees and looked up. "Please, continue. I promise I'll behave."

Zima set the book aside. "Do you recall the last message I sent before you were kidnapped?"

"Oh, right! Something about a surprise, wasn't it?"

"Yes. I was afraid it would no longer be appropriate after your transformation, but it appears I was mistaken."

Anne waited, but Zima continued to stare.

"You're such a tease," Anne said, laughing. "What is it? Or are you going to make me guess?"

Zima gasped — something Anne had never seen her do before.

"Are you okay? What's wrong?"

Instead of answering, she pulled Anne's hand out from its hiding spot and pressed it to her breast. Anne needed no encouragement to run a thumb over her gorgeous swell. Zima shuddered at her touch, and Anne was surprised to feel a stiffened peak through her bra. Zima's breaths became short and shallow. Before Anne had time to wonder at the miracle she had never thought to see, Zima kissed her. Long, deep, passionate, it was exactly what she had been wishing for since the day Zima awoke, the day Anne had confessed her love.

They hastily removed each other's tops and, in a breathless flurry of twisted sheets, Anne was pleased to discover that Zima's anatomy — and her own — were fully functional.

• • •

Hours later, Anne lay naked under the comforter, content to snuggle with Zima and absorb her warmth.

It's so much better skin-to-skin, she thought, caressing the gentle swell of Zima's belly.

"Was my performance adequate?" Zima said. The fiery passion that had possessed her girlfriend earlier was gone, and she was back to her normal, stoic self.

It didn't matter. Anne hugged her close. "Are you kidding? I'd purr if I could. It was like an entire lifetime of sexual repression all coming out at once, and not a single flashback to ruin the moment." She kissed Zima's breast. "You were wonderful. Thank you."

A sharp hunger pain made her wince. *Not again ...* Anne tried to ignore it.

"And my performance? H-how was it for you?"

"If you are asking whether I climaxed: yes, many times. However, I do not feel the desire to purr like a feline. I did not see that in my research of human coitus, but if that is your wish, it is an easy adjustment to make." A low *thrum* emanated from her chest, and Anne laughed.

"Why not? It sounds nice." She ran her fingers along Zima's cheek. "Not that I'm complaining, but where did that passion come from? It was like flipping a switch. One minute you were reading, and the next ... I mean, I wasn't even sure if you could ... you know, then all of the sudden you were unstoppable!" Just thinking about it made her toes curl.

Down to the finest detail and function, Cappa had said about their android bodies. *Boy, she wasn't kidding.*

"You recall the story of my time with the cyborg, and the Desire subroutine that drove me to kill?"

"Vividly." Anne shuddered.

"Although the urge to kill was removed, the pleasure injection framework itself remains. I realized after you kissed me in the lab that you would eventually need more from our relationship than I was capable of giving, so I enlisted Cappa to help me create a new subroutine. It uses the same pleasure-reward system as the original Desire routine, but the triggers are modeled from typical female sexual response instead of homicide."

"You mean ... this whole amazing performance was something you and Cappa scripted?"

"Not exactly. My responses were dynamic and stimulus-based to better resemble human behavior. We chose the Desire routine, which is a pleasure-reward system, over a static decision tree for that exact reason. It allows for more fluid response, albeit at higher risk, but I hope this evening demonstrates it was the right decision."

Anne nodded vigorously. "It's off now?"

"Yes. You would know if it was on."

Another hunger pain twisted her stomach, and Anne suppressed a groan. "So the last few hours, all that passion ... it was just a program, something you wrote to keep me happy."

"My passion was part of the program, but my desire to make you happy was not, nor my pleasure and joy during our lovemaking."

Anne hugged her close, basking in her warmth. "I wish you'd run it all the time, then I could seduce you whenever I wanted."

"That would be detrimental to us both."

"Huh?"

"With the program running, it is I who would tirelessly attempt to seduce you. You would soon wear of my constant need, I suspect. But for me, I fear the results would be similar to my previous experience with the Desire program. Its constant influence overtook my personality until murder was all I craved. The target behavior is far less destructive in this instance, but I do not relish the idea of again becoming a slave to my impulses."

"That sounds terrible! Now I feel guilty."

Zima head-cocked. "Why?"

"You activated the Desire routine because I needed physical affection. Frankly, I ... I'm afraid to even ask you to run it now. I couldn't live with myself if I knew it was causing you harm."

"Neither Cappa nor I believe intermittent use will be detrimental. We are both monitoring closely for adverse effects, and will address the issues if and when they arise."

"Really? So ..." Anne skimmed her finger up Zima's smooth stomach. "Running it just once more today wouldn't hurt?"

"No. In fact, the objective of the Desire subroutine is to incorporate sexual response into my core programming through repeated use. Eventually, I should not require the subroutine at all. I shall have a libido of my own, and you may seduce me as you would any normal person."

Anne smiled. "That'll be nice."

"Yes, but until such time ..." She gasped, and the passion that Anne had been so delighted to see before returned in force. Zima rolled on top of her and, once again, Anne had the pleasant challenge of keeping pace with a lover who never tired.

• • •

The door to the shower rooms opened over an hour later. Anne sagged against the doorway in happy exhaustion.

"You could have warned me you were going to run the program again in the shower," she teased over her shoulder.

Moisture dappled her face. She wiped it away with the sleeve of her pink robe and took a shuddering breath.

"You did not forbid it," Zima said, donning a matching pink robe. "I thought it would please you, since you seem eager for those behaviors to become part of my personality."

"Okay, but twice?"

Zima brow-knit. "The second instance is harder to explain. When I saw you washing with the soap, it just seemed appropriate. Now that we are finished ..." Zima purred softly, which made Anne laugh.

"I'll take that as a compliment, then, and a sign of progress toward my nefarious goal."

A wave of exhaustion made her droop.

Careful what you wish for, Anne, you might just get it.

Calling on her energy reserves, she caught Zima around the waist and kissed her soundly. "I love you, if I haven't said it recently."

"You have not, but rest assured, this moment will also be among my favorite memories."

"You really know how to sweet-talk a girl."

Zima head-cocked. "Shall I run the program again?"

"Heavens, no," Anne said, laughing. "Any more sex today and I think I'll —"

She started at a sharp squeak from down the hall, where a wide-eyed Cappa stood.

Cappa quickly composed herself and continued past, heels clacking on the concrete floor. "Good evening, ladies," she said with a grin, then disappeared down the corridor.

A stabbing hunger pain snapped Anne from her embarrassment. She doubled over and braced her arm against the opposite doorframe.

Zima jumped back. "Have I injured you?"

"No, no, it's just —"

A stronger pain made her cry out. Anne fell to her knees, gasping.

"You are hungry," Zima said, then shook her head. "No, you are starving. Your body is shutting down from malnourishment."

"You ... you can tell all that just by looking?"

"No, I have been monitoring your vital statistics closely through your implant, but your readings are very different from Mark's, and I did not make the correlation until just now. I am sorry."

"Not your fault," Anne said, holding her stomach with a grimace. "A mutant-cybernetic-vampire like me doesn't exactly come with an instruction manual."

"Anne!" Cappa's heels clacked toward them. "Zima, what's going on?"

"She needs to feed. Immediately."

Cappa paused briefly. "Mark's on his way. Hang in there, Anne, you'll be fine in a minute."

She had barely finished the sentence when Mark rushed around the corner, and Anne was so hungry this time that she didn't even try to hide her rapidly growing fangs.

71

STRATEGY

CHARLIE SAT IN THE BIO LAB, staring at the monitor. His body didn't feel tired — it never did — but he still wanted to curl up in bed for a week in the hopes of relieving the exhaustion that had plagued him since his spiritual attempt to help Anne earlier that day. He rubbed his eyes and forced himself to focus on the screen. Sleep was an enticing thought, but now wasn't the time — not when Anne needed him.

Besides, he knew it wouldn't help.

The scene in the lab was a replay from the previous night: Anne lay in a wheeled bed with everyone congregated around her. Even in her weakened state, she looked far more alert than he felt. Zima sat on the opposite side of the bed, her hand a permanent fixture to Anne's.

Charlie scratched his chin.

The pair seemed different tonight. Anne stared at Zima with doe-eyed adoration, face aglow despite her discomfort, and clutched Zima's hand to her chest like a favorite doll. He noticed

Cappa smiling broadly at them, and made a mental note to ask her about it once things calmed down.

A few minutes later, Charlie still wasn't able to concentrate on the confounded screen. He stood with a sigh and joined the others, where he took Anne's free hand, opposite of Zima, and smiled.

"How are you feeling?"

Her adoring eyes found his. Charlie wanted to dive into them and never return.

"My energy's back," Anne said, "but I'm still ravenous. I've forgotten what it's like to not be hungry." She looked over at Mark, who sat with Dela at one of the workstations. "How are you doing over there?"

"Trying to focus on the monitor." Mark rubbed his face. "Your bite packs one hell of a wallop."

"Tell me about it," Dela said with a grin.

Anne looked away and cleared her throat. "Have ... have you found anything yet? I hope the other vampires don't need this much blood to survive, otherwise this city's in *big* trouble."

"You're right on both counts." Mark pulled up a familiar-looking screen. "This video is a microscopic view of the infected tissue sample from Charlie's body. As you can see, the cells are practically inert until they're stimulated, here." He pulled up another video. In contrast to the previous ones, these cells were in constant motion. "These are your cells, Anne. Even at rest, they're in a state of hyperactivity. I think the implant has raised your metabolic rate to human standards, which means your cells don't get the rest they need to conserve energy. Worse, it's trying to match my metabolic rate, which is higher still."

"Well ... at least it's not a tail," Anne said with a sigh.

Charlie squeezed her hand, wishing there was more he could do.

"A tail we could fix," Mark said. "This is trickier. Even if we lowered your metabolism to normal human range, you'd still burn energy like a hummingbird compared to other vampires."

"Any more good news?" Anne said.

"Unfortunately, yes. The metabolic boost only affects the cells your implant has already converted. It's only sixty-seven percent done, which means your metabolism will continue to rise over the next day or so until the conversion process is complete."

"You can't be serious! I … I'll need blood donors lined up around the block just to make it through the day!"

Charlie and Zima each put a comforting hand on one of her shoulders.

"Right," Mark said. "Which is why we have two priorities. Number one is to acquire more blood, and quickly. At this rate, you'll collapse again in an hour."

Anne swallowed. "What happens after that?"

"It … it's hard to say for sure." Mark looked at Charlie.

"A normal vampire's cells would go into hibernation," Charlie said, "consuming little to no energy, and could probably survive for decades in that state. Your cells, however, will continue to consume energy until there's nothing left, at which point …" He looked down, unable to finish the thought.

"At which point I'll die," Anne said softly.

Charlie clenched his jaw. "Not on our watch. We'll get your metabolism under control. That's a promise."

"The trick is doing it safely," Mark said. "Metabolism is touchy. I nearly put myself into a coma the first time I adjusted my own. To make things worse, your new physiology is uncharted territory. We'll need to run detailed simulations before we make any changes."

"Okay," Cappa said, "so back to the first priority of acquiring blood. She just fed from Mark, so he's out. Doris is still recovering, and, given Dela's multiple donations today, she's off-limits, too. Suggestions?"

"Hit the streets," Dela said. "There are plenty of worthless lawyers and stock traders stumbling home from the bars at this hour."

"That is risky," Zima said. "I have observed how the cold ones stalk their targets. It is an arduous process. A hunting party rarely secures more than one victim per night, and it is already past midnight. Regardless, Anne's venom does not contain the same memory-inhibiting chemical as the other cold ones, so unless we are willing to kidnap or kill — which I am not discounting — we will need an alternate strategy."

"Which brings up another point," Charlie said. "She'll need extra blood to get her through the daylight hours."

"Charlie is correct," Zima said. "We must secure an additional supply to be prepared."

Mark shrugged. "Okay, I'll say the obvious one. What about a blood bank?"

"No," Anne said. "As Zima pointed out earlier, we'd be saving my life at the cost of others', and I won't make that trade. I'd rather die."

Dela shot to her feet, waving her hands with excitement. "Oh, oh! What about a hotel? Lots of sleeping people in one place, conveniently in individual rooms for private snacking. Easy pickings for a stealthy vampire, especially if you get your hands on the master room key."

"It sounds dicey," Cappa said. "Besides, Anne's in no condition to go out. Someone else would have to go."

"Actually ..." Anne slipped from the bed. "I'm hungry, but otherwise I feel fine. And if we're looking for a hotel, I know just the one. There's an antiquated place on the coast called the Revelation. They even have an old-fashioned fire escape on the side of the building, which would give us outside room access."

Mark grinned. "A hotel. Why not? Anne and Zima are already dressed for the occasion."

That woke Charlie up. He glanced at the pair, and noticed for the first time their matching pink robes.

And their hair is wet.

"Wait, were you two ...?"

"We showered together," Zima said. "Right after we had sex."

The room fell quiet enough to hear a pin drop, but Dela's laugh quickly broke the silence.

"That's so awesome," Dela said. "Zima, you can't hold out on this one. I've got to know how the first android-vampire shagging session in history went down!" She giggled at her own innuendo.

"We can discuss that later," Charlie said, though he would be happy if the topic never came up again. "After we figure out how to keep Anne from starving to death."

"Agreed." Mark rubbed his head. "So, back to the hotel idea. The biggest risk I see is keeping the, ah ... 'donors' asleep. If even one person screams, it could be game over."

"I have something to help there," Charlie said.

He rummaged through a cupboard, emerging a few seconds later with the small canister he had been searching for.

Dela frowned. "You're going to mace them?"

"It's not mace." Charlie fought an unexpected bout of jealousy when he approached the robed pair and handed the canister to Anne. "This is a mild aerosolized sedative. One whiff will keep an average-sized adult asleep through a thunderstorm and, because the concentration is low, it shouldn't pose a health risk."

"And you just happen to have this lying around?" Dela laughed. "Exactly what kind of experiments do you conduct in this wicked laboratory?"

"It's a long story," Mark said.

"And we're running out of time."

Cappa opened another cabinet, where she grabbed a handful of empty blood bags, tubing, and needles, then shoved everything inside a black canvas bag.

"Here," she said, handing the bag to Zima. "Get going. We can spend all night trying to come up with a better plan, but it won't help if Anne dies of starvation in the meantime."

"Great," Dela said, "I'll get my things!"

She bounded for the door, but Zima stopped her short.

"Anne and I shall go alone."

"But —"

"Your presence will decrease our likelihood of success. I have run two thousand four hundred and twenty-seven simulations using schematics of the Revelation Hotel that I found from public record. We stand the best chance of feeding Anne and acquiring the surplus blood she needs if it is just the two of us."

"Wow," Dela said, "you did all that while we were talking?"

"Yes."

Dela slumped. "Okay, Z, if you're sure. I'd hate to be the one to screw things up."

To everyone's surprise, Zima wrapped her in a friendly embrace. "Thank you for the offer. Please understand that it is nothing personal. I only wish to maximize our chances of success. I promise that I will make it up to you later." She turned to Anne. "Come, we should change into more appropriate clothing."

Zima held her hand out expectantly.

"Right," Anne said, "I guess we'll see everyone later. Hopefully, that is ..."

"Wait, one more thing before you go."

Mark ran from the lab, returning a minute later with a plain metallic rod the length of his forearm.

"Take this with you, it may come in handy. Hold it so the ends are pointing away from you and press the button near the center."

Anne did. With a loud *snap*, the unassuming rod instantly expanded to a full-size *bo* staff. Her shock became a grin. Charlie had missed her martial arts performance in the gym earlier, and was amazed to see her twirl it with deft proficiency.

"It's no plasma pistol," Mark said. "You have Zima for that. But if you're jumped by vampires, it'll keep them at bay until she can get a clear shot. Good luck."

"Thank you," Anne said to Mark, then she put her hand on Charlie's chest and kissed him tenderly. "Sleeping with Zima hasn't changed my feelings for you," she said softly. "Assuming I live through the night, I'll prove it to you later. Okay?"

Charlie kissed her with as much passion as his jealousy would allow. "Okay. Be safe."

She and Zima left hand-in-hand which, despite his reassuring words, left Charlie with a heavy heart.

Mark whistled low once the door had closed. "Well that was interesting. Zima and Anne ..."

"Don't be crass," Cappa said. "I think it's healthy for both of them. It's nice to see Zima finally connect with someone, both emotionally and physically, and Anne was happier tonight than I've ever seen her."

"Basking in the glow," Dela said with a grin. She gave Mark a solid kiss and waggled her eyebrows. "Hopefully you figure this metabolism stuff out soon. After seeing them, I'm ready for some glow-basking myself."

Cappa clasped her hands together and bounced in childish delight. "I know, isn't it wonderful? I overheard them when they came out of the shower. It sounds like Zima wore her out!"

"That sure explains Anne's hunger," Mark said, laughing. "Seriously, though, it wasn't a good idea, given her condition."

Cappa put her hands on her hips. "And if you say that to either one of them — or anything to make them feel guilty about their blossoming relationship — so help me I'll put superglue in your hair gel! That goes for you too, mister," she said to Charlie. "I saw the look on your face when they were making moon-eyes. I'm behind you, Charlie, you know that. But I won't stand by and let you ruin what they have because you've suddenly changed your mind about being okay with their relationship. Anne called you out on it right from the start, but you gave them your blessing anyway — we both did — and now it's time to own up."

"Yes, ma'am," he and Mark said together.

She relaxed. A smile twitched her lips. "As you were, smart alecks."

"And thanks for the reality check," Charlie said sincerely. "I needed that."

"I know, I'm just looking out for you. *All three* of you."

"Well, if you're done threatening my hair," Mark said, "I'll get back to it, shall I?"

He turned back to his terminal, where Charlie joined him. Focusing was still difficult. Mark, despite his drugged state, would probably be far more useful at the computer than Charlie.

"So what do you think?" Charlie said.

"I think we're in for a long night. We have some very complex simulations to build for a physiology we barely understand, and I'm still trying to shake the fun-but-distracting effects of Anne's venom."

"Would coffee help?"

"It couldn't hurt."

Charlie headed for the door. "Don't be so sure. It's been a while since I worked the coffee maker."

• • •

Charlie stood in the kitchen glowering at the infernal coffee machine, so exhausted that he didn't even know where to start.

"I've built androids from scratch," he muttered, "but I can't figure out how to make a freakin' pot of coffee ..."

"So, Mark's not the only one who's kitchen-challenged, I see."

Charlie turned to find Cappa grinning in the doorway.

"You have a habit of lurking, did you know that?"

"I wrote 'lurking' into my job description years ago. It's one of the many documents you signed without reading."

She shooed him from the counter. He backed away, chuckling.

Cappa had the machine happily gurgling in no time. Charlie sat at the table and closed his eyes, trying to remember what fresh coffee smelled like. He gave up with a sigh. Memories of his old life were difficult to conjure now, as if the days of his humanity were just a fading dream.

"You know she loves you," Cappa said.

"I do."

"Zima beat you to the finish line, that's all. The good news is that it's not that kind of race. There's enough room in that giant heart of Anne's for both of you."

"I know. She's very special."

"Then why the long face?"

"It's something you said earlier, about Zima finally connecting with someone."

"Do tell."

"Zima ..." He sighed. "She shouldn't have beaten me to the finish line."

"Now, Charlie ..."

"It's not jealousy. I wish it were that simple. The problem is that I haven't been able to connect with anyone for years. It feels like my humanity is slipping away, and with it, my ability to relate to other people."

"You're exaggerating," Cappa said, sitting across from him. "You two get along great. If it wasn't for her post-traumatic stress disorder, you'd have slept with Anne long before Zima was ready. So, what's really bothering you?"

Charlie stared at the table. "When I projected earlier today, I saw my spirit energy for the first time since the accident. It was so weak compared to what it used to be ..."

"At least you have a soul. That's more than I can say."

"I'm sorry," he said, knowing how sensitive she was about the subject. "The problem is that in helping Anne, I ... I may have hastened the inevitable."

Cappa stared at him. Her lips began to quiver. "Charlie, w-what are you saying?"

"I think you know, and I ... I just want you to be prepared. In case something happens."

Her composure broke. Charlie rounded the table and held her while she cried.

The storm passed a few minutes later. Cappa wiped the mascara streaks from her face with a napkin and blew her nose.

"What about jumping back to your biological body? You haven't tried since the accident."

"Maybe, once things settle down."

She planted a fist on her hip. "You mean after we've solved world hunger, too?"

"Yeah," Charlie said with a laugh. "I suppose there's a big list of things I'd rather do than discover I can't go back, and am stuck in this body forever. The longer I procrastinate, the longer I can hope."

"I think it would be better to try and fail than to die not knowing."

"Not for me. I'd be dead."

Cappa threw a snotty napkin at him. "Not funny!"

"It might not be so bad. You're my sole inheritor, after all. My share of the company goes to you, along with all of my personal assets."

"I don't want any of it," she said, her eyes misting once again.

Charlie leaned in for another embrace, but Cappa turned at the last moment.

Their lips met — not a quick peck, like they sometimes shared, but a lingering kiss with all the passion and tenderness he would normally expect from Anne. When she finally pulled away, he saw neither desire nor regret in her eyes, but sadness.

"Cappa, I —"

"Don't worry," she said. "I'm not trying to steal you from Anne, but I had to know what it's like — just once, with my own lips — the joy she feels when she kisses you, before it's too late."

"And ... h-how was it?"

Cappa brushed his cheek. "Anne is a lucky, lucky girl."

She abruptly grabbed another napkin and gave a great trumpeting blow.

"On second thought, maybe you're right. Since I'm your inheritor, it might not be so bad when you're gone."

"Um ... come again?"

"What can I say? I've had my eye on your rock collection for years."

It was Charlie's turn to throw the snotty napkin.

72

REVELATION HOTEL

THE REVELATION LOOKED just as Anne remembered it. Eight stories and weatherworn, it was a relic from another era. The hotel was nestled right by the ocean and surrounded by open parkland. A narrow path wound from the parking lot to the water, lined by small lanterns, which were the only illumination on the otherwise dark grounds. Even the moon hid behind a thick, high fog, making a stealthy approach easy. Zima wore her usual loose-fit grays, and Anne had dressed to match. Her wardrobe was mostly earthy tones, but she had managed to find black pants and a gray hoodie, compliments of her shopping spree with Cappa.

Zima caught her attention on their way to the beach. "You mentioned that you have been here before," she said quietly. "May I ask why?"

Anne sighed. "My boyfriend from ten years ago, Gary, thought it would make a nice getaway and booked us a room over a weekend. It ... didn't work out like he planned."

"How so?"

"Well, he expected what anyone would who had shelled out money for a nice hotel room, but I couldn't deliver."

"You mean sexual intercourse?"

"Yep. The sad part is that I liked him. I wanted to go all the way, but when he started to unbutton my shirt, it triggered a flashback and I freaked out. We tried a few times, but he eventually got tired of my screaming. That's the night he broke up with me."

"I see."

They walked in silence for a while.

"I would not have left you," Zima said.

Anne smiled. "I know. You have the patience of a saint, and I really appreciate it."

"It is you who has been patient. I am aware of how difficult my continued presence in bed has been."

"Y-you are?"

"Yes. Of the twenty-nine nights we have spent together, your pulse escalated beyond fifteen percent on eighteen of them, indicating moderate arousal, and over thirty percent on six occasions, indicating advanced arousal."

"I, ah ... didn't realize you were keeping track. Why didn't you say something before?"

"For the same reason you did not ask me to leave, I suspect. I did not wish to be apart from you."

"Oh." Anne let that process, flattered that Zima felt the same way she did. "For the record, it was a good kind of torture."

"I have difficulty understanding how that is possible, but perhaps I shall learn soon enough. Do you believe Charlie feels the same?"

"Worse," Anne said softly. "I don't know how he does it. If I were in his shoes, I'm not sure I would have the endurance to stick with me, but he hasn't given up, not even when he discovered that you and I ..."

Anne left the thought unfinished. How she had ever imagined he would be all right sharing her with someone else seemed ludicrous now. He seemed fine on the surface, of course, but she expected nothing less. The Charlie she knew was selfless to a fault. If sleeping with Zima had hurt him, Anne would be the last to know, and that, more than anything, gnawed at her conscience.

Zima turned suddenly. "Do you regret our coupling tonight?"

"What? No, of course not! It was wonderful. The only thing I regret is me not being able to overcome this stupid disorder that plagues me even as a freakin' vampire so I can give Charlie one goddamn night and be the lover he deserves." Anne slumped. "Zima, he's the kindest, most gentle man I've ever met, but I freak out every time he touches me. I feel so bad for him that I can't stand it, but I honestly don't know what else to do."

"Perhaps the issue is that you have not yet addressed the source of your trauma."

As a vampire, Anne didn't sweat anymore — but if she did, it would have been pouring out in buckets.

How did she find out? Did she dig up my hospital records?

It was unlikely. The records were highly confidential, or so they had claimed when she was young and naïve enough to believe everything she was told, but Zima was resourceful and may well have found them.

"W-what do you mean, Zima? What source?"

"Your brother."

Anne was so relieved she almost collapsed. Her darkest secret — her greatest shame — was still buried deep in the closet where it belonged, which meant Anne didn't have to face it, either.

"Dougie? What about him?"

"Cappa has noted you often mistake Charlie for him during your hallucinations. I did not think much of it at first, but your story today has made it clear that your brother was an important person in your life."

"He was, but that ended a long time ago."

"I am not so sure," Zima said. "You spoke of him with great affection, even today, which indicates you still care for him in some capacity."

"So?"

"He betrayed you, did he not? It was a detestable act, yet for some reason you associate him with Charlie, whom we both know would never do such a thing. That leads me to believe there is a deeper meaning behind the association that we have not considered."

"A-are you saying the reason I can't have sex with Charlie is because of some unresolved feelings for my kid brother?"

"Cappa would be a better judge, but yes, it is a possibility."

Anne snapped her hanging jaw shut and mulled the disturbing revelation in silence, until the roar of the ocean caught her attention, and the back of the Revelation Hotel — their entrance point — came into view.

• • •

Anne covered her ears against the deafening surf while they walked along the shore to the side of the hotel facing the ocean. She was pleased to see the old-fashioned fire escape remained. The beach and the rear of the hotel were completely dark, shielded even from the faint city lights. It was well past one o'clock in the morning, so she wasn't surprised that all of the hotel windows were also dark. Zima visually cased the side of the building, the blue lights in her eyes bright to Anne's enhanced night vision.

"Many of the rooms near the fire escape are occupied," Zima said. "It should not take long to feed you and fill the bags we need."

Anne rubbed her hands together in eager anticipation. "What are we waiting for, then?"

Zima shrugged, so the two of them made their final approach.

The hunger pains had returned in force. As they walked, Anne fantasized about crawling between a couple in their king-sized bed, soaking in their warmth, and drinking from their veins to her heart's content while they slept peacefully. It was so enthralling that she didn't notice they had reached the base of the ladder. She bounced off Zima and fell to the sand. Zima stared before helping her to her feet. For once, Anne was glad she couldn't read her girlfriend's expression.

The rusty ladder creaked under Zima's dense mass. Years of salt air exposure had corroded the rivets fastening it to the wall, and a few had already pulled loose. Even Zima's fluid grace made it shake when they reached the first landing. A rivet popped free from above, sprinkling them with plaster.

Despite their rickety perch, Anne was elated when she peered into the first hotel room window and saw a couple sleeping soundly in separate twin beds. Zima slid a thin wire between the windowpanes, popped the latch from the interior, and quietly slipped inside. Anne waited for her signal before following suit.

The smell made her shiver with delight. Each occupant had a unique aroma, but it was like comparing a peach to a raspberry; it didn't matter which she chose, because they were both mouthwateringly delicious. The new muscles in her gums reflexively pushed her canines down, dripping tart venom into her mouth. Her fangs were inches from the man's neck when Zima pulled her away.

In a starved craze, Anne spun on her with a low growl, lip curled into a snarl, but Zima's gentle touch cut through the angry haze; blue eyes beckoned her back to sanity like sapphire beacons. Anne covered her face with trembling hands and tried to clear her mind.

It was difficult. Her hunger was all-consuming and, combined with the smell of the room's occupants, it stirred a powerful predatory instinct that certainly hadn't been there when she was human. With an effort, Anne thought instead of her friends. If she lost control now — if she succumbed to the monster inside who regarded people as little more than food — it would undermine everything her loved ones had done in hopes that the Anne they cherished hadn't disappeared along with her pulse. The anguish and uncertainty they had suffered on her behalf would be for nothing.

That thought, above anything else, gave her the strength to force her hunger aside — to nod to Zima with confidence — because she wouldn't let the monster win. She was in control, and she would fight with her dying breath to stay so.

She would remain Anne.

Taking a deep breath, she pulled Charlie's aerosol canister from her pocket and sprayed a small amount in the man's face. He snorted, causing them both to duck down, but soon settled. The woman hardly stirred when Anne sprayed her with a similar dose.

A severe hunger pain drove Anne to her knees. She was near collapse again and needed to act quickly. With as much decorum as she could muster, Anne sank her teeth into the man's neck. He stirred when her sharp fangs pierced his skin, but once the delectable crimson elixir filled her mouth, she wouldn't have let go even if he screamed bloody murder.

Fortunately, he didn't.

Anne drank deeply, unable to suppress soft moans of delight for each heavenly swallow that eased her ravenous hunger.

Zima tugged her arm, and Anne realized with a start that the sound of his heartbeat had become faint. She hastily stood and mouthed a word of thanks to Zima; Anne had little doubt that she would have accidentally killed him without the subtle cue.

Her concern faded when she saw his smile.

Looks like my bite makes people happy even when they sleep.

She grabbed a tissue from the bedside table and wiped the evidence from his neck, amazed to see the puncture wounds were already beginning to mend.

In and out without a trace, leaving smiles in my wake. Things could be worse, I suppose.

Zima had used a more traditional method to draw blood from the woman: A needle protruded from the crook of her arm, secured with a small strip of paper tape. A short tube led to a full blood bag on the floor. Zima deftly removed the needle, clamped the tube, and put the entire assembly in an insulated pouch of her bag. She then looked at Anne, pointed at her own canines, then at the woman's arm.

Bite her. Got it.

Anne knelt by the bedside, firmly reminded herself the woman had already lost blood, and sank her fangs into the crook of her elbow.

Not drinking was hard. Really hard. Anne's meal had taken the edge off, but she was far from full. She could easily drink as much again and still have room for dessert. And so, when the first drop of blood hit her tongue, Anne pulled her lips away to break the seal, leaving only her fangs attached to the woman's arm. She fumbled for a towel to catch a trickle of blood before it hit the carpet, counted thirty to ensure the woman received an adequate dose of venom, then withdrew her fangs and covered the puncture wounds with the towel. By the time she'd finished erasing the evidence, the woman's arm had stopped bleeding, and the needle mark had already begun to fade.

Anne emerged from the hotel room feeling invigorated, the salty sea air pleasant on her cool skin. Zima followed, shut the window behind her, then used the wire to pull the latch closed with amazing precision.

It's as if we were never here.

Four rooms later, they had six full bags of blood. They would have had more, but Anne couldn't resist sinking her teeth into a woman in the last room who smelled like chocolate and roses. They'd also skipped a room with two small children, whom Anne wouldn't risk inflicting emotional scars upon should they have awoken to the sight of her feeding on their parents.

For the first time since Anne's transformation, her hunger was fully sated, and it was wonderful. She felt energized as she never had when her heart was still beating, as if she could scale the tallest mountain and still be ready for more. She looked at the seven-story drop to the ground and smiled. Yesterday, being this high on a rickety fire escape would have been terrifying. Now it felt natural, like her innate fear of falling had vanished.

Zima looked up to the window of the eighth and final story. "There are two adults in the next room," she said quietly. "That will give us eight bags, which should be sufficient to nourish you through tomorrow."

Zima climbed to the next landing, stairs shaking with every step. Instead of taking the steps, as any sane person would, Anne followed her new instincts. She climbed fluidly onto the outer rail and jumped up. Powerful legs easily carried her the distance to the upper level. She caught the rail and swung onto the landing with a cat's stealthy grace. Zima stared at her with an unreadable expression, then turned to the window without a word.

Spoilsport, Anne thought while Zima worked her magic on the latch.

The landing jerked violently. Rivets popped, plaster exploded. Anne flailed to keep her balance, and realized with terror that the entire fire escape was pulling away from the wall.

Without missing a beat, Zima grabbed Anne with one hand and punched through the window with the other. Before they'd fallen an inch, Zima caught the windowsill and hurled Anne inside.

Anne crashed through the remains of the window in a hail of broken glass. She instinctively curled into a roll that ended with her crouching at the foot of the bed.

The bed's occupant sat bolt-upright, his eyes wide an alert.

Zima climbed inside. Glass crunched under her palms, and again when she landed heavily on the shard-covered carpet.

"Wh-who are you?" the man said, looking at them as if he couldn't decide whether he was still dreaming. "What the hell's going on?"

Zima wasted no words and sprinted for the door. Anne followed, sparing a glance for the man in his pajamas who gawked at the two dark-clad women fleeing his bedroom.

A thunderous crash from outside heralded the end of the rickety fire escape. Zima and Anne hurried down the hall while confused occupants began to emerge.

A middle-aged man with serious bed hair squinted at the lights, but his eyes widened when he saw them approach. "Is ... is that blood on your mouth?" he said to Anne. "Are you all right, miss?"

Anne pulled her hood down over her face and scurried past. "We're going to have a dozen witnesses at this rate," she whispered to Zima. "We have to get out of sight."

The next corridor was blessedly bereft of gawkers. An elevator stood like the gates of salvation a dozen yards away.

"Thank goodness," Anne said, but cursed when the elevator chimed.

Zima shouldered a nearby service door, bursting the frame in a spray of splinters. "In here."

She slipped into the room just as the elevator opened. Anne followed and quietly shut the door behind her.

It was a supply closet, filled with linen and cleaning carts. The only exit was the door Zima had broken, which began to drift open. Anne gently pushed one of the carts against it to prop it closed.

Anne paced in a circle, rubbing her temples. "Crap, crap! What do we do now, wait it out?"

"That is unwise. Our chances of being discovered will only increase once the police arrive."

"They've already called the police?"

"Yes. I have been monitoring police frequencies since we arrived. They have just dispatched units, which gives us only a few minutes if we wish to escape undetected." Zima ran her hand over a rectangle cut into the wall. "What is this?"

"A laundry chute," Anne said. "It's a one-way trip to the basement."

Zima slid the door open and peered inside. "The building plan shows a large service entrance adjacent to the lowest level. We may be able to escape through there."

Anne looked at the narrow chute, then her own not-so-narrow hips. "Seriously?"

"Yes. You will fit as long as the chute does not narrow farther down. It is a long drop, but we can slow our descent by pushing against the walls. Wait for my signal before following." Before Anne could argue, Zima swung her legs in and rattled down the chute.

Seconds later, a low tone that only Anne's sensitive ears could hear drifted up from the hollow depths. It was Zima's signal.

Anne swung a leg inside and gulped. Heights were one thing, but apparently vampires weren't as comfortable with tight places as the movies would have her believe.

That coffin thing must be a myth.

Voices outside of the door launched her into action. She hastily put her other leg in, said a silent prayer that Zima knew what she was doing, and squeezed inside. Sheet metal banged and buckled in a deafening roar. Too late, Anne remembered to push against the walls to slow her descent. She shot out of the chute at ballistic speed and landed hard in a cart of linens. Anne extricated herself from the tangle of sheets and was amazed to find she hadn't broken any bones.

The laundry room was large. Blue carts full of soiled sheets and towels lined one wall, while a row of stainless-steel washing machines and dryers lined another. A swinging set of doors sat on one side of the room. A small rusted door, bolted from the inside, sat on the other.

"That's probably the service entrance," Anne said, pointing to the swinging doors. "Let's go."

Zima caught her arm. "There are people approaching from that direction."

Anne listened but couldn't hear anything over the noisy machinery. Zima examined the smaller door and brow-knit, running her hand along the seal.

"This door is not on the building's blueprints. I feel air moving from the other side."

"It smells salty," Anne said. "Maybe it leads to the beach."

Zima squealed the bolt back and pulled the door open, revealing a dark cement corridor beyond. Anne heard voices from the other side of the room. Shadows moved beneath the swinging doors. She and Zima quickly slipped into the corridor and closed the rusty door behind them.

The smell of the ocean was unmistakable in the long tunnel. Though pitch black, Anne's new eyes allowed her to see well enough to pick out details.

Mineral stains lined the walls where water had seeped through cracks in the concrete. Corroded light fixtures ran dormant along the ceiling. A thin layer of sand crunched beneath their feet.

A feeling of unease came over her, making the hairs on the back of her neck stand to attention. She hugged her arms across her middle and told herself it was just the creepy tunnel.

Besides, I have Zima with me. I'd put my money on her over a cave troll any day of the week.

Anne took Zima's hand for comfort, but it didn't stave off the feeling of foreboding, which grew worse with every step.

73

BUNKER

ANNE'S UNEASE HAD ESCALATED to near panic by the time they reached the end of the dark corridor. A sudden itch on her back made her spin around, but the passage behind them was clear.

A metal door hung from a single hinge before them. Rust had eaten holes through it, revealing a larger space on the other side. A small push from Zima was all it took to topple it over. Anne covered her ears just before it hit the floor with an explosive *crash* that echoed like dynamite from the concrete walls.

The room inside looked like an old military bunker: empty but for a few stone benches. A short flight of stairs led up to a formidable metal door on the other side. Zima climbed the stairs and pushed, but it wouldn't budge.

Another itch made Anne arch her back, as though malevolent eyes bored into her spine, but a quick scan showed they were still alone.

And I'm going crazy to boot. Peachy.

"Great," she said, scratching between her shoulder blades. "We're trapped."

"No. The door is reinforced, but it is not indestructible."

Zima backed to the far side of the room, then dashed up the stairs and rammed her shoulder into it with a thunderous crash. The door buckled, but held fast. "Once more should be sufficient," she said, readying for another run. "I cannot receive police frequencies through the walls of this place, so I do not know if they have arrived yet. Once the door is open, I shall see if it is safe, and will otherwise provide a distraction so you may escape unnoticed. Wait for my signal."

Anne kissed her cheek. "Just be careful." She scratched at the infernal itch on her back, fighting the urge to look behind her once again. "I can't wait to get back to Z-Tech. This place gives me the creeps ..."

"We shall be fine. The police pose no physical threat to either of us, though it would be inconvenient if we were identified."

Zima bolted forward once again. This time, the impact tore the door from its hinges, and she landed face down in the open air of night.

The itch on Anne's back exploded into paralyzing pain, as if someone had stabbed her with a sword. At the same time, four figures piled on top of Zima and pinned her to the ground, each holding a limb firmly in place. Anne fell to the floor with a scream. She clawed toward Zima through a sea of agony, but with every move the imaginary sword twisted, raising her torment to new heights.

She froze when a familiar presence brushed her mind.

William!

Dormant until now, his will flared with terrible radiance. He stepped into view and put his foot between Zima's shoulder blades. Zima twisted and struggled, but even her tremendous strength was no match against five vampires. Anne watched helplessly as William reached under Zima's chin, smiled down the stairs ...

And tore her head from her body.

Sparks flew from dangling wires in her neck. Zima twitched once, then was still.

The crippling pain disappeared. In its place came a black hole of despair that sapped her strength and left Anne feeling numb.

Did that really just happen? Was it an elaborate trick?

Her lover, her protector, her indomitable warrior ... Zima had trained. She had hunted. She was ready. She was the great equalizer — the bane of any vampire unlucky enough to cross her path. She was Anne's shield; the sure-footed destrier that carried her through the darkness, and the lance that vanquished her foes. Zima couldn't have met her end so easily.

Not now.

Not to him.

Could she?

William descended with a haughty grin, tossing Zima's head in the air like a basketball.

"You had me going there for a while," he said. "When that metallic bitch took out half my crew, I actually believed what you said about her being some unstoppable force. If I'd known it was going to be this easy, I would have hunted you down hours ago." He stopped in front of Anne, his face a blur through a growing well of tears.

Zima's head landed next to her with a thump, spattering Anne's face with red liquid.

Not again, not again ...

She gently brushed the hair from Zima's eyes, which stared vacantly at the ceiling.

Just like the last time I thought I had lost her ...

Because of him!

The black hole of despair became a supernova of fury. A feral growl rumbled in the back of her throat. Sheer hatred drove Anne to her feet. She glared at William, fists shaking.

"You ... fucking ... BASTARD!"

His lip curled to match her bestial scowl. He lashed out with the back of his hand.

Mark's implant took over in an instant. Anne stepped inside his reach, grabbed his arm to pull him off-balance, then twisted with all her mighty rage. William toppled face-down to the concrete, arm wrenched behind him in an unbreakable hold.

Anne ground her knee into his spine and snarled. "I'll kill you!" she screamed through bared fangs.

She cranked his arm further, her own muscles straining until he, too, was screaming.

"I'm gonna rip it off and shove it down your goddamn throat!"

William's scream became a demented laugh. "No, you won't."

The flow of his presence in her mind swelled from a moderate creek into a raging river. Anne struggled against the current of his will, fought with every fiber of her being to oppose Zima's murderer, but resisting was as futile as paddling a canoe up a waterfall.

Anne fell gasping to the ground. She tried to rise, but her limbs wouldn't obey.

William climbed to his feet and brushed the sand from his clothes.

"Now that was unexpected. I had you pegged for a skittish house cat, not a honey badger, which will make this next part all the better." His expression darkened. William pointed at his feet. "Kneel."

Her knees bent at his command. A piece of her conscience railed in protest. It flailed in the turbulent waters for something to grab onto, some purchase to brace itself against the raging flow of his will.

And then she found it: a branch in the water, a tiny pool of calm in the rapids. She swam with all her might, grabbed on with both hands, and hauled herself into the sheltered eddy.

Charlie.

She knew without a doubt that this shelter was his doing. Her only refuge was the spiritual protection he had put in place.

That and ...

Anne grasped her amber pendant. The currents around her ebbed further still. She settled into a sitting position on the ground and glared at him.

"No."

That single, defiant word took every ounce of her resolve to utter. Her body shook with the effort to resist rolling onto her knees. It wanted to obey him, but Anne held fast.

William's anger flared for only a moment, then his eyes settled on the pendant grasped firmly between her fingers.

"I see," he said. "I wondered how you had muted your presence when none of the others could. I assumed it was those thick factory walls you've been hiding behind, but it's more than that, isn't it?" He stooped and held out his hand. "Give it to me."

"No."

His will pressed harder. She closed her eyes, straining to shut him out.

"Give it to me!"

"Go fuck yourself!"

Something buzzed in her ear. Anne tried to bat it away, but to no avail; whatever it was seemed intent on adding to her misery.

"You're full of surprises." William unfolded a pocketknife — the same one he had gashed himself open with to force Anne to feed from him. "We can do this the easy way or the hard way, though really" — his fangs glistened in a cruel smile — "I don't care which."

The pressure in her mind was too great. She cried out. The pendant slipped from her clawed fingers and fell against her chest. He yanked it free, snapping Mark's gold chain.

William fastened her with a malevolent glare and squeezed the pendant. Tears streamed down her face when he opened his hand; only the twisted setting of Mark's precious pendant remained. He cast it to the far side of the room, then crossed his arms.

"Let's try this again. Kneel!"

Her earrings and bracelet weren't enough. Without the pendant, his will was a tidal wave that washed away all thoughts of resistance. She meekly rolled to her knees and faced him. The buzzing in her ear was louder now, but her arms wouldn't obey when she again tried to swat it away.

"I'm sure your boyfriend and his partner will be here soon," William said. "But that's all right. I only need a few minutes to send them a message."

His knife gashed her shoulder open. She clenched her jaw against the pain, but couldn't lift a finger to defend herself.

"No matter how clever they think they are ..."

Another flick of his blade opened the flesh at the base of her neck. The buzzing in her ear became static, like a poorly tuned radio station. A crackly voice spoke, although the pain made it difficult to understand what it was saying.

"No matter how safe they think their factory-fortress makes them ..."

The blade bit deep into her cheek, gashing her face open in a mirror of the wound she'd given him in the furniture store. White-hot pain tore a scream from her. Blood dripped from her chin and merged with a rivulet of red that ran from the tubes in Zima's neck.

The heart-rending sight was too much to bear. Anne lowered her head and cried.

ANNE.

She jerked to attention at Zima's voice. A glance showed her girlfriend's body and head lay still.

I HAVE TAPPED YOUR AUDITORY NERVES THROUGH YOUR IMPLANT. CHARLIE AND MARK ARE COMING, BUT WILLIAM MAY CAUSE CONSIDERABLE DAMAGE TO YOU BEFORE THEY ARRIVE.

Anne was so happy to hear her voice that she almost laughed. William eyed her; feelings of suspicion poured from him.

I MAY BE ABLE TO HELP YOU FIGHT HIS INFLUENCE, BUT I NEED MORE DATA. YOU MUST REACH OUT TO WILLIAM THROUGH YOUR MENTAL BOND.

William raised his knife again, turning Anne's elation into fear. She consciously channeled it through the spot in her mind that he occupied.

His breath caught. An obscene smile crossed his face. "Exquisite. Now, let's get down to business. I'm going to let you live, Anne, and I ask only one thing in return." He yanked her by the hair and growled into her ear. "In case your friends still haven't got the message when they find your broken body, tell them to stay the fuck out of my way, or this is just the beginning. Doris, Dela, everyone you ever knew at that shithole diner ... I won't kill them. I won't turn them into vampires like I did to you. I'll hurt them, crush them, cripple them, make the rest of their time on this planet a living Hell."

ONCE MORE, Zima said.

Genuine terror seized her when he pressed his knee to the back of her arm and pulled, threatening to break it at the elbow.

"You will tell them for me," William said, "won't you?"

Anne whimpered her assent and again channeled her emotions through the link. His rapture over her discomfort was sickening, but at least his grip relaxed, relieving the tension from her elbow.

EXCELLENT. JUST A FEW MORE SECONDS.

"Oh, Anne, I'm tempted to keep you for myself. I could do this for hours, but we're short on time, so ..."

Anne cried out when he pulled her arm to near breaking.

Zima, hurry!

BRACE YOURSELF. I DO NOT KNOW WHAT EFFECT THIS WILL HAVE ON YOU.

Nausea hit her like a truck. Anne doubled over and violently retched the crimson contents of her stomach onto the floor, dimly aware that her link to William was going haywire.

William screamed and fell writhing, clutching his head. Others echoed his screams from outside.

CAN YOU MOVE?

Anne tried to straighten, but a stomach spasm dropped her to the floor. She vomited again, unable to draw enough breath to answer.

ONE MOMENT, I SHALL MAKE SOME ADJUSTMENTS.

The nausea disappeared as quickly as it had come, along with the screams of the others. William rolled to his hands and knees, panting, while Anne rubbed her cramped stomach.

ADJUSTMENTS COMPLETE. ACTIVATING.

The spot where William lurked in her mind went haywire again, but the nausea this time was milder. William, however, fell back to the ground, screaming and pounding his head.

RUN, Zima said. I DO NOT KNOW HOW LONG THE EFFECT CAN BE SUSTAINED.

Anne stumbled for the stairs, but took a small detour to grab Zima's head. She had almost lost Zima once. Danger or not, Anne wouldn't risk losing her again. Her prize cradled against her bosom, Anne dashed again for the stairs.

A hand fastened around her ankle, yanking her off balance. Anne tucked into a shoulder roll, came to a crouch, and glanced behind her.

William had stopped writhing, hatred naked on his face.

The nausea vanished again, and Anne realized his presence in her mind had disappeared.

"He's cut the link!"

PLAN B, Zima said. DEFEND YOURSELF WHILE I MAKE OTHER ADJUSTMENTS.

Anne set Zima's head gently on the ground, wiped the blood from her chin, and glared at William as he struggled to his feet.

Defend myself, huh? I have a better idea ...

She kicked with all her might. William flew against the wall and collapsed, shaking his head.

Anne spat in the dirt at his hands.

"How about Plan C, where I kick his ass and send him back to Hell!"

She let another kick fly, but he rolled out of the way and came to his feet snarling.

"You caught me off guard the first time," William said, bracing himself against the wall. "The second time was lucky. There won't be a third."

We'll see about that, you cocky bastard ...

Anne launched a flurry of strikes and grabs, letting her reflexes guide her. He nimbly evaded, then countered with a blinding flurry of punches. Anne blocked and weaved, but was unable to catch his arm as she had before. It soon became clear that, although he was an untrained fighter, his superior speed, strength, and mass put them back on even ground. Anne ducked a heavy swing, saw her opening, and ...

Slipped in her own vomit.

William struck the side of her head with the force of a cannonball, knocking her from her feet. Mark's reflexes guided her into a roll that ended in a fighting stance. Her ears rang, and she shook her head to clear the dizziness.

He's so goddamn strong ...

"Perks of being leader of the pack. I draw strength from my sirelings." William flashed a malicious grin. "Including you."

MODIFICATIONS ARE ALMOST COMPLETE. DO NOT LET HIM KILL YOU.

Thanks for the expert advice, Zima.

Squaring her jaw, she pulled Mark's compact *bo* staff from her jacket. A click of the button snapped it to full size. Anne twirled it in a complex pattern that surprised even herself, then dropped into a low fighting stance.

"You want my strength? Come and get it."

William's first advance taught him a painful lesson on the advantage of reach. He lunged with a fearsome swing, but Anne smacked his head, danced aside, and let him stumble past.

"Oh, I'm sorry," Anne said with mock concern. "Was that the third ass beating you said wouldn't happen?"

He curled his fingers and roared. Twice more he approached: the first led to a crack to his sternum; the second broke one of his fingers. With a snarl, he grabbed his broken digit, snapped it back into place, and advanced again.

When she swung this time, he trapped the staff under his arm, yanked it from her grasp, and threw it into the dark hallway leading to the hotel.

Crap.

"Plan C was a bust," Anne said, skirting the wall to keep her distance. "I'm ready for Plan B, Zima! Anytime now ..."

CELLULAR MODIFICATIONS COMPLETE. ENGAGING.

Anne gasped. A tidal wave of energy surged through her entire body, flooding every pore with raw power. She was a living dynamo — a storehouse of crackling electricity begging for release. Her hands shook. Her jaw quivered. Her eyes darted everywhere at once.

"What ... did ... you ... do?"

I HAVE BOOSTED YOUR METABOLISM BY APPROXIMATELY ONE THOUSAND PERCENT. BE QUICK, I DOUBT YOUR BODY CAN SUSTAIN THIS LEVEL FOR LONG.

Being quick wasn't a problem. Everything around her moved in slow motion. William threw a laughably sluggish punch. Anne slipped inside his reach and kneed him in the stomach with enough force to lift his feet from the ground, then brought her elbow down, shattering the ribs on his back. William crumpled at her feet. She kicked him once, twice, three times and more — each compounding her hatred for the asshole who continually ruined the life she was trying so hard to salvage — until she finally stomped away screaming.

Kicking him wasn't enough. She needed to crush him, destroy him, pulverize him out of existence. Anne closed the distance in long strides, a volcano of fury erupting with every step.

"So, you like inflicting pain, huh?"

Anne ground her heel into his broken ribs, making him holler. The sound of his suffering was sweet and terrible. She wanted more.

"You like ripping people's fucking heads off?"

She stepped on his back and stooped to wrap her shaking hands around his chin.

"You've assaulted me, terrorized me, turned me into a monster. But that wasn't enough! You had to keep hurting me, threaten everyone I love. Doris, Zima …" Anne bared her fangs with a snarl. Her powerful arms tensed, pulling his head back until she heard a gratifying crack. "Well guess what, asshole? This bitch bites back!"

He gurgled and tried to pry her from his windpipe, but her grip was absolute. Anne was fury incarnate — judge, jury, and righteous executioner.

The walking horror story that was William Taplin would finally end.

Tonight.

CHARLIE IS APPROXIMATELY FIVE MINUTES — WATCH OUT!

Zima's warning came just in time. Anne was so caught up in her vengeance that she hadn't noticed the four other vampires enter. One grabbed for her, but she deftly rolled out of his reach and came to her feet.

She was surrounded, just like in her bedroom as a teen.

The hallucination took her by surprise. Chet and the other three jocks took the place of the four vampires. Her anger faltered, and for a moment she reverted into the frightened teenager they had beaten and raped in her own bedroom.

"No," she cried weakly, backing against the wall. "Please, not again. Not again!"

ANNE, SNAP OUT OF IT! YOU ARE NOT WEAK, AND YOU ARE NOT A VICTIM. YOU ARE STRONG, MUCH STRONGER THAN THEY ARE. YOU MUST FIGHT!

Zima's words reached through the flashback, but, instead of pulling her out, Anne transformed from the helpless victim, doomed to suffer the same violation and shame she had almost every day of her adult life, to an avenging angel for her teenage self.

She saw herself lying on the floor, dazed from the door Chet had slammed into her face. The four jocks surrounded her and her younger self. Anne knew what they wanted, how they were going to hurt and repeatedly violate that solitary girl in her own home — the girl who had just gotten out of the shower, who only wanted to make it to work on time and meet her boyfriend later that night.

Eighteen years of hurt and frustration came out in a primal roar. Anne peeled her lips into a snarl and launched into the air with a powerful roundhouse kick. Chet ducked too late; his head snapped sideways with a sickening crunch, and he fell to the ground, his neck twisted at an unnatural angle. Without slowing, Anne dropped into a low sweep that took the first jock from his feet. The second jock grabbed her from behind when she stood, but Mark's reflexes had a solution for that, too. She elbowed his ribs, grabbed his head, and flipped him on top of the first.

He scrambled to his feet. Together with the third jock, they rushed her from the sides. She sidestepped and, with another roar, heaved one into the other with all her might. Their heads collided with a crack of bone, and they landed in a twitching heap.

Her wild gaze turned to the first jock, who had just regained his feet. A snarl was all it took to send him scurrying up the stairs.

Anne glanced at her toweled self on the floor, but the teenager morphed into the thirty-five-year-old version of herself of a few months ago. Her fancy blue dress was scuffed and dirty from struggling on the furniture storeroom's floor, and she was staring in fear at her last remaining horror.

With a snarl, Anne turned her volcanic rage on William.

Except he wasn't there. She frantically looked around, determined to finish this tragic saga by ending his blighted existence, and saw his back retreating down the dark corridor toward the hotel. Anne charged after him —

And the world tilted ninety degrees. She stumbled and hit her head on the concrete floor, dizzy and confused.

YOUR ENERGY RESERVES ARE DEPLETED, Zima said. I HAVE RESET YOUR METABOLISM BACK TO NORMAL.

The world spun — oddly reminiscent of her wine escapade at Gary Danko's. Anne pawed at the floor, trying to figure out which way was up. She eventually flopped onto her back. Her limbs felt like lead, but she couldn't help smiling.

"I've got to hand it to you, Zima. Even without a head, you still managed to save the day."

ALMOST. I AM SORRY WILLIAM ESCAPED.

"S'all right." Anne was so exhausted that she wanted to close her eyes forever. "We did worse than kill him. We humiliated him — made him run like a cowering dog from the woman he'd terrorized." She laughed weakly. "For a domineering misogynist like William, that's gotta hurt."

WHICH GIVES EVEN MORE REASON FOR CAUTION IN THE FUTURE. HE WILL CERTAINLY SEEK REVENGE.

"I hope so, because the next time we meet, he's *not* getting away ..."

ANNE!

Her eyes opened at Zima's voice. Anne hadn't even realized she'd fallen asleep.

YOU MUST FEED. CHARLIE WILL BE HERE SOON, BUT YOUR ENERGY LEVELS ARE CRITICALLY LOW. I FEAR YOU CANNOT WAIT.

Sitting up required far more energy than Anne had left, so she dragged herself over to the satchel Zima had discarded by the stairs. Trembling fingers retrieved one of the blood bags. She punctured it with a fang, rolled onto her back, and emptied the delicious contents into her mouth with large, eager gulps. By the end of the second bag, Anne felt like a new woman. She gathered Zima's head and cradled it to her chest, then climbed the stairs to where her fallen body waited. She turned Zima's body over so it was facing up and placed her head at the top.

"Sadly, you've looked worse," Anne said. "My guess is we'll have you up and running before dawn."

MY POWER REACTOR AND CORE PROCESSORS ARE UNDAMAGED, SO PLEASE DO NOT RUSH ON MY ACCOUNT.

"No, not on your account." Anne gently brushed the hair from Zima's unseeing eyes. "On my account. No one else on this planet could have done what you did to save me. I want to thank you properly, which means those luscious lips of yours need to be in working order."

Zima's body twitched. SORRY. YOUR COMMENT INADVERTENTLY TRIGGERED THE DESIRE SUBROUTINE. I HAVE SHUT IT DOWN — FOR NOW.

Anne kissed her forehead. "Keep it on standby. Once you're back together, I don't want to wait any longer than I have to."

AS YOU WISH. CHARLIE IS TWENTY-THREE SECONDS FROM ARRIVAL.

Right on cue, heavy footsteps pounded in the distance. Charlie was running toward them at a speed Anne wouldn't have believed possible if she hadn't seen it with her own eyes.

He slid to a halt, creating a long trench in the sand, which ended in a large mound that buried him up to his knees. Charlie quickly sized them up, then looked all around, poised for danger. When he found none, he relaxed and returned his attention to them.

"Are you all right?"

"I'm fine," Anne said, though with the bloody gashes on her face and torso, she must have looked a frightful mess. She patted Zima's body next to her. "Ready to go home."

Charlie glanced down the stairs into the bunker. "What about William?"

"Leave him. We have more important things to do." She stood and hoisted Zima's body onto her shoulder, then gently cradled her head. "Like fixing my poor guardian angel."

Charlie smiled. He took the body from her, but left Anne to cradle her head. "Zima, this heroism of yours is becoming a dangerous habit."

ONE I SHALL GLADLY CONTINUE IN ORDER TO KEEP MY LOVED ONES SAFE. DO YOU NOT AGREE?

The look of concern and relief on his face made Anne choke with emotion.

"Wholeheartedly." Charlie glanced at the skyline, which was starting to lighten. "Mark's pulling into a parking lot a few blocks north of here as we speak. We should be home before dawn."

Anne took his hand and led him away from the old bunker, which from the surface looked like nothing more than a weathered concrete dome protruding from the sand.

Home.

Anne could think of no better word to describe the factory that had become her refuge, her solace, and, as soon as Doris arrived, the place where her most cherished people in all the world would soon live together as one odd — but very happy — family.

74

NEEDS MUST

ANNE COULD SENSE WHO WAS GATHERED in Z-Tech's lounge before she opened the door. Doris, Dela, and Mark's heartbeats were easy to pick out; the hums of Charlie, Cappa, and Zima's power plants were different enough in pitch that her sensitive ears could distinguish between them. Anne went inside.

Only two days had passed since her showdown with William. In that time, the previously unused recreation lounge had replaced the kitchen as the central gathering point at Z-Tech. Charlie, Mark, and Cappa were talking excitedly around the coffee table about some new business opportunity in Eastern Europe, while Dela and Doris appeared to be teaching Zima how to play a new board game involving drawing paper, clay, and pantomiming. It was Zima's turn, Anne assumed, since she was making strange waving motions with her hands, although what she was imitating, Anne couldn't guess. She wasn't the only one, apparently.

Dela squinted. "Is it a boat?"

Zima shook her head. The strange motion continued.

"The ocean?" Doris had an equally puzzled look.

"No," Zima said, "and I believe that ends the turn. It is the flow of a graph when plotting a non-repeating quadratic formula where *x* and *y* are inverses of —"

Dela fell back in her chair, laughing. "They have to be real things, Z! Algebra doesn't count."

"Graphs are physical things when drawn on paper. Shall I demonstrate?"

"No need," Doris said. "The point goes to you. It's time for a different game anyway."

Anne gave her usual drive-by kisses to Charlie and Zima, then sat at the computer. Local news held no new clues to William's whereabouts, nor did police activity. He was still alive, Anne was sure of it, but they'd turned over every rock looking for him to no avail. He'd show up eventually; she only hoped it would be on their terms instead of a vampire army unexpectedly appearing at Z-Tech's door. There was little else she could do, so Anne turned to her secondary task and opened an internet search window.

While the others talked, she sifted through pages and pages of results. Twenty minutes later, Anne plopped her head on the keyboard with a frustrated sigh. Like most people, she loved the internet — except when it overwhelmed her with information.

"What are you looking for?" Cappa said from behind her.

"Oh! N-nothing, really, just my, ah ..." Anne dropped her voice to a whisper. "My brother."

Other conversations ceased, as she'd feared they would. Everyone gathered around.

Dela snorted. "You mean Douchebag Doug, who left you to the wolves? Yeah, let's find him. I'll hold him down while you kick the ever-loving snot out of that ungrateful brat."

Cappa shot her a hard stare, which Dela met with defiance, then she gently touched Anne's shoulder.

"Why the sudden interest?"

"It's something Zima mentioned on the way to the hotel, about Doug being connected to my flashbacks. She may be right, and at this point ..." Anne sighed. "I'm willing to try anything."

"Ah," Dela said. "Does this have anything to do with the trouble you and Charlie had getting it on last night?"

Even Mark had the decency to shoot her a look.

"What? We sleep next door to them. The bedroom walls aren't soundproof."

"Um ... y-yes." Anne had long since given up on the idea of privacy inside the walls of Z-Tech, so she wasn't upset at Dela's directness.

Charlie, however, blushed and turned away.

"My flashbacks have lessened, but not enough," Anne said. "I'm tired of suffering. I'm tired of *Charlie* suffering. If facing my brother has even a chance of helping, I'm willing to try." *No matter how scary it sounds.* "I just hope he'll be willing to meet with me alone."

"Alone?" Dela scratched her head. "Sounds like a bad idea. I mean, what if you get a sudden hunger attack, or he just pisses you off, and you accidentally tear him to pieces?"

"Well, thanks to the last round of metabolism tweaks," — Anne gave nods of appreciation to Mark and Charlie — "I'm holding steady at one meal a day. So not only can I sit still for five minutes now without going crazy, as long as I eat before I leave, I should be okay."

"Ain't you worried about William taking over your noggin again?" Doris said.

"No. In fact, I hope he tries. Zima added a new defensive program to my implant that activates when he uses our link. If he does, he and his goons will get the same splitting headaches they did at the hotel."

Dela shook her head. "Z, how the hell did you manage to protect Anne from William, anyway?"

"Using a basic cyber-attack strategy," Zima said. "Endpoints can only process so much data before their behaviors become erratic, often rendering them useless. I simply used Anne's implant to identify the part of her brain connecting her to William, then stimulated her cells to flood him with random information, on the order of seven thousand times what he would normally receive. The results were better than expected."

Mark crossed his arms. "Has William attempted to control you since then, Anne?"

"Once, I think. Nausea hit me before dawn yesterday, which is a side effect of the program running, but it didn't last long."

Anne grinned at the thought of William falling to the ground in agony.

Serves that bastard right.

Her phone beeped, then again, and Anne was surprised to see messages from both Zima and Cappa.

"Damnit," Cappa said. "She beat me by a hair!"

"To what?"

"Doug's contact information. Zima's faster than me at processing large datasets."

"You mean ..." Anne's finger was shaking when she tapped the screen to open the message. "Is ... is this right?"

"Douglas Michael Perrin," Zima said. "Age: thirty-two. Born in Bedford, Indiana to Clive and Linda Perrin. His current address is in Sacramento."

"Hell, that's a two-hour car ride from here," Doris said. "You could make a day trip out of it — er, night trip, anyway. Meet up for dinner or something."

"Except Anne doesn't drive," Cappa said, "and I can't imagine she would trust herself in a bus full of tempting morsels, or even with a tasty cab driver, for that long." She looked at Anne with concern. "Are you sure you want to do this alone?"

"I don't want to, no, but the relationship between a brother and sister ... there are so many topics we need to cover, things only the two of us have shared, I ... I don't know if we'd be able to talk openly if someone else was present."

"Well, all this yapping ain't gonna do no good if he don't want to see her in the first place," Doris said. "You got his number now, hon. Who knows? Maybe he really wants to see you and will drive down here for a visit. Give him a call, and we'll figure things out from there."

"After your snack," Dela said. She tugged Anne out of her chair and pulled her toward the door.

Doris blocked their way. "Hang on, missy. Didn't Anne bite you just before breakfast?"

"So?"

"'So'? Are you trying to put yourself into a coma? Don't be a martyr, red. Let someone else take the hit."

Cappa put a hand on her hip. "I think a 'hit' is exactly what she wants."

"Hey," Dela said, "just because she's using me as food doesn't mean I can't enjoy it. You guys hate the buzz; I don't. I've had two big meals since this morning, and I feel great. Now, if you'll excuse us ..."

She pushed past Doris with Anne in tow, and they went straight to the room she shared with Mark.

Anne emerged several minutes later feeling almost as satisfied as Dela. She hadn't even been hungry, but that didn't make her practically forced meal taste any less delicious.

When she opened the door to her own room, she found Zima sitting on the bed. Zima patted the space next to her and held Anne's phone out.

"I have already entered Doug's phone number," Zima said. "You need only press the button."

"Thanks, but I really —"

"I shall not say a word during or after your conversation. I am aware that this call will be difficult for you, and only wish to be here should you need support."

Anne sat down and kissed her with a smile.

Ever my guardian angel.

"All right, let's get this over with."

Feeling more anxious than when she'd fought William, Anne gripped Zima's hand, and with the other, pressed "Send".

75

REUNION

ANNE STOOD ALONE ON THE THIRD FLOOR of the empty parking structure, fiddling with a shirt button. Fluorescent lights well past their prime flickered in syncopation, which did nothing to ease her queasy stomach.

Doris had been right; not only had her brother Doug been glad to hear from Anne, he'd practically dropped the phone in his eagerness to drive down to San Francisco and see her that very night. He hadn't even questioned her choice of meeting places — which Anne found odd, because she would have.

The parking structure had been Zima's idea and, although Anne had balked at first, she couldn't argue with her logic. It was relatively dark, which would give Doug less opportunity to scrutinize her sketchy makeup job and, unlike the comfort of her first choice of a restaurant, the empty parking lot was as private as meeting spots came in the City. The chill night air also provided a good excuse to leave early should things become awkward.

She heard the car driving up the ramp long before its bright headlights stabbed her eyes, despite her tinted techno glasses. The car pulled into a spot next to her, and the roar of its engine soon stopped hurting her sensitive ears.

Anne forgot about all of that when the brother she hadn't seen in eighteen years stepped out.

Age had treated him well. He was taller and a little heavier than she remembered — as she no doubt appeared to him — but what struck her were his eyes. Gone was the hardened edge beaten into him by their father. He regarded Anne with a genuine delight that made her heart sing; this was the look she had so desperately tried to foster, despite his horrible circumstances, yet Doug had managed to find it on his own. A tear rolled down her cheek, which she carefully dabbed with her jacket to avoid smudging her layers of makeup.

"Annie?"

That single word almost made her lose it.

"Hi, Dougie. Um, th-thanks for driving all the way down here."

"It was no trouble." Doug rocked on his heels, looking as uncertain as she felt. "You look well. How have you been?"

You wouldn't believe me if I told you.

"Life's been ... challenging since I left Bedford, but I'm coping. With help."

"Challenging, huh? Well, I'm glad there's someone in your life to help you out." His eyes softened. "Like I wasn't."

And there it was. Doug had taken the first step onto a swinging tightrope over a pit of hungry alligators, and he was beckoning her to meet him in the middle. Anne took a deep breath, then stepped onto the shaky wire with him.

"Dougie, I-I won't get mad — at least, I'll try not to, but I was wondering if you'd tell me exactly what happened that ... the day I left home."

"You ... don't remember?"

"Bits and pieces. I've stitched it together over the years, but my memories are so fragmented that I honestly can't say what was real, and what my brain might have fabricated to fill in the gaps. For instance ..." Anne bit her lip. Sharp fangs pricked her skin, but the pain helped focus her so she could say what she needed to — the thing that, if Zima was correct, lay at the heart of her disorder.

Her voice was a strained whisper when she finally spoke. "Why didn't you help me, Dougie?"

His mouth worked soundlessly. A range of emotions played across his face, then he finally sagged. "You have no idea how many times I've rehearsed that answer in my head, but now that you're actually here ..."

"Please, just tell me. Even if the reason is because you hated me, w-which I'd understand, at least I'd stop wondering."

Doug flinched. "Hate you? I hated Dad for beating me senseless for no reason. I hated Mom for letting him, though I learned later that she was just as scared of him as I was, but you ..."

He pulled a worn piece of paper from his jacket, which he held out in trembling fingers.

Her breath caught. It was the note she'd written him before fleeing their home in Indiana. The paper was discolored and cotton-soft, but on it were the last words she had imparted to her brother.

I still love you.

Dark glasses hid her welling tears. "Dougie, I ... I can't believe you kept this."

"Are you kidding? This note — your love! — is what gave me the strength to leave home at sixteen and make a better life for myself. Hate you, Annie?" He shook his head. "You were the one person during those awful years who made me happy, even if I didn't always show it. I honestly don't know how I would have made it through without you."

"Then why, Dougie? How could you have stood by and watched them rape me over and —"

"Because Chet said he'd kill you if I tried to stop him!"

Doug took a shuddering breath, then continued in a calmer tone.

"You didn't know him like I did, Annie. He was that sick guy you only read about who kicks puppies for fun. He had a garage full of hunting weapons, and he never missed an opportunity to brag about how brutally his latest kill died."

"I know the type," Anne said quietly.

"Then you know how seriously I took his threat." He gently set his hands on her shoulders. The sorrow in his eyes was heartbreaking. "The hardest thing I've ever had to do was watch them hurt the most important person to me. I would have given my life to save you, Annie. But trying might have cost yours, and I couldn't take that risk. The best I could do was stay close and make sure Chet didn't try to kill you anyway."

The parking lot swam in a wave of dizziness. Doug's grip tightened to steady her, for which she was grateful, while Anne struggled with his words that contradicted everything she had assumed for nearly two decades.

"You ... you didn't hate me," she said, still not sure if she'd heard him right. "You were just trying to protect me from something worse."

"That's right. To this day, I don't know if I'd choose differently if I had to do it over again, but now, at least, I hope you understand that my inaction wasn't because I didn't care."

He cared about me.

She covered her mouth, lips trembling. It was almost too good to believe.

Then his arms were around her, and she could no longer hold back the sobs that had threatened since he stepped from the car and called her by her childhood name. She hugged him as well — too tightly, judging from his grunt — and they stood in the comfort of each other's embrace for what felt like an eternity, until he began to shiver, and Anne realized with a start that her cold body wasn't helping.

She reluctantly parted from his warmth. If Doug had noticed her abnormally low body temperature, he kept it to himself, just as he hadn't commented on her wearing sunglasses in a dark parking lot. He dried his own face, and they shared an awkward laugh.

"So," Anne said, "w-what do you do up there in Sacramento?"

He smiled. "I'm a counselor. I help kids deal with situations even worse than ours, if you can believe it."

"That's wonderful, Dougie. I'm sure the kids love you."

"They're great. Most just want to know they're safe, and that someone actually cares. The best part for me, though, is getting to relive the childhood I wish I'd had through them. I even have a kid of my own now, with another on the way."

Anne grabbed him by the jacket and nearly lifted him from his feet in excitement. "Pictures! Now! Are you married?"

"Four years last October," he said, laughing, then pulled out his phone. "This is my wife, Maria, and the little guy is Nathan, though I doubt he knows it since everyone calls him Natie."

"He looks just like you! How old?"

"Two and a half. He's the textbook definition for the terrible twos, but we're surviving. Hopefully things will be better by the time the next one comes in June."

"Does ... does Mom know?"

"Yeah, I called her a few weeks after Natie was born. She said she wanted to see him, but I haven't heard from her since."

Anne fiddled with her buttons. "How is she doing? I haven't spoken to either of them since I left Bedford."

"I know. The first thing Mom asked was if I'd found out where you were living yet. Not that I blame her. It's the first question I ask when she calls, too."

"I'm sorry, Dougie. I was a mess and couldn't bring myself to face anyone from home."

"I get it. Half the reason I became a counselor was so I could understand, even tangentially, what you might be going through, so that if we ever met, I could maybe help you the way ... the way I s-should ..."

Doug broke down. Anne gathered him in her arms, just as she had when their father had started beating him, and her poor, confused little brother was upset because he couldn't figure out what he'd done wrong.

"It's okay," she said, using the same soothing tone she had back then. "You did what you thought was best for me, Dougie. Part of the reason I've been so messed up all these years is because deep down I knew you wouldn't stand by without a good reason, I just couldn't guess what it was." She kissed his cheek. "Now I know. Thank you."

Her reassuring words did nothing to help his sobbing, so she held him until the fit passed. When he looked at her again, she could see an enormous weight had been lifted. She, too, felt purified of a toxin that had crippled her for so long that she couldn't remember what life was like without it.

Until now.

"Well," Doug said, wiping his eyes, "I always tell my troubled kids that crying is healthy. Glad to know I was telling the truth. So, what about you? Any kids of your own?"

Her mouth went dry. "Y-yes, sort of. She, um ..." Anne tucked her hands under her arms to keep them from shaking. "She should be nineteen in June."

Anne couldn't say what had driven her to admit to Doug, who she hadn't seen since he was a teenager, what she couldn't tell her closest and dearest friends — the only darkness in her past that even Doris didn't know.

It didn't take long for Doug to do the math. "Oh, Annie ... you were *pregnant* when you ran away to San Francisco?"

She nodded slowly. "And I just couldn't bring myself to get an abortion. What Chet and the others did to me wasn't her fault, but I was too unstable to keep her, even though I wanted to, so I ... I gave her up for adoption."

"My God, I'm so sorry. Do you ever see her?"

Anne shook her head. "It was a closed adoption. I only saw her once, when the nurse was taking her away. They wanted me to hold her, but I refused, because I knew if I did, I'd never let her go, and that wouldn't have been fair to either of us."

"A closed adoption ... so you don't even know where she lives."

"No, but it's for the best."

Especially now, Anne thought.

The last thing any kid needed was to learn their real mother actually was that monster lurking in the dark corner of their room.

"I don't know who her parents are," Anne said. "But I did ask the agency about their finances. They were well off, so hopefully she isn't wanting for anything."

"I see."

Doug frowned, as if struggling with something, before he spoke again.

"Annie, I can only imagine how hard it's been for you through the years, but one thing I've helped several adopted kids do is reconnect with their biological parents. If ... if you ever decide that's a path you'd like to take, there are people who can help make it a more positive experience." He smiled warmly. "Like me."

"That's sweet. If I ever decide to, you're the first person I'll call, I promise, but ... she may not even know she's adopted."

"Technically she's an adult now, which means she has the legal right to reunite with her biological parents despite what her adoptive parents might say. Either way, the adoption agency can probably find out for you."

Another wave of dizziness threatened to take her legs out from under her.

An adult?

Of course she would be. Anne had spent so long not thinking about it that in her mind, her child was still that beautiful baby she had glimpsed in the delivery room, but she'd be grown now and probably thinking about college, just as Anne had at that age.

"Thanks, Dougie," she said in a shaky voice. "I'll keep that in mind."

Doug rubbed his arms with a shiver. "Speaking of reunions ... what say we move this one someplace warmer, preferably where they serve coffee?"

Anne did a quick hunger check. Her stomach was holding steady, thanks to a snack from Doris before she had left the factory, so she agreed.

They walked and talked, and eventually ended up in a nearby diner. She was worried the delicious smell of the occupants might push her over the edge, but she was so caught up reacquainting with her estranged brother that Anne soon forgot there was anyone else in the world but the two of them. Her only challenge for the rest of that evening was concealing her fangs when she laughed.

Which, thankfully, happened a lot.

76

BITTERSWEET

CAPPA HURRIED DOWN THE HALL toward the basement stairway as soon as the intrusion detectors went off. It was just Zima returning through the escape tunnel, she knew, so she didn't bother letting Charlie or Mark know.

Especially not tonight.

The basement door opened, and Cappa practically jumped on Zima when she emerged.

"What happened? How did it go?"

"Both Anne and her brother are unharmed," Zima said. "He is dropping her off in the guest parking lot now."

"That's not what I meant! How did their reunion go?"

"I cannot say. My intention in following Anne tonight was not to spy on her, but to ensure her safety, and make sure she did not accidentally do something to her brother that she might later regret."

Cappa was normally patient with Zima, but right now, she wanted to strangle her. "Come on! You must have seen something. How did they act?"

"There was much hugging, crying, laughing, and animated conversation."

"Which pretty much describes any conversation with Anne, but since there wasn't any screaming or running away, I'll take it as a sign that things went well."

Zima shrugged. "Ask her. I am sure she will tell you."

Cappa intended to do just that. The surveillance camera showed that Anne was just approaching the front entrance. Cappa unlocked both the outside and inside doors for her, then hurried down the hall to greet her, with Zima close behind.

They weren't the only ones anxious to learn how the reunion went, apparently. Charlie caught up with them in the hallway, while Doris, Mark, and Dela were already in the lobby, chatting amiably over a pot of coffee.

Anne's eyes widened when she saw everyone gathered through the glass doors, but her surprise quickly melted into a smile.

"This must be a record," she said on entering. "When was the last time Z-Tech's lobby had this many people in it?"

"Four years ago," Mark said. "A bunch of army brass showed up with a bogus excuse to search the factory for suspected use of secret military technology."

"What they really wanted," Charlie said, "was a glimpse of our manufacturing practices, and we all knew it. They spent five hours in here arguing the legitimacy of their claim, but in the end discovered that not only are we not intimidated by soldiers with machine guns — especially with Zima armed and ready on the other side of the door — but that Mark and I are very well versed on both the law and military protocol."

Doris cackled. "I would love to have been a fly on that wall!"

"Speaking of," Cappa said, eager to cut to the reason they had all gathered. "How did it go, Anne?"

"I think it went well." Anne looked pointedly at Zima. "Don't you?"

Zima head-cocked. "You saw me?"

"No, but there was a baking factory a block away with a perfect view of the garage, and ..." She took an exaggerated whiff of Zima's jacket. "You smell just like it."

"I am sorry for not telling you, I only —"

Anne interrupted her with a kiss. "Why would I be upset with my guardian angel for watching over me?"

"Enough with the lovey-dovey," Doris said. "Spill it, kiddo! And don't leave anything out."

"All right! Sheesh. And I thought William was scary ..."

Anne recounted her heartwarming reunion for them. Many faces were tear streaked by the time she finished, including Cappa's.

"I think we're okay now," Anne said in closing. "He even invited me up to Sacramento to meet his family."

"Sounds like the fairytale ending you always wanted," Doris said. "You reckon it'll stop those nightmares and flashbacks now?"

"Only time will tell, but I do feel better."

Dela grinned. "*Only* time? Are you sure about that?"

She bumped Charlie forward — no mean feat for somebody one-third of his weight — which made him blush.

To Cappa's surprise, Anne met him in the middle and took his hand.

"You're right, Dela. It's not." She tugged Charlie toward the inside entrance to the factory. "Please excuse us, everyone. Charlie and I will be busy for the remainder of the night. And tomorrow morning, if we're lucky."

The door closed behind them, leaving those who remained with their jaws hanging.

"Is it just me," Dela said, "or is Anne even hornier now that she's a vampire?"

Mark scratched his head. "Yeah ... that might be my fault. My increased metabolism may not be the only physiological trait she inherited from the implant."

"Ain't a bad thing, if you ask me," Doris said. "She's got two lovers to satisfy now. That girl's gonna need all the help she can get."

• • •

Cappa filed out of the lobby with everyone else. Instead of going to her room, however, she went to the recreation lounge and sat on the couch. Through her Charlie self, she knew that he and Anne had just entered his room. They were both nervous, Cappa could tell, and were doing their usual trick of joking around to break the tension.

Tonight was the night; she could see it in Anne's jubilant eyes.

They were finally going to consummate their relationship.

Cappa wanted to disconnect from her Charlie self, but it wouldn't help. Her minds would simply synchronize when she reconnected, and she would experience the entire ordeal just as if she had been there the whole time. Resynchronizing was a pain anyway, so Cappa did what she always did when they were making out: she made sure Charlie's body was responding appropriately, and suffered her heartache in silence.

Zima entered the lounge and sat next to her without a word. For several minutes, they both just stared at the coffee table.

"How are they faring?" Zima said.

"Just groping so far, but they'll get there."

"I see." Her blue eyes turned to Cappa. "How are you doing?"

"F-fine," Cappa said, caught off-guard by the uncharacteristic question. "Why wouldn't I be?"

Zima continued to stare.

"All right! I'm not fine — not by a long stretch. How about you?"

Zima brow-knit, then her gaze fell. "Not fine."

"We just have to weather the storm, Zima." Cappa held her hand and mustered a smile. "It'll pass."

"No, it will not."

Cappa's smile faltered. "No," she said softly, "I ... I suppose it won't."

A tear ran down her cheek. Cappa laid her head on Zima's shoulder and drew guilty comfort from the knowledge that hers wasn't the only heart aching tonight.

77

AT LAST

ANNE SAT NEXT TO CHARLIE ON HIS BED, fidgeting with the covers. Although she wasn't technically a virgin, at this moment, she certainly felt like one.

Charlie seemed just as nervous as she was. For the first time it dawned on her that while he'd slept with other women in the past, Anne was the first girl he had ever dated in his cyborg body, which technically did make him a virgin.

Oh, the bittersweet irony.

She squeezed his hand, but not too tightly. "Are you ready for this?"

Charlie sighed. "To be honest, even if your trauma has finally been resolved, I'm still concerned about your safety."

"I told you before, I'm not made of glass — especially not now — so what say we save that worry for later, if it actually becomes a problem?" When he still seemed hesitant, she leaned over and kissed him tenderly. "You're kind, gentle, caring, and sensitive. I love you, and trust my care with you more than anyone else on the planet. You won't hurt me, Charlie, because that's not who you are." She grinned. "Plus, I don't think Cappa would let you."

"That's probably true," he said, laughing.

Anne kicked her legs over the side of the bed in child-like innocence. "So, are we going to sit here staring at each other all night wondering what might happen ..." She unfastened the top button of her shirt. "Or are you going to help me take this off and make it happen?"

His answer came in a passionate kiss that left her breathless and hungry for more. With deliberate care, they removed each other's clothes. Hands roamed freely, exploring where they had been afraid to before, until Anne couldn't stand it any longer.

In a frenzy of lust, she rolled on top of him and guided him home.

There was no pain this time, no terror, no flashbacks — just a wonderful aching need that only he could satisfy. Charlie filled her, loved her. For the first time in her life, Anne felt whole. It was a feeling she continued to enjoy throughout the night and well into morning, where they finally settled into each other's arms and lay content for the rest of the day, chatting about anything and everything.

Charlie was still trapped in his cyborg body. Anne was a blood-sucking monster. William was still at large and, with him, the threat of a plague unlike anything the world had ever seen. They knew nothing of the virus's origins, nor how to reverse it, and, to their knowledge, the crew at Z-Tech — Anne's family — were the only ones engaged in the fight to keep it from spreading.

All of this and more came up in their ramblings, but it didn't upset either of them. In fact, lying there naked in each other's embrace after all their hardships and trials, neither Anne nor Charlie could ever remember being happier.

ABOUT THE AUTHOR

Ryan Southwick decided to dabble at writing late in life, and quickly became obsessed with the craft. He grew up in Pennsylvania and moved to a farming town on California's central coast during elementary school, but it was in junior high school where he had his first taste of storytelling with a small role-playing group and couldn't get enough.

In addition to half a lifetime in the software development industry, making everything from 3-D games to mission-critical business applications to help cure cancer, he was also a Radiation Therapist for many years. His technical experience, medical skills, and lifelong fascination for science fiction became the ingredients for his book series, "The Z-Tech Chronicles", which combines elements of each into a fantastic contemporary tale of super-science, fantasy, and adventure, based in his Bay Area stomping grounds. Ryan's related short story "Once Upon a Nightwalker" was published in the *Corporate Catharsis* anthology, available from Paper Angel Press.

Ryan currently lives in the San Francisco Bay Area with his wife and two children. You can get in touch with him and see more of his work by visiting his website *RyanSouthwickAuthor.com*.

YOU MIGHT ALSO ENJOY

CITYFALL

by Lorna Hopkins Keith

After Samanda Lar destroys her ex-husband, the Volen hand her the mission of saving the people of City and establishing their new home.

JUST A BIT OF MAGIC

by Barb Bissonette

Every morning, Jenny Smith stares into her magic mirror, searching for glimpses of two girls. Today, she is joyful with anticipation, knowing that this is the day they will materialize in her village.

RULES OF THE CAMPFIRE

BOOK ONE FROM STORIES IN GLASS

by Paul S. Moore

If you woke up one day and realized you had memories from more than seventy lives, fluid in every language you'd ever spoken, and recalled all the texts you'd ever read, would you wonder why?

www.ingramcontent.com/pod-product-compliance
Lightning Source LLC
Chambersburg PA
CBHW032257020726
47495CB00001B/149

* 9 7 8 1 9 4 6 9 0 7 5 9 2 *